International Praise for Serhiy Zhadan

"*Voroshilovgrad* is an unsentimental novel about human relationships in conditions of brutality in which there is not a single act of betrayal . . . In his prose there is no nostalgia, but there is genuine affection, rough and profound. Even in this brutish habitus, there is trust, loyalty, and love." —**Marci Shore,** *The New Yorker*

"*Voroshilovgrad* is more, however, than an exercise in post-Soviet social realism. There is something deeply mythological about the novel, and, like many myths, it is a story of homecoming . . . Zhadan's language is suitably elastic, swinging from the tough, streetwise irony of a Ukrainian Irvine Welsh to flights of ebullient poetry more reminiscent of Bruno Schulz."

—**Uilleam Blacker,** *Times Literary Supplement*

"A homecoming is by turns magical and brutal in Zhadan's impressive picaresque novel . . . For Zhadan, loyalty and fraternity are the life-giving forces in this exhausted, fertile, near-anarchic corner of the country . . . readers will be touched by his devotion to a land of haunted beauty, 'high sky,' and 'black earth.'" —*Publishers Weekly*

"A dark but funny tale of an urbanite who returns to his hometown to run his brother's gas station. It's a road novel with splashes of magical realism and an embrace of fraternal loyalty. In hindsight, the bleak, disheartening environs and attitudes make it hard not to notice parallels to Trumpian middle America."

—**Jay Trachtenberg,** *The Austin Chronicle*

"With *Voroshilovgrad*, Zhadan has created an authentic poetics of post–Soviet rural devastation. His ragged, sympathetic characters aren't the newly rich post–Soviets of Moscow, the urban oligarchs Peter Pomerantsev has described, who 'sing hymns to Russian religious conservatism—and keep their money and families in London.' They are individ[...] h their place in history and with [...]ngeles Review of Books

"A trippy novel of contemporary Ukraine . . . set far away from the bustle of the metropolis and the Maidan, yet no less representative of the unsettled state of a country unable to transition. A bit meandering—but generally in a good way—*Voroshilovgrad* is an entertaining sort-of-road-novel with quite a bit of depth to it."
—**Michael Orthofer,** *Complete Review*

"Zhadan's canvas is large and is filled with bold characters . . . [he] also tosses into the mix fantastic and surreal flights of prose; poetic descriptions of the still-beautiful parts of the Ukraine, with its rich, black, enduring earth." —**Willard Manus,** *Lively Arts*

"Ukraine's best-known poet and the country's most famous counter-culture writer." —**Sally McGrane,** *The New Yorker*

"Blurring the boundaries between time and space as well as place, *Voroshilovgrad* narrates the journey of Herman, an advertising executive, who returns to his remote home after years of city living to find his missing brother."
—**Recommended Summer Reads 2016,** *World Literature Today*

"An entertaining tale . . . Trouble keeps finding Herman, and it's hard not to root for him."
—**Roman Augustovitz,** *Minneapolis Star-Tribune*

"Zhadan is a writer who is a rock star, like Byron in the early nineteenth century was a rock star."
—**Dr. Vitaly Chernetsky, professor of Slavic Literature at the University of Kansas,** *The New Yorker*

"*Voroshilovgrad* crosses, with tremendous grace, back and forth between lyrical dreaminess and brutal nightmarishness, and Zhadan works in lots of absurdity . . . it's absurdity of the sort that feels normal in books set in the Former Soviet Union, making everything in *Voroshilovgrad* feel paradoxically both real and bizarre."
—**Lisa Espenschade,** *Lizok's Bookshelf*

"A fascinating exploration into a post-soviet Ukraine. Not only does it explore the effects of communism to an industrial city, but also the power vacuum left behind when the Soviet Union collapsed."
—**Michael Kitto,** *Knowledge Lost*

"*Voroshilovgrad* is a road novel that escapes itself . . . [it] evokes the notion that the things we may consider nearest and dearest (romantic love, 'brotherhood' and even more cynical values like materialism) are, rather than the be-all and end-all, just the tip of the iceberg emerging from the more alien depths of human motivation."
—**Elisabeth Cook,** *Lit All Over*

"The book veers from poetic lyricism to brutal realism. And sometimes we get both at the same time, a feat I would have thought impossible, but Zhadan pulls it off." —**Zoe Brooks,** *Magic Realism*

"A strange mixture of magical realism, road novel, and spiritual journey . . . By turns jaunty, hilarious, poignant, and depressing, *Voroshilovgrad* tells an important story about the people left in the wake of Communism›s collapse, and the ways in which they try to build a future." —**Rachel Cordasco,** *Bookishly Witty*

"Zhadan's language is wild and powerful. The rhythm structuring his endless sentences demonstrates his beginnings as a poet."
—**Jutta Lindekugel,** *World Literature Today*

ALSO AVAILABLE FROM SERHIY ZHADAN IN ENGLISH:

Depeche Mode
translated by Miroslav Shkandrij

Mesopotamia
translated by Reilly Costigan-Humes, Wanda Phipps,
Virlana Tkacz, and Isaac Stackhouse Wheeler

What We Live For, What We Die For: Selected Poems
translated by Virlana Tkacz and Wanda Phipps

VOROSHILOVGRAD

—

Serhiy Zhadan

TRANSLATED FROM THE UKRAINIAN BY
ISAAC STACKHOUSE WHEELER AND
REILLY COSTIGAN-HUMES

DEEP VELLUM PUBLISHING

DALLAS, TEXAS

Deep Vellum Publishing
3000 Commerce St., Dallas, Texas 75226
deepvellum.org · @deepvellum

Deep Vellum is a 501c3 nonprofit literary arts organization
founded in 2013 with the mission to bring
the world into conversation through literature.

THIRD PRINTING
Copyright © 2012, Suhrkamp Verlag, Berlin
The original Ukrainian edition was published in 2010 under the title Ворошиловград
by Publishing House Folio, Kharkiv.
English translation copyright © 2016 by Reilly Costigan-Humes & Isaac Wheeler.

ISBN: 978-1-941920-30-5 (paperback) · 978-1-941920-31-2 (ebook)
LIBRARY OF CONGRESS CONTROL NUMBER: 2015960720

—

Cover & interior design by Anna Zylicz · annazylicz.com

Text set in Bembo, a typeface modeled on typefaces cut by Francesco Griffo
for Aldo Manuzio's printing of *De Aetna* in 1495 in Venice.

Distributed by Consortium Book Sales & Distribution.

Printed in the United States of America on acid-free paper.

VOROSHILOVGRAD

PART I

I

Telephones exist for breaking all kinds of bad news. They make people sound cold and detached. I guess it's easier to pass along bad news in an official-sounding voice. I know what I'm talking about. I've been fighting telephone receivers my whole life, albeit unsuccessfully. Operators all over the world still monitor people's conversations, jotting down the most important words and phrases. Meanwhile, psalm books and phone directories lie open on hotel nightstands; that's all you need to keep the faith.

I slept in my clothes—jeans and a stretched-out T-shirt. I woke up and roamed around the room, scattering empty soda bottles, glasses, cans, ashtrays, shoes, and plates with sauce slopped all over them. Barefoot and bad-tempered, I stepped on apples, pistachios, and dates like oily cockroaches. When you're renting an apartment where you don't own the furniture, you try to be careful with everything, since it might not belong to you. I'd filled my place up with so much junk, you'd think I was running a thrift shop. I had gramophone records and hockey sticks hiding under my couch, along with some clothes a girl had left behind and some big road signs I'd gotten my hands on somehow. I couldn't throw anything away, since I didn't know what belonged to me. But from the very first day, the very first moment that I found myself here, the telephone was lying right there on the floor, in the middle of the room. Its voice and its silence filled me with hatred. Before bed I'd cover the damn thing up with a cardboard box, and in the morning I'd take that box out to the balcony. The demonic apparatus lay in the center of the room, its jarring, irritating ring always ready to sing out and declare that someone needed me after all.

Now somebody was calling again. Calling on a Thursday, at 5:00 a.m. I crawled out from under the covers, tossed the cardboard box into the corner, picked up the phone, and went out to the balcony. It was quiet and empty in the neighborhood. A security guard, treating himself to a morning smoke break, came out the side door of the bank. When someone calls you at 5:00 a.m., don't expect any good to come of it. Holding back my irritation, I picked up the receiver. That's how it all started.

"Buddy." I recognized Kocha's voice immediately. It sounded like he had emphysema or something, as though someone had installed a set of old, blown-out speakers in place of his lungs. "Herman, were you asleep, man?" His speakers were hissing and spitting out consonants. It was 5:00 a.m., on a Thursday. "Hello, Herman?"

"Hello," I said.

"Buddy," Kocha said, his tone dipping a bit. "Herman!"

"Kocha, it's five in the morning. What do you want?"

"Herman, the thing is, I wouldn't have woken you up, but some serious shit has gone down here." A horrible shrill whistle came out of the receiver as he said this, and it made me believe him, for some reason. "I haven't slept all night, you know? Your brother called yesterday."

"And?"

"The thing is . . . he's gone, Herman." The sound of Kocha's breathing drew away then, as though removed to a great height.

"Where's he at?" I asked, unsettled. Listening to him was like riding a rollercoaster.

"Far away, Herman." The start of every new sentence was marked by feedback. "He's either in Berlin or Amsterdam. I didn't really catch it."

"Maybe he's going to Amsterdam via Berlin?"

"Maybe you're right, Herman, maybe you're right," said Kocha hoarsely.

"When's he getting back?" I asked, relaxing a bit. I was starting to think that this was all just routine for Kocha, that he was just giving me an update on the family.

"Looks like never," he declared, and the receiver made the feedback noise again.

"*When?*"

"Never, Herman, never. He's left for good. He called yesterday, told me to tell you."

"What do you mean he's never coming back?" I asked. "Kocha, is everything all right down there?"

"Yeah, everything's all right, buddy." Kocha broke into a higher register. "Everything's all right. The only thing is that your brother dumped all the work on me, you got that? Herman, I'm an old man. I can't handle this all by myself."

"What do you mean he dumped it all on you? What did he say?"

"He said he's in Amsterdam and asked me to call you. He said he's not coming back."

"What about the gas station?"

"Looks like the gas station is all on me, Herman. It's just . . ." Kocha's hoarse voice rose to a pleading pitch again. "I can't handle it. I've got sleeping problems. I mean, it's 5 a.m. and I can't sleep."

"Has he been gone for a while?" I interrupted.

"Yeah, about a week already," said Kocha. "I thought you knew. Some serious shit has gone down here."

"How come he didn't tell me anything?"

"I don't know, Herman, don't know, buddy. He didn't say anything to anybody. He just packed his bags and hit the road. Maybe he didn't want anyone to know."

"Know what?"

"That he was taking off," said Kocha.

"Who would care anyway?"

"Well, I don't know, Herman," said Kocha, his voice twisting evasively. "I don't know."

"Kocha, what happened down there?"

"Herman, you know me," Kocha hissed, "I didn't mess around with his business. He didn't explain anything to me. He just packed his bags and hit the road. Buddy, I can't handle it all by myself. You may want to come down, sort things out here, yeah?"

"Sort what out?"

"Well, I don't know, maybe he told you something."

"Kocha, I haven't seen him for six months."

"Well, I don't know," Kocha said, quite flustered now. "Herman, buddy, you get down here, because I just can't handle it all by myself. You see where I'm coming from?"

"Kocha, what are you being so cagey about?" I finally asked.

"Just tell it to me straight, what happened down there at the station?"

"Everything's fine, Herman," Kocha coughed. "It's all good, man. Well, the way I see it, I told you what happened. Now you can do what you want. You know what's best. I'm off, I've got customers. See you, buddy. See you," Kocha said, hanging up.

"Yeah," I thought, "he's got customers. Customers at 5 a.m."

★

We were renting two rooms in a former communal apartment, downtown in a quiet little neighborhood peppered with lime trees. Lyolik had the room closer to the hallway, and I had to walk through it to get to my room, the one with the balcony. The rest of the rooms had been closed off and nobody knew what was hidden behind those doors. Our landlord was a hardened old retiree, a former cash-in-transit driver. His name was Fyodor Mikhailovich, so I called him Dostoyevsky. In the '90s, he and his wife decided to leave Ukraine, so Fyodor Mikhailovich filed for a new passport, but once he got it, he suddenly changed his mind, figuring that this was just the time for a fresh start. So it worked out that his wife emigrated by herself, while he stayed behind in Kharkiv, supposedly keeping an eye on their apartment. Basking in his newfound freedom, Fyodor Mikhailovich rented out his rooms to us, then went into hiding, hunkering down in some other part of town. The kitchen, the hallways, and even the bathroom of this half-decayed dwelling were stuffed with 1930s furniture, tattered books, and stacks of old *Ogonyok* magazines from the Soviet days.

Dishes and multicolored rags that Fyodor Mikhailovich thought fondly of were piled on the tables, chairs, and right on the floor. He wouldn't let us throw any of it away, and we wouldn't throw any of our own stuff away either, so our junk mingled freely with his. Chests of drawers, shelves, and kitchen cabinets were overflowing with dark bottles and jars in which sunflower oil, honey, vinegar, and red wine shimmered (we put out our cigarette butts in the latter). Walnuts, copper coins, beer corks, and buttons from army overcoats rolled to and fro across the kitchen table. Fyodor Mikhailovich's old ties hung from the chandelier. We accepted and even approved, in a way, of our landlord and his porcelain Lenin figurines, enormous fake silver forks, dusty shades, and pirate treasures. The yellow sun slashed through the thick air, herding eddies of dust through the room. Sitting in the kitchen in the evenings, we would read Fyodor Mikhailovich's scribblings on the walls; there were some random telephone numbers, addresses, and bus routes all drawn directly on the wallpaper with an indelible pencil. We looked over cutouts from calendars and photographs of unknown relatives that he had pinned up. These relatives of his looked severe and dignified, unlike Fyodor Mikhailovich, who would wander into our warm nest from time to time in his squeaky sandals and foppish cap to pick up our empty bottles. Once he got his dough for the month, he'd disappear into the lime trees. It was May. The weather was warm and the grass had reclaimed its former territory. Sometimes at night cautious couples would wander in off the street and into the lobby to make love on the bench lined with old rugs. During the day stray dogs would pop in and sniff out all the traces of love. Disturbed by their findings, they would run back out onto the city's central streets. Sometimes in the morning hours the bank security guards would walk over to the bench, sit down, and roll up joints as long as May sunrises, like the one lingering over our apartment building at that particular moment, after I hung up the phone.

★

When I came out to the kitchen Lyolik was already hanging around by the refrigerator in his suit—a dark jacket, gray tie, and pants that drooped over him like a flag on a windless day. I opened up the fridge and studied the empty shelves.

"Hey," I said, flopping into a chair. Lyolik sat across from me with a sour expression on his face, gripping the milk carton tightly. "Let's pop over to my brother's place, all right?"

"Why?" he asked.

"Just because. I'd like to see him."

"What's up with your brother? Something happen?"

"Nah. He's fine. He's in Amsterdam."

"So you want to visit him in Amsterdam?"

"No, not Amsterdam. Let's go to his place, this weekend?"

"I don't know. I was planning to get my car looked at this weekend."

"Well there you go. My brother works at a gas station, he's got a garage. Come on."

"Well, I don't know," Lyolik answered hesitantly. "It'd be better if you just called him." He finished his milk. "Get ready, we're running late."

★

I called my brother a few times that afternoon. No answer. I called Kocha after lunch; no luck there either. I thought, "That's strange. My brother may not be picking up because he doesn't want to pay the roaming fees, or something, but Kocha should be at work regardless." I tried again. Still no answer. In the evening I called our parents. My mom picked up the phone. "Hey," I said, "has Yura called?" "No," she answered. "What's the matter?" "I was just wondering," I said, and changed the subject immediately.

★

The next morning, I went up to Lyolik in the office.

"Lyolik," I asked, "well, are we going?"

"Do we have to?" he moaned. "Are you for real? My car is old, God forbid it breaks down along the way."

"Lyolik," I persisted, "my brother will completely overhaul your car. C'mon, be a pal. You don't want me to have to take a bunch of trains, do you?"

"Well, I don't know. What about work?"

"Get the fuck out of here with that shit! We have the day off tomorrow."

"I don't know," Lyolik said again, "I'll have to talk it over with Bolik. If he doesn't load us up with work . . ."

"Let's go talk to him now," I said, and dragged him into the next cubicle.

Bolik and Lyolik were cousins. I'd known them since college.

We were all history majors. They didn't look related; Bolik was hip: skinny and clean-cut; he wore contacts and it seemed like he even got manicures. Lyolik was pretty ripped, but a bit on the slow side. He wore inexpensive business casual clothes, rarely cut his hair, and wouldn't spring for contacts, so he wore glasses with metal frames. Bolik looked slicker, but Lyolik looked like a simple guy you could count on. Bolik was six months older, so he felt responsible for his cousin; I guess he had some kind of older brother complex. He came from a respectable family. His father had worked for the Communist Youth League, then he made a career for himself in some party or another, got elected head of the regional government, and eventually wound up joining the opposition. During the past few years he'd held some office working for the Governor. Lyolik, on the other hand, came from more humble origins. His mom was a schoolteacher, while his dad had been slaving away in Russia since the '80s. They lived in a small town outside of Kharkiv. Lyolik was the poor relation, so everyone loved him, or at least that's what he thought. After college, Bolik immediately went to work for his dad, while Lyolik and I tried to make it on our own. We worked in an advertising agency, a newspaper that ran free ads, and in the public relations department for the Nationalists' Congress. We even tried our hand at working in a bookmaker's office, which then shut down in the second month of operation. Then, a few years ago, Bolik, concerned about our aimless drifting and thinking back to our carefree college days, invited us to work with him at the regional government office. Bolik's father had registered a few youth organizations under his name, through which various grants were funneled, and small but steady amounts of money were laundered. So that's how we got our start. Our work was strange and unpredictable. We edited speeches, held seminars for up-and-coming leaders and workshops for election observers, constructed political platforms for new parties, chopped wood at Bolik's father's country house, advocated for the democratic process as guests on TV talk shows, and laundered, laundered, laundered the dough being funneled through our accounts. The title on my business card read "Independent Expert." After a year's work I bought myself a souped-up computer, while Lyolik rewarded himself with a beat-up Volkswagen. By this time, we'd moved into our apartment. Bolik often stopped by our place, sat on the floor in my room, picked up the phone, and called up prostitutes. You know, standard stuff for a model employee trying to climb the corporate ladder. Lyolik didn't really like his cousin, or me for that matter, but we had already roomed together for a few years now, so our relationship was easy, perhaps even close. I was always borrowing clothes from him, and he was always borrowing money from me—the only difference being that I always gave back his clothes. He and his cousin had been up to something for the past few months—some sort of new family business. I decided not to get involved, since it was party-sponsored and who knew what that would lead to. The loans were one thing, but I had a stash he didn't know about, a wad of dollars stuck in a volume of Hegel. In general, yes, I trusted them, but I realized it was about time to start looking for a straight job.

★

Bolik was sitting in his office, working on some documents; folders containing the results of some surveys were spread out on the table in front of him. Seeing us, he clicked over to the regional government website in case we peeked at his screen.

"Hey there, you two," he said cheerfully, like a real boss ought to sound. "Well . . . How are things?"

"Bolik," I started in, "we want to visit my brother. You know him, right?"

"Yeah, I do," he said, examining his fingernails.

"We don't have anything planned for tomorrow, do we?"

Bolik thought for a bit, took another look at his nails, and abruptly hid them behind his back.

"You have the day off tomorrow," he replied.

"That means we're going," I said to Lyolik, and turned toward the door.

"Wait up," Bolik said, and I turned around. "I'm going to come along."

"You sure about that?" I asked, a bit incredulous.

I didn't want to drag him along. I could see Lyolik tightening up too.

"Yeah," said Bolik, "Let's all go together. You don't mind, do you?"

Lyolik kept quiet, clearly unhappy with this turn of events.

"Bolik," I said, "why would you want to go?"

"Just because," he replied. "I won't get in the way."

I figured Lyolik wouldn't like the idea of going on a trip with his cousin along—his cousin who was constantly monitoring him, who didn't want to let Lyolik out of his sight even for a second.

"But we're shipping out really early," I said, trying to put up some last-ditch resistance. "At five or so."

"At five?" Lyolik asked incredulously.

"At five!" Bolik exclaimed.

"At five," I repeated, and headed toward the door.

I figured I'd let them sort it out among themselves.

★

In the afternoon I called Kocha again. Nobody picked up. "Maybe he's dead," I thought to myself, and then realized that I actually hoped it was true.

★

In the evening, Lyolik and I were sitting at home in the kitchen. "Hey man," he piped up, all of a sudden, "you think maybe we could just stay here? Maybe you can call them again?" "Lyolik," I said firmly, "we're only going for one day. We'll be back home on Sunday. Chill out." "You chill out," Lyolik retorted. "Okay," I said.

But what's okay about all this? I'm thirty-three years old. I've been living on my own for a while, and quite happily, too. I rarely see my parents and have a good relationship with my brother. I've got a completely useless degree. I've got a dubious job. I've got enough money to support the lifestyle I'm used to. It's too late to get used to anything else. I'm more than happy with my lot. If something's not going to make me happy, I don't bother with it. A week ago my brother disappeared. He disappeared and didn't even warn me. I'd say my life is just grand.

★

The parking lot was empty, which made us look a bit suspicious. Bolik was running late. I suggested we take off, but Lyolik insisted on hanging around for a bit. He went in to get coffee from the vending machine, and struck up a conversation with the security guards who lived right there in the large, well-lit supermarket. The bright and airy morning gave the display cases a yellow tint. The building resembled an ocean liner resting on the rocky bottom. Every once in a while, a pack of dogs would run across the parking lot, scornfully sniffing the wet asphalt and lifting their heads proudly toward the morning sun. Lyolik sprawled on the driver's seat, smoking one cigarette after another and anxiously calling his cousin over and over. They had been talking on the phone a lot lately, exchanging muttered accusations and complaints; whatever pretense to mutual trust they'd maintained till now seemed to be falling away. Lyolik ran into the store one more time for coffee, only to spill it all over himself, leaving him to painstakingly clean himself up with wet wipes and curse his cousin out for being late. That's how it always went with Lyolik—he was uncomfortable year round, either sweating buckets or shivering and sniffling; he was uncomfortable behind the wheel and equally uncomfortable in a suit. His cousin made him feel tense yet had sucked him into another dubious business venture. I told him to keep his distance, but Lyolik wouldn't heed my advice. The possibility of making an easy buck mesmerized him. All I could do was sit back and watch their shady transactions, taking comfort in the fact that I hadn't let myself get wrapped up in this new scheme of theirs.

I went into the store for coffee, chatted with the security guards, and treated the dogs to some chips. It was time to go, but Lyolik just couldn't leave without his cousin.

★

He tore around the corner, helplessly scanning his surroundings while shooing away the stray dogs. Lyolik beeped; Bolik saw us and ran over to the car. The dogs trotted along behind him, tucking their ragged tails between their legs. Bolik opened up the rear passenger door and hopped in. He was in his usual suit with a green and noticeably wrinkled dress shirt underneath.

"Bolik," said Lyolik, "what the fuck?"

"Goddammit, Lyolik," said Bolik, "don't say a word."

Bolik said hello to me and took a few CDs out of his jacket pocket.

"What's that?" I asked.

"I burned us some music," Bolik said. "So we'll have something to listen to."

"Well, I've got my MP3 player with me," I answered.

"No problem, Lyolik and I will listen to my CDs."

Lyolik's face contorted at this.

"Lyolik," I said, starting to laugh. "What's the deal, your cousin decides what music you can listen to?"

"He doesn't decide a thing," said Lyolik, offended.

"Well at least tell us what music you got," I said.

"Charlie Parker."

"And that's it?"

"Yeah. Ten CDs of Charlie Parker. I couldn't find anything else worth listening to," Bolik said.

"Jackass," Lyolik retorted, and we set off.

★

The music made the Volkswagen tremble, like a glass jar someone was drumming on with a stick. Bolik, sitting in the back, loosened his tie and peered out the window at the outskirts of the city, his face tight with apprehension. We passed the tractor factory and some little bazaar, and then we finally broke out onto the open road, heading southeast. Highway patrol officers were sitting at the checkpoint. One of them lazily looked over at us, but failing to see anything of interest, he turned away and walked over to his partners. I tried putting myself in his shoes. A black, used Volkswagen; clearance-sale suits; last year's dress shoes; discounted watches; the kind of cheap lighters your colleagues give to you as gifts; and supermarket-aisle sunglasses—reliable, inexpensive things, not too worn, not too flashy; nothing superfluous, nothing special. No reason to pull these guys over; it's not like you could shake them down for all that much anyway.

★

Green hills stretched out along both sides of the highway. It had been a warm and windy May; flocks of birds were flying about from field to field, diving noisily into new air currents as they went. White high-rise apartment buildings were shining ahead on the horizon, just below the sun that burned red like a fiery basketball.

"We have to fill up," said Lyolik.

"There's a gas station coming up," I answered.

"I could go for a drink," Bolik piped up.

"Have some antifreeze," Lyolik suggested.

We pulled into the gas station, and Bolik and I went into the mini-mart for some coffee. While Lyolik was filling up, we made our way over toward a bunch of plastic tables. A cornfield began on the other side of a metal fence. The sticky, ubiquitous May greenery was burning my retinas. A few trucks were bunched together in the parking lot. The drivers were probably catching up on sleep. Bolik approached the far table, picked up a plastic chair, wiped it clean with a napkin, and took a seat, cautiously. I also sat down. Shortly after, Lyolik came over.

"All right," he said, "we can go now. How much ground do we still gotta cover?"

"About two hundred kilometers," I answered. "We'll get there in a few hours."

"What are you listening to?" Lyolik asked, pointing at my MP3 player resting on the table.

"A little bit of everything," I told him. "Why don't you get yourself one?"

"I have a CD player in my car."

"And that's why you can only listen to what your cousin burns for you."

"I burn him good music," Bolik said defensively.

"I listen to the radio," Lyolik chimed in.

"If I were you, I wouldn't trust the radio's musical taste," I told Lyolik. "You need to listen to the music you love."

"Whatever you say, Herman," Bolik said, unconvinced. "But hey, we need to trust each other, isn't that right Lyolik?"

"Uh-huh," Lyolik said timidly.

"Good," I said, "I couldn't care less. Listen to whatever you want."

"Herman, you don't trust people enough," Bolik added. "You don't trust your partners. You shouldn't be like that. But you can still always count on us. Just tell me—where are we actually going?"

"Home," I answered, "trust me." But I was thinking, "It'd be better if we got there a bit earlier. Nobody really knows how long we'll be stuck there, after all."

★

Bolik pushed some Parker CDs on me. I played them, obediently, one after another. Parker's alto ripped through the air, exploding like a chemical weapon wiping out an enemy camp. He was blowing out a golden flame of divine wrath. His black fingers buried themselves deep in the toxic wounds of the air, extracting copper coins and the dried fruits of his labor. I threw the CDs we had already listened to into my tattered leather backpack. In an hour we passed the nearest town, popped onto a bridge, and found ourselves on the scene of a pile up.

A tractor-trailer was stuck smack-dab in the middle of the road, completely blocking traffic in both directions. Cars were driving onto the bridge and falling into a craftily constructed trap—it was impossible to go forward or backward. The drivers were honking their horns. The ones who were closest to the action got out of their cars and walked ahead to see what had happened. There was an old semi-trailer caked in feathers and leaves and filled to the brim with poultry cages; there were hundreds of them—hundreds of these cages full of large, clumsy birds, flapping their wings and pecking away, all on top of each other. It looked like the driver had crashed into an iron barrier separating the pedestrian walkway from the road. The trailer had flipped over and formed an impromptu barricade. The top cages had spilled haphazardly onto the asphalt and now the bewildered chickens were chilling out around the trailer, jumping on car hoods, standing on the rails of the bridge, and laying eggs under the truck's tires. The driver had fled the scene immediately, taking his keys with him, no less. Two cops were circling around the truck, not sure what to do next. They drove the chickens away furiously, trying to find any scrap of information about the missing driver. The witnesses gave them contradictory answers: one claiming that the man had jumped off the bridge, another saying he'd supposedly fled the scene in a waiting car, while a third witness stated in an insistent whisper that the trailer never had a driver in the first place. The cops were at a total loss, so they tried to radio in to the precinct.

"Well, this will be a while," Lyolik said, returning to the car after talking the matter over with the police. "They want to bring a crew in to clear the road. Trouble is, it's the weekend, who the fuck is going to come?"

A line of cars had already formed behind us, and it was getting longer by the minute.

"Maybe we can go around?" I suggested.

"How?" Lyolik answered sourly. "We can't get out now. We should have just stayed home."

A plump hen hopped up on the hood of the car, took a few measured steps, and froze in place.

"That means death is just around the corner," said Bolik. "I wonder if there are any stores with fridges around here."

"You wanna buy a fridge?" Lyolik asked his cousin.

"I want some cold water," Bolik explained.

Lyolik honked the horn. Frightened, the bird started flapping its wings and hopped off the bridge, soaring into oblivion. Maybe that's the only way to teach them to fly.

"All right then," I said, finally cracking. "You two head back, I'll hoof it from here."

"What are you talking about?" Lyolik asked. "Just sit still. They'll pull that thing to the side of the road soon and then we'll turn around and head back home together."

"You two go. I'll walk a bit and I'll get there somehow."

"Wait up," Lyolik said, concerned. "How the hell are you expecting to do that?"

"I'll get there," I said. "I'll be back tomorrow. Drive safe."

The cops were getting antsy. One of them picked up a chicken, held it by the leg, and toe-balled it. The chicken flew up into the air, soared over a few cars, then disappeared under the tires of one of them. His partner also maliciously grabbed a chicken, tossed it up into the air, and socked it with a right hook, sending it zooming up into the May sky. I hopped over the barrier separating the pedestrian walkway from the road, slipped around the trailer, slid past the drivers, crossed the bridge, and strolled along the morning highway.

★

Then I stopped and stood under the warm sky for quite a long time; the empty highway resembled the metro at night—it was every bit as desolate and every minute there felt just as interminable. After the intersection at the city limits, there was a bus stop that had been intricately vandalized by anonymous sojourners. Its walls had black and red patterns scrawled on them, the dirt floor was thoroughly littered with broken glass, and dark grass grew from underneath the brick foundation where lizards and spiders were hiding. I decided against going inside. I just stood in the shadow cast by the wall and waited. I had to wait a good while. I saw the occasional truck making its way north, leaving dust and utter hopelessness in its wake, while nobody was heading south at all. The shade gradually ran out from underneath my feet. I was already thinking about giving up. I calculated how long it would take and where my friends could be right now, but then a blood-colored Ikarus bus, desperately spewing exhaust as it barreled down the highway, appeared from among the rocks and meadows along the riverbank. It rocked a bit, riding on two wheels momentarily, then stood on all fours like a dog shaking itself dry after a swim. Barely able to catch its breath, it switched gears and crawled toward me. Shocked, I froze and stood staring at this clunky vehicle coated in dust and smeared in blood and oil. It rolled over to the bus stop slowly. The door opened. I caught a whiff of its insides that reeked of death and nicotine. The driver, shirtless and panting from the stifling heat, wiped a bead of sweat from his forehead and shouted:

"Well, sonny boy, you getting in?"

"Yeah," I answered, and did so.

There were no empty seats. The souls who inhabited that bus were a languid bunch. There were women in bras and sweatpants with bright makeup and long fake nails, tattooed guys with wallets hanging from their wrists, also in sweatpants and Chinese-made sneakers, and kids in baseball caps and athletic uniforms holding bats and brass knuckles. They were all sleeping or trying to fall asleep, so nobody paid any attention to me. All of this was accentuated by blasting, crackling Indian music that sounded like a flock of hummingbirds fluttering around inside the bus and trying to escape this sweet death chamber—but the music didn't seem to bother anyone. I went up and down the aisle searching for a seat, but I couldn't find one, so I went back toward the driver. The windshield was covered top to bottom in Orthodox icon stickers, and all sorts of sacred things dangled and flashed there. These seemed to be the only things keeping the bus from falling apart once and for all. Teddy bears and clay skeletons with broken ribs, necklaces made out of rooster heads and Manchester United pennants had been hung all over the place. Pornographic pictures, portraits of Stalin, and Xeroxed images of Saint Francis were Scotch-taped to the window glass. There were also maps outlining various routes on the dashboard, along with a few issues of *Hustler* that the driver used for swatting flies, and then flashlights, blood-stained knives, worm-infested apples, and small wooden icons of the great martyrs. The driver, clutching the wheel in one hand and a bottle of water in the other, was panting in the heat.

"Well there, sonny boy," he asked, "are all the spots taken?"

"Yep."

"Stand here next to me, otherwise I'll fall asleep too. It's all right for them—they can pass out, but I'm the one that's responsible."

"Responsible for what?"

"The goods, sonny boy, the goods," he said in a confidential tone.

He started telling me some sob stories about small-fry entrepreneurs from the Donbas region and their families. Two days ago they picked up the goods (athletic gear, Chinese-made sneakers, and other shit like that) in Kharkiv and headed for home. As soon as they got outside the city, the poor old bus broke down.

"Sonny boy, the suspension is always giving me trouble—the last time it got fixed was before the Moscow Olympics, back in 1980! So we spent the night on the side of the highway." The driver slithered back and forth between the tires while the small-fry entrepreneurs set up camp, lit a fire, sang songs, and played the guitar. They even managed to enjoy themselves. In the morning, the driver went to the closest village and brought some farmers over with a tractor. The farmers hauled them over to the train depot. They spent the next day and night there. The entrepreneurs doggedly stayed up all night, protecting their goods and playing songs on their guitar. They only ran over to the train station once to buy booze and get some new strings. Eventually, the driver fixed the suspension, loaded up the entrepreneurs the best he could, and set off on the ill-fated road back to his beloved mining town in the Donbas region. When he saw the pileup near the bridge, he didn't lose his cool; he cut a quick U-turn and got over to the other side of the river by taking some back roads. Now nothing could hold him back—well, at least that's what he said.

The bus was coughing up a lung trying to crest a gentle rise. Up ahead, a wide, sunny valley filled with light-green cornfields and golden ravines stretched out before us. The driver pushed on decisively. Then he turned off the engine and relaxed a bit, letting the bus coast. It slid down the decline like an avalanche caused by a bunch of Japanese tourists shouting at the top of the mountain. The wind was whistling, brushing against the sides of the bus. Bugs were smashing into the windshield like drops of May rain. We flew downhill, picking up speed amid the hovering voices of those Indian singers promising enduring happiness and a painless death. Once we had rolled to the bottom of the valley, our momentum carried us upward for a while when the land began to rise again. At that point the driver tried to restart the engine. The Ikarus bus stalled with a sharp iron-on-iron screech, and then it came to a complete stop. Desperate now, the driver remained silent—and I felt too awkward to speak up. Finally, he dropped his head onto the wheel. His shoulders heaved from time to time. At first I thought he was crying, which I found oddly touching. After listening in a bit closer, though, I realized that he'd just fallen asleep. All the other passengers on the ghost bus were asleep too, and nobody was so much as thinking about protecting the goods. I walked up and down the aisle once again, then peered out the window. The wind was gently brushing against the young corn; there was absolute silence, and the sun was eating away at the

valley like a grease stain attacking a tablecloth. Suddenly, somebody touched my hand. I looked around. At the back of the bus
there were some dark brown curtains that hadn't been washed
for some time. It had seemed to me that there wasn't anything
behind those curtains except maybe a wall or a window or something like that. But no, a hand was sticking out. It grabbed me
and dragged me easily inside. After slipping through the invisible
entrance I found myself in a tiny room. It was a kind of chill-out
space, a place for meditating and making love, a little cell caressed
by perfume and shadows. Synthetic Chinese rugs bearing strange
ornaments and images depicting deer hunting, teatime, and Bei-
jing pioneers greeting Chairman Mao decorated the walls of the
tiny space. Two small sofas were placed up against the walls. Three
dark-skinned men and one dark-skinned woman were sitting on
these sofas. They were in their underwear, the men's strange and
white, the woman's modern and sporty. Skulls dangled from heavy
necklaces wrapped around her neck. Instead of a comb, there was
a paper knife sticking out of her hair, and she had a thermos resting on her lap. Their skin blended into the darkness; all I could
see was the greedy glint of their yellowish eyes, illuminating the
room like amber. She reached out, grasped my hand and didn't
let it go, looked me straight in the eyes and asked:

"Who are you?"

"Who are *you*?" I countered, feeling the warmth of her palm
and the weight of her silver rings.

"I'm Karolina," she said, and drew back her hand sharply. After
sizing me up, one of the men whispered something to his neighbor, and the latter laughed briefly.

"Where are you going?" Karolina asked, looking me over in the partial darkness.

"Home," I answered.

"Who's expecting you?" she asked, taking the knife out of her hair and letting her flowing locks cover her eyes.

"Nobody."

Karolina laughed.

"Why are you going to a place where nobody is expecting you?" she asked, producing a pomegranate from somewhere or other and cutting it in half.

"Why does it matter?" I was baffled. "I just haven't been there for a while."

"Have some," she said, offering me half of the pomegranate. "What are you going to do there, in this place where nobody is expecting you?"

"I won't be staying there too long. I'm leaving for Kharkiv tomorrow."

"You're that afraid of returning?" Karolina asked, chuckling, lifting her half of the pomegranate to her mouth and sucking on it. "How can you be so sure? You haven't even gotten there yet and you're already planning to leave. You're afraid."

"I've got stuff to do," I explained. "I can't stay any longer than that."

"You can if you want."

"No," I said, irritated. "I can't."

"You only think you'll leave right away because you've forgotten all the experiences you had there. Once you remember, you'll find that leaving is harder than you think. Here."

She handed me a mug filled with something she had poured from the thermos. The drink smelled like a mix of cinnamon and valerian. I tried it. It had an acerbic and spicy taste to it. I drank it all. I was knocked out immediately.

★

Wheat fields surrounded the airport. Some bright, poisonous-looking flowers were growing closer to the runway. Wasps were hovering lazily above, frozen in mid-flight as if there were corpses below them. Every morning the sun heated up the asphalt and dried out all the grass poking through the concrete slabs. Flags were whipping in the wind off to the side, above the air-traffic control station. A bit farther away, behind the administration building, the blistering morning sun touched down on a row of trees woven together by spiderwebs. Strange gusts of wind tore across the fields like animals emerging from the night, attracted by the airport's green lights, only to retreat back into the wheat to hide from the burning June sun. As it warmed up, the asphalt reflected the sunlight, blinding the birds flying over the runway. Gas tanks and a couple of trucks were parked at the fence. Some empty garages, smelling of sweet stagnant water and oil, were just emerging from the darkness. After a while, some mechanics appeared, changed into worn black overalls, and started fiddling around with their machines. The early June sky hovered above the airport, flapping loudly in the wind like freshly washed sheets, rising and swooping down to the asphalt. Around eight, the laborious roar of an engine made itself heard, heaving air in and out of the depths of the atmosphere.

The airplane itself was still hidden behind the sun, but its shadow scurried across the wheat fields, scaring the hell out of the birds and foxes. The surface of the sky shattered like porcelain. A good old Antonov An-2, the pride of Soviet aviation, a model that had seen its share of combat, though this one was almost certainly a crop duster, was descending nearby. Deafening the morning with its prehistoric motor, it spun around the sleepy city, awakening its residents from their light and fleeting summer dreams. The pilots scoped out the fields of crops topped with sunny honey, fresh grass sprouting on the railroad ties and embankments, the golden river sand, and the chalky banks the color of silverware. The city was left behind with its factory smoke stacks and railroad; the airplane was getting ready to land. Light poured into the cockpit and shone coldly on the metal. The machine whipped across the runway, its stiff wheels bouncing up and down on the cracked asphalt. The pilots hopped down onto the ground and started helping the baggage handlers pull out large burlap sacks full of regional and Republic-wide newspapers, letters, and parcels. Once everything had been unloaded, they walked over to the building, leaving the plane to warm up in the sun.

My friends and I lived on the other side of the fields, on the outskirts of the city, in white panel apartment buildings surrounded by tall pine trees. In the evenings, we would escape from our neighborhood, roam around in the wheat, hiding from passing cars and scampering along the fence, and then we'd take a rest in the dusty grass and look at the aircraft. The An-2, with its all-metal airframe and canvas-upholstered wings, looked like something not of this world, some conveyance utilized by demons who burned the sky above us with oil and lead. God's messengers were riding inside it; the mighty propeller was smashing the blue ice of the sky and hurling poplar fuzz into the next world. We came home well after dark, pushing through the hot, thick wheat, all the while dreaming about aviation. We all wanted to become pilots. The majority of us became losers.

From time to time I still have dreams about aviators. They're always making an emergency landing somewhere in wheat fields. Their planes cut at dusk through the thick wheat like razors; all the canvas upholstery gives with a loud ripping sound as the stalks wrap around their planes' undercarriages before they become bogged down forever in the black, dried-up earth. The pilots bail out of their boiling cockpits and fall into the wheat that immediately spins a web around their legs. They stand and peer into the distance as if they're trying to make out something on the horizon. But there's nothing on the horizon except for more wheat fields. They go on for miles; there's no hope reaching the end. The aviators leave their aircraft to cool down in the twilight and make their way west, chasing the rapidly guttering sun. The stalks are tall and impassable; the pilots can hardly make their way through the fields; they forge along nonetheless and smash up against an invisible wall, over and over again, even though they know they have no chance of getting out. They're wearing leather helmets, goggles, flight gloves. For some reason, they don't want to detach their open parachutes; they trail the aviators like long and heavy crocodile tails.

★

I woke to the humming of the engine. The three men were sleeping next to me on the couch, and Karolina was gone. I looked out into the main section of the bus. It was already quite late; to the right, outside the window, the evening sun was speckled with red. I wondered what time it was. I walked up to one of the entrepreneurs dreaming sweet dreams, moved his hand and looked at his watch. It was nine-thirty. "Damn," I thought to myself, "did I really sleep through my stop?" I went up to the driver. He greeted me like an old friend, without taking his eyes off the road. I looked out the windshield. There would be a turn coming up, but I knew that if you kept going straight, then in a few kilometers I'd get where I was going. But the driver was slowing down and was getting ready to take the turn.

"Hey guy, look," I said to him, "why don't you drop me off at the gas station. It's only a few kilometers away."

"The one up on the hill?" asked the driver.

"Yep."

"By the tower?"

"Yeah . . ."

"Nope," he said. "We're turning here."

"Hold on," I said, hoping to strike a deal. "You've got something wrong with your suspension, right? My brother has a repair shop. He'll give you a complete overhaul."

"Sonny boy," the driver responded firmly and convincingly, "that's the city over there, and we can't go into the city. We're hauling goods."

★

I got off the bus. The sun had set; it got chilly right away. I put on my coat and set off along the highway. I got to the gas station in about twenty minutes. The windows at the service station were dark. "Where's Kocha?" I wondered. It seemed completely abandoned, and the front door was padlocked. I decided to wait around a bit nevertheless. I walked behind the building by the grass and raspberry bushes where Kocha's trailer was. I could see a few old, beaten-up automobiles. The trailer was also locked. Feeling my way through the darkness, I found a lonely truck cab, with no trailer in sight. I jumped in and took off my sneakers. The moon was hanging up above, and the asphalt was losing the heat it had soaked up during the day. Right in front of me, in the valley below, was my hometown. I put my backpack under my head and fell right back asleep.

2

The dog was black, tinged with swampy green. It crept forward apprehensively, hunching down as it went, trying to go unnoticed. It approached quietly, its fearsome paws tearing through the tall grass, and then it was looming over me, blocking out the sun. The rays of morning sunlight gave its skull a golden hue. I met its glassy gaze and saw my own reflection looking back at me. It bounded forward, paused, then moved again. It froze for an instant and nudged me with its snout. Its hungry eyes lit up, and the grass behind it curled into an emerald wave, concealing a bloody, sunny thicket. Half asleep and sensing motion, I thrust my hand forward instinctively.

"Herman, hey buddy!"

Putting my feet down heavily on the bent iron rods, I pulled myself up.

"Herman! Pal, you're here!" Kocha said, coming up to me and gesturing vaguely with his long, skinny arms, and bobbing his nearly-bald skull, but he couldn't squeeze through the broken window, so he just stood back a bit in the sun that had already risen and was now ascending to just the height it wanted. "Well, what are you lying around for?" he asked hoarsely, pawing at me. "Hey buddy!"

I tried to get up. My body wasn't cooperating after a night on the hard seat. I stretched out my legs, bent over, and just fell into Kocha's embrace.

"Hey pal!" I could tell how happy he was to see me.

"Hi, Kocha," I replied, and we shook hands, patted each other on the shoulder, and drummed each other on the back for a while, demonstrating just how grand we thought it was that I had spent the night in an empty truck cab and he was there to wake me up at six in the morning.

"When did you get in?" Kocha inquired after the first wave of happiness had passed. Incidentally, he still hadn't let go of my hand.

"Last night," I answered, trying to free myself from his grip, and finally put my shoes on.

"How come ya didn't call?" Kocha had no intention of letting go.

"Kocha, you're a little bitch," I said, finally extricating myself and finding that now that I had it back I didn't know what to do with my hand. "I've been calling you for the last two days. Why haven't you been picking up?"

"When'd you call?" Kocha asked.

"In the afternoon," I said, finally managing to pick up my sneakers.

"Ah, I was sleeping," he said. "I've been having trouble sleeping lately. I'll sleep during the day and then come to work at night. But there aren't any customers at night," he continued, fidgeting a bit and then motioning for me to follow him. "Well, and more importantly, our phone isn't working—we didn't pay this month's bill. And yesterday I was in town. Come on, let me show you around."

★

He went on ahead. I followed behind him. I detoured around a Moskvitch car with burnt tires, and then a heap of scrap metal, airplane parts, refrigerators, and gas stoves, and slipped behind Kocha as he walked over to the gas pumps. The gas station sat about one hundred meters off the northbound highway. The city through which the highway ran was down below, in the warm valley, about two kilometers away. On the other side of the valley, to the south, sprawling fields gave way to the city's outermost neighborhoods. A river flowing from the Russian side of the border toward the Donbas region encircled the city from the north. The left bank was on a slight incline, while tall, chalky mountains, whose summits were covered with wormwood and blackthorn, dotted the right. A TV tower, visible from any point in the valley, soared upward, resting atop the highest hill and looming over the city. The gas station was situated on the next hill over from the tower. It had been built back in the '70s. An oil depot had appeared in the city around that time, followed by two gas stations—one on the city's southern border and the other on the northern one. In the '90s, the oil depot went bankrupt, along with the other gas station, so this one, on the Kharkiv highway, was the only station left in town. In the early '90s my brother got involved, just as the oil depot was on its last legs, and took over. The station itself was looking pretty shabby these days—four old pumps, a booth with a cash register, and an unused flagpole you could hang someone on, if the mood struck you. There was a cold warehouse stuffed with metal out back. Clearly, infrastructure didn't take priority, since my brother invested his money in improving customer service by gathering up all sorts of appliances and mechanisms for repairing everything imaginable. He lived in town, coming to work every morning and descending back into the valley well after nightfall. He had a killer team working alongside him—Kocha and a guy everybody called Injured, both self-taught mechanics who had resuscitated numerous trucks over the years, something they took great pride in. Injured also lived in town, whereas Kocha had been forced out of his apartment, so he hung out at the gas station all the time, sleeping in a trailer furnished according to the principles of feng shui. There was a patch of asphalt with a repair pit near the station, and a few metal tables were sunk into the ground off to one side, under the lime trees. Gullies and apple orchards started behind the gas station, stretching along the chalky mountains; to the north the landscape gave way to steppe, broken up by the occasional noisy tractor. Mangled car parts had been heaped together behind the trailer—stacked tires and the remains of disassembled vehicles. The cab of a Kamaz truck, offering a panoramic view of the sun-kissed valley and the unprotected city, was hidden away in the raspberry bushes. But this business wasn't about infrastructure or old pumps. It was all about location. That was certainly what my brother had in mind when he decided to buy this gas station. The fact of the matter was that the next place to get gas was seventy kilometers north, and the highway ran through several dubious places, places with no government to speak of, and hardly anyone to govern. It seemed as though there wasn't any cell service up north, either. All the drivers knew that, so they wanted to fill up at my brother's place. Moreover, they knew he had Injured working for him, and Injured was the best mechanic around: the god of drive shafts and stick shifts. In short, the place was a gold mine.

★

Two detached car seats had been brought over and planted by the brick booth, next to the gas pumps, covered with the black skins of some unidentifiable animals. Springs were jutting out randomly from the cushions, and a long metal arm or lever had been attached to one of the seats, making the thing look like a catapult. Kocha wearily plopped down onto the seat, took out his cigarettes, lit one of them, and pointed at me, seemingly saying, "Take a seat, buddy." I did so. The sun was beginning to radiate heat like rocks on a riverbank, and the sky whirled along above us, goaded by the wind. It was Sunday, at the end of May—a perfect day for getting the hell out of here.

"You here for long?" Kocha asked, whistling a bit as he spoke.

"Heading back tonight," I answered.

"Why ya leaving so fast? Stay for a few days. We'll go fishing."

"Kocha, where's my brother?"

"I already told you, in Amsterdam."

"Why didn't he tell anyone he was leaving?"

"Herman, I don't know. It wasn't planned, you know. He just up and left. He said he wasn't coming back."

"Was he having problems with the business or something?"

"What problems could there be, Herman?" Kocha replied testily. "We don't have any problems here, or any business either—it's just a mess. You can see that."

"So what's next?"

"I don't know. Do whatever you want."

Kocha put out his cigarette and tossed the butt into the bin labeled "No Smoking." He tilted his face toward the sun and didn't say another word. "Damn," I thought. "What's going on in that head of his? He's probably hiding something—sitting there cooking up some scheme."

★

Kocha was fifty or so. He was pretty energetic for his age, had lost most of his hair, and was decidedly off the grid. The remains of his formerly luscious locks, now surrounded by bald patches, were sticking out every which way. Back when I was a kid, he still had a full head of hair; I remember seeing Kocha a lot back then— he was the first living thing my consciousness registered, aside from my parents, relatives, and our other neighbors. As I grew up,

Kocha grew old. We lived in adjacent buildings in a new neighborhood that was constantly expanding, so I felt as though I grew up on one big construction site. Our neighbors were mostly workers at the small nearby factories (there weren't any big industrial concerns in our city), and then a few railroad men, all kinds of white-collar dipshits (teachers, office workers), military personnel (like my father), and members of the Communist Youth League—the leaders of tomorrow, as they said. As far as I can remember, Kocha wasn't there to begin with; he moved to our street after we did; but it still felt as though he'd lived in our neighborhood his whole life. He had joined the leaders of tomorrow, grown up without any parents, and gotten himself into some trouble with the law, gradually becoming something of a local menace. It was in the '70s that our neighborhood really started expanding, so Kocha's wild adolescent years coincided with intensive infrastructure growth—Kocha held up our new grocery stores, cleaned out the newly opened newspaper kiosks, and broke into the newly constructed civil registry office; simply put, he was keeping up with the times. Acknowledging their helplessness, the authorities handed Kocha over to the Communist Youth League, hoping they would straighten him out. For some reason, they didn't consider Kocha a hopeless case, so they got right down to molding him into a model Communist. For starters, they enrolled him in the local vocational school. Kocha stole a lathe during the second week of classes, and they were forced to expel him. After a year and a half of hanging around the neighborhood, he finally got hauled off to the army. He served in a construction battalion by Zhytomyr, but he came back home with paratrooper tattoos.

These were his glory days. Kocha made his rounds in full uniform, beating up anyone he didn't recognize. All the guys, myself included, worshiped Kocha then since he was such a bad example. This was when the Communist Youth League made one last, pathetic attempt at winning Kocha over by giving him a one-room apartment in the building next to ours. He moved in and immediately made his home a pit of debauchery. In the early '80s, all our neighborhood's young overachievers passed through his apartment—boys became men and girls gained valuable experience. Kocha started hitting the bottle harder and harder, so he barely noticed when the USSR collapsed. At the end of the '80s, when a serial killer went on a rampage in our city, the authorities pointed the finger at Kocha. The neighbors too—everyone was convinced that Kocha was the one raping the girls coming home from the milk factory on starry, perfumed nights, and then stabbing them with a long jagged piece of scrap metal. Nevertheless, no one had the guts to do anything about it—they were too scared of him. In time it seemed he'd earned all the men's respect and the women's affection. Then, at the beginning of the '90s, the authorities had to take matters into their own hands once again, absent the now-defunct Communist Youth League: at the end of a solid week of partying, Kocha burned down a billboard advertising a newly formed joint stock partnership, and this wound up being the final straw. The powers that be had already been at their wits' end; but then they busted into Kocha's own apartment and put him under arrest. A small protest had been organized by the time they led him outside. The guys and I (we were grown-up by then) all backed Kocha, but nobody gave us the time of day. He got a year, and did his time somewhere in the Donbas, where he hooked up with some Mormons. They gave him a bunch of pamphlets, as well as some cologne and cigarettes, at his request. After a year in the can he returned home a hero. Shortly thereafter, the Mormons came around looking to save his soul. They were three young missionaries wearing cheap yet sharp suits. Kocha let them in, listened to their spiel, took a shotgun from underneath the cushions on his sofa, and herded them into his bathroom. He kept them in there for two days. On the third day he rather imprudently decided to wash up regardless, opened up the bathroom doors, and let the Mormons break free. After running over to the police station they tried filing a report; however, the cops quite rationally decided it would be easier to lock up the Mormons for an identity check instead. Over the next few years, Kocha tried, unsuccessfully, to get his act together. He got divorced three times. Moreover, it was the same woman every time. Clearly, his love life was a mess, and Kocha's youthful energy was slipping away from him. It finally slipped away completely in the late '90s, when he wound up in the hospital with part of his finger bitten off and his stomach punctured. His wife had done the biting, during an argument, but Kocha flatly refused to say who was responsible for his stomach. Around that same time, my brother started helping him out by giving him some odd jobs, a little money, and whatever else he needed. He and Kocha went way back, apparently; my brother hinted at this a few times, although he never wanted to get into it. He just said you could trust Kocha—he'd be there if you got into a jam. Some Gypsies forced Kocha out of his apartment a few years ago, so he moved up here, to the gas station. He lived in the

trailer, led a calm, serene existence, spent most of his time remi-
niscing, and wasn't even thinking about getting his apartment back.
He was a mess—his balding head had a soft pink tint to it, and his
glasses made him look like some insane chemist who'd just discovered the formula for an alternative, environmentally-friendly form
of cocaine and decided to test it out on himself, with some very
promising results. He wore orange work overalls and old, beat-up
army boots; most of his clothing came from military surplus shops,
in fact; he even had foreign socks labeled R and L so you couldn't
confuse the right and the left. His wrists were wrapped in handkerchiefs and bloody bandages and his face and hands were always
scratched and cut up. His hands were generally so red he looked
as though he'd been eating pizza with them.

★

Well, now he was sitting out in the sun, answering my questions
rather unconvincingly.

"Fine," I said, "if you don't want to talk, don't. So who kept
the books?"

"Books?" Kocha answered, opening his eyes. "What do you
need books for?"

"I want to figure out how much dough you took in."

"Uh-huh. Herman, we got money out the fuckin' wazoo,"
Kocha said, starting to laugh anxiously, then adding, "You'll have
to talk with Olga. Your brother worked with her. She's got her
office in town."

"Who is she? His squeeze, or something?"

"Squeeze?" Kocha asked, rather huffily. "I just told you—they worked together, that's all."

"Where's her office?"

"You mean you're going to go there right now?"

"Well, I'm not gonna sit around here with you all day."

"Buddy, it's Sunday. She's got the day off."

"What about tomorrow?"

"What about it?"

"Does she work tomorrow?"

"I don't know, maybe."

"All right, Kocha. You handle the customers," I said, surveying the empty highway. "I'm going to get some sleep."

"Go sleep in the trailer," Kocha replied.

★

Light was poking through the shades, filling the room with sunny dust particles. Hot streaks spread across the floor like spilled flour. Some makeshift blinds made out of old tape reels were hanging over the doorway. It must have taken Kocha a while to put them together. I stepped into the room without shutting the door and took a look around. A draft disturbed the curtains, and they started rustling like cornstalks. Two couches, drooping in the middle, had been set up against the walls. A kitchen with a stove, an ancient fridge, and various appliances hanging on the walls was on the right. On the left, in the corner, stood a desk cluttered with all sorts of dubious-looking trash—I didn't want to root around in it. An odd smell topped off the room. I had been absolutely certain that a room inhabited by Kocha would have to reek. Of what? Well, just about anything—blood, sperm, maybe even gasoline—but no, the trailer smelled like any other place where a man was used to bedding down in comfort—it was the same odd smell you always find in the rooms of contented widowers (if one can put it that way) who have no real insecurities. "Well, the Kocha I know has no real insecurities, obviously," I thought to myself as I sank onto the tidier and least droopy-seeming couch. I flopped down, pulled off my sneakers, and suddenly the hassle of this whole trip hit me. All the stop-and-go driving, hitchhiking, drinking Karolina's sweet beverage, seeing the black sky over the raspberry fields, and sleeping in a truck cab. This whole morning seemed like it would have no end to it. I had been operating some mechanism without even knowing it—and it had just malfunctioned. Something just wasn't right. I felt I was standing in a spacious room into which some total strangers had been allowed just before all the lights went out. I had been in that room before, and knew its layout, but the presence of those strangers, who were standing next to me, silently, hiding something from me, made the familiar space foreign.

"Whatever," I told myself. "I can always just go home."

The wall above the couch was covered with old photographs, magazine clippings, and colorful illustrations. Kocha, just like a real serial killer, had pasted up fragments of faces, contours of bodies, and shreds of crowds with some eyes and mouths protruding at random. They were joyful collages; they also contained what appeared to be excerpts of different magazine stories pasted together—random glossy pages and then just plain paper, along with labels peeled from beer bottles, political pamphlets, pictures from fashion magazines, black-and-white pornographic shots, soccer team calendars, and someone's driver's license prominently displayed. From a distance the whole thing ran together into some bizarre pattern, as though someone had been painstakingly disfiguring the wallpaper. Up close, though, the eye was immediately drawn to a multitude of minor details—the faded yellow newspaper clippings, the mannequins whose eyes had been gouged out, freshly-spread glue, and dark crimson drops of strawberry jam resembling dried-up nail polish. A solid light-green, claylike background littered with letters and symbols, broken lines, and contrasting colors wrapped the whole construction together. No matter how intently I looked at the thing, I couldn't figure out what was going on. Eventually, I ran my finger down the wall until I caught a glimpse of Kocha's army photo; I ripped it off. A capital *U* poked out from underneath. It was a map. Probably a map of the USSR—the Carpathian Mountains, the Caucasus, and Mongolia were in sandy clay, the taiga and Caspian Lowland were in light green, and, apparently, the deserts were signified by a chalky dry area, where the sandy clay had hardened. The Pacific Ocean was dark, dark blue and the North Sea was light blue. A naked chick with a severed head took the place of the North Pole. Huh. Perfect for a school geography club. I sank into a deep silence.

★

Some voices woke me up, voices that instantly rubbed me the wrong way. I hopped out of bed and went outside. The sound was coming from the gas station; there were a few people shouting all at the same time, but the only voice I could recognize was Kocha's, and it was trembling.

Two dudes wearing sport coats and jeans were sprawled out on the seats by the booth. One guy was wearing a tie, while the other, who looked like he was the boss, just had his top button undone. The former was in sneakers and the latter was in leather dress shoes. A third guy, though, wearing jeans and an Adidas jacket, had Kocha by the scruff of the neck and was shaking him roughly. Kocha was shouting something in protest, and the dudes sitting in the chairs were chuckling. "Uh-oh," I thought as I moved toward them.

"Hey," I called out, "what's the big idea?" Thinking, "I'll punch the first fucker, and then I'll make a run for it, if I have to. But what about Kocha?"

Taken by surprise, the third dude released Kocha, dropping him onto the ground. The two guys sitting in the chairs gave me the evil eye.

"Guys, what the fuck," I said, choosing my words with care.

"And who are you?" the surly guy who had been roughing Kocha up asked.

"I could ask you the same thing."

"Hey, pansy," the third dude said, giving Kocha—who was sitting on the asphalt and rubbing his neck—a kick. "Who's that?"

"That's Herman," Kocha told him, "Yura's brother—he's the owner."

"The owner?" the main guy asked incredulously as he struggled to his feet. The other one, with the tie, followed his lead.

"That's right," Kocha confirmed.

"What do you mean, 'owner?'" the boss demanded. "What about Yura?"

"Yura's gone," Kocha said.

"Well, where is he?" the main guy asked.

"He's taking some continuing education courses," I said.

Out of the corner of my eye I caught a glimpse of a car pulling in off the highway—I was really banking on it to save the day.

"When's he getting back?" The main guy had also seen the car and was talking with a lot less confidence now.

"Once he finishes his course," I told him, "he'll come back. What's it to you?"

The car rolled onto the patch of asphalt by the gas station and screeched to a halt. The dust settled, and Injured got out of the car. He glared at the group of us and headed right over. He stopped at the booth without saying a thing. He was keeping a close eye on everyone.

"So, what's the deal?" I asked again, trying to assert myself.

"Your gasoline is diluted," the main guy replied spitefully.

"We'll sort that out," I promised him.

"You do that," the guy said, then headed off toward their Jeep, obviously dissatisfied with how our conversation had gone. His two cronies followed suit, though the guy who'd been restraining Kocha wound up to give him one last kick before taking another look at Injured and deciding to back off.

The Jeep had left a black trail across the asphalt. Maybe they'd slammed on the brakes when they arrived. The trail dropped off before the pumps. Apparently, they'd never had any intention of filling up. So the dudes took their seats, put the pedal to the metal, and sped off toward the highway. Kocha got up and started dusting himself off.

"Who were those guys?" I asked him.

"The local gang," Kocha answered anxiously. "The kings of corn."

"What'd they want?"

"Nothing, nothing at all," Kocha said, putting on his glasses, slipping by me, and disappearing around the corner of the building.

"Hi, Herman," Injured said, coming up to me and shaking my hand.

"Hey," I asked him, "what the hell's going on around here?"

"Can't you see?" he replied, nodding his head at the highway. "And your brother's gone, you know."

"But why'd he leave?"

"I know exactly why," Injured said sharply, "I think he was fuckin' fed up with all this shit, so he just packed his bags and left. I'm getting out of here too. I just gotta finish up this carburetor for this one motherfucker from Kramatorsk, and then I'm gone. Why shouldn't I go?" He looked around dejectedly, but after failing to find a sympathetic listener he turned around and stalked off to the garage.

★

Injured's mood came as no surprise. He was always dissatisfied with something, and always seemed to be spoiling for a fight. It was probably just some kind of defense mechanism. Injured was ten years older than me. A living legend, the best striker in the history of Voroshilovgrad soccer. In the early '90s, we wound up playing on the same team, so I caught the tail end of his career. Retiring from the big leagues really hurt his pride—Injured got spiteful and heavy. With his small stature, his foppish mustache, and his substantial gut, he looked less like a striker now than some kind of team massage therapist or sports commentator. When it came time to start a new life off the field, Injured quickly earned recognition as a top-notch mechanic, but he never wanted to work in someone else's garage. My brother was the only one who managed to find some common ground with him—he took Injured on as a full partner, staying out of his hair professionally and refusing to get involved in his personal problems either. Injured was happy with their arrangement. He came and went as he pleased and did what he liked. Still, he had one passion that manifested itself outside of working hours. Since his glory days as a star forward, Injured had always been a skirt-chaser. That's why he'd never married—when you're sleeping with six women at a time, how are you supposed to settle down with any one of them? Curiously enough, the number of his partners hadn't decreased after his athletic career came to an end—actually, it was just the opposite: As Injured aged, he'd honed his charm, meticulously cultivating and maintaining a unique aura, that of a chubby, forty-year-old ladies' man. Women adored Injured, and that son of a bitch knew it. He always kept a metal comb in the breast pocket of his snow-white dress shirt; occasionally he'd use it to straighten out his little mustache. Bottles of cologne and tapes full of romantic melodies— or the "music of love," as he called it—were always on hand. And yes, Injured took the occasional beating from aggrieved husbands on account of his amoral escapades. When that happened, he'd lock himself up in the garage and tinker for days on end. He was a kind man, all in all, if a bit reserved, and he was always a bit of a jerk to everyone. I was used to it, though.

★

So what do we have here? We have some motherfuckers that were roughing Kocha up, and if it weren't for Injured, they could very well have started on me. After all, on paper, I was the owner of the gas station. Five years ago, my brother had gotten nervous about something, so he quite sensibly signed the deed over to me. We trusted one another. He knew that I couldn't hurt his business even if I tried, so he told me not to worry, just sign on the dotted line. Eventually he learned how to forge my signature, so I didn't even know how he was doing, how much he was paying in taxes, what kind of profit he was making. He had his own problems to deal with, while I hadn't had any to speak of, at least up until the last few days. Now it turned out that I had a boatload of problems, and I had to solve them, somehow. (Well, actually, I guess I could have just said, "screw this" and hightailed it to Amsterdam.) What bothered me the most was that my brother hadn't told me a thing. I had no clue where to go from here. Just a few days ago I had been a supposedly free and easy independent expert, fighting for democracy against God knows who. Now I had some property hanging over my head—and I had to do something with it, because my brother was out of the picture and there was nobody to forge my signature anymore.

One way or another, I would have to pay this Olga of theirs a visit to get some kind of information. No matter what, I wouldn't be getting home today. It'd be best to give Lyolik a call and let him know. I stepped into the booth and picked up the phone hanging on the wall.

"It's not working," Kocha said, standing in the doorway and looking at the receiver in my hands. "I already told you."

"You got a cell?"

"Yeah, but it's not working either," he said.

"Does Injured have one?"

"He does. But he won't let anyone use it."

"My ass he won't." I wasn't about to take Kocha's word for it, so I headed for the garage, pushing the old man out of the way.

Injured had already changed into his dark-blue work uniform and pulled on a black beret. Some hunk of junk was elevated on a jack; Injured caressed it like a butcher handling a cow carcass.

"Injured," I said, "give me your cell. I'm staying here until tomorrow. I have to let my guys know."

"You're staying?" Injured replied, looking straight at me. "Okay, fine. But there's no money left on my phone, so you're shit out of luck."

"So where can I make a call?"

"Go over to the TV tower, right over there. And quit fuckin' bothering me, okay?" he yelled as I was leaving.

I walked around the booth, hugging the trailer and following a path. I descended into a gully, climbed a small hill, pushed my way through some raspberry bushes, and popped out onto an asphalt road leading off the main highway. I approached the fence that looped around the TV tower. There was a prominent "Do Not Enter" sign on the gate, but it was open, so I stepped inside. A path led up to a one-story building. It must have contained the control panel, or whatever you call it. The actual tower stood off to the side, buried among flowers and wrapped in barbed wire. An old German shepherd ran out from around the corner, came up to me, sniffed my shoes lazily, then went off in another direction. There was no one in sight. The dog, presumably responsible for guarding the local broadcasting services, had been flagrantly neglecting its duties. I stood still for a bit, waiting for someone to come out. Nobody did, so I went up the rest of the way to the building. The doors were locked. I knocked. Nobody answered, not that my hopes were high. I walked up to the window and peered in. There was nothing to see on the other side, but then someone's face emerged from the darkness. I stepped back, startled. The face disappeared instantly, feet pattered across the floor, and the doors opened. A girl of about sixteen stood at the doorway. She had short black hair, big gray eyes, and was wearing plastic earrings. She had on a short, bright T-shirt, a jean skirt, and light sandals.

"Hi," she said.

"Hi," I said, "I'm Herman, from the gas station."

"Herman? Yura's brother?" she asked.

"You know him?"

"We all know each other around here," she said.

"Do you have a phone? I have to make a call, and ours was disconnected. Kocha claims we didn't pay this month's bill."

"Oh, that Kocha," the girl said, stepping to the side and letting me pass. I walked down a hallway and reached a room with a bed at one end and a desk at the other. There was a phone on the desk. The girl followed me and stood in the doorway, watching my movements with interest.

"Do you mind?" I demanded.

"Not at all," she said, but she didn't move an inch.

I picked up the receiver and dialed my home phone number.

"Yeah," Lyolik said curtly.

"Hey, it's me."

"Where are you?" he asked.

"I'm at my brother's, everything's all right. How was the ride back?"

"Shitty. Bolik got carsick, he barely made it."

"Well, now everything's okay, yeah?"

"Yeah, we're okay. When are you getting back?"

"Listen brohan, there's some stuff I gotta take care of here. I'll be staying for another day. I have to meet up with the accountant tomorrow." I heard the girl chuckling behind me. "So I'll be home on Tuesday. Make sure to tell Bolik, okay?"

"Well, I don't know about that. Maybe you should tell him yourself?"

"You're shitting me. Back me up here, all right?"

"Why don't you just talk to Bolik, huh? So there won't be any problems."

"Get the fuck outta here! What problems could there be, Lyolik? We have to trust our friends, don't we?"

"Okay, sure."

"Next time I'll bring you a chick. A blow-up one."

"Bring me a drive shaft instead."

"So that's how you swing these days?"

"Shut it, douchebag," Lyolik said and hung up.

The girl saw me out. I thanked her.

"Don't mention it," she said. "And tell your brother 'hello' for me."

"He's gone. He took off somewhere."

"And what about you? Are you going to take off somewhere?"

"Why, you want me to stick around?"

"Like I need you," the girl said, completely unruffled.

"You aren't scared up here, all by yourself?"

"No, I'm not," she said. "Now get out of here, or I'll sic my dog on you."

I went up to the gate and then stopped. She was at the window again, keeping an eye on me, probably thinking I couldn't see her. I waved. Realizing I'd caught her spying on me, the girl started laughing and waved back. Then she flashed me, showing off what she had under that T-shirt. She evaporated the very next instant. I just stood there, dumbfounded, waiting to see whether she'd reappear in the window, but no, she was gone. "What a strange girl," I thought, then went on my way.

★

Work was in full swing at the station. Kocha, sprawled out on the catapult chair, was sleeping soundly, his right hand clamped between his skinny legs. I went over to the garage. Injured, shirtless, sweaty, constantly grumbling about something, was circling around that elevated hunk of metal, occasionally rubbing his stomach up against it. He waved when he saw me, wiping beads of sweat off his forehead and deciding then and there to take a smoke break.

"You get through?"

"Yep. I'm heading out tomorrow."

"Sure, sure," Injured said, giving me a severe look.

"Look," I said, "who's that high school girl over there, at the TV tower?"

"Katya?" A warm, dreamy haze appeared in Injured's eyes immediately, and a paternal smile broke out below his thick mustache. "What'd she say?"

"She didn't say anything, really. She's a good . . . modest girl."

"Keep your distance," Injured warned. "It wouldn't go anywhere good."

"Does she work over there?"

"Her dad does. She brings him lunch."

"Just like Little Red Riding Hood."

"Huh?"

"Never mind."

"Herman," Injured asked, "what do you actually do for a living?"

"I'm an independent expert," I said.

"And what exactly does an independent expert do?"

"How should I put it? Nothing, really."

"You know, Herman," Injured said, "I don't trust you. Don't take offense—just let me tell you how I see it."

"Go for it. Lay it all out for me."

"Simply put, I don't trust you. You're going to hang us out to dry—you don't give a fuck about any of this, and Kocha doesn't give a fuck either. You don't even know what you do for a living.

Your brother, on the other hand—he's completely different."

"Well, why'd he leave then?"

"Does it matter?"

"Sure it does. Who were those guys in the Jeep?"

"You scared or something?"

"Why? Should I be?"

"You're shaking in your boots, I can see that. Kocha's scared of them, too. Everyone is. Your brother wasn't, though."

"Your brother this, your brother that. Enough already."

"All right, take it easy," Injured said, putting on his jacket and getting back to work. He started up a car. The noise made my ears ring.

"Injured!" I yelled over to him. He paused and looked over in my direction, leaving the car running. "I'm not afraid. Why should I be? It's just that you've got your lives, and I've got mine."

Injured nodded. Maybe he couldn't even hear me.

★

When evening came, Injured gave the rest of us a mute farewell and went home. Kocha was still sitting on the catapult, covered in orange and blue dust. He seemed to have gotten stuck in some sort of odd torpor; neither Injured's departure nor the various passing truck drivers' repeated requests that he fill up their tanks made the least impression on him. Injured had shown me how to work the pumps, so I was the one who waited on the three larger-than-life tractor-trailers that came by, looking like huge, weary lizards. The sun had floated over to the other side of the highway, and the twilight burst open like a sunflower. Kocha came to life just as the evening did. Around nine he stood up, locked the booth, and wandered listlessly over to the far edge of the lot. With a heavy sigh, he looped around the truck cab I had slept in last night, squeezed himself inside, and sprawled out in the driver's seat, extending his legs through the shattered window. I crawled in after him and sat in the passenger seat. Down below, darkness was enveloping the valley. To the east, the sky was already covered in a dim haze, while to the west, right above our heads, red flames spilled across the whole valley, heralding the arrival of night. Mist rose off the river, concealing the little silhouettes of fishermen and the surrounding houses, rolling out onto the road and drifting into the suburbs. The fog that hovered over the valley the city sat in was white. The valley was fading away into darkness, growing more and more indistinct, until it resembled a riverbed, though up here, in the hills, it was still light. Kocha, wide-eyed and stupefied, was staring down at it all, unblinking, his gaze fixed on the advancing night.

"Here," I said, handing Kocha my MP3 player.

He put the earphones on over his balding head, tapping some buttons to adjust the volume.

"What is this, anyway?" he asked.

"Charlie Parker. I ripped ten CDs' worth."

Kocha listened for a bit, and then put the 'phones down, off to the side.

"You know why I like it out here?" I asked him. "There aren't any airplanes going by."

He looked up. It was true; there really weren't any planes. There were still some lights, though: just reflections, maybe, shooting across the sky; green sparks glowing here and there; golden balls spinning along; clouds massing to the north, giving off little sparkles.

"But there are always satellites up there," Kocha answered finally. "You can see them very well at night. When I'm not sleeping I always see them."

"And why aren't you sleeping, old-timer?"

"Well," Kocha said, every consonant still coming out with a screech, "the thing is, I've got sleeping troubles. Ever since the army, Herman. You know how it goes in the paratroopers—those drops, the adrenaline . . . it sticks with you, for life."

"Gotcha."

"So I bought some sleeping pills. I asked for something that would really knock my socks off. They gave me some kind of weird artificial shit. God knows what they're putting in pills these days. Anyway, I started taking it, but it didn't do a thing. I upped the dose and I still couldn't fall asleep. Thing is, though, I've started sleeping during the day now. It's a real head-scratcher . . ."

"What have you been taking?" I asked him. "Can I have a look?"

Kocha rooted through his overall pockets and took out a bottle; the label was a poisonous-looking green. I took the bottle and tried reading it, but I didn't even recognize the characters on it.

"Maybe it's some sort of cockroach repellent. Who even makes these pills?"

"They told me the French do."

"But look at these hieroglyphs—does that look like French to you? Okay, okay—how about I try one?"

I twisted off the cap, took out a lilac-colored pill, and popped it into my mouth.

"Nah, man," Kocha said, taking back the bottle. "If you only take one you won't even feel it. I take at least five."

Kocha dumped a few pills down his throat, as if to validate this statement.

"Gimme that." I took the bottle back, poured out a few pills, and downed them. Then I just sat there, trying to focus in on my own sensations, waiting for the pills to kick in.

"Kocha, it doesn't feel like they're doing anything."

"I told you so."

"Maybe you need to wash them down."

"I tried doing that . . . with wine."

"And?"

"Nothing. My piss just turned red."

The twilight thickened, slipping through the tree branches and reaching out into the warm, dusty grass wrapping around us. Flaming orange balls hung in the valley, their sharp citrusy light burning through the fog. The sky was turning black and distant, the constellations showing through like a face appearing on a negative. But the night's most salient feature was the fact that I didn't have the slightest desire to sleep. Kocha put on my headphones again and began swaying softly to an inaudible beat.

Then I noticed movement somewhere down below. Someone was coming up from the river, ascending the steep slope. The hillside was buried in fog; I couldn't make anything out, but it sounded as though somebody was herding skittish animals away from the water.

"You see that?" I asked Kocha warily.

"Yep, I sure do," Kocha replied, nodding happily.

"Who's down there?"

"Yeah, yeah," Kocha said, continuing to nod, contemplating the night that had pounced on us so suddenly.

I froze, listening hard to the voices that were becoming more distinct as whoever it was drew nearer in the darkness that clung to everything like some thick, acerbic liquid. Lit by the valley below, the fog now seemed full of motion and shadows. I could see into the space above it, where some bats occasionally whipped by, making circles above our heads then abruptly darting back into the wet haze. The voices got louder, the rustling resolved into individual footsteps, and then, all at once, bodies started swimming out of the fog, gliding quickly across the thick, hot grass toward us. They moved easily up the slope—there were more and more of them. I could already see the first ones' faces; new, distinct voices carried out of the fog now, and they sounded sweet and sharp as they soared into the sky like smoke from fireplaces. When the first ones drew even with me, I wanted to call something out, something that would stop them, but I was at a loss for words. I could only sit there and observe them silently as they came nearly face-to-face with us, only to push on, not stopping or paying any attention to us, disappearing back into the nighttime haze. I couldn't understand what kind of creatures they were; they were strange, nearly formless; men with clumps of fog tucked away in their lungs. They were tall, with long, unkempt hair that they had pulled back into ponytails or else wore in Mohawks. Their faces were dark and scarred; some of them had odd painted signs and letters on their foreheads, while others had piercings in their ears or noses. Some of them had covered their faces with bandannas. Medallions and binoculars dangled from their necks, and they had fishing poles and guns slung over their shoulders. One was holding a flag, while another carried a long dry stick with a dog's head on the end. Somebody was carrying a cross, and somebody else seemed to be carrying all his belongings in a bundle. Many of them had drums; they weren't beating them, however; they were hoisted over their shoulders. The creatures' clothing was striking but bedraggled—somebody was wearing an officer's jacket, while others were decked out in sheepskins. Many were wearing long, simple white garments dotted with cow's blood. One of them wasn't wearing a shirt, and his extensive tattoos gave off a blue light under the glowing stars. Another one was wearing army boots, while somebody else had laced sandals on, though most walked along barefoot, crushing bugs and field mice and stepping on thorns, although they showed no signs of discomfort. Women, whispering back and forth in the dark, and occasionally bursting into laughter, followed the men. Some wore their hair in buns, and many of them had dreads, but the pack even included some bald ladies, their skulls painted red and blue. Icons and pentagrams hung from their necks, and they were carrying drowsy and hungry children on their shoulders, children whose eyes soaked up the darkness around them. The women's dresses were long and colorful; it looked as though they had been wrapped in the flags of some unknown republics. They wore bracelets and baubles around their ankles, and one of them even had little silver rings on her toes. After they too had passed, more dark figures began to burst out of the fog, one by one. They were like nothing I had ever seen before. Some had rams' horns on their heads wrapped in ribbons and golden paper, while other figures were covered in thick fur. Yet another group followed after them, with turkey feathers rustling behind their backs, while the last cohort, the darkest and least talkative, were deformed, each looking as though they'd been created by merging two bodies together—they walked along with two heads on their shoulders, two hearts in their chests, and enough life in them to die twice. Then weary cow heads poked out of the fog; it was unclear how this strange tribe had forced their animals to climb the steep hill, but there they were, plodding along, dragging harrows bearing blind snakes and dead fighting dogs. The harrows erased the tracks left by the incredible procession that had just passed us. Then we saw that the cows were being goaded on by herders in black and gray overcoats. They were moving the animals through the night, taking great pains not to leave any tracks behind. I recognized a few of the herders' faces—the only problem being that I couldn't remember where I'd seen them before. They noticed me too, but they simply looked me right in the eyes, forcing me to give up any last semblance of composure before they pushed on, leaving behind a scorched smell of iron and burning skin. The sky had already started to turn white over wherever they'd come from. As soon as they disappeared, the air was injected with an even, gray light, the new morning filling it up like water poured into a vessel. A red crack ran across the sky, and morning sunlight doused the valley. Kocha was still sitting next to me—he seemed to be sleeping . . . with his eyes open. I sucked in a sharp breath through my nose.

Morning did come, but a bitter aftertaste of the voices that had been there a moment ago remained in the air. It felt as though death or a freight train had just come through.

3

In the morning, Kocha and I drank some tea he had brewed. He told me how to find Olga, and then sent me off with a trucker whose rig he had just filled up.

"Give me your poison," I said. "I'll at least figure out what you've been taking. Where'd you buy this?"

"In the main square," Kocha replied, "at the pharmacy."

★

Down below, just beyond the bridge, a row of lime trees spread out along the highway; the blinding sun fought its way through the leaves. The truck driver put on his sunglasses; I just closed my eyes. A dam, built to protect the city against any possible flood, curved off to the left. In the spring, when the river overflowed its banks, big pools would form; sometimes they'd break through the dam and deluge the nearby neighborhoods. We rolled into the city, drove past the first few buildings, and stopped at an empty intersection.

"Well, that's it, buddy, I'm turning right," the truck driver said.

"Okay," I answered, and hopped down onto the sandy street.

The city was empty. Some slow current seemed to be carrying the sun to the west. As it moved along above the city blocks, the light was settling on the air like river silt, making it thick and warm. This was one of the older parts of the city, mostly crumbling one or two-story red brick buildings. The sidewalks were covered in sand; grass had sprouted everywhere else, making it look as though the city had been abandoned and reclaimed by nature. The grass filled every crevice, reaching upward gently, yet persistently. I passed a few mom-and-pop stores, the smell of baked bread and soap wafting from their open doors. There didn't seem to be any customers around, though. One woman, wearing a short red skirt, was standing there listlessly, leaning up against a doorway. She had heavy, ash-colored hair, tan skin, and large breasts. Beads of sweat, like drops of fresh honey, rolled down the whole warm expanse of her body. She was wearing some beads, and a few necklaces with gold crosses on them. She had gold watches on, one on each hand, or maybe I was just imagining it. I greeted her as I walked by. She nodded in reply, scrutinizing me, but she couldn't recall my face. "She's really paying attention," I thought. She appeared to be waiting for someone. I covered a few more blocks and stopped by the telephone company. It was dank inside, like an aquarium. Two local cowboys, wearing T-shirts that only partially covered their tattooed shoulders, stood in line by the customer service window. Once the cowboys had split, I paid the station's phone bill and went back outside. I turned the corner, walked along a street where all the kiosks were closed, and found myself in the main square. The square resembled a drained pool. Grass was poking up through stone tiles turned white by the rain—the whole place was starting to look like a soccer field. City Hall stood on the other side of the square. I stepped into the pharmacy. A girl with dyed blonde hair, naked except for a white lab coat, stood behind the counter. When she saw me, she slipped her feet into a pair of sandals lying next to her on the cool, stone-tiled floor.

"Hi," I said, "my grandpa bought some medication here a while back. Could you tell me what it's for?"

"Oh yeah? What's wrong with this grandpa of yours?" the girl asked suspiciously.

"You know, he's got some problems."

"What kind of problems?"

"You know, with his head."

She took the bottle out of my hand, scrutinizing it.

"This isn't for headaches."

"You're joking."

"It's for your stomach."

"Does it loosen you or tighten you up?" I asked, just in case.

"It loosens you up," she said, "and then it tightens you up again, but it's past the expiration date. How's he been feeling?"

"He's hanging in there," I replied. "Give me some vitamins or something."

★

Olga's office was right around the corner, on a quiet, shady side street. There was a beat-up scooter parked next to the sprawling mulberry that grew by the doors. When I was a kid, there used to be a bookstore here. Its heavy iron doors were still there, still painted orange. I opened them and walked in.

Olga was sitting by the window on a stack of papers, smoking.

She was roughly my brother's age, although she still looked quite good. She had curly red hair and chalky skin that seemed as though it was illuminated from the inside by fluorescent light; she hardly wore any makeup, which may have made her look younger. She was wearing a long dress and white designer sneakers.

"Hi."

"Good afternoon," she said, waving the clouds of smoke away and sizing me up. "Are you Herman?"

"Have we met before?"

"Injured told me you'd be stopping by. Take a seat," she said, pointing at a chair and getting to her feet. As she did, the papers she'd been perching on spilled all over the floor. I was about to lean over to help pick them up, but Olga stopped me, saying, "Forget it. Leave them there. I've been meaning to throw them out anyway."

She took a seat in her chair and swung her feet up onto the table like cops do in American movies, her sneakers resting heavily on some reports and log books. Her dress slid up for a second. She had some nice legs on her—long, lean calves and high hips.

"What are you looking at?" she asked.

"At the log books," I answered and sat down across from her. "Olga, I'd like to have a talk with you. Do you have a few minutes to spare?"

"I've got an hour. You want to talk about your brother?"

"That's right."

"Okay then, you know what?" she said, drawing her legs back abruptly, so her calves flashed before my eyes again. "Let's go to the park. It's too stuffy in here. Did you drive here?"

"I got a ride."

"No big deal. I've got a scooter."

We went outside. There was a padlock hanging from the front doors; she closed it and hopped on the scooter, which only started on the third try. She nodded to me, and I got on, gingerly holding onto her shoulders.

"Herman," she said, twisting to face me and yelling over the roar of the motor. "Have you ever ridden a scooter before?"

"Sure," I yelled back.

"Don't you know where to put your hands?"

Flustered, I took my hands off her shoulders and put them on her waist, feeling the outline of her panties through her dress.

"Don't get too carried away," she said, and we set off.

The park was just across the street. Nevertheless, Olga tore down the road, drove onto the sidewalk, and darted between the thick bushes. There was a paved path ahead; Olga adeptly squeezed in between the trees and popped us right out onto the asphalt. The rows of trees were sunny and empty, and behind them were amusement park rides and swings, giving way in turn to other, younger trees, a playground whose sandboxes were being slowly taken over by grass, and old ticket booths now inhabited by drowsy, cooing pigeons and skulking stray dogs. Olga rounded a fountain, turned onto a side path, zoomed by two girls walking a dachshund, and stopped by an old bar overlooking the river. The bar had been around for ages; I remembered how back in the late '80s we used to make bootleg tapes in one of the back rooms. In my Communist Youth League days, I'd even recorded some heavy metal here. Oddly enough, the bar was still open. We went into a rather spacious room suffused with the smell of nicotine. The walls were paneled in hardwood and the windows were draped with heavy curtains dotted with numerous burn holes and lipstick marks. A sixty-year-old guy who looked like a Gypsy, meaning he was wearing a white dress shirt and had gold teeth, was manning the bar. Olga greeted him, and he nodded in reply.

"I had no clue this place was still open."

"I haven't been here in ages myself," Olga said. "I just didn't want to talk in the office. It's more relaxing here."

The Gypsy came over.

"Do you have any gin and tonic?" Olga asked.

"No," he said firmly.

"Well, what *do* you have?" she asked, a bit flustered. "Herman, what are you going to have?" she asked me. "They don't have any gin and tonic."

"Do you have any port?" I asked the Gypsy.

"Yeah, white port."

"Oh, I'll have that," I said. "What about you, Olga?"

"Well, fine," she agreed, "we'll have port. So, have you seen your brother lately?"

"The last time was about six months ago. Do you know where he is?"

"No, I don't. Do you?"

"Nope. What are you to him, anyway?"

"I'm his accountant," Olga said, taking out a cigarette and lighting it. "Isn't that why you wanted to talk to me?"

"I didn't mean to imply anything."

"Who said you did? Don't worry about it."

The Gypsy came back over, carrying our port in the squat

glasses they use to serve tea on trains, though their new role had allowed them to shed the metal holders meant to keep passengers from burning their fingers.

"Well, what's your next move?" Olga asked, taking a cautious sip.

"I don't know," I answered. "I'm only in town for a few days."

"I see. What do you do for a living?"

"Nothing really. Here, take a look," I said, pulling my business card out of my pocket and handing it to her.

"So you're an expert?"

"Yep, sure am," I said and downed my port. "Olga, you know the whole business is in my name, right?"

"I know."

"What should I do?"

"I don't know."

"Well, I can't just leave everything as is, can I?"

"Maybe you can, maybe you can't."

"Would that be a problem?"

"Maybe."

"So . . . what should I do?"

"Haven't you tried getting in touch with your brother?" Olga asked after a short pause.

"I've tried. But he hasn't been picking up his phone. I have no idea where he is. Kocha says he's in Amsterdam."

"That Kocha . . ." Olga said and motioned for the Gypsy to bring her another.

Visibly irritated, the Gypsy hauled himself up, placed the unfinished bottle of port on our table, and went outside—clearly, he didn't want to be bothered anymore.

"The gas station, is it even profitable?" I asked.

"How should I put it?" Olga replied after I had poured another round and she had downed her glass. "Your brother made enough money to keep the place afloat. But he never made enough to open another station."

"Uh-huh. My brother didn't want to sell it?"

"Nope."

"Did anyone make him an offer?"

"Yeah," Olga said.

"Who?"

"Well, we've got some local hoods."

"So I noticed. Whose hoods are they?"

"Marlen Pastushok. He's a corn guy."

"I might know who you're talking about."

"He's also a member of the Parliament, from the Communist Party."

"He's a Communist?"

"Yep, he's got a chain of gas stations in the Donbas, and now he's buying up everything over here too. I don't know where he lives. He offered Yura fifty thousand, if I remember correctly."

"Fifty thousand? For what?"

"For the property," Olga said.

"Why didn't Yura take it?"

"Would you have taken it?"

Finally, I just said, "Well, I don't know."

"I do. You would have."

"Why do you say that?"

"Because you're a wimp, Herman. And stop staring at my tits."

I had indeed been inspecting the front of her dress for some time—it was rather low-cut, and Olga wasn't wearing a bra. Some wrinkles were developing under her eyes, but the effect was pretty cute. I still probably wouldn't peg her as forty.

"Olga, this just isn't my thing, you know what I mean?" I said, trying to be diplomatic. "I've always stayed out of his business."

"Now it's *your* business."

"Olga, would you sell it, if it was your gas station?"

"Sell it to Pastushok?" Olga asked. "I'd burn it to the ground before I did that, and I'd throw all that scrap metal on the pyre as well."

"But why? What's the problem?"

"Herman," she said, finishing another drink, "there are two kinds of people that I really hate. First and foremost, I can't stand wimps."

"And the second kind?"

"The second kind are railroad workers, but that's strictly personal. Well, you do what you want. At the end of the day, it's your call."

"It seems like I don't have a choice, do I?"

"It seems like you just don't know whether or not you do."

I didn't have anything to say to that, so I poured the rest of the wine. We clinked glasses, without saying a word.

"You know," Olga said after the silence had dragged on long enough, "there's a disco around the corner."

"I know. That's where I had sex the first time."

"Oh yeah?" she said, for want of anything else to say.

"By the way, I also had sex in this very bar one time. On New Year's Eve."

"Maybe it was a mistake to bring you here," Olga said, after thinking a little.

"Nah, everything's fine. I like this park a lot. We would always come here after soccer games. We'd climb over the stadium fence and head over here . . . to celebrate."

"I can only imagine."

"Olga," I said, "if I wound up staying, would you work for me like you did for Yura? How much was my brother paying you?"

"In any case, you'd have to pay me more." She took out her phone. "Oh," she said, "it's twelve already. I gotta go."

She paid for the port. She ignored all of my attempts at picking up the tab and said she made a good living so there was no need for my poor show of generosity. We went outside. I didn't really know what to do next, though I did know that I had no real desire to ask her any more questions. Her phone rang as we stood there.

"Yeah," Olga answered. "Uh, yeah." Her voice immediately took on a distant, professional tone. "Yes, he's here with me. Should I give him the phone? You want to talk to him? All right, if that's how you want it. By the fountain."

"Well," she said to me, muffling the phone with her hand, "now you'll have a chance to talk to them in person."

"With who?"

"The corn guys."

"How'd they find me?"

"Herman, there aren't that many people in this town, so it's pretty easy to find someone when you want to, you know? They want you to wait by the fountain. I'm off. Enjoy!"

She hopped on her scooter, which emitted a thick cloud of smoke, then disappeared into the depths of the municipal park.

★

"But how will I recognize them?" was the thought that popped into my head as I waited on the brick ledge of the dried-up fountain—there was more grass growing on the bottom. It seemed to be sprouting just about everywhere in this city. In fact, there wasn't anybody else in the park besides me, the two high school girls walking the dachshund, and the Gypsy. Nobody, that is, until the black Jeep from yesterday came barreling around the corner, scattering the pigeons and honking to high heaven. "I'll know them when I see them, all right," I thought.

The Jeep did a victory lap around the fountain and stopped across from me. The back doors opened and a petite bald guy wearing a light-colored polo shirt and white pants leaned out of the car at me. He hadn't been at the gas station yesterday. He smiled, exposing his fine collection of metal. He wasn't getting out of the car, though.

"Herman Korolyov?" he inquired.

"Good afternoon!" I said, holding my ground as well.

"Have you been waiting long?" The bald guy was sprawled out on the leather seat in a way that was clearly intended to suggest an easygoing disposition.

"Not very long!"

"My apologies," he said. By now the dude must have been pretty uncomfortable in that position, but he refused to sit up.

Who would budge first had become a pissing contest now. "We had a hell of a time getting here."

"No worries," I answered, making a great show of how relaxed I was.

"I was trying to figure out if you were the one I was looking for," the bald guy said, breaking into laughter. His body began to jerk, and suddenly he was sliding down the slippery leather seat and onto the ground.

I darted toward him, but he clambered back to his seat quite adroitly, assuming a more comfortable position and extending his hand resolutely. All I could do was jump into the Jeep next to him and shake his hand.

"Nikolay Nikolaich," he introduced himself, producing a business card from somewhere underneath the seat, "but you can just call me Nikolaich."

I took out my own card and handed it over. His read, Assistant to Member of Parliament Marlen Pastushok.

"Where are you headed?" Nikolaich asked.

"Don't know," I said, "home, maybe."

"We'll give you a ride, it's along the way. Nick, let's go."

Nick . . . so the driver's name was also Nikolay. Maybe that was one of the prerequisites for getting hired in this outfit—non-Nikolays need not apply. Anyway, I saw an old Makarov pistol with notches on the grip lying brazenly on the seat next to "Nick." And I thought to myself, "This sort of cavalier attitude toward handling weapons might well get someone killed."

"The door," Nikolaich barked.

"What?" I asked blankly.

"Close the door."

I did, and the Jeep tore off into the bushes. Nick was driving headlong, paying no real attention to the road in front of him, as though relying on a compass. We plowed through the playground, looped around the disco where I first had sex, hopped the curb, then landed on the main road. But Nick wasn't going to take the easy way out—he spun the car into a dead-end side street paved with cracked bricks instead of asphalt, dragged us through a construction site, soared over a ditch, and pulled out onto the highway. All the while, Nick had been listening to some heavy guitar-based music—Rammstein, or something along those lines.

"Are you hiding from someone?" I asked Nikolaich.

"Nah, nah, it's just that Nick knows all the shortcuts around here."

We rode on for a while without speaking. Then Nikolaich cracked:

"Nick!" he yelled up to the driver, though Nick couldn't hear him over the music. "Nick, fuck man! Turn those fascists off!" Nick turned around rather grumpily, but he did turn the music off.

"Mr. Korolyov," he said.

"Just call me Herman," I told him.

"Sure, sure, of course," Nikolaich said. "I'd like to have a talk with you."

"Okay, so let's talk."

"Okay, let's."

"I don't mind."

"Excellent! Nick!" Nikolaich shouted. We had just driven onto a bridge. At the sound of his name, Nick hit the brakes, halfway across, then turned the engine off. Silence.

"Well, how do you like it in our neck of the woods?" Niko-laich asked, as if we weren't parked in the middle of a bridge.

"It's fine," I answered hesitantly. "I have to admit, it's good to be back in my old stomping grounds. Aren't we going to go any farther?" I asked, looking out the window.

"Nah, nah," Nikolaich reassured me, "soon we'll take you wherever you need to go. How long will you be in town for?"

"Don't know," I said, starting to get anxious. "We'll see how things play out. I'm sure you know my brother's gone . . ."

"Yeah," Nikolaich interjected, "Mr. Korolyov and I . . . I mean Yura, had a professional relationship," he said, finally making eye contact.

"That's good," I said rather feebly.

"It's excellent," Nikolaich agreed. "What could be better than a professional relationship?"

"Don't know," I admitted.

"You don't know?"

"I don't."

"I don't know either," Nikolaich said. A milk truck pulled up behind us. The driver honked. I saw another driver pulling up behind the milk truck. "Nick!" Nikolaich shouted.

Nick hopped out of the car and walked over to the milk truck. Then he jumped onto the running board, stuck his big head through the open driver's side window, and said something. The driver shut off his engine. Nick hopped down onto the asphalt and walked over to the next car.

"Herman, what I'm getting at is . . ." Nikolaich continued, "You're a young, energetic guy. You have a lot of ambition. I'd like to establish a professional relationship with you too. What do you think?"

"That would be excellent," I agreed.

"I don't know if Olga told you, but we're interested in purchasing your business. You understand what I mean?"

"I do."

"Well, it's good that you understand me. Your brother and I couldn't reach an understanding."

"Why?"

"Well, you know, we couldn't sort out all the details."

"Well, when he comes back, you'll sort them all out."

"When's he coming back?" Nikolaich asked, really starting to scrutinize me.

"I don't know. Hopefully soon."

"And if he doesn't come back?"

"What do you mean?"

"Well . . . it may play out that way."

"Don't be silly, Nikolay Nikolaich," I said. "It's Yura's business— he'll definitely come back. I'm not planning on selling anything."

A line of cars had formed behind us. The drivers coming our way in the other lane were stopping and asking Nick if everything was all right. Nick would say something, and the cars would just take off.

"Don't get anxious," Nikolaich said in a conciliatory tone. "I realize you aren't going to sell your brother's business to someone you hardly know. I completely understand that. Think it over— you have some time. We weren't able to reach an understanding with your brother, but I hope with you everything will work out the way it's supposed to. You've only got one option. Your business is failing—I know that for a fact. I see where your brother is coming from; he really did build his business from the ground up. But a business needs to keep growing, you got that, Herman? Take the money and split it with your brother. That's if he comes back. Think it over, okay?"

"Will do."

"Promise?"

"I swear," I answered, hoping to wrap this conversation up and get traffic moving again.

"Well, sounds like a deal," Nikolaich said, kicking back in his seat. "Nick!" he yelled.

Clearly in no hurry, Nick casually sat down in the driver's seat, started up the engine, and we headed out. A whole column of cars followed suit. We crossed the bridge, crested the hill easily, and veered off toward the gas station. Nick slammed on the brakes as soon as we pulled in. I opened the door. Kocha and Injured were soaking up the sun, sitting in the chairs by the booth. They exchanged a look full of surprise when they saw me.

"Well then," Nikolaich said as I took my leave, "I'm glad we've already found some common ground."

"Hold up," I said, as if I was trying to remember something. "What would you do if I were to turn you down?"

"Do you really have a choice?" Nikolaich asked incredulously. Breaking into a wide grin, he added "Okay, Herman, I'll stop by in a week. Have a good one."

Kocha had unbuttoned his overalls down to his chest; he sat there tanning a body as withered and pale as some dusty relic. Injured was wearing a foppish snow-white dress shirt, meticulously ironed black pants, and polished, pointed shoes. He looked like a farmer who was marrying off his only daughter. Both of them were glaring at me disapprovingly—Injured's eyes were burning right through me as he ran a finger over his mustache, and Kocha's glasses flashed in the sun, making me think of a dog baring its glinting fangs.

"Herman, what was all that about?" Injured asked.

"Did they rough you up?" Kocha added.

"Are you kidding? Nobody laid a finger on me. We just had a talk, and then they dropped me off."

"They're your new buddies?" Injured asked grimly.

"Uh-huh. We're good buddies, all right. They want to buy the gas station."

"Herman, we know," Injured said.

"You already knew?" I asked. "That's just great. How come you didn't tell me?"

"You didn't ask," Injured said, a bit offended.

"What was I supposed to ask you?"

"You weren't supposed to ask us anything," Injured said grumpily.

"That's just what I thought."

"Well, what did you think?" Injured asked after a short pause.

"I don't know. I think that 50k for this heap of scrap metal is a good price."

"You call that a good price?" Injured asked, getting up and sticking out his large gut.

"I'd say so."

"Sure, sure." Injured was mulling something over, examining

the pointed tips of his shoes, "Herman, watch it," he said eventually, "if you screw up too many times you'll be sorry. So you figure the easiest thing is to sell all this shit, do you?"

"It could be," I agreed.

"It could be, it could be," Injured repeated, before turning around and walking over to the garage.

I flopped down on the chair next to Kocha. He was hiding his eyes behind his glasses and looking up at the sky. Heavy clouds had begun moving in, and now they were drifting along over the hill, nearly beaching themselves on the booth's lonely pole like overloaded barges coasting in shallow waters.

"Here," I said, giving Kocha the vitamins. He inspected the bottle, holding it up to the sun.

"What's this?" he asked suspiciously.

"Vitamins."

"For my insomnia?"

"For your insomnia."

"Who makes them?"

"A Dutch company. You see those hieroglyphs? That's Dutch. They put shrooms in there . . . you know, the white ones, so you'll sleep like a rock."

"Thanks, Herman," Kocha said. "And don't mind Injured. So what if you sell the gas station? It wouldn't be the end of the fuckin' world."

"You think so?"

"I know so."

A leather ball flew out through the open garage doors—it landed heavily and rolled down the warm macadam. Then Injured emerged from the dark garage. He wasn't even looking at us. He came up to the ball, chipped it up with his polished shoe, moving pretty easily for a guy his weight, popped it into the air, and started juggling just as easily with his left foot. His movements were easy and effortless; he sucked in his stomach adeptly so the ball wouldn't hit it as he kept it afloat, occasionally heading it or tapping it with his shoulder. Kocha and I froze, observing these miracles of motion. Injured still had it—he'd hardly even broken a sweat, though his eyes were a bit red from exertion and his breathing slightly labored. And there was his stomach, twisting and turning and always seeming to get in the way, despite his best efforts.

Three trucks pulled in off the highway as the performance continued. The drivers hurried over, greeted Kocha, and joined in watching Injured.

"Injured!" one of them yelled, clearly dying to play. "Pass!"

Injured glanced at him, and kicked the ball in his direction. The driver stepped on it, took one slightly awkward touch, and booted it as hard as he could back to Injured. Injured trapped it and then clamped it between his legs. The drivers could no longer contain themselves, and they all bolted toward him, howling like wild animals. It was on. Injured spun away from the drivers' embraces and did circles around his opponents, forcing them to fall and trip over each other—holding onto the ball all the while. The drivers were charging at Injured like dogs going after a sleepy bear, but they were utterly hopeless. They started smacking each other in frustration, clearly trying to assign blame. Injured was starting to get short of breath, so he dropped far back on the macadam strip. He'd been kicked in the shins a few times and now was limping a bit. Smelling blood, the drivers pressed their attack with fresh vigor. Injured faked out one of them out, causing him to ram his head into his teammate; both dropped to the asphalt like bowling pins. The third driver ran over to help them up. Injured caught his breath and looked over in our direction.

"Herman," he yelled, "get in here—it's three against one, ya know . . ."

I dashed over onto the strip. Injured passed the ball to me; I took possession and carried it across the "field." The drivers too were running out of steam after circling a few times, so they stopped, rested their hands on their knees, and tried catching their breath. Their tongues lolled like the tongues of corpses, or tickets poking out of trolley machines. I stopped, waiting for a response from Injured. He motioned toward the drivers, as if to say, "Let them play a bit." I booted the ball to the tallest guy; he was standing the closest to me. Elated, he dashed for the ball, turned around, and hammered the leather sphere as hard as he could. The ball shot into the sky, slicing through the air and seemingly brushing against the clouds before disappearing into the grass behind the macadam strip. The drivers' spirits were nearly broken, but after a brief team meeting, they decided to venture off into the thicket. Injured and I followed them. Even Kocha got up. We moved into the dust and enveloping warmth like African hunters trying to lure lions into the open. The ball was sitting somewhere in the brush; you could hear its muffled growling, its faintly beating leather heart. We advanced cautiously, trying to catch a glimpse of it—occasionally we'd call out to each other and have a look at the sky, where more and more clouds kept rolling in.

It all reminded me of something—men wading warily through waist-high grass, pushing the blades back, gazing fixedly at the texture of the plants around them, listening to the sounds coming out of the brush, goading skittish animals out of the foliage, slowly crossing an unending field. I'd seen this before. Tense backs, silhouettes standing still in the twilight, white dress shirts shining in the darkness.

When had I seen it before? Back in 1990, I think. Yeah, 1990. In the summer. We'd just won a home game against Voroshilovgrad. Injured scored late in the match. It may have been his best game ever. We were at a restaurant called Ukraine, over by the park, across from the fire station. It was evening, and we were celebrating the victory: our players as well as local gangsters, women wearing fancy dresses and men wearing white dress shirts or track suits, waiters—budding capitalists, all of us, sitting together with all kinds of crooks, hot waves of alcohol breaking over our heads. It made me think of when we'd dare each other to run into the sea at night: a bittersweet, black wave washes over you and then you run back out onto the beach, no longer a boy, but a man. Boxes of vodka; an endless table seating everyone you know; loud, crappy music; blue, damp twilight shining in through the window; drenched trees; voices blending together and reminding you of the rain; men and women talking, the overwhelming feeling of approaching some precipice with hot, unbearable drafts rising from beyond to take your breath away and make your pupils dilate, the underlying sensation of invisible vessels pumping the whole world's blood. Suddenly, there's the sound of shattering glass amid all that golden shimmering, and the air burst into a million crystal pieces—some Voroshilovgrad fan had tracked us down, and he threw a brick through the restaurant window. The dark blue night poured into the room, chilling our blood and knocking our spinning heads back into sobriety. Next came a short silence, followed by general movement, angry voices, everyone suddenly bursting with courage, loud shuffling through the doors, more broken glass, the stomping of shoes on the wet asphalt, white dress shirts standing out sharply as men sprang into the lilac-colored night, female silhouettes by the window peering anxiously into the darkness. Gangsters and capitalists, soccer players and the neighborhood crew—all of them spilling out through the darkness and combing the wasteland beyond the park, chasing their invisible quarry toward the river, refusing to let it get away; an odd pursuit full of excitement and joy—nobody wants to fall behind, everyone stares into the overwhelming darkness of the summer, ducking around and trying to catch a glimpse of the enemy. Distant electric lights burn beyond the river as if yellow-green suns are burying themselves in the grass; we want to lure them out, so they can dissolve the surrounding darkness—it's thickening like blood, hot blood shot into an internal combustion engine by the effort of our breathing.

4

Kocha slept soundly that night, as if he wasn't dreaming but just lying there while someone herded dreams through his mind. They rolled through him like trains passing a junction, and he inspected each of them as though he were the station manager, focused and earnest. He took his vitamins and went to sleep outside on his beloved catapult. I lugged an old overcoat out of the trailer and draped it over him. I also got up a few times during the night and went over to check up on him. The stray dogs that had been roaming the lot slept at his feet, and the wind pushed paper bags along the macadam strip. Birds sat on Kocha's shoulders and ants crawled up onto his open palms, licking off the red residue of the vitamins. The last of the clouds rolled off to the north, and constellations spread out across the sky. It was starting to feel like June again. June was always fleeting and eventful around here—stems would fill up with slightly bitter juice and leaves would turn rough like skin exposed to the cold. Each passing day meant more dust and sand—it got in our shoes and the creases of our clothing, grated in our teeth, and rained from our hair. In June, the air would heat up like army tents, kicking off the season of sluggish men in the streets and rowdy kids in streams. It was already clear by morning that we should be bracing ourselves for a merciless summer that might continue until the end of time and scorch everything in its wake, including our skin and hair. Not even the rain would give us any relief.

Kocha usually took a while to wake up, and he felt lethargic in the morning, like a kid dragged out of bed when his parents are running late. He'd get up, walk around by the garage, feed the dogs some black bread, gaze pensively down into the valley, and then eventually wake me up. He'd flop down on the couch next to me and tell me long, random, fragmented stories about his ex-wife, taking out old pictures and digging his old army photo album out from under the couch. I'd fend him off feebly, trying to fall back asleep, but that wasn't too easy to do after looking at the army photo album. Eventually, I'd get up, wrap myself in an itchy hospital blanket, and start listening. Kocha would tell me about love, about dating his wife-to-be, and about sex in the front seat of an old Volga-model car.

"But why didn't you just do it in the back seat?" I asked him.

"Buddy, everybody did it in the back seat," Kocha explained. "There's a joint seat in the front of old Volgas, just like in the back, so it makes no difference where you do it, you dig?"

"I sure do, Kocha," I answered him, "it makes no difference." He nodded appreciatively, as if to say, "Buddy, you know what's up." And then he went to brew up some super-concentrated Chifir tea to start off our day with a swift kick in the head.

A bit later the first car pulled up to the station, beeping its horn. Irritated, Kocha threw on his glasses and rushed outside.

"Kocha, let me help."

"Forget about it, Herman," he said, waving me off. "You're not my idea of good help."

"Well, I'm all you've got."

"All right, fine, you can come along," he said, standing by the doorway and waiting for me to find my clothes. "Just put something else on. What are you doing wearing those jeans? I've got some old clothes over there under the bed. Try to find them, okay?" With that, he went outside.

★

He had two suitcases stuffed with ratty clothes. They gave off a strong smell of tobacco and cologne. I rooted around squeamishly in the first suitcase and found some black army pants that were patched at the knees and stank as badly as everything else. Nevertheless, they still looked presentable. I opened up the second suitcase and pulled out a camouflage Bundeswehr coat, wrinkled, but not yet ripped. I pulled it over my shoulders. The coat was tight on me—that's probably why Kocha, who had roughly the same build, didn't wear it. But I didn't have much choice. I looked out the window. The sun broke up my reflection and shredded it into scattered rays. I could only make out some outlines and shadows, but I must have looked like a tank driver who still had a lot of fight in him, though his tank had long since gone up in flames. With those thoughts rolling around in my head, I set off to start work.

★

Injured showed up at nine. He cast a judgmental glance at my work clothes, harrumphed, and took his post in the garage. I tried to help, but I basically just got in the way. I spilled gasoline a few times, talked at length with a truck driver heading to Poland, and was constantly bumping into Kocha, keeping him from performing his duties. Finally, the old-timer couldn't take it any anymore, so he sent me over to Injured, who caught on right away: he gave me a gasoline-soaked rag and instructed me to scour some piece of metal caked with silt, rust, and oil paint. I was decisively bored thirty minutes in; I hadn't done any manual labor in years, and it showed.

"Injured, let's take a smoke break," I said.

"You can't smoke here," Injured responded. "This is a gas

station, in case you hadn't noticed. But all right," he went on, "go take a break, and then come back." Which is just what I did.

★

They turned the phone back on at around twelve. I called Bolik. His voice sounded wrong, he was agitated.

"Herman! How are you doing down there?"

"Fine," I said, "it's like a resort. There's a river nearby stocked with pike."

"Herman!" Bolik yelled over the static. "We've got the convention coming up this week, and you're fuckin' going on about pike. Herman, screw the pike. Listen bro, we've got so much fuckin' work to do—we actually really need you back at the office. When are you getting back?"

"Oh, Bolik!" I yelled back. "That's just what I'm calling about. Looks like I'm going to be hung up here a bit longer."

"What? Herman, what'd you say?"

"I said I'm gonna be hung up here a while."

"What do you mean hung up? For how long?"

"A week, max. No more."

"Herman," Bolik asked, suddenly serious, "are you doing all right down there? Maybe we can help somehow?"

"Nah, man," I said, trying to affect a carefree and convincing tone, "relax. I'll be back in a week."

"You aren't going to stay there for good, are you?" Bolik sounded concerned, or suspicious, or maybe just hopeful.

"Nah, what are you talking about?"

"Herman, I've known you for a long time . . ."

"Right, so quit talking nonsense."

"You wouldn't do that, would you?"

"Don't worry about it—I just told you I was coming back."

"Herman, think twice before you do anything stupid, okay?"

"Okay."

"Think about us, your friends."

"I am, I'm thinking about you guys."

"Before you do anything stupid."

"Gotcha."

"Think first, Herman, okay?"

"Obviously."

"All right then, bro. We love you."

"Bolik, I love you guys too. Both of you. But I love *you* a little more."

"Quit blowing smoke up my ass, fucker," Bolik said, finally hanging up.

"Yeah, yeah," I yelled, hearing the dial tone, "I miss you, too! Very, very much!"

★

I called my brother again a few times after that. He refused to pick up. Sunlight poured into the room; dust hovered like river water disturbed by a passing fish. I looked out the window and felt the steaming guts of June settling on the surface of the tarmac, touching every living thing on the highway. What's next? I could descend into the valley once again, try to find friends and acquaintances I hadn't seen for years, chat with them, and ask them about their lives. I could hitch a ride out of here, extricating myself from this hellish place with its sunbeams and memories that clogged my lungs and blinded me. Naturally, the easiest thing would be to sell all of this, then split the money with my business partners. I doubt my brother would take it the wrong way. And if he did, what difference would it make anyway? He really hadn't given me much choice. I could chill with Kocha a while longer, while it was still warm and the river was stocked, filling up trucks, and pretending I wanted to help. Still, soon or later I'd have to handle the documents, taxes, and all that junk that I've avoided my whole life. The whole episode where my brother registered the company in my name seemed odd and illogical now. My brother must have foreseen this scenario; unlike me, he always calculated everything well in advance—I just don't get why he had to leave me in the lurch like this. Most importantly, why'd he disappear without explaining anything or leaving any instructions? He seemed to be saying, "Do what you want. Sell it and save yourself the headache if you want to, or donate it to the poor or some orphanage—let them fill up all these outlaws' vehicles, or just torch the booth and throw the deed into the fire and head on home, where your real friends and an interesting job are waiting for you." But no, he hadn't left me any instructions. He just disappeared like a tourist from a hotel, dragging me out into these smoldering hills; ever since I was a kid I always felt out of place here, from early childhood up until that wonderful last day when my parents and I finally got away, when our father—a retired serviceman from a now-insignificant army—was given a house near Kharkiv. That was when my brother decided to stay; he didn't want to leave—he didn't even want to talk about leaving. He'd been planning on staying from day one, and it seemed as though he'd never really forgiven us for running away. He never came out and said it, but I always felt his coldness, especially toward our parents, who gave up on this valley with all of its sun, sand, and mulberry. He stayed, hunkered down in the hills, and fought valiantly to protect his land. He was incomprehensibly stubborn. He would be capable of fighting to the death for this empty land, while I have no trouble letting go of emptiness, trying to rid myself of it. That was the difference between us. Life had its own plans, though—he'd run off to Amsterdam, and I was stuck on this hill from which you could see the end of the world . . . and I wasn't liking the looks of it much.

★

Kocha had worn himself out completely; he sat on his catapult and lazily fended off this truck driver, an old acquaintance, who was trying, just as lazily, to get Kocha to stand up and actually do his job, fill the truck up before a long haul. I went outside and relieved the old guy. The sun smelled of gasoline, it hung over our heads like a pear full of oil.

★

Work diffused my confusion by giving my daily routine a defined rhythm and some semblance of order. When you're keeping busy you think less about the corridors of the future that you'll inevitably have to walk down. I helped my business partners, bobbing around under the orange June sky. In the evenings, Kocha would take out his canned food, roll a few cigarettes, and put on my headphones. We would sit under the apple trees, silent and relaxed, our skin telling us that the sun was sinking and the cool air was rising off the river. After dark, Injured would start getting ready to leave, washing his hands at the yellow sink and dousing himself with cologne. He'd put on his foppish white dress shirt and head down into the valley, toward the golden electric lights and lilac-colored shadows of the city's alleyways—his lovers would be waiting there for him, opening up their windows into the cool black night.

★

The colder air and sweet wool covers made our sleep deep and smooth, like an old riverbed; our skin, scorched by the sun, would cool off by the morning, but our blankets would retain the heat of our bodies for a while. In the morning Kocha would wake me up with some tall tales, make breakfast, and kick me outside to brush my teeth. Our routine reminded me of some kind of extended school field trip—I had lost all sense of time. I was on an unexpected vacation, a visit to a gas station, and now I was roaming these little hills in bewilderment, tangled in the grass, wandering between the field birds' rusty iron hideouts. Injured continued to look at me with just as much suspicion, although he had softened up a bit; the next evening, on Wednesday, he took out the ball again, as well as the paint cans, put me in his makeshift goal, and spent a long while perfecting his left-footed shot. One of the drivers recognized me, said hello, and asked how I was doing, whether I was here for long and where my brother was. I avoided giving any direct answers, saying that everything was all right, insincere though this was. But what difference did it make?

★

On Thursday, Olga showed up after lunch. She arrived on her scooter, carrying a large wicker basket over her shoulder. The basket was constantly swinging forward, hitting up against the wheel, getting in the way. Olga passed a truck gracefully, turned off the highway, darted toward the gas station, and pulled up in front of us. Kocha and I were sitting in our chairs, swatting away the pesky wasps, intoxicated by the smell of tobacco and cologne. Olga hopped off her scooter, greeted Kocha, and nodded at me.

"You're still here?" she asked.

"Yeah, I decided to take a vacation. An unpaid vacation."

"Oh, I see," Olga said. "How are your buddies doing?"

"What buddies?"

"The guys in the Jeep."

"Ah, those guys. Excellent. They wound up being awfully nice people."

"For real?" she asked.

"They played me some music and they want to be friends."

"And?"

"The music? It was shit."

"What about being friends?"

"I'm still thinking about it," I admitted.

"Sure you are," Olga said coldly. And then, "Kocha, this is for you," handing him the basket and heading over to the garage to visit Injured before Kocha could even get out a thank you.

The basket contained fresh bread and milk in a plastic Coke bottle. Kocha eagerly broke off a piece of the bread and sank his teeth into it; they were yellow and robust, like an old dog's teeth. He offered me the bottle of milk. I turned him down. The scooter's white sides were reflecting the light, heating up quickly under the sun's rays. The valley was quiet; the birds roamed between the trees, looking for cool spots to settle down in.

Olga came out of the garage a little later. Injured, huffing and puffing, wearing his work clothes and wiping the sweat from his neck with a snow-white handkerchief, followed behind her. He was holding some papers. Clearly, Olga had just given them to him, and he was waving them around, trying to explain something to her. She wasn't even listening to him.

"Injured," she said, "what do you want me to do about it?"

Injured crumpled up the papers, stuck them in his coat pocket, and vanished back into the garage, waving his fists.

"What's going on?" I asked.

"Nothing," Olga answered curtly. She hopped on her scooter, started it up, stood still for a second, and then shut off the engine. "Herman," she said, "are you busy now?"

"Generally speaking, yes," I said, a bit flustered. "But at this particular moment I'm on break."

"Let's go for a swim in the river," she suggested. "Kocha," she asked the old-timer, "do you mind?"

Kocha expressed his consent with a big gulp of milk.

"Well then, are you coming?" Olga asked, hopping off the scooter once again and charging down the hill. All I could do was get up and follow her.

She took the lead, searching for the trail between thick black-thorn bushes and unripe mulberries. The path dropped sharply; blades of grass were getting in her shoes, butterflies and wasps were flying off stems, and little emerald lizards were scurrying around beneath us. Exhausted from running through the scorching air, I could hardly keep up with her. There was more greenery here, we could only see the valley through the gaps between the branches. The trail simply disappeared a few times—when that happened Olga would just glide over into the grass and push on. Finally, my legs gave out, and I tumbled down onto the bitter wormwood, cursing cruel fate.

"Hey, what's going on over there?" Olga called out from down below. "You doing all right?"

"Yeah, yeah," I answered mutinously.

I didn't like that she had picked up on how tired I was, my skidding into the tall grass, my inability to keep up with the pace she'd set at the top of the hill. "Well," I thought, "come on back and give me a hand then. Why'd you drag me down this over-grown trail anyway? Come on back here."

But she wasn't even considering coming back for me. She was standing down below, somewhere beyond the branches; I couldn't see her, but I could sense the heat of her blood pumping from her short run. I could feel her waiting, so I had to pick myself up, empty the sand out of my pockets, and move forward, following the sound of her breath. We walked on in silence. The river wasn't actually that close to the gas station; it would have been easier to take the highway down, but Olga stubbornly forged on, dodging trees and bushes, fighting through weeds, and leaping over burrows and ditches—and then the trail dropped off abruptly into the river shining below us. Olga advanced; skidding down the steep chalky incline, she stepped softly into the water. Resigning myself to following her obediently, I too skidded into the water. The bank had a small patch of sand surrounded by reeds.

"Just don't look," she said. "I'm not wearing a swimsuit."

"I can see that."

She slid out of her long dress, exposing a pair of white panties, and stepped deeper into the water. I really did want to turn away, but I'd missed my chance.

"I don't know how to swim, by the way," she said, standing in water up to her neck.

"Me either," I answered, slipping out of my tank driver getup and wading through the water toward her. The river was warm; the chalky hills reflecting the sun's rays had heated it up, so I just felt sleepy and lethargic.

"I used to be a camp counselor. At a Young Pioneers camp about fifty kilometers from here. My partner and I had to pull kids out of the water every day."

"Dead kids?" I asked, a bit confused.

"What? No, regular, alive kids. Nobody drowned, but they'd swim out to the reeds and hide out until the evening. They knew we couldn't swim. Can you imagine the kind of pressure I was under?"

"Sounds like no fun," I said. "My friends and I used to go dynamite fishing in this river."

"There are fish here?"

"Nah, but we still tried blasting them."

"I see," Olga said, droplets shining like copper in her red hair. Her skin was wet and warm, which made it look smooth: the wrinkles under her eyes had disappeared. "Do you have a lot of friends here?"

"Yeah, a lot of childhood friends."

"What's so special about childhood friends?"

"They still remember a whole lot."

"Herman, you're too self-conscious."

"Yeah, yeah, I'm really self-conscious. Like about not being able to swim."

"I can't swim, either, but I'm not self-conscious about it." Olga's voice was stern.

"So you might drown, but you won't be self-conscious about it."

"I won't drown," Olga said confidently. "You can't drown in a river you've been going to your whole life."

"Sure you can. Plus, I haven't swum in it for a long time."

Bugs skirted across the surface of the water, like fishermen hurrying along wet gray ice.

"What are you going to do?" Olga asked at last. "About the gas station, I mean."

"I don't know. I've decided to sit on it for a little bit. I've got time. My brother may come back, after all."

"Gotcha. How long are you going to wait?"

"I don't know. Summer is long."

"You know, Herman," she said, swatting some wasps away, "I'll be here to help, if you need me."

"Thanks."

"But don't take it the wrong way—it's just business."

"Got it."

"Then why are you staring at me like that again? Are you *trying* to make me feel self-conscious?"

The current was carrying away some branches and twirling the black grass that ran along the river's sandy bottom. Insects still hovered above the water, sticking to its pasty surface—the thick and clumpy afternoon river wasn't flowing so much as simply continuing.

A little while later, we climbed out onto the bank and started putting our clothes back on. Once again, Olga asked me not to look—she slipped off her wet panties in one swift motion, rolled them into a ball, and started pulling on her dress. We moved out, ascending the chalky cliffs, following the evening sun that had already rolled out behind the hills. Olga walked ahead of me, squeezing her panties tight in her left hand, her dress clinging to her wet body; trying not to look at her occupied most of my attention. At the gas station, she took the empty basket back from Kocha, discretely tossed her underwear into it, whispered something to Injured—who promptly glared at me—hopped on her scooter, and vanished into the evening air, as if she had never been there at all.

★

In the evening, Kocha's hoarse voice told me about his women, their treachery, their illogical behavior, and their tenderness—all the things he loved them for. Our canned food had run out, so I gave Kocha some money to get groceries. He hitched a ride with a guy in an old Ukraina car and went down into the valley. I stayed put in the chair, looking at the red currents flowing above the highway; the dust and twilight were weighing down the air, and the sky was starting to look like tomato sauce.

★

These were strange days—I found myself surrounded by old friends and complete strangers both, all of whom looked at me apprehensively, expectantly, waiting for me to take some action—it was if they were frozen in place, forced to listen to what I would say and watch to see what I'd do next before they could make a move themselves. This made me particularly anxious. I was used to taking responsibility for my own actions, but now I faced a different level of responsibility. It had just fallen into my lap like a surprise visit by relatives; and it wasn't even as though I absolutely *had* to assume this new role—it's just that shirking my new responsibilities wouldn't have sat right with me. I had been living my own life, sorting out my own problems, and trying not to give out my number to a lot of random acquaintances . . . and suddenly, I found myself among all these people, knowing that they wouldn't let me go too easily. I'd have to find out where I stood, clear the air, and reach some sort of solution. It seemed as though people were really counting on me. Frankly, I didn't like that one bit. All I really wanted was some hot pizza.

★

Friday evening rolled around, bringing with it an odd new character. He zeroed right in on me, and I noticed him too, arriving in an old UAZ car—the type of car agronomists and warrant officers used to drive back in the day. He'd come in from the north, and was dressed just like me, in army pants and a camouflage T-shirt. He was also wearing a peaked cap with the SS lightning bolts on it. He looked at everyone suspiciously and inquisitively. He greeted Kocha silently, motioning for him to fill up his tank, saluted Injured, and walked with him to the garage. Around then he took notice of my Bundeswehr jacket, came over to me, and struck up a conversation.

"Nice jacket," he said.

"Yeah, it's holding together pretty good," I agreed.

"That's some fabric. Are you Herman?"

"Yeah," I answered.

"Korolyov? Yura's brother?"

"Uh-huh."

"You might not remember me. Your brother and I did some business together."

"Everyone in these parts did business with my brother," I pointed out, annoyed with having to go through these preliminaries again.

"We had a special relationship," he said, placing special weight on the word "special." "He used to buy fuel for airplanes from me and sell it someplace in Poland . . . to some farmers."

"What do you mean he used to buy it from you?"

"Well, at the airport."

"So, you work at the airport?"

"What's left of it. Ernst," he introduced himself, extending his hand.

"What sort of name is that?"

"It's a nickname."

"Well, is that what you go by?"

"Sure it is. I'm used to it already. What'd you major in?"

"History."

At this, his expression changed completely. He sized me up, took me by the elbow gingerly, led me out of the garage, and guided me off to the side, away from Kocha and Injured, who both looked bewildered by this situation.

"You know, Herman," he said, continuing to hold onto my elbow and tugging me farther away from the gas station, "I majored in history too. I just fell into the job at the airport. Where'd you get your degree?"

"Kharkiv."

"History major?"

"History major."

"Where'd you do your field work?"

"The usual, just outside the city."

"Digging?"

"Digging."

"What can you tell me about the *Death's Head*?"

"What head?"

"The *Death's Head*. That was the name of a German division."

"Well," I hesitated, "nothing good."

"You know what, Herman," he continued, pinching my elbow now enough to make me wince. "You have to come visit me at the airport. I'll open your eyes."

"To what?" I asked.

"A whole new world. You don't get it yet."

"And you do?"

"Sure I get it. Herman, I've dug up every field from here to the Donbas. So, I'll be waiting for you on Monday. Why don't ya stop by, all right?"

"All right," I agreed.

"You'll figure out how to get there?"

"I'll figure it out."

"Sounds good."

He turned back decisively and headed toward his car. He walked up to Kocha, handed him some dough for the gas, and hopped inside.

"Monday!" he yelled as he was leaving. He pulled out, kicking up clouds of dust. Then I walked over toward Kocha.

"Who is that guy?" I asked.

"Ernst Thälmann," Kocha answered with a great sense of satisfaction.

"What's with his name?"

"It's a perfectly normal name," Kocha chuckled. "He's a mechanic at the airport. And he's the namesake of the famous German Communist."

"I think I might know him from way back."

"Everybody here knows each other," Kocha said, as though he was repeating someone else's words.

"He used to give us grain alcohol. It was stored away somewhere at the airport. That was about twenty years ago." I was starting to piece it together.

"See?" Kocha said. "He's dug up a good part of the valley. He's looking for German tanks."

"Tanks?"

"Yep."

"What does he need tanks for?"

"I don't know," Kocha admitted. "Maybe it's a self-esteem thing. He says that there are still a few tanks buried in our neck of the woods. Well, he's looking for them. He's got a bunch of fascist memorabilia at home—automatic weapons, shells, medals. But he's not a fascist," Kocha warned me. "Who ever heard of a fascist named Ernst Thälmann?"

"Gotcha," I said, comprehending at last.

"A German tank would be worth a lot of money," Injured added, coming over to us. "But it's not like he's gonna be fuckin' digging one up anytime soon."

"How come?" I asked.

"Herman," Injured said irritably, "it's not some sack of potatoes. We're talking sixty tons of metal. What's he gonna dig it up with, a shovel? Come on, let's get back to work."

Disgruntled as usual, Injured turned around and vanished into the garage. I followed him in. "Sixty tons," I thought, "nope, that's no sack of potatoes, that's for sure."

★

I had discovered one thing—work can give you, if not a sense of satisfaction, really, then at least a sense of accomplishment. The last time I felt anything like it was in third grade, when they took us out to an orchard to gather apples for the collective farmers— searching conscientiously for heavy windfall fruits in the cold September grass. . .

On Saturday, there were more cars than usual. They were heading north, toward Kharkiv. Kocha counted up our money gleefully, although he was concerned whether we would have enough gas to last us until next week's delivery.

★

After the morning rush, when the sun had rolled up to its apex, I took off my heavy gloves, told Kocha I was going to take a little break, and I headed out along the hill, turning off the highway. I had no clue where I was going—I probably just needed to get away from it all and take in the bucolic scenery. I descended into the gully then climbed up another hill. Soon I reached the endless cornfields that stretched out to the horizon (well, apparently they kept going even after the horizon). There wasn't any road to guide me, so I simply kept moving forward, trying to keep the sun at my back and not in my eyes. The unripe corn made the landscape a light shade of green, tinted black by the dry earth between. I encountered some depressions here and there—the whole area looked like a golf course where someone had taken it into his head to plant corn. Suddenly, up ahead, about two hundred meters in front of me, I noticed some sort of silhouette. Somebody had stopped dead in their tracks, listening to the enveloping silence. I didn't get a good look at whoever it was, and I thought that if someone saw the two of us out there, in the middle of a cornfield, in the middle of all those accumulations of black soil, we might make an odd picture—odd and suspicious. I approached the figure and recognized Katya. She was wearing denim overalls that must have felt smothering in this heat, with a bright yellow T-shirt on underneath and the same sandals as the last time I saw her. She had also noticed me—she was just standing there, waiting for me to come over.

"What are you doing here?" I demanded in place of hello.

"Well, what are *you* doing here?" Yet it seemed she wasn't too surprised to see me.

"I was looking for you."

"Yeah, sure . . ." she said, eyeing me coldly.

"Hi," I replied, extending my hand to her. She hesitated for a second, then took it. She even threw in a smile, though it was more dismissive than friendly.

"So what are you doing here?" I asked again.

"I'm looking for Pakhmutova."

"For what?"

"For Pakhmutova, my German shepherd. She's always running off into the fields."

"She'll turn up. Dogs are wise."

"She's just so old. She's forgetful. She's already run onto the highway a few times . . . I was lucky I found her the last time. It's just a good thing everybody around here knows her, so they just leave her alone." Katya was beginning to show how upset she really was.

"Why not tie her up—that way she won't run away."

"How about I tie you up," Katya said angrily. "That way you won't run away."

"Okay, chill." I did my best to sound conciliatory.

But Katya wasn't listening. She had turned her back on me and was calling for her German shepherd: "Pakhmutova!" she yelled out into the empty fields. "Pakhmutova-a-a!"

When she stopped shouting, we noticed an odd sound. It grew increasingly distinct, breaking down into individual clanging notes as it slid through the air, cutting through the silence like an icebreaker through a frozen river. Katya tensed up immediately and looked into the sky. There was something there, moving toward us, and soon enough I realized it was a biplane, an An-2. Katya leaped toward me, dropping to the ground and yanking me down by my sleeve. I fell on top of her. "Well, how about that," I thought. Katya whispered:

"Lie flat and don't move. And cover me up. My shirt is bright—they might spot it."

"Who might spot it?"

"The corn guys."

"That's their plane?"

"Yeah. Make sure they don't see you. They don't like people coming on their land. There could be trouble."

"Yeah, whatever," I said, trying to get up.

Truly frightened, Katya tugged me back onto her, repeating, "Don't move!"

I buried my face in her shoulder. The ground beneath her hair was dry and cracked; I could see ants scurrying up the nearby cornstalks, and Katya's black hair was trapping the dust that floated past us, taking on its color, and her eyes were also the color of dust. It was as if she was trying to blend in with her surroundings. Meanwhile, the plane was still approaching, letting out its desperate and ominous roar. I was shielding Katya from view, but soon found my nose in her hair and my body pressing into her and the grass alike. Her breath was quick and nervous, and she was clinging to me, one hand slipping underneath my shirt.

"You're drenched in sweat," she said, surprised.

"That's from the sun."

"Don't move," she repeated.

"These damn overalls," I said, trying to undo her side buttons and slide my hand underneath her shirt, but all I was managing to do was jerk vainly at the catches and pull her against me. I started getting anxious and angry as she went on touching my skin softly and disinterestedly, not even looking at me. She was focused solely on the plane whipping by and casting a deep shadow over our bodies—its roar becoming deafening before the machine finally soared away, leaving behind smoke, fumes, and emptiness. By this time, I'd even managed to undo one of Katya's buttons, but she evidently felt the coast was clear, so she pulled her hand out from under my shirt and lightly pushed me away.

"Okay, that's enough," she said and got up.

"Wait a second. Where are you going?"

"Get up."

"Where are you going? Wait up."

"That's enough," she said calmly and did up the button I had been struggling with for so long.

"Damn," I thought, but was immediately distracted by a new sound: heavy breathing just over my head. I got up and saw a German shepherd had materialized next to me without my noticing. It was Grandma Pakhmutova, standing there and looking at me, seemingly asking, "What do you want from us, anyway?" And I didn't know how to respond.

"Okay, let's go," Katya said, and headed toward the TV tower sticking up from beyond the horizon. Pakhmutova trotted happily behind Katya. I picked myself up, dusted off my shirt, and fell in behind them with a bit of a hangdog expression on my face.

Katya kept quiet all the way back, paying no attention to my feeble attempts at striking up a conversation, either muttering to herself or talking to Pakhmutova. She stopped by the gate of the TV tower and extended her hand to say good-bye.

"Thanks," I said, "sorry if things got . . ."

"Whatever," she said calmly, "everything's fine. Make sure not to wander into the cornfields again."

"Are you *that* afraid of them?"

"I'm not afraid of them," she answered. "I just know what they're like. All right, I'm outta here."

"Wait. What are you doing tonight?"

"Tonight? I'll be doing my homework. And tomorrow morning, too," she added, turning and heading inside. The German shepherd sniffed my shoes in farewell, then followed.

"Hard day's night," I thought.

★

Injured looked at me even more suspiciously than usual when I got back, as though he knew exactly what had happened, but he kept quiet. Just as he was about to leave he came up to me and said:

"Herman, here's the thing," his tone was flat, though not unsympathetic. "We're going to need you tomorrow."

"Who's we?"

"You'll see," he said. "We're gonna stop by around eleven. Make sure you're ready. This is some serious stuff. Can we count on you?"

"You bet your ass you can, Injured."

"That's what I like to hear." He hopped into his car and pulled out onto the highway.

"Here we go," I told myself. "And don't even try to say you weren't expecting this."

5

I thought long and hard about the whole situation. How did they wind up dragging me into this turf war of theirs? What was I doing there anyway? Why hadn't I left yet? Most importantly, what was Injured cooking up? Knowing him as I did, and given his somewhat loose relationship with reality, one could expect just about anything. But just how far was he willing to go? "We're talking about holding on to our business here," I thought, "so how willing is he to take a stand?" And what part has he cast me for in this script of his? What was in store for me the next afternoon? Would I live to see tomorrow evening? Should I just have high-tailed it out of there right away? Who could say what might happen, whether things could be resolved without any bloodshed; it seemed to me that everyone in this part of the country was all too willing to fight for their principles. Injured and the biplane pilots were far too determined and stubborn to find a solution that didn't involve body bags to what were, after all, just some administrative problems. It seemed as though it was all coming back to me—my school days and the real, adult world that was right there beside me. It felt as though somebody had opened a door, and now I couldn't help but see what was going on in the next room. Most importantly, I could see that there was nothing good about it, but since the door had been opened, I was involved in the whole mess. And it was terrible, mulling all of this over—I needed some sort of solution, and told myself that I shouldn't be the only one responsible for finding it. A solution would only be found when your brothers in arms were standing alongside you. But where are my brothers, I wondered, and who are they anyway? I was standing alone in the dark, but I could already feel apprehensive breathing and the fiery beating of warriors' hearts. The night was heating up like fresh asphalt. I had run out of time and patience—I told myself I couldn't afford to wait till morning to make a decision. That may have been my one real chance to go. And I slept right through it.

★

I got up early, realizing that I'd blown my opportunity to turn back, and that there was absolutely nowhere else for me to go. It just seemed impossible to walk out into the sunlight that was pouring abundantly into the room and leave this place behind. I could have done it at night, I thought, but not now. Which made things a lot simpler, in a sense—I got up, trying not to wake Kocha, and started getting ready. I put my tank driver pants on and found a pair of heavy army boots under the bed—they were worn, yet quite sturdy. I figured some tougher footwear was in order if today's engagement was going to be as bloody as I expected. I pulled on a T-shirt and went outside. I found an iron rod in the pile of scrap metal out back. I picked it up it, estimating its weight. "Just what I need," I thought, and set off to face the unknown.

The unknown was running late, however. After tanning in the chair for two hours I was feeling sleepy and hungry, thought I was trying not to think about food—any solider will tell you that you shouldn't eat right before going into combat. That was roughly the state of mind I was in when I slipped into a sweet morning sleep.

The air popped open right next to me, letting in a strange, hot, and heavy draft. It felt as though it was rising from somewhere deep in the earth. Its heat ate into my dream, and there was a moment when I thought I'd escaped, pulled myself together and fled, returning to real life. Even after waking up, this feeling still lingered—the sunny, torpid feeling of being on the road, and a smell like flame and ash, sweet but tinged with menace. Without even opening my eyes, I understood what was going on, knew what I'd find standing in front of me, exhaling this hellish air when I did at last look around. Heavy and hot like the air in September, parked in front of me, right by my chair, was a bus. An Ikarus model. That smell is unmistakable—it lingers in the air when someone's been resurrecting the dead. It was parked, with its engine turned off; the windows were tinted so I couldn't see

what was going on inside, although there most definitely was
something going on. I heard muffled voices and nervous breathing, so I got to my feet and tried to look inside. That was when the
door opened. Injured was standing on the steps. He was wearing
a white and blue Argentinian national team jersey and he looked
at my army boots, quite perplexed.

"You're gonna go in that?" he asked.

"Well, uh . . ." I answered, trying to hide the rod behind my
back.

"What do you need that thing for?" Injured asked, seeing it and
looking even more perplexed. "To keep the dogs away?"

"Just because," I said, getting flustered and tossing my weapon
into the tall grass.

"Okay, then," Injured replied, and, stepping off to the side, he
nodded, seemingly saying, "Come on, hop in."

I greeted the bus driver, who nodded apathetically in reply,
then climbed the next step surveying the inside of the bus. It was
dimly lit—at first I couldn't even make out who was sitting there.
I stood in place for a second, watching Injured get on, then surveyed the bus, submerged in twilight, then waved sheepishly, greeting the passengers of this sepulchral vehicle. That was the signal:
the bus exploded into cheerful whistling and shouting, and somebody yelled out:

"Herman, my boy, what's goin' on!"

"Herman, you magnificent bastard!" some other voices
chimed in.

I smiled cautiously, yet warmly, just in case I actually knew
these people, even though I still had no idea what was going

on. Injured came over and shoved me lightly, and a bunch of friendly embraces broke my fall. Only now could I discern the faces of my fellow passengers—they were all there: one-eyed Sasha Python; Andryukha Michael Jackson with the dark-blue onion-dome churches tattooed on his chest; Semyon Black Dick with his bitten-off ear and his right hand with all its fingers sewn back into place; Dimych Conductor with his tattooed eyelids; the Balalaeshnikov brothers, who had always gotten by with one cell phone for the three of them; Kolya One-and-a-Half Legs with his Hitler mustache and his bald spot painted white; Ivan Petrovich Fodder, his head boxlike from getting busted up too many times; Karpo Disc Grinder, who was holding a disc grinder; Vasya Negative with his bandaged knuckles; Gesha Accordion; Siryozha the Rapist; Zhora the Sucker; and Gogi Orthodox were sitting there too. Pretty much all the stars of the Meliorator '91 club—the dream team that ripped through every rival from here to the Donbas on their way to the championship. They were the elite athletes of this particular sunny valley. They were all sitting there, right in front of me, thumping me on the back, messing up my hair, and laughing, their gold and metal teeth flashing in the darkness.

"What are you doing here?" I asked after the first wave of excitement had subsided.

The bus went silent for a second, but then a loud roar broke over my head—my friends, exchanging looks, laughed heartily and took great pleasure from looking at my bewildered mug.

"Herman!" Gogi Orthodox yelled. "Hey buddy, you're too funny! You're a riot!"

"Herman, you're too funny! You're a riot!" the Balalaeshnikov brothers echoed, kicking back in their rickety seats. "Bro, you're too funny!"

Then the rest of them chimed in, bellowing and patting me on the back some more. Sasha Python even choked on his Camel, while Siryozha the Rapist was laughing so hard he was crying right on top of Vasya Negative, who didn't look too happy about it. Zhora the Sucker was pointing at me and laughing, as was Karpo Disc Grinder, who was waving his disc grinder around in the air, demonstrating that he was ready for battle. Then Injured came up behind me and placed his hand calmly on my shoulder. The gang piped down.

"Herman, do you know what day it is?" he asked. Someone burst out laughing again, but he was promptly smacked on the back of the head, which quieted him right down.

"Sunday," I answered, not quite getting the picture.

"Exactly," Injured replied. "Exactly. So what does that mean?" he asked, looking around at our friends.

"IT'S GAME DAY!" they chorused.

"Got it?" Injured asked me.

"Got it," I said, without actually getting it. "I thought you guys stopped playing years ago."

"Well, we don't really play much anymore," Injured replied, "but today, Herman, is a special occasion. We are PLAYING today. More importantly, we're playing against the GAS GUYS today!"

Once again, the whole team roared excitedly.

"So, come on, bro," Injured said, pushing me along, "Have a seat. We need you today."

I walked down the aisle, sank into an empty seat, and took a look around. Meanwhile, we were setting off, the bus rattling along the battered asphalt, dodging numerous potholes, and finally crawling out onto the highway. Not knowing which way to go, the driver braked.

"Hey, pops," Vasya Negative yelled up to the driver, "put some music on!"

"Come on, pops!" the Balalaeshnikov brothers backed him up cheerfully. "Let's get some music up in here. Let's hear some music!"

"Come on, guy," Gogi said, bellowing along with the chorus, "let's hear some music!"

The rest of our team started buzzing too, demanding music. When the cranky driver turned around, he was bombarded by old, ripped T-shirts and soccer socks, crusty with dried sweat. He couldn't take it any longer, so he popped in some AC/DC, circa 1981, and their terrible guitar licks sent us back into a black pit, back to nowhere, from death to birth, closer to God and the devil who were sitting in the back of this boiling bus and singing along with the rest of us. Then the Ikarus jerked forward abruptly, and the players fell back into their seats, yelling happily over the speakers, pulling off their striped vests and sweaters, taking their jerseys with stenciled numbers out of their big athletic bags, looking for their black athletic briefs, bandages, shin guards, all their gear, moving around in the darkness, knocking heads, and falling back into their seats when the bus would hit yet another pothole.

"Hey, what about Herman?" asked the youngest Balalaeshnikov brother, Ravzan.

"Oh yeah, what about Herman?" Everyone suddenly remembered that I'd need gear too, and started rooting around in their bags once again.

Zhora the Sucker tossed me a jersey, as damp as the blankets they give you on crummy sleeper trains. Then Andryukha Michael Jackson slipped out of a pair of athletic briefs, revealing another pair beneath, and gave the extra one to me, as though he was parting with something he truly cherished. Sasha Python, his one eye flashing, took out a brand-new pair of soccer socks and tossed them to me. "Come on, Herman, get dressed," everyone was shouting. "We're going to fuck those gas guys up, fuck them up real good!" I slipped out of my tank driver getup and put on my uniform. The jersey was oversized, and I looked like a boot camp trainee in my athletic briefs—I couldn't have cared less, and yet, just the same, I felt as though something was missing: I didn't feel quite ready for the game. I looked underneath the seats in vain, as if that would help me understand what was going on.

"Guys!" Ravzan yelled out again. "He doesn't have any cleats!"

"Ah, that won't fucking do," the guys agreed. "Yeah, you're right. Give him a pair of cleats! Somebody give him a pair of cleats already!" they all entreated each other.

But nobody had an extra pair of cleats—not Sasha Python, not Semyon Black Dick; not even Andryukha Michael Jackson, who had peeled off another pair of black briefs and given them to the oldest Balalaeshnikov brother, could help. Disappointment consumed us. All of their planning had come to naught—what use would I be without a pair of cleats? It's not as though I could take the field in my boots. I looked at Injured and threw my hands up, apologizing for my shortsightedness. The rest of the team looked at Injured, evidently waiting for a miracle, hoping he'd be able to feed the whole team with only five loaves of bread and give all eleven starters magical cleats that would lead us to a decisive and indisputable victory. Injured felt the tension; he must have realized how crucial this moment would be. It might very well undermine our team spirit, dampen our bloodlust, so he bent down and picked up a tattered briefcase, like the ones Young Pioneers, engineers, and officers carried in the '80s, balanced on one leg in the aisle, put it on his knee, and opened it up—taking his time—and pulled out his old spare pair of Adidas cleats, the same ones he'd worn fifteen years ago. The team looked at them in mesmerized awe. They were, indeed, Injured's gold cleats. They were patched up with fishing line in a few spots and missing two spikes. The leather reeked; the juice of all the grass that had worked its way into these shoes had been eating away at it for fifteen long years of retirement. Injured handed them to me and said:

"Herman, here, these are for you."

The team cheered its captain with a roar of brotherhood and camaraderie. I took the cleats and sat down.

Meanwhile, the bus was flying down the highway. A sharp, prickly ray of sunlight was poking through the windows, making my friends' eyes light up hungrily and giving their skin the blue tint of drowned corpses. The Balalaeshnikov brothers were getting changed right in front of me. The younger brother, Ravzan, had a cat's head tattooed on his left shoulder, a woman burning in a bonfire on his right hip, and then some sort of demon being stabbed with a sharp knife on his left hip. The cat, which was supposed to look fierce and self-reliant, I imagine, looked rather harmless and thoroughly domesticated; possibly because Ravzan had put on a lot of weight since getting the tattoo, so the cat had stretched out along the whole length of his upper arm. As for the woman in the bonfire, she looked like our high-school chemistry teacher. The middle Balalaeshnikov brother, Shamil, had a few stars, like the ones on cognac bottles, tattooed on his chest, below his left nipple. The words "There is no God but Allah" were written in a gothic font below the stars. The oldest brother, Barukh, also had stars, crosses, and crucifixes scattered across his skin, while an eagle carrying a suitcase in its beak was depicted over his abdominal area, which was supposed to symbolize Barukh's predilection for attempting to escape from wherever he happened to be incarcerated. It looked just like Injured's old briefcase. I looked more closely at the rest of my old friends, their bodies battered by hard lives and the fists of their rivals. The black markings on their backs, chests, and shoulder blades stood out in the bright sun, skulls and sickles, women's faces, and incomprehensible cyphers, as well as skeletons, Virgin Marys, gloomy curses, and lofty quotations. Semyon Black Dick's tattoos were the most minimalist— his chest just read "Adolf Hitler is my God," and his back boasted "The thief in law rules the prison."

The team gradually quieted down. Everyone was waiting, anticipating the impending battle and asking themselves whether they were really ready to do it again—outdo themselves, give it their all, keep playing through the pain, and fuck the gas guys up. Meanwhile, the driver slowed down and veered off the highway onto a pothole-ridden asphalt road that disappeared over the

nearby hills. I peered out the window, looking for some familiar terrain. When was the last time I was here? Fifteen years ago,
in the spring, I was riding with the same crew, but back then my
friends didn't look like tattoo-parlor zombies—they were younger,
but just as rough. How many times had we driven along this road,
looping up and down the hills, trying to reach the gas guys' cursed
and forgotten land? How many years had the gas guys been camp-
ing out there like polar explorers huddling on the ice?

★

They showed up here in the late '80s. It turned out that there
were natural gas reserves out there where it was driest, in the dry,
black soil between rivers—where the Soviets hadn't ventured, out
where the paved road trailed off. A large cohort of gas guys from
somewhere by the Carpathian Mountains was sent here; they
were supposed to get down in the trenches and start pumping gas
for the Motherland, figuring out the logistics as they went along.
Like Gypsies, they arrived in a long caravan, coming down from
the northwest and crossing the Dnieper River down by Kremen-
chuk. They lived in trailers hauled by heavy, swamp-colored military eighteen-wheelers. They brought a whole field kitchen with
them too. Finding themselves surrounded by endless fields, the
gas guys were taken aback by the vastness of the black soil and
all-pervading absence of anything living. They weren't in the Car-
pathians anymore. They stayed put, of course, because the country needed gas, but gas eluded them like a legion of mujahideen,
luring them deep into the sweet blue steppe, toying with them,

teasing them, but never letting itself get cornered. In the early '90s they put their search on hold for a while. Shortly thereafter, a new government boss took control of the land, ensuring that the gas guys' colony would be kept intact. Initially, the locals were wary of the gas guys—whenever one of them came into town in one of their eighteen-wheelers to buy some bread or go to the movies, gangs of locals would lie in wait for them, ambush them, and beat the shit out of them. They'd get kicked out whenever they ventured into our discos, too. Still, you have to give the gas guys credit—they adapted to their new habitat, began only coming into town in larger groups, and managed to hold their own in their periodic brawls with the townies. From time to time, some of our local gangsters considered burning down their trailers, along with their gas towers, but the police advised our boys to leave the gas guys alone, especially since they reported directly to the ministry, meaning they got their orders straight from Kyiv.

★

They also formed a soccer team pretty much immediately. They set aside a spot between their towers, amid those sun-scorched fields, and they crushed every other team that passed through. They not only played dirty, but were fearless—nobody dared lock horns with them. Nobody, that is, besides us. We held our own against them, and if we lost to them on their turf then we would most definitely get them back when we played at home. Our encounters were more than just games—they were a matter of principle. The gas guys would drive their silt-caked trucks into our city like a battalion on a reprisal raid, looking to level everything in their path. They were so accustomed to trouncing everyone that if the opposing team put up any meaningful resistance, they'd leave the stadium in a hurry, making for the steppes where they would vanish into the blue haze of ghosts and natural gas. Sometimes they'd start fights right on the field. Whenever something like that happened, the ministry in Kyiv would call our regional politicians and berate them hysterically. Eventually, the gas guys went off the grid; they hardly ever even bothered to set foot on the highway. When they were first sent here, they got periodic deliveries of movies and library books (they used to roll their cigarettes with the latter); but after the towers changed hands, a helicopter started coming by to drop canned food and tabloids: management was concerned with job satisfaction, after all. The majority of the gas guys had grown accustomed to the loneliness and the homogeneous landscape. After all, they had no home to return to—and is returning from nirvana really even an option? I had no idea what kind of lives they had been living in the years since I left home. It was very odd; everything seemed to be coming full circle, turning back—back to nowhere, back to emptiness.

★

The large yellowish red sun crawled along above our heads, rubbed against the roof, sprang over to the nearby hill, then pushed off to the west slowly, dragging its rays along behind it, which drifted like seaweed being pulled out into the open sea. It was already about three—we were crawling along the dirt roads, circling up and over the green fields, and trying to catch a glimpse of the gas towers on the horizon. The driver supposedly knew the way. Everyone knew these parts quite well, after all, so for a while nobody was paying attention to where we were relative to where we were trying to go. The driver was urging our bus confidently up yet another hill, plowing between the thick, cool grass, dodging blackthorn bushes and pits hunters had dug to catch animals. It was getting hotter out; dust was floating in through the bus windows and settling on the passengers' shaved heads—while the driver got progressively angrier and more anxious, goading his vehicle along the road toward some emerald city but getting lost along the way in the infinite, ominous landscape stretching out around us. The sun was blinding, and some birds landed on the roof of the Ikarus when it was stopped at yet another intersection—still no towers in sight. A few minutes later, Injured got up, stood at the front by the driver, and started directing him, peering out the windshield nervously. That didn't help either, though—we were just moving through space with nothing promising on the horizon, space that just continued, without any coordinates, just grass and corn, dust and gas—the gas our rivals had been hunting so doggedly all these years. Yes, sitting in that Ikarus among my drowsy friends, in that deadly silence, I could sense the gas, somewhere down there with the groundwater—I pictured it filling up all the cracks and crevices, moving along underground channels, bursting to the surface at midnight and igniting, burning the sky like grain alcohol burns your throat. The gas was the only thing anchoring this place in the vast emptiness all around us, maintaining the delicate balance between something and nothing. That's what came to my mind.

The gas, like spring water, was looking for a way out, forcing its way up through wells and out of old foxholes.

★

In the late afternoon, the driver stopped on a flat stretch in the valley and refused to go any farther. Injured let him be, since we really needed to get our bearings. The team, feeling listless and doomed, started seeping out of the Ikarus, which was as hot as the inside of a microwave by now. The Balalaeshnikov brothers took out a two-liter bottle filled with grain alcohol. I looked at Injured, wondering, "Are they actually going to start drinking? What about the game?" But Injured glared at me and was the first to take a swig. The rest of my teammates had already flopped down on the grass—they didn't even want to talk anymore. The driver stayed on the bus, since he must have felt he was to blame. It was quiet and sultry, although the heat was gradually subsiding. The sun was rolling farther and farther away, making our shadows long and forlorn. Swallows were flying around above the grass. The Balalaeshnikovs took out another bottle of grain alcohol. I went over to Injured.

"Injured," I said, "give me a boost."

At first Injured didn't understand what I was getting at. Then he walked over to the Ikarus and leaned up against it. I hopped onto his back and stood on his shoulders, holding on to the side-view mirror.

"Fuck man, be careful up there," Injured said a few seconds later, without much conviction.

I still had to hop a bit in order to make it onto the roof, given how short Injured is. I swung my leg onto the mirror, hauled myself up, and crawled on top of the bus. And maybe I had a good idea just then of how a fish feels when it's been thrown into a frying pan—the euphoria of having survived the journey is quickly overshadowed by a certain degree of discomfort. The roof was covered in a thick layer of dust and was burning hot. I stood up.

"Hey, Herman," Ravzan yelled, standing on the ground below. "Wait a sec, I'm coming up, too."

"Oh, me too," Shamil chimed in.

"Me too, me too," Barukh said, getting all excited.

They picked themselves up out of the warm grass and clambered onto the roof like lizards. Shortly thereafter, the four of us were still standing there, trying to catch sight of a road, or at least something vaguely resembling one.

Long, hot rays of light streaked down crookedly from the west, burning the grass and cornstalks. Our shadows were sprawling out in the evening sun, like grease stains on wrapping paper. The sky overhead hadn't gone entirely dark yet; it glowed ever so slightly, like water in an aquarium. There was a haze hanging on the horizon, as if there were invisible bodies of water out there it had evaporated from. It was hard to make anything out—those last, long sunbeams were cutting through the glistening air, whiting out the image. Once my eyes began to adjust, though, I could sort of see a dull, light-blue background, tinged by the evening darkness, peeking through the glare. From this distance, at this hour, whatever I was seeing looked like a huge concentration of light made solid—light that had piled up on itself, that had grown, hoisted by some strange frames that cut through the air vertically.

"What are those things?" Shamil asked, pointing at the light's nearly indiscernible masts.

"Towers," I said.

"You're right, they're towers," Barukh answered and started laughing gleefully.

By the time we finally got there later that evening, the sun had sunk behind the corn plantations; warm air was rising slowly, and the atmosphere was serene. The gas guys hadn't bothered to wait for us, and had apparently decided that we'd effectively forfeited the game, if their bonfire in the middle of the field was any indication. All huddled around the flame, they were boiling some sort of stew in big pots. Behind them, I could see the towers reaching upward, and the dirty eighteen-wheelers and trailers parked along the perimeter of the field. German shepherds and sheep were roaming around, coming up to the fire and eating food out of the gas guys' hands. There was still some lingering daylight, so the bonfire wasn't as impressive as it might have seemed without those last rays of sun playing around it. The gas guys were sitting on the trampled soccer field and cooking their lamb. They looked like Tatar Mongols resting up after conquering the gas towers of Kievan Rus. Upon seeing us pull up and brake hard between the eighteen-wheelers, the gas guys grew tense, picked their Tatar-Mongolian butts off the ground, and waited silently to see what would follow. Almost all of them were short; almost all of them had buzz cuts, and most of them were shirtless and wearing tracksuit bottoms. Many of them had gold teeth, some of them had crosses around their necks—none of them had tattoos. They wore identical hostile and suspicious expressions.

"Well, here we are," Injured said, stepping out of the bus with his briefcase in his hand.

We piled out of the bus after him and ventured across the field, sticking together in one big group. The gas guys were heading toward us. Eventually, we came face to face. The gas guys were spitting on the grass and glowering at us. Our crew was cracking their knuckles menacingly. The dogs were standing off to the side, barking fiercely. Finally, the gas guys' boss, a short-legged, golden-toothed tough guy wearing a white T-shirt and blue tracksuit pants, broke the silence:

"Scram!" he yelled at the dogs, and they trotted over behind the eighteen-wheelers rather reluctantly. It got quiet.

"Hey, ball guys," Injured said.

"We're the gas guys," the boss corrected him, making a big show of being offended.

"That's the same fuckin' thing," Andryukha Michael Jackson said, and all of our guys nodded pleasantly, as though to say, "Yeah, it *is* the same fuckin' thing."

"You're late," the boss stated, rather sharply.

"And your point is?" Injured asked.

"You've already forfeited the game," explained a guy with glasses and scars on his stomach, clearly their accountant.

"Who says so?" Injured countered.

"The Federation," the accountant answered again, quite boldly.

"What federation?" Injured looked at him. "Federation of Ball Guys?"

"The Federation of Gas Guys," the boss corrected him, again.

Our team laughed heartily, but insincerely. The boss waited for the laughter to subside, then continued.

"Injured," he said, "quit waving your dick around. You were late for the game."

"So now you're not going to play us?" Injured was unruffled.

"You've already forfeited the game." The boss sounded less confident this time.

"Let's cut to the chase," Injured said, putting on the pressure. "Are you going to play or what? Are you too scared to play us?"

"We're not scared!" the boss shot back. Clearly, Injured knew what buttons to push.

"Yeah, that's right, we're not scared!" said the accountant, backing him up.

"Then let's play already," Injured replied.

The boss turned to face his guys. They huddled up, whispering to each other, their foreheads converging. Eventually, the boss turned back to us.

"Okay," he said, "we'll play you. We're not scared, but you were still late!"

"Take it up with the Federation."

That settled things; it was time to play.

The gas guys put out their bonfire, put away their pots, and readied themselves for battle. Our driver wound up being the referee. The gas guys only had twelve players, including their accountant. Just like the apostles. You could say their bench was fatally short because their accountant, whom they didn't let play due to his poor vision, was their only sub. Anyway, the gas guys spilled out onto the field, leaving their accountant on the bench. They looked so much alike that we had no hope of telling them apart. The boss put on a pair of women's leather gloves and assumed his position in goal. Injured gathered us together and put his briefcase down at his feet.

"All right, guys," he said, "focus on trapping the ball cleanly. Got it?"

"Got it, Injured," Vasya Negative answered for all of us.

"Got it," the Balalaeshnikov brothers confirmed.

"Got it," I added.

Injured had the tall, skinny Semyon Black Dick play goalie. Semyon ran over to the goal, sprang up, and started hanging from the crossbar. The Balalaeshnikovs were supposed to be playing defense. The rest of our players assumed their usual positions. Injured told me to play up with him. Karpo Disc Grinder and Vasya Negative, who weren't included in the starting roster, trudged dejectedly off the field, joining the rest of the backup players behind our goal. Karpo waved his disc grinder threateningly, while Vasya flopped down onto the warm grass, placed Injured's briefcase under his head, and fell asleep as if he didn't have a care in the world. The captains faced off in the center. The driver was bobbing around by them, holding a heavy, old-school leather ball.

"Injured, here's how it's gonna be," the boss declared. "No brawls on the field. Save your complaints for after the match."

"Whatever you say, whatever you say," said Injured, who apparently saw no point in objecting.

The last glimmers of reflected sun were dying away. We had to get a move on. We kicked off.

★

The game got off to a rocky start. The gas guys were lethargic, possibly due to the meat they'd been eating, so they weren't moving up the field. On the other hand, the Balalaeshnikov brothers were all jittery for some reason—they'd wind up and completely miss the ball. Also, they were constantly getting in each other's way and arguing with the referee. Five minutes in, Ravzan whiffed again, and got hit upside the head by Shamil. The referee blew the whistle, but couldn't think of anything better to do than giving the opposing team a free kick. He even wanted to card Shamil for unsportsmanlike conduct, but Ravzan himself stood up for him, saying that it was a family affair. He advised the referee to keep his distance. One of the gas guys took the free kick, the ball slid along through the thick grass and slipped past someone into our goal, which by the way was probably a total fluke. The gas guys started celebrating—the dogs roared in reply to their triumphant cries and their sheep bleated too. This elation was short-lived, however—on the very next possession, Injured ran halfway down the field and smashed the ball past the boss, who had timed his jump pretty poorly. He tumbled awkwardly back into his goal and got tangled up in the net like a big catfish. It took both teams to help extricate him. Gradually we started up again. The gas guys doggedly refused to attack—our guys opted for positional play, and as soon as one of our opponents got the ball, we'd knock him off his feet and run over to the referee to contest the call. Our referee didn't exactly have the best eyes—he couldn't see the ball at all in the twilight, so he'd just take our word for it. Shortly afterward, Injured scored again. It was rather unexpected—it was so dark by now that one of the gas guys mistook Injured for a teammate and lost control of the ball; scoring from twenty meters out was a matter of pride for Injured. We took the lead. At this point the gas guys finally got into the game and went on the offensive, leaving their goalie alone with some hungry sheep whimpering by the goal. Injured scored his third goal in a blistering counterattack. He just came running all the way back to our goal, stole the ball from the gas guys, dribbled it down the whole field, burned past the goalie, and careened straight into the pack of sheep, carried by his momentum. Right after that, the Balalaeshnikovs knocked over three guys inside the penalty area—Ravzan took down one guy, while Shamil handled the other two. The referee had the gas guys take a penalty kick. They scored. Injured was pissed, but he didn't want to sub out the Balalaeshnikovs. Basically, it looked like we were all just getting in his way. He faked out the boss and scored two more times before the end of the half; however, Semyon let two goals whiz by him. If there were a commentator, he would have remarked that the fans must be loving this high-scoring game. The accountant was the only one in the audience, of course, but to be fair, he was clearly soaking it up. During halftime, the home team drove their eighteen-wheelers closer, started up their engines, and flooded the field with their headlights. The field looked like a stage, bright and ready for a show, and the German shepherds' eyes and the accountant's glasses were shining through the darkness. Injured gathered us around, crouched down, and put his briefcase down in front of him. He took out a bottle of grain alcohol, and sent it around the circle. Everyone was looking at our captain with deep reverence.

"Guys, remember, clean touches," Injured said, and then again: "Clean touches."

We all took a swig and nodded. The Balalaeshnikovs were standing off to the side arguing about something, but I couldn't hear what they were saying.

The same dynamic continued into the second half. Siryozha the Rapist, who subbed in for Python, tried calming the Balalaeshnikovs down—he yelled at them, told them to push up the field, told them to pay closer attention, started playing their positions, and generally just got in *their* way. Trying to clear the ball, he wound up slamming it into our own goal. He asked to be subbed out after that. Karpo Disc Grinder took his place, but his contribution wasn't especially meaningful either. The game drew to its logical conclusion—the gas guys had dropped back; apparently, they were quite satisfied with a tie. Our team had run out of steam and couldn't get a decisive advantage. Injured was trying his best to crack the gas guys' tough defense, but you can't stop a column of tanks with a bayonet, and one player can't break past eleven angry gas guys six times in a row, even if that player is Injured.

The game should have already ended, but the referee, squinting and straining his weak eyes, just couldn't make out how much time had passed, so we played at least five minutes extra. Everyone had already started peering over at the bus parked off to the side, black and nearly invisible in the night, trying to figure out whether we'd be able to escape in one piece. It seemed as though even Injured had resigned himself to a tie. During the last possession, Semyon punted the ball into the opposing team's half—Andryukha Michael Jackson trapped it, burst past two gas guys, and ran down the field. He was almost one-on-one with the goalie, but at the last second, one of the gas guys kicked the ball out of bounds—we were set to take a corner kick. Both teams bunched up by the boss's goal. Even Semyon ran all the way up the field, sliding off his goalie gloves. Injured went over to take the corner. He chipped it up with his weak left foot, and the ball, following some implausible trajectory, curved into the gas guys' penalty box. It bounced off of one of them and his teammate dropped it back to the boss. The boss kicked the ball with desperation, and it whizzed up like an artillery shell, bouncing off my head and into the goal. I didn't even see how it all happened because I had my back to the goal. We had won the game. The exhausted gas guys collapsed on the ground; the boss wiped off some sweat and tears trickling down his cheeks; our guys hoisted me up on their shoulders and ran across the whole field to our bench. The referee, fearing the gas guys' wrath, led the way. Injured brought up the rear, limping along with a satisfied grin. The German shepherds came running along after him, howling morosely into the dark skies that not even the eighteen-wheelers' headlights could pierce.

Joy filled our hearts, joy and a feeling that justice had prevailed—everything played out the way it was supposed to. Who could have doubted that we'd come out on top? This journey could only have ended in triumph, so nobody was particularly surprised. I shook my friends' hands, relishing this adventure, which had ended so well, and genuinely surprised that so many years had passed and yet everything seemed to be returning to how it was—everything was behaving according to the laws of motion again. This thought calmed me and wound me up at the same time: it was this kind of joy, precisely the joy of recognition and the joy of returning that I'd been missing all these years . . . since our last match, really. Immersed in those thoughts, I spotted the gas guys out of the corner of my eye, moving toward us, slowly but surely. They had already started to recover from their defeat. It looked like they weren't planning on letting us go so easily. I exchanged glances with one of my teammates, and he too noticed their approach. Our triumphant cheering cut off all at once. Our guys started walking toward the gas guys. The teams faced off. Of course, that's how it was always going to go down. Even the accountant was coming at us, though he didn't have his glasses on. Evidently he didn't want them to get broken, so he had to grope blindly across the field. The gas guys stopped, breathing heavily. Our guys halted too. Their headlights were directed right at us, blinding us and making all our shapes seem transparent, barely visible, as though we were ghosts standing in the middle of the field, trying to settle things with other ghosts. Gold teeth and tattooed crosses flashed periodically in the electric glare. The boss took a step forward.

"Injured, that last goal doesn't count."

"Why the fuck not?" Injured asked cogently.

"Time had already run out," the accountant explained.

"You're a doofus," Andryukha Michael Jackson said, "I'm gonna feed you to your sheep."

"Quit waving your dick around," pronounced the boss solemnly. "Time was already up."

"Time was up?" Injured asked.

"Time was up," the gas guys repeated obstinately.

"So what," Injured replied, pulling a pair of brass knuckles out of nowhere.

The rest of our guys were also taking out brass knuckles, nun-chucks, and baseball bats. The gas guys also whipped out some boards, lead-lined army belts, and bricks. Something like overtime was about to get underway, but then two of the Balalaeshnikov brothers, Ravzan and Shamil, stepped forward:

"What the fuck?!" yelled Ravzan, though it was more of an answer than a question. "Time was up, you say? But it was only in the first half that we scored after time was up!"

"No we didn't, not in the first half," Shamil interrupted to correct him.

"What do you mean we didn't?" Ravzan asked incredulously. "We did. It was way past time."

"No fuckin' way." Shamil wasn't backing down.

"Bro," Ravzan said, getting anxious, "you're lying out of your fuckin' ass. You weren't even there during the first half. I saw it with my own eyes, it was way past time."

"Nope," Shamil persisted.

"Bro, be quiet, all right?"

"We didn't score after time," Shamil said.

"What are you lying out of your ass for?" Ravzan asked again. Neither team dared get involved.

"So what?" Shamil asked, braced for whatever would follow.

"What? What?" Ravzan's blood was boiling over.

"I'll show you what!" Shamil's blood was doing likewise.

"I don't fuckin' think so," Ravzan replied, and socked Shamil in the jaw.

Shamil went down, but he sprang to his feet quickly, grabbed a baseball bat out of someone's hands, and chucked it at his brother. Ravzan ducked; the bat whirled by him, right past his ear. He cried out and charged at his rival. He socked his brother a second time and then started pummeling him, but Shamil soon managed to escape, climb on top, and now he was the one pummeling Ravzan. Then Barukh flew toward them unexpectedly and kicked them away from each other; he grabbed them by their shirts, slammed their heads together, knocked both of them down, and then started pummeling both of them at once. Shamil and Ravzan, not expecting anything like this from their brother, lay there and took it for a moment or two, but then, sure enough, the fight came back into them and they grabbed Barukh by the legs and toppled him. They straddled him and they both started pummeling *him*. This didn't last long, though—Barukh slithered out from under their heavy bodies, got them both in a headlock, and went back to flattening them into pancakes. About five minutes later, utterly exhausted, they were all rolling around in the grass, panting and spitting up blood. The gas guys were watching this whole scene, stupefied. They stood there in silence, too scared to move a muscle. Eventually, the boss called out warily:

"Hey Injured!" His voice was expressionless, petrified. "What the fuck is with you guys? Just beat it already."

"And what about the last goal?" Injured asked, just in case.

"It counts," the boss assured him, "it counts."

★

We pulled out onto the highway in the darkness. The moon had rolled out to meet us, and its yellow light poured into the bus, falling onto my friends' faces—most of them were already asleep. Their eyes drooped in the dim light; their cheekbones had become more defined and their heads bobbed in unconsciousness. The driver stopped at the gas station. I waved, but pretty much no one was awake by this point, so there wasn't anybody to say good-bye to. Injured was the only one still awake—he came up to me and shook my hand without saying a word. I hopped out of the bus. The doors closed and it moved out, disappearing slowly behind the trees.

6

Ernst called before I even had the chance to think over our recent conversation. He called to see when I planned on coming by. I tried rescheduling, saying I was busy, I had an important meeting today, I was waiting for a special customer, I was feeling under the weather; I suggested we meet another time. Ernst listened to my spiel and countered with the following remark:

"Herman, sometimes people don't know what they're passing up, so it's best not to pass anything up. You see what I'm getting at?"

"Yeah."

"So when should I expect you?"

"I'll shoot for two o'clock," I conceded.

"Let's make it one-thirty," Ernst replied and hung up.

I went over to the garage to tell Injured. He heard me out and got angry, like usual. He said that instead of giving him a hand, just once, I was always dicking around and hanging out with shady motherfuckers. He told me he wouldn't take me anywhere and that I needed to get my shit together.

"Herman," he shouted, "do you really wanna get mixed up in this tank scheme? What the fuck for? What would you even do with a tank if you found one?"

"I'll use it to cut the grass," I answered irritably. "You want me to pay for the gas or something? You greedy bastard . . ."

"No, it has nothing to do with the gas . . ." Injured replied, sliding off his gloves and heading outside to start up his car.

We rode in silence, descending into the valley, speeding over the bridge, and entering the city. Injured would occasionally nod at women who recognized him. We passed the bus station, the grain elevator, and then pulled up at the railroad crossing. Injured stopped and said:

"All right, this is as far as I go. I don't want anyone seeing me over there."

"How come?"

"I've got a girl down there," Injured explained. "She thinks I'm in Poland. I told her I was going there on business, you know? I don't want to blow my cover. You can walk from here—it's not too far."

"I know," I said, shutting the door behind me.

The sparse buildings on the outskirts of town gave way to fields of crops—there were fewer and fewer people here, more and more animals. Cows, tied down with durable ropes, like blimps, were grazing in the fields. The road leading off the highway toward the airport had become thoroughly overgrown. A few poplar trees stood orphaned and abandoned; the metal gate at the entrance was covered in rust and black metal stars hung there like dead planets. I walked up and pushed on the gate. It screeched loudly and swung open. Ernst was already standing outside the building. Apparently, he had spotted me coming down the road, and now he was waiting for me in full uniform. He was dressed in a British fireman's jacket on top of a black army T-shirt and jean shorts held up by an old German belt with "God with us" on the buckle, with a pair of Keds on his feet. He looked like an Iron Maiden fan. He came up to me and shook my hand.

"It's a good thing you decided to come," he said.

"I'd like you to know that it was quite a hassle getting here—we really should have rescheduled after all."

"Time, Herman, time," Ernst replied, "who knows how much of it you've got left . . ."

"What are you getting at?"

"I mean that we need to walk through those doors that others have opened for us."

He said that with a pensive air, then started walking. I followed. We trod through the thick grass and grapevines that surrounded the airport. We went past a garage, cut behind the small administration building, and found ourselves next to a large structure that looked like a hangar. A flat lot, empty as a highway in the early morning, had by now become visible behind the various structures—this was the runway. A sense of neglect pervaded everything. Now Ernst struck me as looking like a man who'd gone AWOL after falling behind his unit. He was hiding out in abandoned warehouses, awaiting court martial. He opened the metal doors and motioned for me to come in. It was an old cafeteria where, as far as I could gather, the airport employees used to eat. I could picture it now—gallant pilots, all-star rural aviators returning home after completing hazardous flights over a vast sea of corn to their quiet and cozy haven where they would be greeted by their loyal mechanics, their wise dispatchers, and some warm compote. The room was spacious, lined with old tables and metal chairs. There were propaganda posters on the walls—a testament to the might and constancy of Red aviation and doubtless the product of some committee dedicated to improving the public perception of using planes to apply chemical agents to crops in peacetime. Not much had changed over the past twenty years. Aside from the fact that I was wearing a German army jacket and Ernst a British one.

Ernst invited me to take a seat at the table, produced a ten-liter metal canister from somewhere by the wall, sat down across from me, plonked the canister down at his feet, and took two crummy table glasses marked with red oil paint out of his pocket. He put the glasses down and I peered inside of them—the bottom of mine read 7 and Ernst's read 12. Ernst hefted the canister, opened it up, and filled up both our glasses with red liquid.

"It's wine," he said, handing me the glass. "I make it myself." We clinked glasses. "I use the grapes that grow right here at the airport. One could say that this is all that's left of Soviet aviation."

"Let its memory live on," I said and downed my glass.

The wine was acerbic and hot.

"Let me tell you." Ernst downed his glass too and started pouring another round. "Killing aviation might be the worst thing they ever did. Democracy can't exist without aviation. Airplanes are the cornerstone of civil society."

I suggested we drink to that. Ernst was all for it. Anyone watching us would probably have thought we were drinking gasoline.

"How's Injured? Hanging in there?" Ernst asked after a short pause. An awkward silence had set in while he was pouring. I never know what to say to break the ice. He'd clearly felt my anxiety, so he was trying to change the subject to something more neutral.

"All right," I answered, "he's been playing some soccer."

"Soccer?" Ernst was genuinely surprised. "He's still at it?"

"They're all still playing. We beat the gas guys yesterday."

"What do you mean *they*?"

"Well, all the guys I used to play with. Python, Conductor, Andryukha Michael Jackson." Ernst was giving me a strange look. "The Balalaeshnikov brothers too," I added, less confidently.

"The Balalaeshnikovs? Aren't they the guys who died in a fire at their movie theater?"

"What do you mean they died in a fire? I was playing soccer with them yesterday."

"Of course you were," Ernst said. "Since when has dying in a fire ever kept anyone from playing soccer? So, how's Injured hanging in there?" he asked again.

"He's doing all right. He didn't wanna give me a ride over here. He said your whole tank scheme is a bunch of baloney."

"That's what he said?"

"Yep, what's that he said."

"And he was talking about the *tanks*?"

"Yeah."

"Hmm," said Ernst, turning sullen. "Injured is rather impulsive, that's his personality type—he can't concentrate on any one particular thing. He's got the same problem with women. You know that, right?"

"I figured as much."

"Actually," Ernst went on, "a few years back, Injured was helping me try to dig up three German grenadiers."

"What do you mean, 'dig up'?"

"Well," said Ernst, apparently not sure how to explain, "digging them up, you know, from the pitch-black void. I'd find them with a metal detector—they had metal crowns in their teeth, they'd set it off. Incidentally, Injured offered his help, straight away. I figured he was in it for the *Reichsmarks*. But why would grenadiers have *Reichsmarks?*"

"How'd it all play out?"

"Badly," Ernst replied, pouring us another round out of the canister. "We found them and exhumed them. But it turned out that they'd actually been properly buried after the war, but they hadn't put down any markers. So, I was accused of desecrating military burial sites. I barely got off. But I still wear the belt I found." He showed me. "Ever since then, Injured has been skeptical about the whole thing."

Ernst poured another dose into his face. I followed suit, trying to keep up.

"Gotcha. So what now? You really want to find a tank?"

Ernst gave me a shrewd and attentive look. I started to feel a bit uneasy.

"Herman," he said, "what would you do if you suddenly came into a lot of money? Like a million . . ."

"A million."

"Uh-huh."

"*Reichsmarks?*"

"Dollars."

"I'd buy myself a house . . . in Africa."

"What would you do with a house in Africa?"

"I've always wanted to live in a country where there's no racism."

"Got ya." Ernst nodded wisely. "You know what I would do?"

"What?"

"I'd buy an airplane, Herman. And I'd bring local air travel back to life."

"But why?"

"Why, you ask? Because I can live just fine in a city where there's racism. But I just can't live in a city where there's no aviation."

"It's really that important to you?"

"You see," Ernst said, having to tilt the canister even more to fill up our glasses now, "it's not just a matter of air travel. If not for me, the damn corn guys would have bought up this property a long time ago." He gestured around at his domain. "They would have ripped up the asphalt and planted this whole area with corn. Herman, you see all this? Everything they built here—it'd be cornfields."

"Why haven't they done it yet?"

"Because it's still technically state property. But trust me, as soon as they let me go, everything's going to get bought up. Because they don't care about anything but their damn corn, you know what I mean?" Ernst was already rather drunk, so he was getting less lucid but more effusive as he went along: "All they need airplanes for is to look after their corn. They don't care about air travel, Herman. For me, airplanes aren't just a job. You know, when I was a kid, I would dream about the sky. In school I'd draw airplanes in my notebooks—the same models that were soaring up there, over our heads. Herman, think about it. When we were kids, we all wanted to be aviators. We wanted to fly and touch the sky! Dude, we were all named after astronauts!"

"Especially you, Ernst Thälmann . . ."

"Whatever," he said, not losing any momentum. "What happened to our dreams? Who took our tickets to heaven away from us? I ask you, why have we who love the sky been ostracized? Why have we been forced into seclusion?"

Ernst shook his head anxiously and went quiet. I also went quiet because I didn't know what to say to all that. Finally, he perked up again:

"For me," he said, "it's a matter of principle. I want to revive air travel in this city where the only choice is pushing people around or getting pushed around yourself. They're letting those fuckers tell them what to do. You could say that this is my life's work."

"All right," I tried encouraging him, "but where does the tank come in?"

"Herman, you're a history buff, right?"

"Sure."

"Then you probably know how many Tigers were produced in the Reich?"

"What model are we talking about?"

"All the models put together."

"Around fifteen hundred."

"Well, thirteen hundred fifty-five, to be exact," Ernst said jubilantly. "Would you say that's a lot?"

"Not really," I answered after thinking for a bit.

"No, it's not many at all," Ernst concurred. "You know how many are still intact?"

"About a hundred," I guessed.

"Six, Herman, just six. What do you think? How much would a Tiger be worth today?"

"A million."

"Or more."

"And you know where you can find one?" I asked, trying to keep the doubt out of my voice.

"I don't know, but there's got to be one around here. I can just feel it. I'll dig it up one day, and then I'll tell all those businessmen buying up scrap metal from state companies where they can stick it. Those assholes! They've sold out and ruined the aviation industry," he concluded, pouring another glass.

I was only then realizing just how drunk he really was, so I didn't see any point in arguing. I thought, "Why *not* aviation? Not a bad dream for a guy who lives in an old cafeteria."

"All right, Herman," Ernst said, coming back to life, "time is on our side, or history. You know, history doesn't teach us a thing. A tank war—can you picture it? A tank war is a great migration of peoples. Think of those simple German mechanics, those young boys—the majority of them hadn't ever been away from home before, let alone crossing a continent. Say you were born and raised in a small German town. You went to church, to school, fell in love for the first time, and stayed loosely informed about politics, at least enough to know who the chancellor was. Then the war starts and you get drafted. You get some training and become a tank driver. Then you start moving east, farther and farther east, crossing borders, taking over foreign cities, and destroying your enemy's resources, both material and human. You come to realize that you're seeing the same cities and same landscapes here as you saw back home, and the people too—they're essentially the same, if you don't count the communists and Gypsies. The women are just as pretty, while the kids are just as naïve and carefree. And you take over their capitals, not really too concerned about what awaits you, where the war will take you tomorrow. With that attitude, you cross through Czechoslovakia, then Poland, and finally, your tank has rolled across the border into the USSR, the country of developed socialism. At first everything was going smoothly—blitzkrieg, your generals' genius strategies, a quick advance eastward. You even crossed the Dnieper pretty much problem-free. But that's when things go bad—you suddenly find yourself in an absolutely barren landscape: no cities, no people, and no infrastructure. Even your enemies have disappeared—they're somewhere out there, hiding. In a place like this you'd be relieved to see *anyone*, even them, but no, they've disappeared, too, and the farther east you advance, the more worried you get. And when you finally find yourself here," Ernst said, his finger circling in the air, "you get this eerie feeling, you realize how good you had it until then, because here, right on the other side of the nearest fence, as soon as you get three hundred meters away from the railroad tracks, everything you thought you knew about war, about Europe, about landscapes, is nullified, because endless emptiness begins right on the other side of that fence, emptiness without content, form, or connotation. It's real, absolute emptiness, and there's nothing to hold on to. And what's waiting for you on the other side of all that emptiness? Stalingrad. That's what a tank war is, Herman."

Concluding his speech, Ernst tipped the canister right over.

★

In the evening, he led me out to the gate. He could hardly stand up, but he had a sly twinkle in his eye. He clearly realized that his whole performance with the wine and the tank had hooked me, not to mention his little digression about emptiness—a grain of interest had worked its way into my heart, and now it was only a matter of time before it would ripen and he would reap his harvest. Ernst patted me on the back and shoved me off the compound. I took a look around. The road leading out to the highway was drowning in twilight and darkness had swallowed up the stars hanging over the gate. Just as I was getting used to the dark, a harsh light struck me right in the face; I shielded my eyes with my hand. The black Jeep was there, parked off to the side of the road. I headed toward it. The wine sloshing around in my stomach gave me a sense of carefree anticipation, like when you take your seat on a Ferris wheel—after all, what's the worst that could happen? Even if you get sick at the top, nobody will give you a hard time, because it's an amusement park—and if throwing up on a Ferris wheel isn't amusing, then what is? So I walked up to the Jeep, opened the rear door, and hopped in, uninvited. Nikolaich, sprawled out on the wide backseat, was taken aback by how willingly I'd climbed in. Still, he more or less managed to compose himself, stretching his face into a delighted smile.

"Herman!" he began in his most polite tone of voice.

But I didn't let Nikolaich finish, since I was already giving him a big bear hug, outwardly demonstrating how great it was that they'd found me here. The wine was sloshing around in my head now.

Nikolaich was completely bewildered. Maybe he had pictured today's meeting differently. Maybe he had rehearsed some tough talk—but my gregariousness had thrown him for a loop.

"We've been looking for you," he said finally. "Well, shall we?" he added, pushing me ever so slightly away.

"Let's go," I said lightheartedly.

"Doors!" Nick yelled back at me from the driver's seat.

"Go fuck yourself," I replied just as lightheartedly.

Silence. Nikolaich curled up into a ball, Nick started breathing heavily, and I smiled generously, trying to convey just how delighted I was to see them.

"Nick!" Nikolaich exploded.

Nick got out of the car, walked around to my side, and slammed the door without saying a word. He got back behind the wheel and we headed out. We pulled onto the highway, turning toward the city. That was a good sign—it meant they weren't planning on burying me in the cornfield by the airport.

"How are things?" Nikolaich began.

"Excellent," I answered. "We beat the gas guys yesterday."

"Really?" He frowned. "When are you heading home?"

"Not sure," I said. "I'd like to stick around a bit longer."

"Really?"

"Uh-huh. I've got some paperwork to take care of."

"Really?" Nikolaich was trying to ape my good-natured tone. "Herman, do you really need all that hassle? Why not just go on home?"

"Nikolaich, were you bullied as a kid?"

"Now why would you think that?" Nikolaich asked with a hint of anxiety.

"Well, your build . . . you don't exactly look like you've done a lot of fighting, you know what I mean? What size shoe do you wear?"

"Nine," Nikolaich answered apprehensively. "Nobody bullied me," he added. "I could always get them to cooperate."

"I got beat up a few times," I admitted, "by this bunch of guys. I mean, I also beat some guys up myself. But the thing is—I have no hard feelings about it all. I don't hold any grudges. Because when you're duking it out with a guy, you take a few punches, that's just how it is, right? There's no reason to hold a grudge. You catch my drift?"

"Yeah," Nikolaich said. "So, you don't want to cooperate with us?"

"Nope."

The Jeep pulled up onto the railroad crossing. The tracks were shimmering in the moonlight.

"Nick!" Nikolaich called sharply.

Nick slammed on the brakes and turned off the engine. We were stopped right in the middle of the tracks. A railroad man wearing an orange jacket hopped down out of his booth and ran over to us. Nick stuck his head out the window and said something, which was apparently enough to make him slink right back to it.

"Herman," Nikolaich said coldly, evidently trying to recall the threatening speech he had prepared. "You know, I'm a businessman, so I'm used to dealing with all kinds of clients. But I just can't stand people who . . ."

The lights near the booth flickered, indicating that a train was coming. The metal barriers dropped, shutting the Jeep in on both sides. Nick let out a gasp. Nikolaich tensed up too, but he tried to keep his composure and continued:

" . . . who don't want to find common ground. Do you see what I mean, Herman?"

"Huh?"

"You don't see what I'm trying to say?"

"Not exactly."

"I'm trying to explain . . ."

"Nikolaich," Nick interrupted.

"The thing is . . ." Nikolaich continued, trying to ignore him.

"Nikolaich," Nick said more assertively—I could hear the growing alarm in his voice.

"Nick, go fuck yourself," Nikolaich snapped, irritated at losing his momentum. He turned toward me again, trying to pick up where he'd left off. "It's just . . . What I'd like to say is . . ."

"Sorry, but could you give me a sec?" I asked.

I hadn't been feeling too hot for the last few minutes—now the wine was rushing upward through my body like natural gas shooting up from the depths of the black Ukrainian earth. I'd been trying to block it out and listen to Nikolaich, but the sensation was getting worse by the minute.

"What?" Nikolaich asked, going for a steely tone again but still failing to pull it off

"Give me a sec," I said, opening the door and leaning outside.

I threw up, instantly. Then I was gasping for air. It was over, but I decided to wait a bit longer, leaning out the door, just in case.

Nick was cursing me up and down, while Nikolaich was looking tensely out the window—the Moscow train could pop out of the twilight any second now. As he stared, Nikolaich seemed to be going back over some phrases he had rehearsed especially for this conversation. When I finally caught my breath, I flopped back on the leather seat, utterly exhausted, and closed the door.

"So, Herman," Nikolaich said, starting his speech once again, albeit a bit faster than before. "I do business—"

"Give me a sec!" I yelled again, opening up the door frantically and leaning out.

"Motherfucker!" Nick cursed desperately, while Nikolaich curled up like a hedgehog.

Soon I flopped back onto the seat again, gasping for air and favoring Nikolaich with a whiff of wild grape. To our left, a train rolled out of the fog. It was still a few hundred meters away and, from afar, its joyous light was flashing in the evening air.

"I'm fuckin' out of here!" Nick yelled, starting up the engine and putting the pedal to the metal. The Jeep jumped forward, miraculously circumventing the barrier before flying down the asphalt.

Nick stopped the car and turned around:

"Nikolaich," he barked, "get rid of this fuckin' faggot! Kick him the fuck out of the car!"

"I can get out myself," I said and stepped into the air. But before taking my leave I leaned in toward Nikolaich. "I don't think this is going to work out. This isn't the way to do business. Good-bye."

I closed the door, leaving nothing but rich grape fragrance behind me.

7

Even though one look at me must have made it clear what I'd been up to, even though you could see the treachery of home-made wine glistening in my eyes, even though my clothes and hair still had a wild grapevine scent, Kocha didn't say a single word to me. He just paced around timidly, like a cat in someone else's house, taking in the new smells. He brewed tea and fended off the wasps that circled my head like seagulls hovering over a sunken tanker. He was talking the whole time, more to himself than to me, telling stories about his wife. These stories continued to haunt him, and they haunted me, even though I was hearing them for the nth time.

"Women, Herman, fuckin' women, at the end of the day it's always their fault," he said, with his usual audio feedback.

"What do women have to do with it?" I asked, but Kocha simply shrugged disaffectedly, drinking his oil-black tea.

"I see exactly what's going on here," he added. "Herman, buddy, you're a mess and it's all because of them."

I shook a few pesky wasps out of my hair and grabbed hold of them, but they flew out of my rather anemic fist as Kocha went on and on, soothing away my headache.

"Did you know her?" he asked. "My wife, I mean."

"Yeah, I knew her—she was dark-skinned and a lot of fun, yeah?"

"Yep, that was her." Kocha's hoarse voice seemed cheerier. "She was five years younger than me. But I woulda never thought she was younger than me. She was seventeen when we met . . . but damn, she knew her way around in the sack . . ."

"Where'd you meet?"

"At the athletic fields," Kocha said after thinking a bit, "in the summer. She moved to the city to study to become a doctor. I met her for the first time by the medical college. They always have the same skin color—I mean women from down south. They don't really tan, you know?"

"I didn't realize she was from down south."

"She was from Georgia. She had these long, long legs . . . And she had black hair back then too."

"Yeah, I remember that," I said.

"And when she was studying at the medical college she would always wear that snow-white coat . . . Tell me, Herman, do women doctors turn you on?"

"Nah, I'm afraid of doctors."

"Well, they sure turn me on. One time I was getting a check-up at the health center, and . . . well, I was so turned on I could hardly stand it. But look, I wanted to tell you about Tamara. Buddy, I'm going to tell you the whole story."

But I don't think he actually told me that much. It was more that I started remembering things as he talked, or when I thought back to his story later on. I'm always genuinely surprised by how much a typical person's memory can store, and yet how difficult it can be to find anything worthwhile in there. How does a memory really form? What did Kocha actually tell me? Something about her clothes, yeah, something about her clothes. Long hair, dark skinned but not tanned, and her clothes. Not tanned—what did he mean by that? And then I saw her: she had this black dress—nobody else in the city wore that kind of dress. When you saw her, your heart skipped a beat—that's what happened to all of us guys from the crappy apartment blocks on the edge of town. Her dress was so black that her skin looked pale by comparison, even when she was wearing her snow-white coat. But how could we know anything about her tan or lack thereof? Kocha had seen much more than us—he'd seen all of her, with clothes on and without, so he was the man to ask. And I remembered the evening twilight, the warm sand on sidewalks turned red by the mulberries, and Kocha. He was dragging two Azeri guest workers by the hair, shoving their faces into the fence in front of some endless factory wall; and there we were, standing off to the side, not interfering—Kocha had to fight his own battles. Tamara was yelling something, shrilly, anxiously, trying to stop him. She was yelling that nobody had laid a finger on her, and the Azeri guys were also yelling that they hadn't laid a finger on her, but Kocha continued banging their heads against the fence. Then she ran away and vanished into the darkness. Kocha ran after her. We helped the Azeri guys up and treated their wounds with vodka, because we knew that they really hadn't laid a finger on her.

"Uh-huh," Kocha said, bringing me back to reality. "Buddy,

you know, when we met she was only seventeen, but let me tell you—I'd never seen some of the stuff she could do, not even in brothels."

"And you've been to a lot of brothels?" I asked skeptically.

"Well, not a lot," Kocha said, a bit offended at having his heroic biography questioned, "I was a paratrooper, Herman. We could have any girl we wanted."

"Gotcha."

"I fought for her for three years," Kocha continued. "I couldn't leave her alone, not even for a second, not even for a second. Can you believe that?"

"I can."

"Finally she just decided to run away. Her parents wouldn't let her marry me, no matter what. Mountain people—they've got their own rules."

"Well, did she run away?"

"Over my fuckin' dead body," Kocha said, rather self-satisfied. "I found out about her plan and got on the same train as her. The same exact car, too. The two of us bounced around, from station to station, from here to Rostov. She tried hopping off a few times, but I caught her. We slept at train stations, drank champagne in dining cars, and fought like cats and dogs—can you believe that?" Kocha was kicking back in his chair and peering out the window now, enjoying this talk of his glory days. "Then she gave up, came back with me. That's life. We stayed together, though her parents never stopped giving us trouble. They just hated me. But then we told them she was pregnant, so they gave up too, and we got married."

"Was she actually pregnant?"

"Nah, are you kidding? The last thing I wanted was for her to get pregnant!"

"How come?"

"I was afraid the kid wouldn't be mine. Buddy, I'm telling you, she was an animal in the sack . . ."

Kocha got quiet, evidently still daydreaming about the past. Then he started up again:

"It didn't work out, all the same. Her parents came down for the wedding. I mean, they moved in with us. So, it didn't work out. Those damn Gypsies . . ."

"Gypsies?"

"Uh-huh, Gypsies."

"What did they have to do with it?"

"Everything." Kocha didn't bother explaining. "It's all because of women —I see what's going on with you, buddy. I know why you're all riled up."

"All right, all right, that's enough," I said, putting up some feeble resistance.

"Herman, I see what's going on. I see what's going on."

He caught a glimpse of something through the window and went outside.

She had done something that stuck in my memory, but what was it? Sun was pouring in through the windows; the blanket was stiff and hot, like a stray dog drying out after a rain shower. I was lying there in an empty room, my eyes closed to see fragmented images, the trees swaying rhythmically back and forth in the park, the lilac-colored darkness sticking to the damp leaves, the gold light flickering on the windows of the fire tower, and the scattered, sharp silver of broken glass in vegetable bowls—but that wasn't it; there was something before that, some climax to this memory. What happened? Didn't Kocha tell me about it? What did he remember that everybody else had forgotten? What could she have done? There was only one way out of there, out the side doors, through the kitchen. That way you'd go straight out into the park, and the trees would surround you, wet and wary—you had to be careful because the grass was littered with broken glass and you could get cut, though nobody ever was careful; blood was pumping through invisible channels in the cool night air and it was going to be shed, one way or another. It was only a matter of who was going to bleed. Toward the end of dinner, I went out those side doors. But why? I don't know why anymore. I was supposed to meet somebody. But who? It was pitch black, and nobody saw me come outside. And there she was, her skin luminous in the wet twilight air—she hadn't even taken off her dress. Oh boy, you should have seen what she was doing! There were two of them, and Tamara was taking both of them on; she was facing one with her back to the other. She hadn't even taken off her dress. I was stunned. I mean, I would have figured that a dress would get in the way in that kind of situation, but no, not this time . . . I couldn't make out the guys' faces, but Kocha definitely wasn't there, and anyway, it's ridiculous to imagine Kocha doing such things, in public no less. After a while, she tore herself away from the first guy, lifted her head, and asked for a smoke. The flame shone brightly, so I opened the kitchen doors and slid back inside so they wouldn't see me. Returning to the party, I bumped into Kocha, all gloomy and angry. From the way he looked at me,

I realized he already knew. Suddenly, the darkness lit by electricity burst into hundreds of silver shards, and the evening air exploded into the room, mixing with the smell of alcohol. That's when I knew this wouldn't just blow over.

"What'd I tell you?" a concerned Kocha asked, running over to his trailer. "Get over here. She's on the phone."

★

"Herman!" I was standing there holding the warm receiver to my ear. "How are you doing?"

"Fine," I said, trying to sound convincing. I don't think it was working. "I saw our competitors yesterday. We had a chat."

"Uh-huh." This clearly wasn't news to Olga. "I don't know what your little chat was about, but they're trying to have the station shut down, Herman."

"I'll be right over." I draped my headphones around my neck and ran out onto the highway.

★

The familiar Jeep was parked outside her office—Nick was in the driver's seat as usual, giving me a completely unruffled look, as if to say, "Oh, it's you, I didn't even notice you left." I waved and stepped inside. Olga was sitting at the table in her yellow-rimmed sunglasses. She was wearing ripped jeans and a T-shirt with some political slogans in Polish. Her orange bra was peeking out from underneath. Two chubby ladies with perms and skin-tight dresses were sitting across from her. These bitches were well over the hill, but they hadn't lost that youthful spark, that Young Pioneer spirit that seeks the joy and inclusion that come only from collective labor. Now they were breathing heavily in this oppressive heat, reminding me of two robust Spanish women, fanning themselves with accounting ledgers.

One of them had a perm the color of cigarette ash; she was wearing massive bronze earrings that dangled like medals from a general's coat, and enormous coral beads were wrapped around her neck. She had squeezed her flabby, sweaty body into a dark, ancient dress, which was stretching every which way, tracing her every bulge, and her powerful, work-worn feet were jammed into slippers. Now she was holding a ledger in one hand and a pencil in the other; she'd stick the latter in her perm from time to time, probing intently for something. Her friend, drooping just as much from the heat, had a copper-colored mop, tinted red by the sunlight, neatly arranged on her head. She wore big emerald stones in her ears, like the ones used in bus station mosaics, and though she didn't have any beads on her neck, her skin there folded into a few hefty layers concealing amber droplets of bitter female sweat. She was wearing a multicolored sundress dating back to the Soviet days, peppered with images of tropical flowers and herbs, and she too was wearing slippers. She looked more alert and reproachful than her counterpart; her sharp shoulders were twitching, causing her dress to tighten in some areas and loosen up in others, like a sail flapping in the wind. The women turned toward me as one, with identical hostile looks on their faces.

I greeted them, giving Olga an inquisitive look. The women

introduced themselves, albeit unwillingly. The ash-colored one's name was Angela Petrovna—she had a heavy and languid voice, and her expression as she spoke was obviously accusatory, yet somehow hard to read. The other woman, the copper-colored one, spoke anxiously and unintelligibly, as though with a mouthful of rocks, introducing herself as Bhalynda Bhedorobna. Clearly she meant to say *Halyna Fedorovna*, or something along those lines. I thought of her as Brunhilda Petrovna, and from then on my mind refused to give her any other name. Why Petrovna, not Fedorovna? Maybe I wanted to give them the same patronymic because they were so similar as to be indistinguishable, like two half-sisters—both women had acquired some valuable experience, some experience that they weren't planning on sharing with anyone.

"Ah, good thing you've finally decided to show up," Olga said, not looking remotely happy to see me.

"I had to catch a ride," I explained to all present.

The two ladies watched me coldly and implacably, Angela Petrovna twirling her pencil in a predatory manner, Brunhilda Petrovna puffing up her flabby neck like a cobra.

Olga briefly filled me in about the problem at hand. As far as I could gather, it all boiled down to the fact that Angela Petrovna and Brunhilda hadn't retired when they were supposed to, so now they had nothing better to do than mess with me. Like funeral keeners, these two signified death, forecasting interest rate hikes and mounting utility bills. I tried getting to the bottom of things, but it was a struggle, since Angela Petrovna and Brunhilda Petrovna's voices had a debilitating effect on me, making me depressed and wistful. I could only glean one thing from our conversation—they had been sent by the tax service, and the social security fund, as well as the sanitation department, and the veterans' association too, in addition to the independent small business owners' association, and, finally, the housing department. It turned out that we were in deep trouble—my downtrodden private enterprise had owed the government an exorbitant amount of money for years, and it'd be best for all concerned, it seemed, if I simply hung myself, liquidating my business before doing so, and transferring all my worldly wealth to the fearless retirees. Angela Petrovna did most of the talking, spinning a web of confusing accounting jargon around my head. Brunhilda Petrovna rolled colored marbles anxiously along the roof of her mouth, periodically interjecting with such linguistic mutants as "betirees," "bygenic," or the utterly incomprehensible "balfolcol bovelment," so I could never quite get to the bottom of things. Olga persisted, trying to explain something to the women and taking some papers out of her drawer. She was saying that things weren't actually that bad, that all of our documents were in order, and that there weren't any legal grounds for banishing me to deepest layer of hell. But Angela Petrovna and Brunhilda Petrovna paid her no mind, waving Olga's arguments away with their ledger books, holding their ground by citing some amendments or other, reading aloud choice excerpts from some recent decrees, and pointing out inconsistencies in our tax forms. All of Olga's attempts at easing the pressure applied by these two passionate, sultry Spanish women were to no avail—the old-timers were clearly spurred on by their own wailing as they exhibited their vast knowledge of both the criminal code and accounting standards. At some point, Olga stopped trying. This caused the Spanish women to pipe down as well, though they went right on glaring at us. I got the sense they were waiting for me to react. I decided I had to say something:

"Listen," I began, in an exceedingly conciliatory tone, causing my voice to take on an emotive note that was unusual for me. "Maybe we can smooth this all out together? Huh? We're all grownups here, aren't we?"

The ash-colored lady squinted at me formidably, while the lady the color of copper launched lightning bolts out of her aging eyes.

"What do you mean?" the ash-colored lady asked me slowly, like a professor during an oral exam.

"Bha?" went the copper-colored lady.

"Herman," said Olga, frightened by my brashness, trying to rein me in.

"Well, I don't know," I cut her off, getting frustrated. "People can always find common ground, can't they?" I asked. And then I added, for some reason, "Couldn't we smooth things out?"

"You're completely out of line!" Angela Petrovna shouted, or tried to shout; she was raising her thick voice as though it were a rock she was rolling up a hill. Brunhilda nodded along with her. "Who do you think you are? Maybe that's how you do business UP THERE! Maybe that's how you talk UP THERE!!!" Now her voice had reached the peak, and was about to crash down the other side—and there it went, barreling down the hillside, leveling everything in its path. "Do you even realize what you're saying? You think this is some sort of a joke? UP THERE it's a free for all! But HERE you're on our turf!" She turned to address Olga: "Ms. Volkova," she said, "I won't stand for this!"

The old ladies rose haughtily to their feet, said their contemptuous good-byes, and disappeared out the door. They vowed to return tomorrow.

★

I was starting to feel uneasy.

"It looks like you rub them the wrong way," Olga said, sorting through some papers.

"Could that put the business in jeopardy?"

"You betcha. Herman, if those old vultures get a hold of you somewhere in town, you could be in some real deep trouble." Her voice was grim.

"What exactly do you mean?"

"I mean they'll cook up a sexual harassment case. Come on, use your head," Olga said, tucking away her papers. "Well, now we're getting audited. Those hags are going to come in here every day and try to get me to shut down your business."

"What are you going to do about it?"

"Herman, I'm an accountant. I'm going to do what I'm paid to do, so don't you worry."

"But it's no coincidence that they started this audit today."

"Ya think?" Olga took off her glasses and sized me up. She looked a bit tired.

"I talked with the corn guys' representative yesterday."

"With whom exactly?"

"Nikolaich—the small guy. He's their representative."

"Small guy?" Olga asked.

"Yeah."

"That little shit . . ."

"That's the one."

"He's their computer guy."

"What do you mean?"

"Well, he's the guy who fixes their computers."

"You're kidding me, right?"

"I'm afraid not. I guess they aren't taking you very seriously. I would think about that if I were you."

"Huh, imagine that, he does computers. He seemed like a decent enough guy to me."

"In any case, we've got problems."

"What exactly is the main problem?" I asked.

"Let me explain."

★

We had a boatload of problems, of course, but one above all. As far as I could gather, we didn't have any copies of the minutes from the oil depot's workers' association meeting. My newly acquired property belonged, in fact, to that oil depot, and not to my brother or me. It seemed my brother didn't care too much about paperwork. He just wasn't that kind of person—generally, he did business by using his connections and his fists, so it didn't come as much of a surprise that he was missing some important documents. Clearly, the sanitation department ladies had been briefed on this weak point before they were sent into the enemy camp. According to Olga, all of our other documents were in good shape; our licenses, on the other hand, might actually cause some trouble, so we needed to do something about them fast. I had no idea what we should do.

"It's all very simple," Olga told me. "We need to get ahold of the former director of that oil depot—he's a pillar of the community, just so you know . . . we'll convince him to backdate a copy of that fuckin' rotten minutes form." She sat down and started dialing him up.

I walked over to the window and peered out. The black Jeep was still parked outside—its tinted windows were rolled halfway down, and I could have sworn I saw Nick and Brunhilda Petrovna in the throes of a passionate make-out session in the front seat, as Angela Petrovna sat in the back and poked them with a sharpened pencil.

★

After making a few calls, Olga ascertained that things would be even more complicated than she'd assumed. It turned out that our pillar of the community didn't actually live in the community anymore. He had moved to a medical facility by the salt lakes that were a few dozen kilometers away from here. We had no clue what condition he would be in, what kind of treatment he was getting, or even whether there was any scientific basis for him being out there in the first place. In short, we didn't know what we were getting ourselves into. I found myself remembering the harsh tone that goddamn computer guy had tried to take with me the day before. And then, as I was remembering the old ladies' unfriendly stares in turn, a bitter and unsettling sensation overcame me—for the first time since my arrival at the station, I really wanted to go home, back to my white-collar job, back to my mundane routine as a party functionary. I regained my composure quickly, though.

"Well? Ready to go?" Olga asked.

"Where to?"

"To visit the director. Where else?"

"Do you need me to be there?"

"Not really," Olga replied, "but in this particular case it'd be better if you came."

"I feel like a real capitalist. I've got interests to protect now. I feel like George Soros."

"Quit your blabbing. I'm trying to think here," Olga said, getting ready to go.

★

The road flowed up and down the green, sun-plastered hills and valleys. The asphalt was falling to pieces, so we were driving cautiously, taking our time. I held onto Olga firmly, her T-shirt flapping in the wind; she didn't seem to care. We passed a few bars scattered along the way. Black, dusty trucks were out in their parking lots with some kids and prostitutes, weary from the extreme heat, sleeping inside. Olga looked around with a severe and concentrated expression, but she only stopped to ask for directions once, from a prostitute. The woman didn't even get out of the truck to answer—she just pointed the way with her bare foot. As we were climbing yet another hill, Olga stopped and looked apprehensively to the south. "It might rain," she said, uneasily, before we forged on.

A bit later, a vast pine forest stretched out before us.

★

The director was undergoing treatment at an old, timeworn sanitarium. According to Olga, he was practically being held there against his will, because what the old guy really wanted was to go on being a productive member of society. According to Olga, he'd led a heroic life, and had a reputation for being quite the curmudgeon, so she warned me that he might have a problem with me. This didn't exactly put my mind at ease, but we'd come all that way—I had to have a talk with him.

The forest was sparse around the sanitarium. Salt marshes stretched out along the perimeter—the sick, the humiliated, and the insulted were swimming in them. We drove through the gate and turned toward the main building. Olga parked her scooter and went ahead. I fell in behind her, watching the patients. There was something unsettling about them. They looked at me mistrustfully, stepping back, whispering among themselves, and pointing their long, skinny fingers at us. The salt marshes gave off an odd smell—a mix of silt and brimstone. The receptionist recognized Olga, nodding happily and informing her that Mr. Petrovsky was in an especially bad mood today; he'd been acting up all morning: hadn't touched his breakfast, had made a scene at lunch, and was refusing to go to the bathroom. Basically, he was being a real pain in the ass—just like yesterday and the day before that. They told us to be careful and not turn our backs on the old-timer. Wishing us luck, they slammed the window down. Olga headed down a hallway, and I tried to keep up, glancing at the patients peering out of the procedure rooms. The walls were lined with odd medical posters warning about the dangers of overheating in the sun, catching hypothermia in the water, and having unprotected sex. Unprotected sex was depicted as something like an act of trespass against God, an offense that would get you excommunicated, and stoned at Party meetings. Posters like that make you want to swear off sex altogether.

Mr. Petrovsky's ward was on the second floor. Olga knocked on the door resolutely, opened it, and stepped into the room. I collected myself and followed suit.

"Hello, Mr. Petrovsky! Hello, my dear!" Olga chirped, addressing the old-timer lying in the bed by the window, giddily running up to him and kissing him on his shiny, bald head.

"Olga, my sweet little butter crumpet, hello there," Mr. Petrovsky extended his slobbery lips, trying to land on her cheek. He gave me the suspicious look I'd come to expect around here. "Who's this snot-nose you brought along?"

"Herman," Olga answered, "the businessman."

"Hello." I stayed put by the door.

"Businessman?" Mr. Petrovsky asked skeptically. "Well, to hell with him. Tell me how you've been doing," he said, turning to Olga.

Olga started telling him about their mutual friends, about the state of the stock market. Meanwhile, I was sizing the old-timer up. Mr. Petrovsky was alert and energetic, with a little twinkle in his eye. Saggy gray curls sprinkled his predominately bald head; dirty, shaggy eyebrows crowned his face, and his nose was hooked. When Mr. Petrovsky spoke, his dentures made a predatory clicking sound somewhere inside his skull. He was lying on the unmade bed in his suit, a snow-white, starchy shirt poking out over the top of a jacket festooned with union member badges and Hero of Labor medals. Incongruous rubber beach sandals stuck out at the bottom. The whole ensemble made him look like William S. Burroughs being admitted to the Writers' Union. A big, busty nurse was sitting on a chipped, dark blue stool beside the director. He called her Natasha and treated her like utter garbage, not seeming to care that we were watching him do it. Natasha clearly knew her place in the party hierarchy, however; she would hand Mr. Petrovsky his metal mug of rum, fill his silver hookah with tobacco, swat away the moths hovering over his bald skull, rub down the geezer's feet with French perfume, and take his adult magazines away from him as needed. She performed all of these duties without speaking a single word, or even looking directly at her charge. He wasn't the only man in the ward, though: there were two other patients there to enjoy the show. One heavy-set fellow was lying across from Mr. Petrovsky, panting profusely. His bulging eyes were fixed on his venerable neighbor, absolutely fuckin' floored by his brazen attitude and willingness to break the rules. This one was wearing a modest outfit—striped hospital pajamas and warm soccer socks—and was holding a newspaper over which he'd cast the occasional apprehensive but curious glance at Natasha. The ward's third inhabitant was stationed closer to the door, exhibiting no signs of life. Judging by the smell, I'd have guessed he had died roughly three days ago, although I might have been off by a couple of days.

Meanwhile, nervous shuffling and whispering could be heard down the hallway—some of the other patients were standing at their doors, frozen and suspicious, trying to catch bits of our conversation. I didn't like this one bit—I wanted to escape from this crematorium as quickly as possible.

Olga was trying valiantly to change the subject to our paperwork problems. She complained to the old-timer about the corn guys making trouble for us, told him about the old Spanish women, and the corruption-ridden local government. Every time, however, Mr. Petrovsky would veer off topic, pretending he hadn't caught what she'd said, drinking his pirate rum, pinching Natasha ferociously, and gobbling down these pills that turned his eyes happy and pink, like those of a fighting dog in a bad photograph.

"Mr. Petrovsky," Olga said, finally breaking down. "I'm asking you to do me this one favor, please."

"Do *you* a favor?" The old-timer looked legitimately surprised. "But you don't need this favor—*he* does," he pointed at me. "That businessman of yours does."

"Yes, Mr. Petrovsky," I hastened to add. "I'm also asking."

"Why the hell should I?" The old-timer seemed to be trying to provoke me. "Sonny boy, what do you want me to do, exactly?"

"Mr. Petrovsky," I moved closer to him. "You know my brother, don't you?"

"So what?" The old-timer was holding his ground. Hope just about gone, Olga stood there pursing her lips. Meanwhile, Natasha placed the mug filled with rum off to the side.

"I just thought," I continued, "that you could help me out, since you once worked with my brother and all."

"Sonny boy, you're not answering my question: *why* should I help you?" Mr. Petrovsky took his horn-rimmed glasses out of his jacket pocket, rested them on his nose, and looked at me long and hard.

"Well, we're in the same business after all."

"Sonny boy, you're the one doing business," he said. "There's no 'we' here. And I'm the one who has pull with the government. You got that?"

"Got it."

"Just so you know, I'm an honored retiree. I've been working for the Party since '52. Do you understand what that means?"

"Roughly."

"And you say you're a businessman . . ." The old-timer calmed down, snatched at his mug, and sucked its contents down past his dentures. Then he kicked back on his pillows smugly and cast a languid look at Olga.

I realized that this engagement wasn't quite going in my favor. I had to do something, and fast.

"Mr. Petrovsky . . ." I approached him and sat down next to him on the bed. He wasn't expecting such familiarity, so he tucked his legs back anxiously. "Please give me five minutes of your time. I'd like to say something, okay?"

"Fine, fine," he said, shifting back toward the wall, pressing the empty mug up against his chest.

"Could I have a sip?" I reached for the mug. This softened the old-timer up immediately and he willingly handed it over. "Pour me a little?" I held out the mug for Natasha. She looked at the old-timer inquisitively; he ignored her, but she poured me some rum nonetheless, and I gulped it all down. It caught in my throat like a hairball. I swallowed hard and started talking, leaning in for an intimate word with the old-timer: "Mr. Petrovsky, let me say just one thing, then we'll be on our way. You know, I haven't actually been in the business for long. I mean I only just took the reins. Frankly speaking, I have no experience managing gas stations. I couldn't even say I especially like the job. All that gasoline—it's toxic, after all, which you know as well as I do. So, what am I getting at? If I were the only one involved I would just sell the station and get as far away as possible, you see what I mean?"

The old-timer nodded.

"But it just so happens that I'm not the only one involved, and one way or another, I have to sort this whole mess out. Because, no matter how you slice it, we're not just talking about me. What we're talking about is much more important. I'm not even sure why yet. But Mr. Petrovsky, I'm looking at you now, and I feel that there's something at the station that I can't just walk away from."

Mr. Petrovsky clicked his dentures loudly.

"I realize that you probably don't like me very much. Look, Mr. Petrovsky, I can see why you might not want to trust me—I'm not a businessman, after all, I have zero experience, I'm a total stranger, and I've never had anything to do with the Party. But, goddamn it, Mr. Petrovsky, is it absolutely essential to have worked for the Party to keep yourself from fucking up something that really matters? Tell me, do you really need to have worked for the Party?"

"Give me my mug back," Mr. Petrovsky responded quietly.

"Huh?"

"I said, give me my mug back," he repeated.

He hid the empty mug under his pillow and took off his glasses pensively.

"You seem like a decent guy," he said after a short pause. "I'll be honest with you—I underestimated you. All right." He clapped his hands, apparently signaling his readiness to begin an important task, and that odd twinkle appeared in his eyes again. "I'll help you out."

"Thank you," I said, relieved, though my relief proved to be short-lived.

"Under one condition," he added. "You have to play a game of Gorodki with me."

"A game of what?"

"Gorodki," Mr. Petrovsky repeated, deriving great satisfaction from seeing me so bewildered. "Gorodki. Ivan Pavlov and Tolstoy's favorite game. What's your take on Tolstoy? You like him?"

"Yeah, I do."

"Excellent. If you beat me, I'll help you out. If you lose, then you go your merry way and let me get back to recuperating."

"Uh . . . how about you just help me out, and we skip the game of Gorodki?" I asked, just in case.

"Nope, sonny boy," Mr. Petrovsky said severely. "There's no way we're skipping Gorodki."

I looked over at Olga. All she could do was roll her eyes. Behind her, the patient holding the newspaper was relishing our anguish. The third, unidentified man was still decaying steadily off in the corner. I had to make a choice. "Gorodki it is," I thought.

After all, I was probably easily a match for this old-timer. I had youth and vigor going for me; all he had was Party discipline. I decided to take the risk.

"Okay," I said, "I guess let's play some Gorodki. You're not going to cheat me, are you?"

"Sonny boy, you really think I'd do that to you?" Mr. Petrovsky answered resolutely, hopping onto the floor and scurrying across the room. "Gorodki!" he yelled enthusiastically. "Gorodki!"

His sudden transformation was remarkable. He was all fired up now, really strutting his stuff, like a fight dog, zooming around the ward. He took a pair of golf shoes and a black T-shirt with NY on the front in white letters from underneath the dead patient.

"Gorodki!" he shouted again, his rubber sandals forcing open the door with a powerful kick. "Let the games begin!"

All the doors in the hallway flew open, and a crowd of patients who had clearly been eavesdropping on our conversation and anticipating some really riveting entertainment, which was presumably a rarity here, spilled out of their rooms toward Mr. Petrovsky. He was the hometown favorite; they were undoubtedly putting their money on him. Me they regarded with openly mocking and skeptical expressions. The whole boisterous pack was dressed identically, in hospital robes and tracksuits, though one of them was covered in army medals, while someone else was wearing a battle-worn Soviet-era tunic. Men on crutches gnashed their brittle yellow teeth, while the women, whose arms were almost all in casts, smiled effusively, their thick lipstick making them look like sadistic clowns. This whole cluster of chronic ailments on legs limped on outside and over to the sanitarium's recreation area, past the older buildings, through a well-trodden courtyard between apple trees. Olga, Natasha, and I rushed out behind them—Natasha carrying the old-timer's inhaler in one hand and in the other the iron bats that would allow us to settle this matter once and for all. Any hint of competitive drive had quickly dried up and fluttered away. Judging by how she was looking at me, Olga wasn't optimistic about my chances; she kept quiet, however, probably because she didn't want to scare all of the fight out of me.

Mr. Petrovsky was already warming up in the recreation area, putting his leg behind his head and crouching like a cat in the thick grass, showing off how limber and energetic he was, clearly trying to intimidate me. I probably don't have to say that I'd never played this Gorodki thing before. All I knew about this game was that Lenin, as well as Tolstoy and Pavlov, were all avid players, which didn't really do much to lift my spirits.

Everyone took their places. Mr. Petrovsky, Olga, Natasha, and I stood behind the line, gearing up for the game, while our audience spilled across the recreation area, gathering up the pins and setting them up in the correct order. All business, Mr. Petrovsky walked up to Natasha, grabbed a handful of acidic hard candies, tossed them into his metal-filled face, ground them between his armor-piercing dentures, and started explaining the rules.

"Listen up, sonny boy," he said, waving one of the bats, "it's simple. There are fifteen shapes made out of pins, or Gorodki. Whoever knocks all the pins out of the square first wins. Whoever loses gets audited."

"Spot me a few points?" I suggested, hopefully.

"No way, no how," Mr. Petrovsky shot back. He stepped up to the line. "First round—cannons!" he yelled out.

Like rats, his cheerleaders scurried around under the apple trees on the far side of the court—the rickety old fossils were shuffling through the grass, stacking the pins into the shape of cannons for us to knock down.

"All right, sonny boy. Godspeed," Mr. Petrovsky said, stepping out of the way.

I picked up a bat. "Well now," I thought, "let's see who's top dog."

My first bat plummeted into the ground, far short of my target. The crowd squealed with joy, anticipating a quick victory by the home team. So when I threw my second bat, I let myself be guided by their voices more than anything else. The projectile soared into the sky and came down hard on one of those rickety old dinosaurs with a satisfying thump—right in the back of the neck. He grunted and collapsed into the sand. His fellow patients immediately dragged him under the apple trees, glaring at me.

"Well then," Mr. Petrovsky said dryly. "Not a bad start."

He nimbly whirled his first bat up into the air. It made a miraculous half-circle and knocked down the cannon. Now that some of the pins were out of the square, he could move up to the closer throwing line and finish off the cannon with his second bat; he gave Natasha a triumphant look, and yelled out into the June sky:

"Second shape—fork!"

The fork was quickly assembled. The game followed the same pattern—I continued to harass the patients with my throws, as well as knock down tree branches, forcing my elders and betters to roam through the tall grass in search of my missiles, while the old-timer effortlessly knocked down each of his figures, becoming more exhilarated after each throw. Occasionally, Natasha would come over and he'd inhale some magical vapors from his inhaler, making his hands firm and his eyes razor-sharp. There was some sort of elixir of youth in that thing; our distinguished citizen was scattering those pins like they were a neighbor's chickens in his garden. No matter how I tried, however, no matter how much I strained and cursed myself, I couldn't bounce back—my bats were flying every which way, just not at my target. Shortly thereafter, I lost the first set, utterly disgraced.

"Second set, second set!" Mr. Petrovsky crooned joyously, and the patients chimed in, repeating his chant and setting up the figures once again.

I walked over to Olga. She sighed and refused to make eye contact.

"Herman," she said, "for a Soros, you sure are a loser."

I didn't have a good comeback, so I picked up a bat for the next set. Which I lost even more quickly than the first. The old-timer was happy as could be, doing a little victory dance—his fellow patients were now forming a circle around him, yelling out their congratulations. I walked up to Mr. Petrovsky despondently. He was wiping off his sweat with a Mickey Mouse towel, trying at the same time to swallow some oblong, light green pills.

"Well then, sonny boy," he said, squinting playfully. "I won, fair and square."

"Yep, fair and square," I was forced to admit.

"Come by again some time."

I shook his hand, leathery from years of service to the Party, and turned around to leave.

"Hey," Mr. Petrovsky called out. "You really are a shitty businessman. Are you actually just gonna dust yourself off and leave? What about your documents?"

"Well, I lost."

"Come over here," Mr. Petrovsky ordered.

I did.

"What have you got there?" he asked.

"Headphones," I said, not sure what he was getting at.

"Do they work, or you just wear them like that?"

"They work."

"Let's make a deal." Mr. Petrovsky's eyes had lit up like the proverbial kid in a candy shop. "You give me the headphones, and I'll help you out."

I removed my headphones, took out my MP3 player, and gave them both to the old-timer. He fondled them in the palm of his hand.

"What's wrong with you, sonny boy?" he asked. "Why do you give up what's yours so easily?"

"But you asked me to . . ."

"And what if I were to ask you to suck my dick—would you do that too?" Mr. Petrovsky asked, intrigued.

I didn't know what to say. The old-timer was really rubbing it in.

He handed back my MP3 player. "You need to protect what's yours. Otherwise, you'll be left without any headphones, businesses, *or* Party experience. Got it?"

"Got it," I answered, trying not to look at Olga.

"All right then, let's go," Mr. Petrovsky said wearily. "The documents are in my ward. Let's go save that damn business of yours."

8

The rain and the twilight were running together, currents of water were moving in fat, coarse strands, weaving themselves into the air. It was as though we were riding along the bottom of the river when its surface was suddenly blanketed by darkness. Shadows and rays of light moved all around as invisible water dwellers rose up from the silt and came dangerously close to us, two drowned fishermen on a scooter. The rain was warm, like water at a river's mouth. Waves were crashing down on the scooter, and we nearly skidded off the road a few times. Olga stopped and desperately surveyed our surroundings. "We gotta get out of the storm!" she yelled. Sheets of rain were breaking over her face, and I could hardly hear a thing, but I knew what she was getting at—we had to stop somewhere, the storm was too heavy to go back or push through. "How?" I yelled back. She thought for a second, then: "There's a turn up ahead, we'd better try it!" she yelled, and we forged on, fighting through the waves and scaring away the river ghosts. Occasionally, the scooter would get bogged down and stop—still wearing her sunglasses, Olga could barely see the road ahead, so we were moving blindly. Nevertheless, she made the right turn, and we found ourselves on a side road. The narrow, overgrown asphalt track slalomed between clumps of pine trees. We continued deeper into the forest; the scooter's wheels kept getting tangled in the grass, and it was slow going, but Olga now appeared to know the way, so she was able to dodge bushes and potholes with confidence. We soon found ourselves in front of a dark fence.

I hopped off the scooter to open up the gate, which was just a metal sheet held in place with wire, and Olga pushed her scooter inside. The rain had flooded everything in sight, so we were standing in water up to our ankles. Evidently this was an old Young Pioneers camp from the Soviet days. Off in the distance, I could just make out some old metal buildings—sheets of rain were falling on them too. There was a little square with some sort of peeling monument in the center; pine trees stood tall above it, with the rain presiding over everything. We rolled the scooter up to the nearest building and rested it up against the front wall. Olga, who had been here before, ran under the cover of the next building over, the largest of all of them, and turned the corner, passing under a line of windows. There was an entrance there, covered by a patch of soaked, sprawling flowers that almost completely concealed the doors. She hunched over the lock, started spinning something, and the door popped open. We sprang inside, as if we were diving into a tin cookie jar while kids happily drummed on it with sticks. The rain beat loudly on the building's metal walls, a sweet rattling sound that shook the entire structure. We couldn't even hear ourselves breathe over that constant, wet drumming. We walked down a hallway and found ourselves in a spacious room. Shelves of old books stretched along walls covered with children's pictures; dark vases of dried flowers rested on the windowsills and a tattered couch had been dragged out into the center of the room.

"This is the Lenin room," Olga said and walked over to the

bookshelves resolutely. She browsed for quite some time, but couldn't seem to find anything interesting.

"How do you know?"

"I worked at this camp for a few years. We had counselor meetings in here. Nobody used the library, from what I remember. Listen," she turned toward me, "I have to do something about my clothes. I'm absolutely soaked. Would you be okay with me hanging up my stuff?"

"I could just leave. But I'd rather stay, of course."

"Just don't look at me then, all right?"

"Well, where do you want me to look?"

"All right, damn it, look wherever you want," Olga said. "Just don't be weird about it."

She slid off her shirt, stepped out of her jeans and threw everything on the windowsill, neatly placing her sunglasses on top. There she stood, in her orange underwear, glaring at me.

"Okay," she said, "I realize that this could look a bit odd, but you can hang up your clothes, too. We have to wait out the storm anyway."

"Look odd to who? Are there security guards here?"

"Technically, yes," she answered. "But what's the point of guarding the place in the middle of a storm? They're in town, probably. Don't be scared."

"I'm *not* scared."

Nevertheless, I decided against getting undressed. Who knows how she would have taken that. I flopped down on the pullout bed, which squeaked in response, and lay there in the twilight, taking in the steady sound of the rain—it was like old ship engines humming. Olga bounced around the room, looked over the children's pictures, found a stack of Young Pioneer magazines somewhere, then brought some over and lay down next to me. It was hard to see in there, the air was so damp it seemed to have congealed around us in the dark, so Olga just skimmed through their pages, looking at the bright images. I leaned in toward her and started looking too. Olga noticed my interest, and began lingering on each page so I could get a good look at everything.

"When I worked here," she said, "we would read these magazines out loud before bed."

"Why don't you work with kids anymore?"

"Well, it just didn't pan out. I didn't like the Pioneers. They could be real pieces of shit."

"Really?"

"Uh-huh. Although I guess it might be inappropriate for a former camp counselor to talk like that."

"Maybe so."

"Did you go to camp as a kid?" Olga asked. "I mean a Pioneer camp."

"No, because I didn't really get along with other kids. That's also why my teachers never really liked me."

"Let's talk about something else, then, you wouldn't find it interesting," Olga said. She tossed the magazines on the floor.

"That's not true. I wanna hear it. You know, I often think back to my German class. It sure was weird studying German in the Soviet school system. There was a kind of unhealthy, anti-Fascist pretentiousness that went along with it. In like fourth or fifth grade we got this one assignment—we were given postcards with pictures of different cities on them. You remember those? Back then they were sold at every post office, whole sets of them."

"Nah, I don't remember them."

"Well, they were at every post office. Like postcards with pictures of Voroshilovgrad on them. That city doesn't even exist anymore. It's called Luhansk now. But I talked about it in German for years. Funny how that works, don't you think?"

"Oh yeah. Hilarious."

"Generally, those postcards had government buildings or maybe monuments on them. But what kind of monuments could there be in Voroshilovgrad? Well, presumably there was one to Voroshilov . . . Honestly, I can't remember anymore. I had to talk about what I saw on the postcard. But what was there to see? The monument itself, a flowerbed around it, and then there would always be somebody walking by, and maybe a trolley in the background. There might not be, though, and that would make it a little harder, since there would be even less to say. The sun might be shining. There might be some snow on the ground. Voroshilov might be on a horse, or on foot, but that'd be worse, for the same reason . . . I could have told a whole separate story about the horse. Well, you just had to start talking. But what can you really say about something you've never *actually* seen? So, you start making stuff up. At first you could talk about the monument itself—I mean about the real person it's a monument to. Then you'd just have to move on to the random people passing the monument. What could you really say about them, though? Well, that woman is wearing a yellow sweater and a black dress. Maybe she's carrying a bag. With bread in it. Then, after you've covered all of the people, you could say a few words about the weather. Mostly, what I'm getting at is that it was all so artificial—all those pictures, all those stories, that language, a handful of canned phrases, that silly accent, and your pathetic attempts to put one over on your poor fuckin' German teacher. Ever since, I just haven't been able to stand German. And I never went to Voroshilovgrad, either. And now there's no such thing as Voroshilovgrad."

"Why are you telling me all this, anyway?" Olga asked.

"What do you mean?" I was disappointed that she had to ask. "Well, take this whole situation with my brother," I said. "It reminds me of German class. It's like I'm being asked to talk about what I see in the pictures, and I really don't like talking about things I know nothing about, Olga. I don't even like the pictures! And I certainly I don't like being backed into a corner, and told to play by someone else's rules. Rules only have meaning as long as you're abiding by them. As soon as you start ignoring them, it turns out that you don't owe anyone anything, you're not obligated to make up all kinds of silly stories about things you actually know nothing about. Then it turns out that you can get by just fine without all those made-up stories, and there aren't any rules—what they're showing you doesn't exist anymore, so there's nothing to say. It's all a sham, they're just trying to use you . . . and it's all perfectly legal, of course. It's like school all over again. The thing is that we all grew up a long time ago, but we're still being treated like kids, like unintelligent, deceitful, irrational bastards who need to be coerced and corrected and have the right answers beaten out of them."

"What do you mean it doesn't exist anymore? You exist, don't you? And I do too."

"Yeah," I said, "I exist. But there's no Voroshilovgrad anymore. We have to come to terms with that."

"It's pretty much the same thing with the pioneers," Olga replied. She fell asleep after that, I'm not sure exactly when.

★

The rain didn't sound like it would be letting up anytime soon—it continued to rattle against the tin box of the Lenin room, filling the darkness with its monotonous tapping. The longer the storm continued, the colder it got in that damp Pioneer room. My clothing, wet and heavy, was dragging me down; I felt like a scuba diver, and when I finally hit the ocean floor, where the rain ended and a thick, inky darkness set in, it was even colder. No matter how hard I tried to ignore the cold, I couldn't warm myself one bit. Olga was still lying next to me in her orange underwear, shivering in her sleep. Her skin was shining; I touched it, and it felt like river water, receptive and cool. "Just make sure she doesn't wake up," I thought.

I touched her wet hair, and again it felt as though my hands were penetrating the surface of a river, and that surface was calm and clouded so I couldn't see anything beneath it. I caught hold of some shells, trying to reach the bottom. I was afraid my hands would snag on fishing hooks someone had left behind. Her eyes were closed and her eyelids were translucent. They were like ice through which you see the forlorn shadows of the drowned and the dark green seaweed drifting like tumbleweeds along her body's underwater currents, drifting due south, toward her heart. Sliding down those green channels, I cautiously touched her soft cheekbones—beneath her skin was shadowed and particularly thin, like a spiderweb being stretched by the wind. She was whispering something in her sleep, something I couldn't make out, her lips barely moving as if she was talking to herself, asking herself some tough questions she didn't want to answer. The luminous lines of her collarbone showed through the darkness, like rocks by the coast with the waves wearing their angles down. As I touched them, I tried to feel the motion of the seaweed down below. I could hear her heart; its beating was as steady as the turning of a sunflower following the day across the rainy sky. I carefully slid my hand farther down, only grazing her breasts to avoid disrupting her breathing. Her skin was firm yet yielding, like flags flapping in the sea wind, directing the movements of clouds and birds. Guided by the blood flowing through her capillaries, I slid down her legs, her fragile porcelain knees, her nearly weightless calves. I reached her toenails, speckled with polish, like shards of broken tea sets, then moved up slowly, as if my palms were full of sand lifted from the bottom of the river. Without opening her eyes, Olga turned toward me and cautiously placed her hand on me, sliding underneath my T-shirt, touching me as though she were touching empty air. We were lying on a worn-out couch, indoors, with darkness and water pouring out of the sky, embracing sheepishly, like young pioneers. She was talking to herself, and I was trying not to interrupt—"Let her talk," I told myself as I touched her breasts. She took off my shirt and said something to me, nestling up against me and seemingly reading a message written on my skin, some sort of code only she could comprehend. I can't recall anyone ever paying such close attention to my skin. She was examining it thoroughly, pensively, as though she were looking for traces of injections or old burns that had healed long ago but still caused me pain. I even thought that she might have mistaken me for someone else, someone she really wanted to talk to. She was hovering over me, incredibly close, and I pulled her against me. But she extricated herself smoothly and wound up somewhere behind me instead. She leaned over me.

"Listen," she said, not using my name, "as long as we're just touching each other we haven't crossed the line. You got that?"

"What line is that?" I asked.

"The red line. Everything is fine now, but if we start kissing, like, you know, making out . . . that'd mess it all up."

"Mess it *all* up?" I asked.

"Yep, that'd mess it *all* up," Olga confirmed, "so just try to sleep."

Then she sprang off the bed and went outside.

★

But I couldn't fall asleep. I was just lying there, contemplating the spots on the ceiling, listening to the rain drumming on the walls, and sensing the trees encircling our little building. I didn't quite understand where Olga had gone, why she had stopped. I turned over so the sky and the ground switched places, and looked at the wall covered in children's pictures. They were dark and mysterious against the white wall. The Pioneers primarily used watercolors—their lines were heavy and thick, as though they were drawn in cow's blood or colored clay. Eventually I realized that the pictures had been hung in a deliberate order, because they formed stories, or parts of them, like on church walls, but, of course, in watercolor. Strange men, carrying weapons and wearing animal masks, were depicted in the top pictures. They were razing whole cities, cutting down tall trees, and hanging pets on balconies. They were cutting merchants' ears off and gouging their eyes out, goading heavy, fire-breathing elephants out of a wasteland—and those elephants had folded wings, like bats. The lower pictures showed women building fires and burning toys and dead people's clothing, and also branding each other with odd symbols that glowed in the dark, attracting herons and owls. They chose the most beautiful woman among them, put her in a big cage, and lowered her into the river—newts and water demons gathered around to hear her sing and watch her do card tricks. In another picture, a woman was giving birth to a little, two-headed girl who started speaking right away—speaking two different languages nobody could make any sense of, and so she was sent to a faraway land to find people she could communicate with. When she got there, a terrible plague broke out—dead birds fell out of the sky, delirious snakes slithered out of their holes; her words drove men to insanity, and women hopped into the river, swimming downstream balancing bundles of clothing and scripture on their heads. The last picture showed some sort of funeral procession; children and old people were carrying open caskets, but there weren't any people in them. They were arguing about which coffin they were supposed to bury. Oxen and herons were standing next to them, and the stars above their heads were following unfamiliar routes. The children, unable to decide which coffin to bury, shoved a big, tired ox into the grave instead, and covered it with thick and pasty earth the consistency of peanut butter, like a buried German tank; unintelligible signs were pouring out of its mouth, but the children couldn't read them because they were illiterate. They simply stood there, holding their spades and listening to the animals that were trying to tell them something important and ominous.

★

What I'd seen there made me uneasy, so I got up and went looking for Olga. Rain bombarded me as soon as I opened the outside door. I tried calling to Olga, but I threw in the towel right away. Where could she be? I turned the corner and ventured over to the next building. I headed toward the gate and saw Olga standing on the playground, getting soaked, her shoulders drooping oddly. She was letting the rain wash over her face, and then she was raising her hands into the air, as if trying to catch the raindrops. I called her name, but she didn't hear me. Then it hit me—she was actually trying to warm up. It was now a lot warmer outside than in the cold, metal Lenin room. She'd just stepped outside to get the chill out of her bones. She was letting the warm sheets of rain fall on her freezing skin. It seemed as though she couldn't see me at all; she was walking over the asphalt, wringing the shivers out of her body . . . an odd scene. Her eyes were still closed, as if she had been sleepwalking the whole time. I had to catch her before she wandered out through the gate and vanished into the woods. Good luck trying to find her out there, come morning. I walked up to her and touched her hand. She opened her eyes and gave me her full attention. In the dim light her eyes were a dark shade of blue, thick like the lines of the pioneers' paintings, thick like clay. She kept looking at me for some time. Eventually she let go of my hand and headed back toward the buildings.

"Are you going to try and get some sleep?" she asked, taking a last look at the rain-soaked forest.

"Yeah, *sure*," I said, trying to hold her placid, clay gaze.

"And stop looking at me like that," she added.

We slept poorly, obviously.

★

In the morning, the jubilant sun was driving rainy fog out along the line of pine trees; the puddles were steaming like open freezers, and the birds were drinking water out of the dark green leaves. Olga was wringing and shaking her shirt, trying not to make eye contact with me. I wasn't feeling too hot either, overwhelmed with doubt and pangs of conscience—I was blaming myself, thinking, "Maybe I did something wrong," or "Maybe we should have had sex after all." But why exactly? What for? Basically, I felt exactly like a young pioneer who hadn't gotten lucky last night, not that he was really expecting to.

"Herman," Olga said dryly, "I hope you didn't think yesterday was weird or anything."

"Nah," I assured her. "I enjoyed those magazines, the pictures were great."

"Glad to hear it," she said in a flat detached voice, "glad to hear it."

Then she walked toward the door.

"You forgot your sunglasses," I called after her.

"You can have them for now." Olga didn't bother to turn around.

So I took them with me.

★

The pine forest ended a bit down the road, giving way to wide open landscapes where cold damp fog gathered at every low point, and beyond that a sunny haze, a light and deep emptiness that unfolded all around us, sprawling out to the east and south, stretching out and soaking up the last drops of water and patches of greenery, grass filled with light, encompassing the earth and lakes, the skies and the gas shining under the earth like gold veins standing out on the Motherland's skin. Somewhere down south, beyond the pink sunrise, on the other side of the cloudy emptiness, the gates of Voroshilovgrad sliced cleanly through the sky, promising a welcome that was nowhere to be found.

★

Alarm and confusion prevailed in the gas station parking lot. Injured was sitting in his chair, apparently thinking something over, his head in his hands. Panic-stricken, Kocha was looking every which way, sprawling out on the catapult next to Injured. Some new, little guy, wearing a singed, battle-worn sailor's shirt, was curled up on the ground next to Kocha. This little guy was also looking around in terror, occasionally hiding his head under the blanket he'd wrapped around himself; it looked like the same one I was used to sleeping under. Katya, clearly petrified, stood off to the side, holding an equally petrified Pakhmutova by the collar. Pakhmutova was rubbing up against Katya's bare calves and jean shorts. Everyone looked pretty miserable. Evidently they had been waiting for me, although now that I'd finally shown up, they were avoiding eye contact and keeping quiet, waiting for me to say something.

"What's going on here?" I asked, genuinely concerned.

"Something real bad happened, buddy," Kocha's voice screeched like microphone feedback.

The little guy sitting on the ground gave a kind of aggrieved shudder, obviously recalling something unpleasant.

"I'm done with this fucking business!" Injured interjected abruptly. He got up out of his chair and disappeared into the garage.

"What's all this about?" I asked.

"Herman, they torched our tanker truck. Petrovich got a little burned, too."

The little guy popped his head out from underneath the blanket and nodded readily.

"They pulled up right over there. Well, their guys got out and chucked two firebombs right in the truck. They almost killed our old pal here," Kocha said, patting Petrovich on the back. "Good thing Katya saw them and called us over, otherwise they would have barbecued him."

"I was taking Pakhmutova for a walk," Katya explained.

"Have you called the cops?"

"Sure we did," Kocha said, nodding. "But what do you expect? Like the fuckin' cops are going to do anything. Everyone already knows who did what. Try and prove it, though."

"But didn't Petrovich see them?"

"Petrovich's too much of a pussy to talk to the cops," Kocha declared genially. "Isn't that right, Petrovich?"

Petrovich gave a submissive nod and set off toward the booth, the blanket still wrapped around him like an army poncho.

"Kocha, how could they just burn the tanker?" I asked.

"We're not the first ones they've done this to. We're lucky they didn't burn down the whole station along with it."

"So what do we do now?"

"I don't know, Herman," Kocha replied candidly. "We gotta shut down the station for now."

"Get outta here with that shit!"

"Buddy, they'll be back, and nothing will be left by the time they're done—I'm telling you. They'll stop at nothing. They saw Petrovich was in the truck and they went right ahead anyway. And Petrovich has been working this area for the past twenty years or so."

"I'm not going to shut the place down—no way," I declared.

"Sure, sure, whatever you say," Kocha said.

"Are you going to stick around?"

"We'll see. I'm too old to get knocked around like this."

"What are we going to do about the gas?"

"We gotta have some more delivered."

"Do we have any dough?"

"No, Herman, we don't have any dough, and I don't see how we're gonna get any for a while, either."

Kocha had had another sleepless night, it seemed, as he kept nodding off during our conversation. I went over to see Injured in the garage. He looked a bit distraught too, and he agreed that we needed to shut down the station for a bit. The corn guys had already blown up the gas tanker; it was highly unlikely they would stop there. That's just not how they did things—they never left unfinished business. Obviously, the fuzz weren't going to do anything, and it didn't seem like city hall was on our side, so Injured couldn't see any reason to be optimistic.

"Well, what if we don't shut down the station?" I asked.

"We don't actually have to," Injured answered. "You think I'm scared of them? I don't give a fuck. It's just that *you* can pick up and leave anytime you want. Kocha and I are staying, and they'll roast us in our sleep."

"What makes you think I'm going to leave?" I asked, a bit offended.

"Your past history," Injured replied.

"What do you know about my past history?"

"Herman," Injured said, patiently, "who are you trying to fool? It's easy for you to say you're gonna stick around, because you know you can always leave. But what about Kocha and me?"

"Here's how it's gonna go down, Injured—I'm staying put and we're keeping the station open."

"You're staying put?"

"I'm staying put."

"Well, we'll see. Today you're staying, tomorrow you could be miles away."

"Injured, I said I'm staying—that means I'm staying."

"Well, we'll see," he repeated.

"But what are we going to do about gas?"

"We'll have to buy some, but we don't have any dough. Don't think for a moment we'll get any insurance money for the last delivery."

"Well," I said after thinking for a bit, "how about I pay for it out of my own pocket, and then we make that money back."

"You've got money?"

"Yeah, not much, but I've got some.

"All right, sounds like a plan."

I asked him for his phone and called Lyolik.

"Lyolik," I yelled as soon as I made out his sullen breathing on the other end. "How are my pals doing up there?"

"Herman!" Lyolik began a bit anxiously. "Man, you're unreal. You've been gone forever and haven't even called. Who does that? When are you coming back?"

"Lyolik," I said, "hey, listen. I'm in a bit of a jam here."

"You getting married?"

"Nah, not yet. But I need my money."

"How come?"

"Lyolik, it's for the station. For the business."

"You have a business?"

"It's my brother's business—remember? I already told you all that."

"And?"

"And nothing. I need my money. Can you bring it down?"

"Herman, do you realize what you're asking me to do? I can't just drop everything and bring you your money."

"But I really need it," I said. "Otherwise, I'll be in even more of a jam. Lyolik, help me out, this one last time."

"Herman, what do you need the money for?"

"I just told you."

"No you didn't. I don't know, man. Come back home and we'll talk. You can count on us, we've been through thick and thin."

"That's exactly what I'm saying. How soon can you get me the money?"

"But why do you need the money? You're not making any sense."

"They torched my tanker, okay? I don't have any money here to pay for the next delivery. So Lyolik, get your ass moving and bail me out here."

"Well, I don't know," Lyolik said. "I'll have to talk to the boss first. I definitely can't leave right now. Maybe in a couple of days or so."

"Come on, bro," I yelled into the receiver. "Any minute now they'll torch me too! You know where I keep my money, right?" I asked.

"I know," Lyolik answered gloomily. "In Hegel."

"Yep," I confirmed, "volume two."

"I know, I know, don't worry," Lyolik said, and signed off.

"Who were you talking to?" asked Injured, who had heard our whole conversation.

"Some Party colleagues," I replied giving him his phone back.

"Should I wipe their number or keep it?" he asked.

"You can wipe it. These guys can find anybody they want."

Injured picked up a hammer and started bending some piece

of metal. I went outside and looked up at the sky. It was deep and cloudy. The clouds looked heavy and overloaded. Just like a tanker truck.

9

That day the conversation kept drifting back toward the burned truck. Katya and the dog were sent home and instructed not to leave the tower grounds. I felt like a real businessman, and somewhere deep down I was even glad that everything had unfolded the way it did. Now nobody could be like, "Brohan, you're just getting in the way, so step aside and let us handle the real work." It was my gas tanker too, after all. Moreover, I had decided to invest my modest savings in the business, so now I was putting my own neck on the line. Kocha, who had bounced back after a morning bout of weakness, just sat there in his catapult chair, smoking one joint after another, shooing away customers, listening to my MP3 player, and telling tall tales about the emergence of small business in our region. Petrovich sat next to him, chain smoking cigarettes, and treating his cuts and his sorrows with grain alcohol. Evidently, the alcohol was demolishing him—after lunch he was piss drunk, and around three Injured called the ambulance. They came and took Petrovich back home to rest. That's just the way things were done around there. I sat there listening to Kocha. I was still on an emotional high, and the old-timer, having found an appreciative listener, started going on about one particularly tough gang that worked the highway about ten years back.

"Yeah, that's how it was." Kocha inhaled deeply, making his

voice even more hoarse and thick. "Herman, I knew all of them. They were a great bunch—working-class guys. It's just that they smoked a shitload of weed, and that costs a lot of money, you know? They picked up a bunch of Kalashnikovs. They thought about selling them, but then the default hit, back in '98. Well, what were they supposed to do with the guns? It's not like they could just throw them away. So, they started hijacking Kharkiv buses. Two of them would buy tickets and ride in the bus. The other guys would be waiting outside the city in their car, right around here," Kocha said, motioning at the highway. "They'd steal old cars so they could just dump them afterward. I'm telling you, they were real good guys, ya know? They'd wear those goofy ski masks. Well, they'd flag down the bus, put the masks on, and clean out the whole thing. They'd even rob their own guys that were on the bus, so they wouldn't blow their cover."

"Why'd they have their own guys ride the bus anyway?" I asked.

"So they could jerk the detectives around," Kocha explained. "They'd purposely contradict each other and feed them a real line of bullshit."

"Ah, I see."

"This was all during the winter and they'd walk around in the same ski masks they wore on jobs, that's how they got busted in the end. Still, they got three buses under their belts," Kocha concluded, looking out toward the highway, at the shadows from Rostov. They were holding athletic bags stuffed with large bills and nodding to Kocha, like he was an old friend.

★

We decided that we had to take turns watching over the pumps to make sure they wouldn't get blown up too. "Uh-huh, pal," Kocha remarked, "they'll burn the pumps down in the blink of an eye. Just so you know, I'm not going to sleep at all tonight. What am I, stupid or something? Buddy, I got no intention of letting them fry me." He had already biked down into the valley, brought back a few bottles of port, settled in on the catapult, and built himself a barricade of booze. He went on and on about how he wouldn't let them tie him down in his sleep or barbecue him, about how he'd seen much worse as a paratrooper, about how he could handle "these civvy brats."

"Don't worry," he said, passing me a bottle. "If I gotta, I can take them out with a knife or my nunchucks." In the evening Kocha lit a bonfire right by the pumps. I tried stopping him, but he got all worked up, shouting that he knew best: rolling over empty metal barrels from somewhere out back, filling them up with old newspapers, and setting them on fire. The newspapers stank more than they burned. Injured ran over, berated Kocha for a while, and asked me to put the fire out. Before heading home, Injured tried convincing Kocha to go to bed, but the old-timer stubbornly refused; his behavior was getting more and more erratic. He called Injured an old fag and then tried kissing him the very next instant. Finally, Injured gave up and he took off, his eyes shining angrily in the dark. Kocha cursed him up and down, all the while blowing him kisses and drinking straight out of a bottle. I settled in next to him, gearing up for a long, sleepless night. Kocha conked out at ten o'clock on the dot, though, and all of my attempts at waking him were futile. I picked him up as though he were a child and carried him over to the trailer. Then I locked the door from the inside and fell asleep too, without a care in the world. As I was falling asleep, I thought to myself, "They'll be able to identify my body by my headphones." And then, "They'll identify Kocha's by his paratrooper tattoos."

★

Injured woke me up early in the morning and stood there leaning over me judgmentally, taking in my rumpled and disheveled appearance. Kocha was gone. It was seven o'clock by my watch.

"Where's Kocha?" I asked.

"How would I know?"

"Why are you here so early?" I asked, staggering to my feet, barely awake.

I was wearing Olga's yellow-rimmed sunglasses. I had slept in them. Which might explain why I didn't have any dreams. I took them off and put them in my jacket pocket, next to my MP3 player and headphones.

"I couldn't sleep."

"You were worried?"

"Yeah, *real* worried," Injured said, instantly offended. "I was at this girl's place. In the early morning I thought to myself, 'Maybe I'd better go check to make sure those bastards haven't burned everything to the ground.' Well, I ditched my girl—acted like a real jerk and kicked her out. All because of you guys, Herman," he added, spitting. "And I couldn't tell you why the fuck I did it."

He got a call right then. Startled, Injured put the phone up to his ear.

"Ah, it's you. Where are you? What?" he asked. "Why? Okay, fine."

"It's for you," he said, handing me the phone.

I took the phone from him, no less startled.

"Hello?"

"Yeah, buddy," it was Kocha, even more hoarse than usual. "This isn't good. Open up the gate."

"Where are you?"

"It's Masha . . ." Kocha said.

"Who's Masha?"

"Masha, you dope," the old man hissed back. "Tamara's mom. She's dead. They called me last night."

"They who? And why'd they call *you*? What are you, the coroner?"

"Buddy," Kocha said dejectedly, "she was like a mother to me. And now she's just lying here, dead. She's given up the ghost. And their whole Gypsy tribe or whatever the hell you call it, they're already here. They all got in last night, you know? And Tamara's absolutely devastated—people like her, I mean, people from the Caucasus, they take these things especially hard. It's a real mess over here."

"We'll be right over. Should we bring anything?"

"Get my suit for me. I feel like a scientist with no lab coat."

★

"Kocha's really taking this hard," I said to Injured as we were coasting down into the city toward Kocha's old apartment. I was holding the old-timer's dark blue suit. "And it's such a blow for Tamara."

"Why would she care?" Injured asked.

"What do you mean? It's her mom, after all."

"Whose mom?"

"Tamara's mom," I explained. "Tamara—Kocha's wife."

"Damn it, Herman," Injured said, losing his temper. "Kocha's wife's name was Tamila."

"So who's Tamara?"

"Tamara is her cousin."

"She's Georgian?"

"She's a Gypsy, from Rostov."

"Why'd Kocha say she was from the Caucasus?"

"Kocha thinks everything south of Rostov is the Caucasus," Injured replied. "That sly dog lived with the both of them. He'd always get them confused. That's why their parents didn't like him, you know? And now he's all like, 'She was like a mother to me.'"

I was at a loss for words, and Injured seemed to have run out of things to say on the subject. So we kept driving in silence.

★

The family, who looked more like Serbs than Georgians, were standing outside the apartment building. The men were wearing black suits with brightly colored dress shirts underneath—yellow and pink ones, primarily. The women were dressed all in black, thumbing rosary beads with such intense concentration it looked as though they were texting. The children, who were also wearing little black suits and running all over the place, had wet, neatly combed hair. I recognized Ernst, clad in an Austrian policeman's coat and Russian army boots he had polished until they gleamed. Nikolaich was walking through the crowd too, with a black wallet dangling on a chain from his right wrist. The two fiery Spanish women were there too, and stood out from the crowd—they were both holding wreaths, one from the worker's union and the other from the Chernobyl Disaster Fund. Ernst graced me with a dignified salute, Nikolaich was shaking his birdlike head feverishly, and the Spanish women were intent on giving me the cold shoulder. Injured plowed his way through the Serbian-Georgian relatives toward and into the main entrance. More members of Tamara's family were standing on the landing between the third and fourth floors, smoking pot right out in the open, like they thought they were too cool to get caught. We went up to the fourth floor. The apartment door was open, and we stepped inside.

A muffled yet slightly anxious buzz of voices filled the room, the kind of atmosphere you might expect at a shotgun wedding. Women with black hair to match their outfits were running every which way, carrying dishes and bottles. Men with chairs, axes, and shovels were also hurrying past us, and children clutching mint candies and severed chicken heads were playing, scurrying around our feet. We went into the kitchen. Kocha was sitting on an old stool, wearing a long, white T-shirt and black army briefs. The women were buzzing around him, doing their very best to please him. It was very obvious that our old friend was loved and respected here. They swarmed around him, affectionately calling him *gadjo*. Kocha was lazily keeping up a conversation with the whole room, calling one or another woman over, giving out instructions, cracking jokes. Evidently, he was the head honcho. On seeing us, he gave out a warm if restrained "Hello" before dragging us into the bathroom, where he whispered:

"Fuck, man," he said, "what a goddamn shame. She was like a mother to me . . . but she just wouldn't listen . . . what should I have expected? She never came home before midnight. She was always at her bar."

"She worked at a bar?"

"What are you talking about?" Kocha asked, confused. "Buddy, that's not how we do things. We look after our parents. They don't work—come on man."

Kocha took the suit from me and put it on there and then, but all it did was make him look like some farmer who had to dress up to go to court.

"Let's go pay our respects," he said, combing back the remains of his once luxuriant hair. "I really have to be by the old lady right now."

Tamara's mom lay in the living room, sprawled out across a few stools. She was wearing her Sunday best, a gray suit jacket, black skirt, and red, polished high heels. Makeup had been applied meticulously, and she looked rather content, aside from the fact that her lower jaw kept flopping open. When it did, one of the relatives would carefully close her mouth, as though they were punching a tram ticket. Two beautiful, worn-down women, both wearing black dresses, black stockings, and black shoes, were sitting by the deceased. One of them had countless rings on her fingers, while the other had beads, necklaces, and two or three gold crosses hanging around her neck. The two decrepit beauties looked rather severe, sitting there with their legs crossed, watching us coldly and attentively.

"Who are they?" I asked Injured quietly.

"That's Tamara to the left, and Tamila to the right," Injured explained.

"I can't tell them apart at all."

"You're not the only one," Injured said.

Tamara pulled out some handkerchiefs, as though she were sliding out marked cards, and rubbed her dry eyes, taking great care not to smear her mascara. Occasionally Tamila would glance at her two gold watches, one on each wrist. Meanwhile, Kocha was drifting from room to room, coming up to Tamara and Tamila from time to time; they would light up whenever he approached, lean in toward him, and pat him on the hip or back mournfully yet enthusiastically. The other women were gradually bringing the deceased's possessions in from the other rooms and placing them around the stools to form a circle. A coffee machine and a Japanese sound system lay at the corpse's head, while a few pairs of shoes were lined up by her feet. In addition, lamps, clothing, and sewn portraits of Taras Shevchenko and Jesus Christ surrounded the deceased. She was holding a compact and a hair dryer, while Kocha had considerately stuffed her jacket pockets with coins, medals, and tokens. Tamara and Tamila looked at him despondently, continually muttering to themselves, "*Gadjo*, oh, *gadjo*." We stood around for a bit, then Kocha pulled us out onto the stairs. Ernst was coming up holding a metal pot. Someone took out a mug and grabbed it with an air of affected purposefulness, moving past the relatives and taking stock of the calm crowd:

"They haven't renovated this apartment since '91," he said. "And it's still holding up just fine." Having made this pronouncement, he downed his drink.

Everyone nodded their heads approvingly, commiserating with Kocha. An ambulance rolled up to the building a bit later. A young man hopped out wearing a formal black suit and tucking a folder under his arm.

"The priest is here," someone said, and everyone hurried to the main doors to greet the new arrival.

The priest came in, and as soon as he did, the mourners began rushing at him to get his blessing. He patiently blessed everyone who approached him, accepted a full mug, carefully made the sign of the cross, cocked back his head like a child, and drank.

"Where's Mom?" he asked Kocha.

Kocha took him by the arm and led him up the stairs. The priest handed out Xeroxed copies of some text as they headed toward the apartment.

"What's that?" I asked Ernst, who was pouring everyone the last of the wine.

"The hymn," Ernst answered. "He gets them off the Internet."

"What kind of hymn? Are they Catholics or something?"

"Nah, they're Shtundists," Ernst replied succinctly, taking a copy and heading back up the stairs.

Not everyone could fit in the living room. Distant relatives, colleagues, and distinguished guests all bunched together in the hallway or stood in the bathroom. There were even people gathered two whole floors down. The priest handed out his hymn, told everyone what to do, and broke out into high-pitched song, wasting no time on a sappy eulogy. The deceased's family chimed in right away, followed by the distinguished guests, and then the neighbors and other fellow tenants. Down below, a wedding band joined in, the trumpet player, drummer, and violinist picking up the tune, adding their music to the singing, though they were playing more for those living on the lower floors than for the wake itself. The priest really went all out, reaching for the high notes, but sometimes Kocha's screeching voice would drown him out nonetheless.

The hymn went like this:

> When the Lord takes you by the hand and leads you down the yellow brick road,
> When you leave this strange country where the weather and utilities cause constant vexation,
> When your young and handsome face yellows in photographs from your trip to Gurzuf,
> Our loving family, including all the sons-in-law, daughters-in-law, and more distant relations, will follow your lead,
> Wearing our Sunday best, dressed as if for Election Day,
> We'll raise our voices to praise Jesus, so he'll hold your hand firmly and won't lead us astray as we make our way to the Holy Father!

"Sing to the Motherland, home of the free," was the refrain, and everyone belted it out in unison. "Sing to our celestial Jerusalem, bulwark of peoples in brotherhood strong. The word of God, an invisible power, *sare manusha de taboro yavena, romano zakono pripkhenela sare lent e priles!*"

> When you come before the Lord in your new suit, boasting of your pull,
> And fall into his sweet, tattooed, and gold-bejeweled arms,
> The Savior will say to you:
> This is your new home, Masha—you're one of the gang, so relax.
> nalache manusha phendle, so roma jyuvale; lache manusha pkhendle so ame soloviy.

Once again everyone chimed in for the refrain, and then continued:

> Live on Romanistan, the magnificent and free land untainted by the pernicious influence of transnational corporations,
> *sare manushende kokale parne, rat loli.*
> Free amongst the free, equal amongst the equal, recognized by the world community and a special OSCE committee on the spiritual and culture heritage of Europe's minority groups,
> The Lord holds you in his arms, so listen to the vibrations of his hot heart!

When the hymn was over, everyone in attendance joined in for some slightly more familiar church songs—and further songs as well as off-key if energetic violin screeches accompanied the departed as she was carried out of the apartment, feet first. Her immediate relatives brought along her personal possessions. As Ernst explained, it was unacceptable for anybody else to touch them. Mom was shoved in the back of the ambulance, while Tamara and Tamila, as well as Kocha and the three-man musical ensemble, took seats in the front. The rest of the relatives, friends, and acquaintances took their own cars over to the cemetery. A tractor with an open trailer was provided for the very poorest relations—roughly two dozen Georgian Gypsies jammed themselves into the back, and then the funeral procession got underway.

As I was leaving, I noticed that Kocha was already a few drinks deep—some sort of scene was inevitable. At the cemetery, he got out of the ambulance even more loaded than he was getting in. He was haranguing the musicians, demanding they play some sort of polka, and then started in needling the ambulance driver, trying to get him to take the body all the way up to the grave, saying he would pay him whatever he wanted. The old cemetery was tucked away in a pine forest. The trees encircled the rows of graves, and there was hardly any unused ground left, so we had to creep like partisans, between the trunks and headstones to the freshly dug plot. It was a rather spacious hole. The walls of the grave were faced with brick and the bottom was covered with meticulously placed boards. Mom was carefully lowered in, and afterward came her possessions, passed down the line and placed in the grave beside her. Portraits of Shevchenko and Jesus had been fixed to the walls somehow. Kocha pushed through the pack of relatives, gave them some brusque instructions, ripped some dishware out of their hands so he could put it in the grave himself, ultimately lost his balance, and tumbled, of course, right into the pit, still holding a coffee machine. Some of the mourners reached to help. They wanted to pull him out, but he wasn't having any of it, saying he wanted to be closer to Mom.

"Let's just make sure they don't leave him in there," Injured remarked, genuinely concerned.

After the hole had been filled with flowers and the deceased's possessions, completely concealing her, the priest walked up to the grave to pay tribute:

"Why go to a place where you're not welcomed? Why run away from those who love you? If you can't stand up for yourself or your friends and family, what gives you the right to complain about your lot in life? Did you try to do anything before throwing up your hands and giving up? How will you be judged by those who went before you and who are now counting on you? How will you answer the questions posed by those who follow in your footsteps? Life, good people, is an ongoing cycle, and actions taken in the name of love justify any mistakes you may make. The economy is grounded not in force, but in justice. If you can't feel the presence of the living, then why have you come here to part with the deceased? Masha lived a long and heroic life, doggedly fighting for the happiness of her people, her friends and family, and her colleagues. Her persistent struggle to promote the common good and secure equality ennobled her mission, her spiritual journey and her painstaking efforts to build a better tomorrow. Her commitment to the principles of brotherhood, genuineness, honesty, and Romanipen, which she upheld consistently and staunchly throughout her entire life, will serve as a timeless example for generations to come, as they take the baton from their parents in the eternal fight for a brighter future. In that sense, Masha's industry and resilience should inspire us to perform heroic tasks of our own, to refine our professional skill set, and tune in to the positive vibrations sent by the Savior as a reward for our years of wandering and our endurance in the face of discrimination."

"Amen," the crowd cheered amiably.

I didn't know the deceased, but it seemed as though the priest might have idealized her life story just a tad. A lot of the mourners were invisible, standing behind the pines; one could easily have thought that he was speaking to the forest itself.

"One more thing," the priest added after gathering his thoughts for a moment. "What does death teach us? It teaches us that we must remember everything that has happened to us and to those closest to us. That's the main thing. Because when you can remember everything from your past it's not so easy to let go of it. That is all," he said, ending his eulogy, and everyone broke out into song once again.

Before the mourners could belt out yet another hymn about the brick roads that we walk down alongside the Savior, about the trying hardships that will pay off tenfold down the line, you know what I'm saying, yesterday's black clouds rolled back in and an unexpected deluge drenched us. Everyone scattered, trying to find shelter under the tall, barren pine trees, hopping over old, sunken tombstones, and running to their cars parked out on the asphalt. The rain gushed into Masha's pit, threatening to flood the grave completely and turn the whole cemetery into a lake. Now Kocha climbed out as quickly as possible and ran after everyone else. I dashed to find Injured's car, but I must have taken a wrong turn somewhere, veered a little off course, or maybe chased after the wrong person: I quickly got lost in a labyrinth of pine trees, running between them, choking on the water that ran into my mouth, feet sinking into the wet sand. Eventually I stopped by some more tombstones to catch my breath. My eyes settled on their inscriptions. I couldn't quite take it in, at first. I moved a bit closer and read them again. The names of the Balalaeshnikov brothers were carved on the tombstones. All three of them. The rain was drowning their portraits; they were looking at me like sharks peering up from the ocean floor. It really was them. Barukh Balalaeshnikov, 1968–1999. Various sacred signs, such as stars of David, gold half-moons and pentagrams, crowns and bird's wings, rose stems and old revolvers, were engraved next to Barukh's face. The next plaque read: Shamil Balalaeshnikov, 1972–1999. Something written in Arabic was engraved near Shamil's picture, while some scenes depicting birth, hunting, and last rites could be seen at the bottom of the plaque. They were hunting deer. As expected, Ravzan Balalaeshnikov, 1974–1999, was next in line. A sad woman, her hair down, wearing a short skirt, had been drawn on the plaque below the deceased's portrait. The woman was sitting on a riverbank under a tiny birch tree, clearly pining for Ravzan. Bewildered and drained, I continued my run, trying to escape from this black hole and remember where I'd come from. However, the farther I ran, the more despair overwhelmed me, because I soon came across Sasha Python's grave, featuring carved horses bearing insane riders; then Andryukha Michael Jackson's tombstone, with a marble column and gold letters; and then heavy granite plaques with the names of Semyon Black Dick, Dimych Conductor, Kolya One-and-a-Half Legs, and Ivan Petrovich Fodder; as well as small yet ornate plaster sculptures of Karpo Disc Grinder holding his plaster disc grinder in his right hand and Vasya Negative with thuja trees planted all around him; and then there were Gesha Accordion and Siryozha the Rapist's graves; and finally Gogi Orthodox's tomb with crosses painted all over it.

At last I fought through some blackthorn bushes and popped out onto the road, where I was nearly run down by Injured's car. He wasn't too surprised—he just stopped and waited for me to get in. After I was safely inside I immediately started telling him about what I had just seen, but he cut me off, asking grimly:

"Where have you been? Olga called. She's worried about you. And she was asking about some sunglasses."

"About some sunglasses?"

"Yep, about some sunglasses. She told me to make sure you're being careful. This is some serious shit we're talking about."

He was right—I immediately recalled the burned truck, thinking that they were probably just getting started. My mounting dread was accompanied by an odd excitement. For the first time since I'd come back, my heart was resonating with those odd, sweet vibrations that filled the sky. Suddenly I could feel them all—the musicians playing their old instruments, striking their false, piercing notes; the two relatives in black suits driving a crane into the cemetery and covering the freshly-dug grave with concrete slabs, so nobody would be tempted to desecrate the final resting place of an eminent public figure like Masha and make off with her Siemens coffee machine. I also felt the two Spanish women wailing for the deceased, squeezing each other's hands, and felt the two cousins, Tamara and Tamila, who had gotten soaked to the bone, their clothing sticking tenderly to their shoulders. I could feel Kocha, with his hoarse, whistling cries as he tried to get the ambulance driver to drop him off right in front of the apartment. I felt the children clutching their mint candies—I felt them, so carefree, so remote from death and hardship, running in the rain as hymns sounded around them. This happy and terrible feeling thrust me forward, forcing me toward the group packed into Kocha's apartment; I had to join in without delay. The crowd spilled out onto the stairs and landings—nobody was even thinking of heading out early, and Tamara's relatives wouldn't have let them go anyway.

"Look," Injured said, "don't take what you see in there to heart, because who knows what you'll wind up seeing. That's the main thing."

We were heading up the stairs. Olga had called again before we'd reached the apartment, asking me how I was doing and telling me to watch out. But she didn't want to stop by for some reason. The party was flowing out onto the stairwell; bottles of wine and vegetable platters were being passed down the line. Everyone was talking loudly, recalling the deceased's professional achievements, yelling over one another. The band was stationed between the third and fourth floors, and as soon as we approached them, the trumpet player nodded at me and started playing a Charlie Parker song, which I took as a bad omen. We continued plowing through the crowd, up the stairs, but then, right at the doorstep, a slim, dexterous arm jerked Injured away from me. Some middle-aged woman, with a hefty backside, led him farther up the steps. Injured looked back at me and managed to shout out some sort of warning, but I couldn't make it out, as I was already diving into the jam-packed apartment. A bunch of the deceased's closest relatives as well as the most esteemed guests were sitting at the table in the living room. I picked out Kocha's bald spot, between Tamara and Tamila, and steered heedlessly toward it, crushing kids underfoot and shoving half-blind grannies out of the way. Kocha turned around, saw me, and yelled excitedly:

"Herman!" hitting a high note, even for him—it must have taken every one of his internal whistles—"Buddy, thank God you're here. Well," he went on, introducing me around, "this is Tamara, the deceased's daughter, you know. And this is Tamila, she's like a sister to me. Herman, you know how hard it can be growing up in a big family and all."

Tamara and Tamila didn't bother to disguise their interest; the way they looked at me suggested a challenge. Kocha spun, bobbed around the table, gave up his seat to me, and disappeared into the sea of people. Tamara and Tamila started taking care of me right away. Two hands poured me some wine, and they scrutinized my every move, making sure I kept drinking and stayed quiet. I had no clue what I could have conveyed to them, so I was more than happy to sit there, drinking to the deceased's memory. I still didn't know how to tell them apart, either. I thought I had seen Tamila last week by the store, downtown. As far as I could remember, she had been wearing a short, red skirt, but I wasn't absolutely sure about that, so I didn't bother asking.

After a while the party started getting amorphous. A few people hurried out of the apartment, while others started showing up and proposing elaborate toasts to love and fidelity. The priest was going on about something or other—he and Ernst seemed to be having a lengthy argument about race relations, and soon Kocha's insensate body was carried out of the kitchen into the next room. Tamila and Tamara lit up like fireflies when they saw this. Bitter, dark wistfulness flooded their eyes, and I gazed intently into their bitterness, remembering more and more of the stories I had so conscientiously tried to forget. The number of guests gradually increased, although I couldn't figure out where exactly these new people were coming from and how they could possibly fit inside the apartment. By midnight, I was dazed from all the yelling and singing, so I excused myself and went looking for some place where I could take a leak—but some old women were smoking heavy clay pipes in the bathroom. One of them offered me a hit. I accepted and breathed in deep. The pipe was hot, like the heart of a long-distance runner. I passed it back and wandered off.

"Where can I take a leak around here?" I asked a man wearing a rubber raincoat standing in the hallway and drinking some Moldovan brandy straight from the bottle.

"This way," he said, slinging his arm over my shoulder and pulling me along.

We walked over to the next apartment. The man whipped open the doors and shoved me inside.

"It's on the left," he yelled from behind me, "but it's dark in there, the light doesn't work."

I groped my way down the apartment's hallway, bumped into something, squatted down to take a closer look, and recognized the musicians all sleeping on the moonlit floor. Their drum sat on its side in their midst, heaped with bottles and sliced bread. Moving on, I felt for the doorknob, found it, and stepped into the bathroom. There was a window up on the wall that clearly looked out onto the kitchen. Yellow, wavering streaks of moonlight were pouring inside; my eyes took a long time to adjust to the darkness, but I was gradually starting to make out individual objects. I pissed and went over to the tub, which was filled to the brim with cold water. I scooped some into my hands and dunked my face in it. That's better. I blinked heavily; there were dark glass bottles down there on the bottom of the tub, glimmering in the moonlight like carp, flapping their booze-soaked fins. It was time to go home. Then the door opened and shut, and a shadow slid into the bathroom, barely visible. All I could tell was that it was a woman. She approached me apprehensively, touched my face, and sank her hands into my hair. She pushed her body at me, and her hot lips sucked me even closer. The taste of her lipstick only intensified the wine fumes on her breath. There was something predatory in the way she kissed me; she really knew what she was doing, neither hurrying nor drawing things out. Her hands slithered under my shirt, her nails scratching my skin. She removed my pants quite handily and pushed me back up against the edge of the tub, turned, smoothly lifted her dress and got on top of me. It was sweet and painful—difficult to get inside her. She winced keenly in answer to my every movement, but she persisted, breathing deeper and deeper, as though her lungs were somewhere deep, deep down, where the sun's rays couldn't reach and there wasn't enough oxygen. I touched her face, feeling her warm lips, wrapping my hand around her neck and closing it around her throat, which didn't faze her, incidentally. When I touched her hands, locking them together and pulling them toward me, my fingers rubbed up against something sharp; I realized she was wearing rings on almost all her fingers—they were glowing in the yellow light that trickled into the bathroom and digging into my skin as I squeezed her hands. Then, all at once, she froze, extricated herself nimbly, pulled down her dress, and slipped out into the hallway without making a sound. I didn't know whether I should chase after her or stay put . . . but before I could settle on any sort of action, the door opened, and a shadow was moving inside the bathroom again. I decided not to waste any time, so I grabbed her and bent her over the edge of the tub. I heard her voice for the first time when she let out a nearly inaudible screech. She sounded hoarse and mistrustful. I pulled up her dress hastily. This time I slipped into her smoothly, her fiery body bent over the tub as she stared down at the green and black bottles that our movements goaded along beneath the water's cold surface. It must have looked as though she was washing her hair, or trying to catch a fish with her hands. And I was trying to catch her. She kept whimpering, like she was surprised or something, leaning closer and closer to the surface, until her long hair, which smelled of pine trees and tobacco, dipped underwater. When things were drawing to a close, I tried pulling back to help keep her head above the surface. She caught her flowing hair and tossed it back. Our hands interlocked. Suddenly, I felt that she wasn't wearing any rings. I clutched at her other hand, but there weren't any rings there either, although she had two watches, one on each wrist. Feeling me tense up, she tried extricating herself, but I grabbed her by the neck and bent her back toward the water, finishing up and feeling numerous necklaces and chains on her neck which hadn't been there the first time around. They were all hopelessly tangled now.

She caught her breath, collecting herself, then grazed her lips across my cheek before disappearing into the hallway. I stood there for a bit and then went out too. I walked over to the front door of the apartment and opened it a crack, peering through to the stairwell. It was packed, same as before. I joined the throng, and nobody noticed me coming back, but then Kocha unexpectedly popped out of the apartment behind me—I was taken aback, but he didn't seem to notice, grasping my hand firmly and dragging me down the stairs. I submitted, following behind him and thinking about how to tell him about what had just happened. We stumbled out into the street and Kocha stopped.

"Kocha," I said, fumbling for words, "I ought to tell you, I kinda wound up . . ."

"Whatever, buddy," he whistled back jauntily. "Just chill man. Go home, otherwise you'll drink yourself to death. I'll see you tomorrow."

"I just wanted to tell you . . ."

"Forget about it, buddy," Kocha replied. "It's not like you can tell me anything I haven't heard before. You better get going before those alcoholics in there get hold of you again."

"Okay, okay," I said. "Thanks, man. It's a damn shame what happened to Masha."

"Everything's dope," Kocha answered in a severe yet candid tone. "Mom's already walking down the yellow brick road. She's long gone," he added and disappeared back inside.

I turned around and headed home. The sand underneath my feet was wet, and the city's buildings were dark, as if they were filled with black paint. I walked along, trying to remember everything I could from that night after the game. The more distance I covered, the more distinct my memories became. I remembered the women's frightened and slightly hysterical voices begging us to stay put, not to go anywhere, not to venture out into the darkness lit up from the inside by electrified evening air. I remembered Tamara running up to us and standing in Kocha's way, flat out refusing to let him pass. I remembered how she fixed her dress discreetly, how she was scrutinizing me, how I immediately realized that she had seen everything, that she'd noticed me but wasn't the least bit scared I would go and tell Kocha everything. The fact that she didn't even feel awkward around me hurt the most—I was upset with her, but there was no way I could have said anything. Most importantly, I remembered that light: the yellow, thick light coming off the lampposts, and the anxious silhouettes carrying on about something, trying to come to a decision. Who was there? I remember my brother, and Kocha of course, and someone else too. But who? Kocha was trying to convince my brother to give him the knife, but my brother was just standing there in some kind of stupor, and it seemed like he wasn't listening. All he could do was wipe the blood off the blade. The fragments came together and I could see it—Kocha finally grabbing the knife out of my brother's hand, cutting himself in the process, and then tossing it far away into the darkness. And then Kocha walking somewhere with two policemen, as Tamara tried to stop them, shouting that Kocha had nothing to do with it and they should let him go. The last thing I could remember was her standing there by the broken glass, her head in her hands, her rings shining silver against her thick black hair. Now I saw the morning sun cropping up in the sky and the mulberry trees all around me starting to soak up the darkness, like sponges soaking up the black soda that had spilled all over the sky.

10

"Where have you been?!" Katya shouted, dressed in her long rain-coat and baggy athletic pants, standing beside the catapult. "They killed her!" she shouted.

"Who'd they kill?" I asked, horrified.

"Pakhmutova! They hanged her!"

She wouldn't budge, as though afraid to leave the cover of the fog that had descended on the station. Everything in the area looked as though it was dissolving into the damp air. I turned off the highway and walked up to the gas pumps as she let out a ter-rible cry.

It had taken me a long time to climb the hill, peering into the morning murk all the while, in search of passing cars that might give me a lift. By the time I had made it out of town, it was already getting light outside. The remaining darkness had settled on the bottom of the valley like silt. Here on the hill, the air had filled up from the inside with white fog. It was so opaque that I didn't see Katya until she was right in front of me, both palms pressed to her face. She went on shouting hysterically, her frightened eyes bulging at me as though I was the one who'd hanged her dog.

"Where is she?" I asked. Katya continued shouting, ignoring me. I grabbed her by the elbow, trying to shake some sense into her. "Are you even listening to me? Where is she?"

"Over there," Katya said, after a moment, gesturing vaguely.

I pushed her aside and strode into the fog, but I couldn't see a thing. It was as though a brick wall was stretched out behind the catapult; all I could make out were some trees and part of the trailer out back.

"Are you listening to me? Where is she? Show me!"

"She's right over there," Katya said, pointing up.

I looked up. There was Pakhmutova, swinging over my head in the foggy mass, hanging from the pole. She looked like a flag raised for a state holiday. I went over and tried uncoiling the metal line. It was taut and resilient; the wet metal cut into my fingers but I managed to loosen the knot. I carefully lowered the dog onto the ground and leaned over her. Katya was behind me, whimpering now. I finally got the knot undone. The line had dug into her neck—bloody clumps of fur were still clinging to the metal. I set her down on the asphalt. Katya couldn't muster the courage to come any closer, so she stayed where she was, staring at her dead dog.

"How did you find her?"

"She'd been missing since yesterday," Katya answered. "I was looking for her all night. I came over to the highway a few times, then decided to check at the station again, because she runs over here all the time. But she wasn't here. No one was here. I decided to wait for someone. I sat on that thingy over there," she said, pointing at the catapult. "I couldn't see anything in the fog. Well, I fell asleep. Then I opened my eyes again and saw her. I thought I was dreaming."

She was crying again. I hugged her and felt how sweaty she was in her heavy raincoat. I tried calming her down, but she went on crying and whimpering, burrowing her face into my shoulder. She wasn't listening.

"Let's move her someplace else," I said finally. "We have to bury her."

Katya stepped back obediently and sniffled, waiting for me to pick up the dog. Pakhmutova didn't turn out to be too heavy— after all, she was really getting up there. The last few years seemed to have sucked out any excess weight. I carefully carried her over to the trailer. Katya followed me without a word. I took the path along the side of the trailer, where the grass was particularly thick and cool, and lowered Pakhmutova onto the ground. She looked almost happy, lying there in the cool grass. Katya was still crying. I hugged her again and took her back over to the trailer. I opened the door, stepped in ahead of Katya, drew her in, and sat her down on the couch. Then I went to make some tea.

Strong and sweet tea—it burned her throat and fogged her vision, ignited her from gullet to heart, making her cry even more bitterly. Then she put her mug on the floor, off to the side, and started kissing me, wrapping her hands around my neck. Her rain-coat was hampering her movements; she looked comical and awkward—the two of us started sliding it off. She jerked suddenly, kicking over her mug, which gave the air a sharp, minty scent. I kept taking off her clothes, working methodically; she was wearing different colored socks—maybe she got dressed in a hurry to go looking for her dog, who might very well be coasting down the yellow brick road at that very moment, I thought, falling in right behind Jesus and Masha. Then I tried peeling Katya off me for a second, just long enough to slip out of my own clothing. Her expression became serious when she let me in. She was consumed by this new activity; it was a task she performed calmly and conscientiously, but not too meticulously, like a schoolgirl who does all of her homework because she likes the teacher, but not his subject. I saw she had a tattoo on her calf. Odd that I'd never noticed it before. I could hardly see it. It was as if the rain had nearly washed it all away. She rolled me over on my back and got on top with a carefree bound, rocking the couch and goading the old odors of dust and love out of it. Occasionally, she'd get caught up in her own thoughts, dropping onto my chest and starting to cry again, but crying contentedly, without commentary, without complaint. When she was done, she used my sweaty T-shirt to wipe away her tears.

★

"Now I'm definitely getting out of this place," she said and started rooting around in my pockets.

"What are you looking for?" I asked.

"Don't you have any smokes?" But no, she didn't find any. Then she pulled the yellow-rimmed sunglasses out of my jacket, put them on, and fell back onto the pillow by our heads, gazing up at the ceiling.

It was already late morning, and incredibly bright outside. The fog had drifted off somewhere toward the river, and it now looked like it was going to be a dry, sunny day. Our clothing was heaped together on the floor; the room smelled like cold tea.

"Where are you going to go?" I asked.

"Odessa," Katya answered, "to live by the beach."

"What are you going to do there?"

"Go to college."

"And what do you want to do when you graduate?" I asked, like a helpful upperclassman.

"I'll be a prostitute," Katya said, and laughed. "Why are you asking such dumb questions? What about you?" she asked. "When are you leaving?"

"Never."

"What are you going to do?"

"I'll open up a barbeque joint. It's a sure thing. Maybe you should stick around here with me?" I suggested. "We'll get married and all."

"You're a goof," she replied, very amused. "They'll take you out too, any day now, just like Pakhmutova." She was crying again.

"Please, don't," I said, trying to comfort her. "You're wasting your tears anyway—I can't see them through those sunglasses."

"It's a good thing you can't," Katya said, and fell asleep as though on cue, her head resting against my shoulder.

"It's a bummer she's leaving town," I thought. "Although I guess it'd be much worse if she stayed."

★

The lethargic afternoon sun was hanging high up in the sky, but I still couldn't get to sleep. It was as though I were fighting some unknown force, trying to stay on my feet as long as possible, waiting for the crucial turning point in our fight. And, you know what—the crucial turning point did in fact arrive. Someone pulled up to the pumps—I heard it. It could have been anyone. What popped into my head was that I should find a baseball bat or something to defend the sanctity of private property . . . I felt strangely detached from the danger, apathetic—I didn't want to do anything at all. I didn't want to defend myself, didn't want to snap any necks, didn't want to put my own neck on the line. "Sure, maybe death is coming," I thought, "But not for me. I'll remember his face for next time." I heard some footsteps, the door opening, and there was Olga. She stood in the doorway for a bit, surveying the sun-kissed room. Seeing Katya sleeping next to me, she froze for a moment, then began fixing her hair. She came over and sat down on the couch next to me. I was unable to sit up or say a word. "Well," I thought, "this really couldn't get any worse—dying probably would have been better."

"Hey," Olga said, trying to be nonchalant. "What's going on here?"

"She's sleeping. You called yesterday?"

"Yeah, a few times," she said, looking even more anxious.

"Let me wake her up," I suggested. "I'll send her home, and then we'll be able to talk."

"You're a real scumbag, Herman. What's the point of waking her up?" She didn't know what to do with her hands.

"But we have to talk, don't we?"

"What makes you think that?"

"Well, why'd you come over here then?"

"I came over here to make sure they hadn't burned the station down. For your information, I work for you—remember? As far as I can tell, you're doing just fine, so I'm gonna get going," she said, standing up abruptly and heading for the door. But then she stopped, turned around, and came back over to me. "Oh, and there's something else," she said, as if suddenly remembering. "I want my sunglasses back."

She carefully slid her glasses off of Katya's nose, then darted out of the trailer, slamming the door for emphasis. Katya didn't move a muscle. I sprang to my feet and put my tank driver's uniform on as I ran out the door after Olga.

"Olga!" I yelled, trying desperately to catch up to her. "Olga, wait up please. Let's talk."

"Sure," Olga answered. "But the only talking we'll be doing will be at my office, during regular business hours. Oh," she added, pointing at my collarbone, "and she bit you. You're incredible." After that she hopped on her scooter and flew out of the parking lot, kicking up hot dust.

★

Pakhmutova's burial came after lunch. Kocha and I worked tenaciously to dig a pit back by the raspberry bushes, while Injured constructed an odd sort of marker out of scrap metal. It looked just like a TV antenna, but he claimed it was a sunflower.

It was hard to dig the grave because the ground was so hard. We had to rip up tree roots, thick as underground cables, and toss away all the wet stones our shovels kept striking. Katya stood silently next to the hole. Pakhmutova lay at her feet, as she did when she was alive, and Katya would bend down occasionally to pet her.

I was standing waist-deep in the hole, looking around at all the little rocks and patches of grass trickling down around me, the yellow ball of sand, and the white ball of clay that had accumulated as we dug. The roots we'd exposed and slashed with our shovels were tough and ropey, and the stones we removed from the grave were drying out quickly in the sun. Hard as we hacked away at it, though, the earth at the bottom of the hole just wouldn't budge any further, save what little stuck to the soles of our shoes. It was as if the ground out back had been packed down—it wouldn't let us in for the longest time, then it stuck to our shoes, refusing to fall off.

The clay we'd exposed had a sweet and piquant smell. I had dug up something valuable, something I'd always suspected was there. I never would have imagined that it was right there under the surface this whole time. Shortly thereafter, we lowered Pakhmutova in as far as we could manage. "My second funeral in twenty-four hours," I thought as I tossed some dirt over her body. We filled in the grave, Injured planted his antenna, and now our work was done.

Katya stood at the grave for some time. Then she said goodbye to everyone and ran home, holding her raincoat in her hands like a kite.

★

Kocha's relatives came by the station in the late afternoon. They drove into the parking lot in their beat-up Mercedes. A big piece of cellophane, attached with Scotch tape, covered the rear window. Seven people were jammed into the car. They had sobered up after the funeral but hadn't changed clothes yet, so they were all still in their black jackets and colorful dress shirts; they had taken off their ties, though I could see them hanging out of their jacket pockets like boa constrictors. Kocha's relatives were speaking loudly and using a lot of incomprehensible words; they kept calling him *gadjo* and kept him away from the Mercedes when he eagerly tried hopping inside it. They greeted Injured respectfully, though they were a tad too familiar with him. They shook his hand and kissed him three times, as per the Orthodox tradition. After that they came up to me. Kocha and Injured stood off to the side, giving us our space. They greeted me, one by one— their handshakes were short yet firm.

"Hey Herman," said Pasha, their leader. "A friend of our mother's is our friend, too."

"Huh?"

"You. You buried our mom with us yesterday," Pasha explained. "Tamara told us about you."

"Great," I thought, "now these guys are gonna slice me up."

"She said you needed some help?" Pasha asked.

"Some help?"

"Herman," said Borman, Pasha's right-hand man, a fat, bald dude, stepping forward. "We heard about everything."

"About everything?"

"About everything. About the tanker and all that. We just wanted to say that if you need any help we've got your back. All right?"

"Okay."

"So, don't let anyone push you around," Borman continued. "Just give us a call if you need anything. We'll be there for you if you need us."

"Now the ball is in your court," Pasha added. "It all depends on how you act. You see what I mean?"

"Yeah," I answered. "Thanks."

"Don't mention it, bro," Pasha said, extending his hand. "Hang in there."

The rest of them shook my hand too, exchanged kisses with Injured, kicked Kocha off the hood of their car, started up the motor, and pulled away, heading back down into the city. As they hit the highway, they crossed paths with a black Volkswagen, which had pulled onto the side road and was now flying toward the station.

"Who's that pulling in?" Injured asked, irritated.

"It's for me," I said.

Injured looked at Kocha gloomily and headed over to the garage. Kocha stood next to me, examining the newcomers, clearly intrigued. The Volkswagen rolled over to the gas pumps and stopped. Lyolik and Bolik stepped out of the car, looking around anxiously and stretching their legs after their long trip. They weren't in a hurry to hug me; they just watched me attentively, waiting for me to say something. Bolik wiped some sweat off his forehead with a damp handkerchief. Lyolik was tense, fiddling with his glasses.

"Hey, I'm glad you guys could make it."

"Hello, Herman," said Bolik, a note of concern evident in his voice.

"Hey," Lyolik said, avoiding my eyes.

"Herman," Bolik said, "let's talk."

"Okay, what would you like to talk about?"

"Just the three of us, I mean." He nodded in Kocha's direction.

"He won't understand anything anyway," I reassured them. "He's Georgian."

"Gotcha," Bolik said, apprehensively. "So, Herman, how are you doing down here?"

"Fuckin' shitty," I answered.

"Fuckin' shitty?" Bolik asked.

"Uh-huh. Fuckin' shitty. They torched my tanker truck and hanged our dog."

"You have a dog?" Lyolik asked.

"Not anymore. We just buried her. Kocha and I did," I said, nodding at the old-timer. He nodded back.

"Herman," Bolik said, clearly struggling to follow his initial train of thought, which my interaction with Kocha had derailed. "Well, basically . . . we came here to take you back home. We're up to our eyeballs in work. Ya know . . ."

"You guys are good friends and all, but I'm not going anywhere," I said after a moment's thought.

"What do you mean you're not going anywhere?" Bolik asked, looking dumbfounded.

"I mean just that. I'm not going anywhere."

"What about your job?" Bolik asked.

"Say that I've quit."

"What do you need all this hassle for, Herman? Come on, let's just go home. This isn't even your business." Bolik was almost trembling now.

"They torched my tanker truck and hanged my dog. This isn't about business anymore."

"Listen man," Bolik said, getting heated, as usual. "Who does this to his friends? You're really letting us down."

"Did you bring my money?" I asked.

"Huh?"

"I said, did you bring my money? And Lyolik, why are you being so quiet?"

"Herman," Bolik said, "well, look. Things aren't so clear-cut with your money."

"Yeah, Herman," Lyolik said. "We've been meaning to tell you."

"You gotta be kidding me."

"We borrowed some of your money. We had to pay off some bills right away. The thing is, Herman, well, we were flat broke, so we borrowed your money. So now you pretty much gotta come with us. We'll pay you back, don't you worry."

"Herman, we'll definitely pay you back," Lyolik added.

"So you fuckin' blew all my money?" I asked.

"Herman, we'll pay you back!" Bolik said, almost yelling. Clearly his feelings were a bit hurt.

"Herman," Lyolik interjected, "honest to God—we'll pay you back!"

"Just come back with us! You'll see, everything will fall into place!"

"I already told you I'm staying."

"We're not going anywhere without you," Bolik declared in the most decisive voice he could manage.

"Hey, numb nuts," Kocha piped up suddenly, "you heard what the boss said—he said beat it!" He took a sharpened screwdriver out of his suit pocket and starting to pick the dirt out from under his nails. "If I were you, I'd listen."

The word "boss" took the wind out of Bolik's sails. He couldn't take his eyes off the screwdriver. Eventually he turned around and headed back toward the car in silence. Lyolik stayed put, however. He hesitated a moment, then said:

"Herman, I'll pay you back, don't you worry."

"Okay," I answered, "sounds good."

"Seriously, you have nothing to worry about."

"All right."

"Maybe you wanna come back with us, after all?" he asked hopefully.

"Nah, I'm not going anywhere. I'm where I need to be. Here, I've got something for you," I said, pulling my MP3 player and headphones out of my pocket and handing them over. "A little going-away present."

"What are you doing?" Lyolik asked. "What are you going to listen to without these?"

"I've already listened to everything I wanted to. You have to listen to music *you* like and not let other people take your headphones away. All right, now get out of here, man."

Lyolik gave me a firm handshake and headed back to the car.

"Lyolik, hey," I called out.

"What?" he asked, looking back.

"Do you have unlimited calling?"

"Yeah . . ."

"Can I use your phone real quick?"

Lyolik came up to me and handed over his cell. I called my brother. At first it seemed as though no one would pick up, as usual. Then there was a click, and I heard a woman's voice on the other end.

"Hey," she said, "how are you hanging in there?"

"Who? Me?"

"Who else? How've you been doing?"

"Pretty decent," I answered. "And who is this?"

"Who were you calling?"

"My brother."

"Well, I'm not your brother. What did you want?"

"I wanted to chat."

"Well, why don't you chat with me," the woman asked, laughing. "You want me to tell ya a story?"

"You definitely have unlimited calling?" I asked Lyolik. He nodded, so I told the woman, "Okay, let's hear it."

"Ever since I was a kid I've been afraid of heights, and I was always scared of flying too. When I grew up I decided to overcome my fear. I'd buy airplane tickets and fly—a lot."

"And?"

"Well, nothing's changed. I'm still scared of heights, but I've seen the world, at least."

"And how are you holding up now?"

"Fine," the woman said. "I realized it was never really about fear. I just had to let myself relax, so I started feeling better. Why don't you try relaxing, too, all right?"

"All right."

"Okay, then," she said, laughing again. Then she hung up.

"Here." I handed Lyolik his phone back.

"Is everything okay?" he asked.

"Yep," I answered. "Everything's all right, everything's fine."

★

"Kocha, do you remember that big fight in the park by the restaurant, back in 1990?" I asked.

"In 1990?" he asked suspiciously.

"Yeah, June 1990."

"Nah, man," Kocha said, after thinking for a bit, "I don't remember any fights. I spent June 1990 in Gurzuf with Tamara, buddy. There was a real serious fight down there, though, let me tell you, Herman. On the beach. See, I'd barely turned my back for a second, and then . . ."

★

At night, the sky looks like black fields. The air, akin to black Ukrainian soil, is teeming, fecund. The endless landscapes that spill out across the plateau seem to follow their own laws of motion and acquire their own rhythm. Stars and constellations are buried deep in the sky, while stones and roots are buried in the earth. Planets rest in the sky, while the deceased rest in the earth. Rain flows down from the sky and rivers flow out of the earth. Once the rain reaches the earth, it flows down south, filling up the oceans. The sky is always changing—heating up or cooling down or soaking up the wet August heat. Grass and trees exhaust the earth's soil, spreading out under the flat skies, like a herd left behind by its owners. If you choose just the right spot, sometimes you can feel all these phenomena together—roots intertwining, rivers flowing, oceans filling up, planets soaring across the sky, and the living moving along the earth's surface like the dead move beneath it.

PART II

I

The priest from the funeral—the "presbyter," as he was officially called—was looking up at the morning sun as the three figures emerged from the yellow cornstalks that swayed in the wind like hangers in an empty closet. For a while it was hard to tell who precisely was pushing their way out of the thick crops—the only clues were a black jacket flashing by, the creaking of the corn, their cool breath rising. Stomping some sand-colored leaves and mowing down the morning dew, they finally popped out onto the road: two adults and one teenager. The man in front was wearing a winter AC Milan track jacket that went down to his knees. Army boots too. The club's black and red colors seemed faded against the troubling October sun. The man was unshaven and had long hair. He cast a shrewd yet unfocused glance at us. Another man, short and pot-bellied, wearing white work overalls stained with yellow paint, followed behind him. He had short, gray hair and was wearing Chinese-made Nike sneakers. The teenager looked the worst of all. He was wearing knockoff Dolce & Gabbana jeans and a shiny black jacket with scattered cigarette burns, square-tipped dress shoes, and had some Koss headphones on his head—which also looked like knock-offs. All three of them headed toward us without a word. I looked at the presbyter out of the corner of my eye.

He was just about holding it together: was doing his best to conceal his distress. I started rooting around in my pockets, but then I remembered I was wearing someone else's clothes. Digging around in my jacket pocket, I was surprised to find Kocha's screwdriver. The tips of my fingers felt its sharp edge. "God's watching out for me," I thought, smiling at the presbyter. But he wasn't looking at me—he was watching the strangers, quite concerned. Admittedly, there was cause for concern—the tallest guy was holding a hunting shotgun, come to think of it, while the pot-bellied one was expertly flourishing a machete. The teenager was the only one not holding anything, but he had his hands in his pockets, so one could only imagine what he was hiding in there. The distance between our two groups closed. The tall guy unexpectedly swung the gun off his shoulder, cocked it, and fired a blast into the sky. Then he spread out his arms, holding the weapon with one hand, and came over. The rising sun flashed behind his shoulder. The October air was dry, like gunpowder.

He stopped, dropped his hands, and shouted amiably at the presbyter:

"Father?"

The presbyter was doing his best to exude an air of self-importance.

"It's me, Tolik," the guy in the AC Milan jacket said to the presbyter, dashing over to embrace him.

The presbyter tolerated his affection with surprisingly good grace, and then the soccer star headed over to embrace me.

"Tolik," he forced out his name, nearly hugging me to death.

"Herman," I answered, freeing myself from his grip.

"Herman?" the soccer star asked. "Yura's brother?"

"Yep."

Tolik broke out into amiable laughter. Then he remembered his fellow travelers and started introducing me to them.

"That's Gosha," he said, pointing at the pot-bellied man. "He showed us the shortcut. We were like plantation owners," Tolik said, pointing at the machete, "cutting our way toward you. Yeah, and that's Siryozha, Gosha's son. He's studying at the local community college. He's going to be an engineer—well, maybe."

Siryozha, continuing to listen to his music, waved at us. Gosha gave the presbyter a long and heartfelt handshake.

"We went straight through the fields on purpose," Tolik explained to the presbyter, "to cut you off. It'd be best to turn here, otherwise we could bump into the farmers farther down. We're at war with them."

"What are you fighting for?" I asked.

"Isn't it obvious?" Tolik asked, surprised. "To expand our sphere of influence. Sure, in all honesty, sometimes we do cross over into their territory now and again. But, you know, we have to hide our shit somewhere," he explained. "We leave everything out in their fields. That's capitalism for you. Anyway . . . they're waiting for us out there," Tolik said, looking off into the distance.

Only now did I notice that his right eye was glass. Maybe that's why he'd looked so mysterious to me. Now he was laughing heartily again—he was an easygoing guy, it seemed, despite everything—living in a warzone wasn't getting him down, at least.

"Well then," he said, his real eye directed at the pot-bellied man, "let's give them a call and get going."

The pot-bellied man handed me his knife and started digging around in his overall pockets. They seemed bottomless. He kept taking things out and handing them to Tolik and me to hold: I got two red autumn apples, and Tolik got a handful of spark plugs. Then, much to my surprise, I got a hand grenade covered with nail polish; next came a few old, battered cassettes for Tolik, whose glass eye twinkled joyfully. Finally, the pot-bellied man reached all the way down past his knee and came back up with an old Sony Ericsson phone, one with a short antenna. He walked a few steps away from us, pulled out the antenna, and turned the thing on. After a few minutes of struggling with the ancient apparatus, he called back, dejectedly, "I don't have any bars. We'll have to drive up to the top of the hill."

"We're down in a gully here," Tolik explained. "We'll have to drive up to the top of the hill," he repeated. "We'll take a little detour. We'll be there in no time."

Gosha collected his toys and dropped them into his cavernous pockets, wiping the grenade off on his sleeve before tossing it back in. He also took back the machete. The three of them just started milling around, seemingly expecting something to happen.

"What's the deal?" Mr. One Eye blurted out at last. "Are we going or what?"

"What are you going to drive up there in?" the presbyter asked, clearly confused.

"What do you mean?" Tolik asked, chuckling. "We're going with you. We can all fit."

Seva, our driver, who had been sitting in the car this whole time watching through his sunglasses, took them off to admire the spectacle of us all jamming into his old, white Volga, which seemed to be rusting more and more the farther we traveled. The presbyter took a seat up front, next to Seva; Mr. One Eye squeezed himself in right behind the presbyter, insistently nudging him toward the driver and miraculously getting the door shut behind him. Tolik's puffy Milan jacket engulfed both himself and the presbyter like an airbag. Pot-bellied Gosha and his son hopped in the back; seeing a woman already sitting there, they started apologizing profusely, albeit without surrendering even an inch of space. I was the last one in, and Siryozha had to sit on my lap. He was so close I could hear the music playing in his headphones—I thought it was shit, so I just did my best to ignore it. Seva put his sunglasses back on and looked at the presbyter inquisitively. Tolik's hand emerged from under his Milan jacket, waving the driver on. The Volga shuddered and started along the dirt road. At times, the corn came right up to the edge of the road, rubbing up against the sides of the car. Tolik directed the driver, flapping his arms. The car was crawling up the hill, up to where we would have more bars and where the farmers would presumably be waiting for us. Then, Tolik was motioning off somewhere to the left. Seva braked and looked askance at his one-eyed passenger, but Tolik persisted in his waving. Our driver obligingly spun the wheel, and we dove into a dry, rustling expanse of corn, shining in the afternoon sun and cutting off our view in every direction. It seemed there was a path hidden there, nearly invisible to the untrained eye, though obvious enough once we were on it; it ran through the heart of this corn jungle, protecting us from the evil eye. We drove slowly, pushing through the cornstalks and tuning in to the random sounds scattered out in the sun-drenched fields. It felt as though the Volga was barely moving—the thick dust on the dashboard jumped every time we hit a ditch.

Eventually we emerged into stubble fields. Then we crossed over a strip of fallow ground between two fields and rolled onto a brick-paved road. It was completely empty out there, just the dew sliding down blades of grass, and the sun rising higher and higher. The drive seemed to be going on forever. Maybe Mr. One Eye wanted to make sure our trail would be hard to follow, who knows. Soon the fields ended abruptly and we found ourselves in front of a wide gully stretching out to the east. The road dropped sharply, and about a dozen identical two-story structures, which looked like they'd been built back in the '80s, stood at the bottom of the hill. At the edge of this settlement I saw rows of warehouses, followed by gardens, then there were yellow meadows sprawling out to the horizon. Far to the east I could just about make out what might have been a dam or a huge earthen wall stretching out along the horizon. It had a well-defined shape, though I couldn't quite decide what I was looking at.

"What's that?" I asked the pot-bellied man.

"The Russian border," he answered succinctly. Then he retreated into his own thoughts.

Seva shut off the engine, and we coasted down the hill. The bricks under our tires were all broken up. The road was crushed, like the spine of a dog that had been run over by a truck. Having descended into the valley, we stopped in the middle of a small lot. There was a relatively spacious building there with a slate roof and fake columns on one side. About forty locals were standing on the front steps. They seemed to have been waiting for us.

I could instantly sense the atmosphere of a grand, festive gathering. The men were mostly wearing dark, inexpensive suits, bizarrely colored ties, and thoroughly polished shoes. The women had a less uniform appearance—some of them were in dresses, some of them in white blouses and black skirts; others, mostly the younger ones, were wearing jeans studded with masses of rhinestones. Some women had winter coats around their shoulders, some were wearing leather jackets, and a few others had raincoats on, although the autumn air had had already been thoroughly dried out and warmed up by the sun. It was actually rather cozy down here in the valley, like on the southern Crimean coast. The locals greeted us with a joyful roar. We all crawled out of the car, smoothing our wrinkled clothes. Tolik, wearing his Milan jacket, and the presbyter, wearing a black jacket and holding a folder, took the lead, followed by Seva, who was also wearing a suit, albeit a red and rather dubious looking one, as well as his sunglasses, of course. Then the rest of us spilled out—Siryozha, wearing his knockoff jeans with the letters *D* and *G* on the back pockets, and me in my reflective blue suit that made me look like a '70s Soviet pop star. Then came Gosha, decked out in his white, paint-stained overalls, and finally Tamara, surveying her new surroundings anxiously. She was wearing a cherry-colored sweater and a long skirt. On her feet she had thin high heels that immediately sank into the sand outside. Our whole crew headed over to meet the assembled locals.

They were glad to see us. A short dude, wearing a suit and colorful handkerchief instead of a tie, and clearly the one in charge, came down the steps and kissed the presbyter five times in a row, a custom that was unfamiliar to me. It seemed as though they were old friends; they had some catching up to do, but, instead, the boss invited us in, saying that we didn't have much time, and needed to get everything done nice and snappy.

"*Then* we can catch up," he added, and headed up the steps.

The presbyter fell in behind him. The locals parted respectfully, making way for him and the rest of us. Our driver moved quickly down this living corridor, then Tamara, sending a concerned glance my way. I turned to Gosha and Siryozha.

"Are you going in?" I asked.

"I'm going to stop home real quick," Gosha said, standing still and keeping his machete hidden behind his back. "I'm going to get changed. It's a holiday after all."

"What about you?" I asked Siryozha, raising my voice to be heard over his headphones.

He just waved his hand amiably. Then again, maybe he didn't even hear my question. Meanwhile, the locals were cramming themselves through the front door. I went up the steps too.

I found myself in a dark hallway with a cool scent to it; the building appeared to be their town hall, or something along those lines. Various doorways could be seen at the end of the hallway— the locals who'd preceded us inside were bunched up around them. There was a rather large— given the size of their community— auditorium on the other side. The interior was modest, the room was lined with neatly arranged rows of wooden pews, and the stage was decorated with red velvet. Up above the proscenium I could see the clear outline of Lenin's profile. His picture had probably been hanging there for a while, and then it was taken down, but the fabric had faded and molded around the outline of his face. Now a crucifix had taken his place; at a distance it looked as though somebody had crossed out the tenets of Marxism-Leninism once and for all. Most of our crew was already on the stage—the leader, with his handkerchief tie, was bobbing around them and explaining something. The locals took their seats all around us. Tolik came up to me.

"What do you think? You like it?" he asked.

"Is this your club or something?" I asked.

He slid out of his heavy jacket, exposing a striped woolen navy shirt. He carefully leaned his gun up against one of the benches.

"It's our church," he said.

"Seriously?"

"Uh-huh, it's our church. Well, and our club too. We've combined the two, you see?"

"Gotcha."

"Our religion says it's okay," Mr. Glass Eye assured me.

"Good to know."

"The presbyter knows what's good."

"Uh-huh."

"For real."

"Okay, chill."

Now the presbyter was calling me over. He seemed completely focused now, and was handing out clear instructions. I pushed through the crowd as Seva took out a leather bag containing all the necessary supplies. Tamara was fixing her hair, standing silently at the back.

"Well then, Herman. You ready?" the priest asked.

"Yep. Are we going to get started?"

"Of course," he said confidently. "This is exactly what we came here for. This is exactly what we came here for."

★

Three months of plentiful sunshine. We had sand in our clothes and teeth, and silence that stopped our blood and thickened our dreams so they ran one into another; it made waking up a long and uneasy process. Black bread and green tea that marked time and framed space. We had sugar in our pockets and on our bed sheets, the smell of grass and diesel, hoarse conversations in the mornings, the smooth operation of rain falling slowly like factory workers trudging home after a tough shift, passing empty tin cans. We listened to border radio stations, giving us news from both countries, alternately informing us about clear days and calling for precipitation. Women's voices came through the speaker, telling us about the heat waves battering distant, unreachable places, complaining about the stifling heat and the unending racket in the city and dreaming about travel and cool weather. It all seemed so artificial and intoxicating from where we were—we listened greedily to their smooth breathing, their short yet frequent bursts of laughter. We wanted to look them straight in the eye as they reported the day's exchange rates.

The summer was so dense that it was impossible to push through to the other side. Every evening after work, we'd lock up the booth, flop down on our couches, and listen to the radio—one of the truckers had hooked Kocha up. I'd fall asleep to the music request show and wake up to long, sad conversations between radio evangelists. The latter were particularly earnest in the early mornings when things were light and easy and I couldn't even think of falling asleep again. Around that time they'd generally be holding forth about the importance of fasting and reading excerpts from the prophets' holy books. Occasionally, they'd break for weather reports, which made their sermons all the more comprehensive. Three months of good sleep, a healthy appetite, and sentimental feelings. I'd always thought that it would probably serve a person well to change their social circle, daily routine, name, and hair color every once in a while, and now I'd had the chance to test that theory. My hair had gotten lighter and grown out—in July I started combing it back, and then in August Kocha cut it with his prized German scissors. My old clothes had gotten all greasy and they stank of wine and gasoline now so I bought myself some black army T-shirts and a few pairs of pants with countless pockets to store all the bolts, keys, and light bulbs I came across at work. I had become more sensible and self-assured—maybe changing my daily routine did the trick, or maybe it was the fact that I was working with some serious people. Fresh air really can cool your head and light a fire inside you. I reconnected with all of my old acquaintances, all my old loves, all my teachers and enemies. My old acquaintances were genuinely happy I had come back, but it didn't go any further than that. My old loves introduced me to their kids, reminding me of the diffuse passage of time that makes us wiser, though this newfound wisdom is inevitably accompanied by cellulite. My teachers looked to me for guidance, while my enemies asked me to lend them a little cash so they could continue leading their worthless lives. Life is cruel, but fair. Well, sometimes it's just cruel.

On the weekends, Injured and I would play some soccer. A bunch of community college guys would stop by the station, guys who considered playing on the same team as our chubby living legend a great honor. We had a lot of work, but I'd gotten used to it. Olga and I still weren't on speaking terms. My former Kharkiv friends never came back. I forgave their debt. Kocha's Gypsy relatives gave me enough money to keep going. I stopped trying to contact my brother. At night I'd dream about airplanes.

Surprisingly enough, my gas station worries had just evaporated somehow. At first, I sat around anxiously awaiting their next move—waiting for arson, corpses, and so forth. I even tried to rally my old acquaintances in town. Nothing ever wound up happening, though, and I was told not to make a big deal about it, and just take things as they came. I gradually calmed down, despite Injured's constant warnings that our problems wouldn't blow over so easily, and that one day somebody was going to get his neck snapped. "Maybe," I told myself. "And then again, maybe not."

In the early fall, everything was set into motion again, everything was reactivated—caravans of trucks pushed out to the north, delivering the fruits of the harvest to local markets. This golden September was warm. The sun would seem to halt right above the gas pumps, and then it'd get it into its head to roll away as quickly as it could, heading along the highway to the west, lighting up the road for the truckers. Sometimes Ernst would stop by and hold forth to Injured about differences in the tactics of tank combat in daytime and nighttime conditions. Injured would soon lose his temper and disappear into his workshop to dismember some more fresh automobile carcasses. Occasionally, when it wasn't too hot, the clergyman with whom I'd struck up a friendship during the funeral would stop by on his bike. We'd have long conversations. Sometimes he'd stay late, and we'd listen to the evangelists sitting in faraway radio stations—much like us, they clearly had no idea how to pass the time on those black nights, ignited by indolence. Other times, the presbyter would bring me some books to read. Once, noticing my Charlie Parker discs, he asked me if I was really interested in jazz. On the very next day he showed up with a greasy scholarly work on the emergence of the New Orleans jazz scene. And then there was a long period during which he tried talking to me about Shtundism, but I couldn't help but demonstrate a total lack of respect for religious symbols whenever the topic came up, so he finally decided to let me be.

By this time, Kocha's Gypsy relatives already saw me as one of their own. They too would stop by from time to time, trying to draw me further into their community. Kocha and I even went to their religious services a few times, but we could never manage to sit through an entire Mass. Each time, Kocha would drag me over to the kitchen where he'd start pillaging the wine supply. Tamara also came by the station sometimes. She'd always greet me with a certain reserve, as if she wanted to tell me something but couldn't quite find the right words. Frankly, I had no real interest in trying to pry any information out of her. Certain things are best observed at a distance, including other people's intimate relations.

After those three months of sun and shade, of sandstorms and plentiful if withering greenery, came October. The mornings were sunny yet cool; every day it felt as though a cyclone was just about to touch down. I would get out of bed with great reluctance and wander outside, shivering, to wash up at the sink. Our toothpaste would freeze overnight like vanilla ice cream. Patches of fog would gradually clump together by the gas pumps, with only individual trees still visible, poking through. Fall was already gathering momentum; we needed to start gearing up for months of darkness and snow.

That's when it happened. The presbyter had to make a trip all the way out to the border to perform a wedding ceremony for some members of his congregation. He had to go God knows where, so he decided it'd be best to travel with a big group. The church provided him with a driver and an old, rotting white Volga, and asked Tamara to go along, since having a woman there would make the whole affair look a bit more legitimate. Kocha was supposed to join the group, help out at the ceremony, and generally serve as backup. One of his pals from the can paid us a visit a few days before the trip, though: The two of them loaded up on wine and sang prison songs deep into the night, paying no mind to the first breaths of frost that blew through those deceptively warm, early autumn nights. By the next morning, Kocha had nearly lost his voice, while his former cellmate, who had agreed to bike into the valley for some medicine at some point during the previous night's festivities, had failed to reappear as promised, meaning there was little chance of getting the bike back, leaving the old-timer distraught. All he could do was lie around on the couch, drinking hot tea and pouring generous doses of grain alcohol into his mug. So I had to go to the ceremony instead of him. I guess that's just how it goes sometimes in a big family.

"Can't they get by without me?" I asked. "I don't know a thing about their church stuff."

Kocha, who was still quite sick, replied hoarsely, "Look, you don't have to do a thing. They'll handle it, so just chill, dude. All you gotta do is hang around them, that's it." His voice fizzled out then like a dying car battery. He couldn't manage more than a feeble mumble when he went on: "I just can't—you see I'm hurting."

"What I don't get is why they needed you in the first place."

"It'd be bad news if we only sent Gypsies over. They need a regular person there, you know, just in case the shit hits the fan."

"What's their beef with the Gypsies?"

"Herman, they're uncivilized people. They already don't trust each other, and then you throw Gypsies into the mix? Listen, if this weren't so important to the family I wouldn't have asked you. The thing is, you're like a brother to us now. Just make sure you wear my suit. You look like some sort of POW in that getup. Come on, Herman—you gotta take life by the horns."

"Who are we doing all this for, anyway?" I asked.

"Smugglers," Kocha explained. "They live by smuggling. The border's right there, see. They just get by however they can."

"They ever get caught?"

"Yeah, of course. Some of them get locked up and others are let go."

"How'd they wind up here in our neck of the woods?"

"They do business with our guys," Kocha said. "Our guys hook them up with Chinese-made bathroom fixtures, they take them across the border, repackage them in Rostov, and then ship them out to China, passing them off as Italian-made. Remember, Herman, business and faith go hand in hand."

"Sure."

"They come to our services sometimes, take some of our pamphlets, donate some money to our church. But it's not just about that."

"Really?"

"Of course. We have to spread God's word. Who else should we be spreading it to? Why not them?"

"What sort of creed does their presbyter preach, anyway?"

"None that I know of, he just does things his own way. All that matters is that you're at peace with yourself . . . and that you keep your feet warm," Kocha said, tucking his ailing body underneath the blanket.

They came by to pick me up early Saturday morning. I put on Kocha's dark blue suit, laced up a pair of worn boots, and hopped in the car. If I had known from the get-go how the trip was going to play out, I probably would have been a bit more cautious. But who could have guessed how it was all going to go down, and what kind of trouble we were going to get ourselves into? When you're taking life by the horns you don't really think about the consequences of your actions.

★

Their songs sounded like national anthems being performed at the Olympics—their voices rose in a heartfelt chorus, even though they didn't exactly know how to sing. They may not have been hitting the right notes, but the joy in their voices made up for their musical shortcomings. I remembered the singing at Tamara's mother's funeral: you might have thought that there would be a mournful, wistful air of solemnity about the ceremony, but no, everyone was singing uplifting songs, thanking the heavens for all the kindness they had been shown, and asking for further intercessions on behalf of those they loved. Now the presbyter was standing on the stage and launching into couplet after couplet as his congregation joined in gladly and sang the Lord's praises. Tamara and the driver were both inspired by all this melodious thanksgiving to lift their voices as well. I felt like a soccer player from some third-world country at the Olympic Games—I opened up my mouth and caught the beginning of the words, latching onto them and spitting out the endings as loudly as I could, so one could hear my voice, too, on longer phrases like "the righteous" or "burning bush." The bride and groom were standing in the first row with one-eyed Tolik to their right and the head of the local community to the left.

The words they were singing warmed the roofs of their mouths as they belted them out, so by the time they began exalting Zion's golden hillsides, tucked away in the green woods beneath the icy blue sky, they were practically breathing fire. "Oh, Zion," they cried, "golden Zion, the hidden chamber of our passion, golden Zion, the anthracite coal of dusk. We have ventured toward you, forty times in forty years, our elusive Zion. Boarding trains and barges, fording the mighty river, passing demarcation lines. Oh Zion, you're still so distant and unattainable, you remain elusive, never in reach, never letting the Israelites return unto you. A thousand birds soar above us, showing the way toward you, Zion. A thousand fish swim behind us, straining to burst out into your sweet, shady embrace. Lizards and spiders, dogs and deer undertake this journey of faith with us. Lions of Judah, with dreads and stars on their heads, stand guard over our places of refuge. Owls fall into pits of darkness, losing their way during our endless journeys. How much longer must we endure? How much longer must we follow the rivers flowing south, closer to you? Callous farmers drive us from their fields like foxes. Blue rains flood our houses and our kitchen bowls, but those valiant, dark red lions lead us onward through the storm, black as tarnished silver. The lions of joy and enlightenment carry our sleepy children. The king of kings among the fish of the sea and the beasts of the land, whom we will recognize as soon as we reach your priceless hills, walks hidden somewhere among us. He will break out of this emptiness and overcome all the barriers in his way, traveling the roads of desperation to reach you. Yellow-green birds will lift him up by the hair so he can survey the twilit valley. Red-brown whales tuck him under the roofs of their mouths. He beats his drums, drawing to him the whole of the animal kingdom to teach them the value of patience and attention. Whosoever listens to him will know that from here on the roads will be firm and the grass will be fresh. Whoever hears his teachings will sing, along with the mad beating of the drums, hymns to your advent, oh Zion! Go to a place where you're welcomed and stay clear of any false teachings. And make sure to remember your divine mission and the people who love you, Zion!"

★

After all the songs had been sung, the bread had been broken, the wine had been drunk, and the presbyter had given a long and emotional sermon about piety, everyone left the auditorium for the reception. We were invited too. We walked down the only street of their strange settlement, passing nearly identical buildings. The smugglers led an odd life. It was as if they had settled permanently in a busy train station—their yards, roofs, trailers, and decks were occupied by goods wrapped in rags and brown paper and packed away in cardboard boxes and athletic bags. Dark curtains and tin-foil lined the windows of their houses; it was as if they were blacking out their settlement in preparation for an impending air raid. Tolik walked alongside me, his gun slung over his shoulder. He said they had a lot of work these days, that they were constantly on the move, spending their nights on the road. But they were used to all of that—it came with the territory, and their jobs were what kept them going.

The reception was held in their orchard, under the trees. Red apples lay in the sun-dappled grass, and spiderwebs were inching down the leaves as they moved with the wind. The presbyter, clearly an honored guest, was given a seat next to the bride and groom. The guy with the handkerchief tie sat next to him, and the two of them would occasionally toast the bride and groom, encouraging everyone to be hardworking and considerate of others, and to file their taxes in a timely fashion. One-eyed Tolik kept me entertained. Later on Gosha joined us, wearing a red dress shirt. The smugglers turned out to be a simple, hospitable bunch of folks; they preferred Mediterranean cuisine (at least that's what they were calling it), but by the end of the reception they started chasing Moldovan cognac with soda. I thought to myself that it was a good thing for the whole congregation to get together for weddings and funerals. There was something primal and positive about it all—about the presbyter joining in their celebration and chasing his alcohol with the same soda as his parishioners, about how everyone was taking their turn dancing with the bride, about how everyone was kissing the groom out of brotherly love, some people even giving him enormous, grateful smooches, as though he were their best friend in the world, and had just gotten them out of some serious jam.

The newlyweds were given a boatload of gifts, mostly German household appliances—most notably ones manufactured by Bosch. Tolik told me that they'd received a fresh shipment from Bosch's Western Ukrainian partners a few days ago; they manufactured their own handy household and garden tools, and now had the right to slap Bosch labels on all of their products, having recently struck a clever deal with them. He said they'd be shipping the latest batch out to the northern Caucasus tomorrow night, since Bosch goods are usually in very high demand down there. For the time being, though, all of the smugglers' closets were simply bursting at the seams with Bosch lawn mowers and chainsaws, while refrigerators and microwave ovens were stowed away in their cellars, waiting for their time to shine. Maybe that's why nearly all of the wedding presents were the same items—the newlyweds received two identical drills, two sets of garden shears, several electric scissors, and even a matching pair of tripod-mounted laser levels. I expressed a certain degree of doubt as to whether they would actually need all of those things, but Tolik explained that they would, saying that the groom was in the smuggling business too, after all. He'd unload all of these tools quite handily somewhere in Ossetia or Ingushetia and make enough profit to build a brick house for his family.

Nightfall set in quickly; they laid out an extension cord from the nearest house, and soon the dark apple branches were lit by a soft band of electricity. Tolik and Gosha had already started saying their good-byes. They each gave the groom a long, sloppy kiss, shook the bride's hand, wished the presbyter sweet dreams, and exchanged tender farewells with Tamara. The presbyter decided to stay the night. The smugglers, most of whom were quite intoxicated by then, remained peaceful and amiable.

"Where you off to? It's still early . . ." I asked Tolik.

"We have to get to work," he answered and pointed somewhere toward the east, where a ball of darkness had accumulated and some blue and yellow stars were shining.

"How about I come along?" I volunteered.

"All right," he said. "But it's really dark out there. You won't be able to see a thing."

"I'll be just fine."

★

We looped through the black apple orchards, tromping all the while through dry grass mottled with spiderwebs. Tolik and Gosha strode along confidently, speaking softly to one another. They weren't rushing me—when I would fall behind they would freeze in the grass and wait patiently. Eventually we reached some empty meadows. Clouds had blanketed the sky like soot from a chimney, making the night truly dark. Tolik and Gosha found a trail and moved further into the night. I lost sight of them; all I could hear was their footsteps, and then their once-quiet voices, which had begun to carry, their volume rising the longer our trek continued. Soon enough it sounded as though there was a large group of hikers up there in front of me. While moving through the all-encompassing blackness, I kept trying, albeit unsuccessfully, to remember the way, so I could get back if need be. I don't know why I believed I could ever manage to navigate through the gloom just as long as I didn't lose sight of my escort and wind up all alone in the cool darkness of the border. Impossible though I would have thought it, the black abyss seemed to be getting even deeper, up ahead: it looked as though the soot that had been pouring into the sky since we left had hardened.

"Be careful up here," Tolik said, out of nowhere, as he started climbing up something I also couldn't see.

It looked like we'd reached the earthen wall I'd seen that afternoon. Once I'd climbed up after the smugglers, I realized that we were actually on top of an embankment leading down to railroad tracks.

"There's a railroad here?" I asked.

"Well, yeah," Mr. One-Eye answered.

"Where does it go?"

"Nowhere."

"What do you mean 'nowhere'? It must go somewhere."

"Nope. It doesn't. They were building it here in case of war. But they started building it from the center, laying track in either direction. Well, they never wound up connecting this line to any-thing at either end. They just stopped."

"So you're saying that no trains run on these tracks?"

"We run on these tracks. The border's right over there. That's Ukraine," he said, pointing to the left, "and that's Russia over there," he said, nodding toward the black abyss.

We stood on the tracks for a bit, peering into the gloom.

"Why don't you take these apart and sell them as scrap metal?" I asked Mr. One Eye.

"These tracks keep our business running," he explained. "The border guards on the other side cruise around in big trucks. If you can sneak by them on the tracks with some goods in hand, you're in the clear. They won't chase after you because they'd just get caught up on the rails."

"Gotcha. But you can't see a thing out here."

"Brohan," Tolik said, laughing. "This is the sickest time for a smuggler. Isn't that right, Gosha."

Gosha may have nodded in the darkness, but I couldn't tell.

"Well, what about you guys? How can you make anything out?" I asked. "It's pitch black out here."

"Brohan, when you can't see, you gotta follow your heart. Then you can see just fine," Tolik replied, putting his hand on my shoulder. "Herman," he said, changing tack, "you head on home now. We're gonna keep going."

"What do you mean 'head on home'? I don't know the way back."

"You'll find it if you want to. You shouldn't come any farther. You could get shot. And it's not your business, after all. See you soon, brohan," he said, punching me affectionately in the shoulder and diving into the dark void.

Gosha shook my hand and then disappeared too. I was left standing there alone on train tracks that went—literally—nowhere. The only piece of advice I'd been given was to listen to my heart. But my heart was telling me that I wasn't going to be getting out of there anytime soon, and that my only other option, following those two smugglers with only three eyes between them, probably wasn't the greatest idea in the world. My heart was telling me: "You got yourself into this mess, now you get yourself out of it." So I got to thinking it might be best to stay put and wait out the night. And that's what I did. I just stood there. A gust of smoky wind came over from the east; the inert clouds overhead finally got moving, floating west and crossing the Russian border. A round, red moon cracked the darkness, appearing in the turbulent air above me, drenching my surroundings with radiant light and stretching long shadows out along the valley. I could finally see again, at least in my immediate vicinity, though the void was just as thick as before, if I looked too far ahead or behind, leaving me none the wiser as to the origin of the voices and muffled footsteps that could still be heard echoing out of the abyss from time to time. Now, standing here and gazing at the red, moon-kissed meadows, I caught a glimpse of a caravan of gas tankers inching past my position, heading west, toward the border. There was an old, dark-colored Kopeika model car out front, meticulously smeared with mud. There were four people inside, wearing black jackets and black winter hats. The guy in the passenger seat was holding a Kalashnikov. The gas tankers were wrapped in swamp-colored canvas and camo nets. From this distance they looked like elephants meandering out of some desert land with valuable and aromatic fuel supplies in their black wombs. The caravan stretched out into the distance, its tail somewhere far behind. It was hard to spot it over the hills and blackthorn that peppered the valley. I could just about make out a small crowd of people waiting on the border for the tankers to arrive—silhouettes were hurrying down the embankment, and a few trucks were sitting parked on the Ukrainian side. The silhouettes descended to meet the trucks, unloaded some boards and ready-made wooden frames, and placed them over the tracks to form a makeshift bridge. They clearly knew what they were doing; brief commands would reach my ears occasionally, after which someone would run over to the other side of the railroad tracks and carry another board over on his back. A makeshift bridge had already been assembled by the time the lead car rolled up to the embankment. The Kopeika rode up onto the boards gingerly. Then some of the silhouettes scurried down, formed a circle around the car, and started pushing it over. Shortly afterward, I saw it coasting to a stop on the other side of the embankment. The gas tankers followed suit. A few of them crossed problem-free, while others stalled a bit, and so had to be pushed or towed. The crossing continued for quite a while; eventually, the entire motorcade wound up on the other side of the tracks. From atop my hill, the whole scene resembled a sort of odd military maneuver—a column of tanks stopping under cover of night, afraid of being spotted. The tanker drivers, the outriders from the Kopeika, the guys who built the bridge, and the men from the Zil model trucks all gathered around, standing between their vehicles, sitting on the hoods, crawling underneath them and climbing on top of them to keep watch on their associates as well as the surrounding landscape. Then some of them started arguing, yelling and carrying on about something. One small group, arguing in a particularly animated fashion, waving their arms and ripping off their sweaters, stepped away from the tankers. Another group, calmer and more focused, opposed them. The rest of the crowd stood there in anticipation, not knowing which side to join. I didn't have any way of figuring out what the argument might be about, from my vantage point, since I couldn't make out a word they were saying. Still, I heard it clearly enough when one of the guys I'd pegged as being calm and reasonable pulled out a sawed-off shotgun and fired into the air. I crouched low, involuntarily. Then I saw what I had not seen before; black stars were glinting up in the sky, cutting through the thick air and igniting the dry grass so I could see the birds nestling between its blades, hiding from the cold and our unfamiliar voices. Animals were crossing the border, all the while apprehensively surveying the valley, thick with breath, where countless shadows were suddenly moving across the high embankment, sprinting into the adjacent country like people sprinting into the ocean in summer. Snakes slithered onto the tracks that were shining in the moonlight, slithering over the rails, undulating down into their émigré burrows to lose themselves amid the elaborate and tenacious roots below. Spiders scuttled across the sand, reaching upward, toward the other side of the moonlight. Red foxes scowled threateningly as they approached the railroad tracks that were the last thing separating them from the unknown land beyond. Ravens circled above, as if hesitant to give up this territory they have claimed, meandering through the sky like Gypsies roaming along a train platform. I saw the roots fighting doggedly to tunnel through the parched, early autumn ground, striving toward the water that was hidden deep beneath the surface like magma. I saw silver pockets of water reaching upward to meet them, intruding into the black earth, skirting around the bodies of the dead that were buried there who knows when by who knows who, moving into the dark unknown. I saw the black anthracite heart beating deep in the body of the valley, giving life to everything around me, and the fresh milk of natural gas accumulating in nests and underground channels, hardening and watering dried-up roots—insanity and resilience ran through those roots, turning blades of grass to make them face the wind. I turned with them and a gust of wind slapped me in the face, bringing me back to reality. I looked back to the commotion down below. Three men wearing long coats had grabbed one of the most vocal guys from the loud, angry group and carried him by his arms and legs over to the closest gas tanker. They tossed him to two of their guys who were standing on top of it and they bound his hands with rope. He tried to break free, but to no avail. Then his captors opened the hatch, dropped him into the tank, and hopped back to the ground. I didn't quite want to believe what I'd seen. "What was that for?" I wondered. "He'll drown in there." I pictured him swimming in that thick blue gasoline juice like a man inside a whale's stomach, kicking off the bottom of its metal lining. Afterward, both groups quickly dispersed. The argument had quieted down—apparently, all their issues had been resolved. The driver of the Kopeika took out a heavy road flashlight and started shining it at the nearby hills, checking to make sure nobody was around. The fat stream of light moved slowly across the grass in my direction. It had already crept past the embankment and was coming at me quickly. "Drop!" my heart advised me. "Come on, drop!" So I followed my heart right onto the railroad ties. The stream of light slipped by over my head and kept going. The driver turned around and started walking by the trucks. My heart wasn't stingy with additional advice: "Now get the hell out of here!" The tankers revved up and continued west. I got up, ran down the embankment, then went off at a quick walk, slightly hunched over, toward the lights coming off some buildings in the distance. Once I was in the clear, I looked around—the wind was still goading the clouds across the sky; by now they looked as heavy as bags stuffed with coins, they moved so slowly, blanketing the horizon. The moonlight was gone; gloom had settled on the grass like silt on a riverbed. It was as if a mother had turned the lights out as she left her child's bedroom.

2

Early fall mornings—late stars, golden grass, and the air drying out and hardening like fresh sheets hung out in the frosty air. In the mornings, everyone would be busy with their own work. Hardly anyone would pay any attention to us—they'd pack up their Jeeps like fishermen loading up their boats before heading out into the bountiful eastern waters. Women would come up to the presbyter, whisper some tender words in his ear, and he'd chuckle a bit, giving them printed hymns, pencils and scraps of paper where he'd written his phone number. Seva looked tired—he hadn't exactly been practicing temperance the night before, despite all the presbyter's exhortations. Today his entire body seemed to be exuding contrition. Tamara, for her part, anxiously bombarded me with questions: where had I wandered off to, who could I possibly have made friends with out here, why had I let everyone get worried sick about me. I told her that despite having spent the night God knows where with God knows whom, I was thinking about her the whole time. Tamara wasn't angry, but she wasn't too happy either. She took a seat in the car and slammed the door, causing flakes of rust to flutter off like snow from a fir tree.

It was time to go, and the head of the friendly smugglers' association wanted to see us off. We were all standing by the Volga—Seva was already at the wheel, warming up the engine, when the newlyweds came out of the house and headed over. They were truly glad they had been afforded this last opportunity to thank us for yesterday's reception. In fact, the groom took out two champagne bottles filled with homemade cognac that he had somehow stuffed into the pockets of his formal wedding pants, placed them on the hood, and tried to convince us to stick around and continue celebrating. I declined his offer, taking a seat next to Tamara. Seva joined this impromptu extension of the party, although he didn't shut off the engine, because he wanted to preserve the illusion that we were indeed about to part ways any minute now. The presbyter was glad for the delay, since he liked the smugglers' company—probably because they were attentive listeners and provided him with a constant flow of alcohol. The groom now took a Finnish knife and a few heavy onions from his pockets as well, spread them out between the bottles, and started dicing the ripe vegetables furiously. At one point, he went a little overboard and stabbed the knife into the hood of the Volga. The driver was mesmerized by the groom's slicing and dicing—he just stood there, not saying a word, taking occasional swigs from one of the bottles of cognac.

"When are we going to get moving?" Tamara asked wearily.

"What's your rush?"

"Herman, I want to get home already," she answered with a sigh.

"We're going to get moving soon," I reassured her.

Then: "How's life treatin' you?" she asked out of the blue.

"Fine," I said. "How's it treatin' you?"

"Can't complain."

"Why do you ask?"

"Just curious," she said. "I just wanna know how you're holding up."

"Well, I'm doing just fine, just dandy."

"Well, that's good to know," Tamara said, and turned away, toward the window.

We finally headed out about an hour later.

Seva got into a groove. He said he knew the way by heart and getting us home would be a snap. The first obstacle was this big hill. It took forever. The Volga kept stalling and rolling back—at which point the locals would surround our clunker and push it till it got going again. Eventually we managed to crawl out of the valley and started bouncing along a dirt road studded with bricks, red and firm like pine roots. Some time later, we stopped.

"We come out down here, right?" Seva asked us, doubting himself.

"You sure about that?" I asked. "This doesn't look right to me."

Tamara sighed anxiously; the presbyter waved his hand list-lessly, seemingly saying, "It shall be as God wills it. Go wherever your heart desires. If need be, we'll start gathering the harvest and they'll find us eventually." Seva took his advice, listened to his heart, and veered onto another gap in the corn that only faintly resembled a road. He stepped on the gas and we moved into the cornfields, where we lost ourselves. Dry leaves rubbed up against the bumpers, tangled around the windshield wipers, and crept in through the open windows. The cornstalks were crackling grimly. The smell of warm death permeated the fields and found its way into the car. We all flew up in the air when we hit yet another pot-hole. Tamara's hand landed on mine, but she pulled it away quickly. Maybe even too quickly. I tried taking it back, but she snatched it away decisively and wiggled as far away from me as she could manage. The journey was long, slow, and hopeless. Typical for a ride through cornfields.

But we weren't lost. Seva, perhaps accidentally, perhaps inten-tionally, got us out of the golden thicket, and we found ourselves on the right road. The only problem was that we didn't know which way to go. We thought for a bit and then turned right, following the sun. Nobody was talking. Tamara's sighs got more dejected with each passing mile, while the presbyter kept trying to get the radio to work—the problem being that our antenna, out of its depth, was gasping for signal in those rolling hills, like a scuba diver with an empty tank. Seva, seeing the presbyter struggling, leaned toward him to start flipping the dials too. It seemed that he had completely forgotten about the road, only casting an occasional lazy glance at it . . . before, of course, desperately slamming on the brakes, responding to some half-seen movement up ahead. I flew into the front of the car. The presbyter had slid under the seat. Tamara let out a piercing cry somewhere above me. It was Tolik, standing in the middle of the road, his hand bandaged and yesterday's Milan jacket over his shoulders. He stood there, smiling at us like we were old friends.

"Hey Herman, you guys asleep at the wheel?" he asked after I'd gone over to talk to him.

My traveling companions were still in the car—Tamara was crying, pretty shaken up by the near miss, while Seva was characteristically impassive, and the presbyter was whispering some hymns about submariners and pilots to himself.

"Tolik," I said, seeing the reflected sun floating across his glass eye, "what are you doing dicking around in the middle of the road? We could have run you over."

Tolik merely cackled in reply. He had corn silk stuck in his long hair and his bandaged hand was bleeding.

"What's up with your hand?"

"It's nothing," he said nonchalantly. "I was out shooting yesterday, and my piece kicks like a mule, it nicked my hand a little. I came back in the morning, but you were already gone. I taped up my hand and headed out to look for you."

"But why?"

"Herman, the thing is . . . well, let's just say it's good that I caught up with you guys. We gotta talk."

"You couldn't have just called?"

"I don't have any fuckin' bars out here," Tolik said, seeming more and more restless. "You know that!"

"What'd you wanna talk about?"

"Your soccer player friend called."

"Injured?"

"Yeah, Injured. He was trying to get hold of you. At first he called her," Tolik said, nodding in the direction of the car, which I assumed meant Tamara. "You don't have a fuckin' phone. Well, and you guys had already left. So, he called me, asking for you."

"Couldn't he wait for me to get home? Did you tell him we'd be back in the evening?"

"I told him, Herman. He said it'd be best for you not to come back for a few days."

"What do you mean 'not come back'?"

"I mean, don't go home without calling him first."

"What happened at the station?"

"He wouldn't say. Actually, he said you should give him a call. Then he'll tell you what's up. Just make sure you call, all right?"

"All right. You got a phone?"

"Well, yeah. But, you know, I just don't have any bars out here. Come over to our place."

"To your place?" I asked, with a wince. "They're gonna start drinking again," I said, nodding toward the car. "Let's figure something else out."

"You're the boss. He wants you to call him ASAP. He said you've got some problems."

"Damn. Where else can you get reception around here?"

"You can drive over to the farmers' place," Tolik said after a second's thought. "Just don't tell them you know us."

"And where do they live?"

"Over there," he pointed out into no-man's-land, "on top of the hill. You'll see."

"Maybe you can take us there?"

"You think I'm fuckin' nuts?" he said, laughing. "Anyway, I'll see ya."

"See ya," I said, shaking his hand and heading back to the car.

"Hey," he called out behind me before I made it more than a few steps. "This is for you," Tolik said, coming up to me and handing me an odd-looking object. "Electric scissors. Top quality, Bosch ones. There's no warranty on them, though."

"Thanks. I don't need any warranties. I'll have them blessed instead."

"Good idea," Tolik said, waving to everyone and disappearing into the shifting haze of corn.

"What was that?" Tamara asked.

"I don't really know how to break this to you," I began, speaking to the presbyter more than her. "Long story short, I've got some problems on my hands. I have to make a call."

"Okay, go for it," Tamara said, taking out her pink Nokia.

"There's no reception here. That's part of the problem."

"And it can't wait?" the presbyter asked.

"It can't wait, Father," I assured him.

"What now?"

"Let's head up to the farmers' place."

The presbyter remained silent for a bit, engrossed in his thoughts.

"Well, all right," he said finally. "Let's go if we're going."

We turned around and headed up the hill. The sun rolled out in the opposite direction.

★

A deserted and disquieting landscape, churned by tractor wheels— dry, black earth, low-hanging skies spread out like a map of a theater of war, garages facing east like churches and their grated windows facing west, paralyzed combines, and the remains of agricultural equipment, muddy and red as beef. There wasn't a living soul in sight—no farmers, not a single person. What looked like a jackal but was probably a dog came around the corner of one of the buildings, ran across black earth saturated in fuel oil, sniffing assiduously. Then he quickly darted back, startled by something. He looked around and ran off in the other direction. I figured there must have been someone standing around that corner—somebody who had knocked that jackal-dog off course.

We pulled into a bumpy, black-smeared lot, and Seva shut off the engine. It was quiet. Spooky. It seemed we'd wound up somewhere we weren't supposed to go. I held Tamara's Nokia in my hand and flipped it open. A shape flashed in front of the car, but we couldn't get a good look at it.

"Someone's out there," Tamara said, frightened.

"Maybe another dog," Seva suggested.

The presbyter, possibly already regretting that he had agreed to take this detour, remained silent. The Nokia reported that there was indeed reception up here. I tried to remember Injured's number. "But how could you remember it if you never knew it in the first place?" I asked myself. And then, "Look, what are you getting so worked up over, anyway?" Out of the corner of my eye I saw other shadows scurrying from one garage to another. Evidently, Tamara noticed them too.

"Let's get out of here," she said quietly.

"Just give me a sec. Could you dial Injured's number for me?"

Somebody was standing behind one of the combines. I could feel eyes on me.

"Come on already." Tamara snatched the Nokia out of my hand and started looking for Injured's number.

"I just saw someone back there," the presbyter said, nodding at the rearview window. "Now he's gone."

I checked. Nobody. Except the dog again. He was leaving the area, crossing the lot. He clearly knew better than to come back in our direction.

"How's it going?" I asked, leaning toward Tamara.

"It's ringing," she said, apparently relieved. "Here."

I reached clumsily for the phone, but wound up knocking it right out of Tamara's trembling hand. It went down somewhere between our feet. I leaned over to try and fish it back out.

"Herman," I heard the presbyter say. His voice had gotten strange.

Finally finding the cell, I looked up and found everyone staring apprehensively at the rearview mirror. Four men were standing silently behind the car, keeping a close eye on us. I shut the cell phone and stuffed it into my pocket. Tamara squeezed my elbow, gesturing for me to follow her gaze. Three other men, also quiet, also examining us intently—as though trying to read the tiny names etched into the stone marking a mass grave for fallen soldiers—were now standing right in front of the car. The dog too was back after all, hunched over, scowling, behind them. Well, I got the picture. It smelled like we were in some deep shit. Fuel oil, too.

The farmers looked like a biker gang—beards, dirty looks, and implicit threats. Some of them were decked out in black track-suits and leather jackets; others were in camo and leather dress shirts. One guy had a red bandanna, another was wearing sun-glasses, and a third farmer wore a tattered sheepskin coat over his bare chest; yet another, who seemed to occupy a position of prominence, standing out in front, was holding a rusty metal rod, tossing it between his big, meaty hands. After a few moments of this, he suddenly wound up and slammed the rod into the hood of the Volga. Metal rang like church bells on Easter. Seva hopped right out of the car in reply; the presbyter followed him, neither of them even bothering to shut the doors behind them. Tamara yanked firmly at my sleeve, hanging on for dear life.

"Calm down," I told her, feeling for her cell phone in my one pocket and the Bosch electric scissors and old screwdriver in the other. "Just calm down."

Seva was standing across from three farmers, trying to say something. They were eyeing him scornfully, like a pack of preda-tors. They weren't so much listening to him as waiting for a reason to mash him up and mix him in with the fuel oil.

Seva eventually managed to stammer out a question to the farmer with the rod: "What do you think you're doing, anyway?"

"I do what I want," he said, wiping his hands on his leather pants.

"Well, what the fuck are you wrecking my car for?" Seva asked, trying to sound stern.

"Well, I could wreck you instead," the farmer answered, stepping forward, his fat belly gradually edging into Seva's personal space. Two other guys moved to positions on Seva's left and right.

"Hold on there for just a second." the presbyter said, seemingly waking from a trance.

The three farmers threatening Seva stopped and spared the presbyter a glance.

"There's no reason for violence," he continued in a conciliatory tone. "We were just on our way back from a wedding. I'm the presbyter. We decided to stop by your place to . . ."

"You're a presbyter?" the farmer in leather asked. "Where were you coming from?"

"From over there," the presbyter said, pointing to the east, "from the border."

"There aren't any churches over there," the fat guy said, tossing the rod from his right hand to his left.

"You don't need a church to get married," the presbyter replied.

"You Baptists or something?" the leather one asked.

"Shtundists," one of his friends suggested.

The farmers' faces got even grimmer.

"Fine," said the guy with the rod. "Let's go have a talk with our agronomist. You'll tell him all about your church."

"Actually," the presbyter said, still trying to be as diplomatic as possible, "we have to get going. We don't want to keep our friends waiting."

"Hey," the rod man replied, "they can wait a bit. Now you're going to have a talk with our agronomist. Got it?"

"All right then," the presbyter said feebly.

"Do you have any phones on you?" he asked.

"Huh?" went Seva, sounding rather dense.

"Give us your phones," the rod man barked.

"You're not for real, are you?" Seva asked. It was all the resistance he had left in him.

The farmer's reply was to grip the rod with both hands and strike Seva with it right in the stomach, folding him up like a lawn chair. The presbyter was about to dash over to help him up, I think, but one of the farmers cut him off. I bolted out of the car to help, and Tamara slid out behind me, but we were immediately surrounded by the four men who had been standing behind the car. A short, young farmer with some sort of punkish Mohawk, wielding this season's tire iron, was standing closest to us. I stopped, making sure I was between him and Tamara.

"Give us your phones," the rod man ordered Seva once again.

Seva took out his cell and handed it over. One of the farmers hopped in the Volga, took the keys out of the ignition, and put them in his pocket.

"Now give us *your* phone," the farmer said, pressing the rod up against the presbyter's chest.

"I don't have one," the presbyter replied timidly.

"How do you keep in touch with your congregation then? And check them, too," he told the punk, pointing at Tamara and me.

"Hey," the punk said, eager to get at Tamara. "Give us your phones."

Tamara let out a frightened squeal.

"Take it easy," I said, intercepting his hand. "She doesn't have a phone on her."

"You lookin' for trouble, tough guy?"

"Are you?" I asked, sticking my hand in my pocket and grasping the electric scissors.

The punk could see I had something in there. He decided not to risk it.

"Fine, whatever you say. What about you? You got a phone on you?"

"You wanna search me?" I asked him.

"Fuck that. I don't need your shit," the punk replied. "Vlad!" he yelled over to the chubby guy, "all clear over here."

"Well then," Vlad replied. "Shall we?"

He gave Seva's cell to the punk and took the lead. We followed him, leaving the Volga empty and open out in the middle of those black, well-trodden pits. I started walking, thinking to myself, "Phone, please don't ring, please, don't ring." The dog sniffed each wheel, his fur soaking up the October sun.

★

We passed the garages, went around the combines, and found ourselves next to a big cinder-block warehouse. There were a few more farmers hanging around by the door. Seeing us, they all started talking at the same time.

"Well Vlad, you've got some hostages?" shouted one of them, tall and bald and wearing a long leather jacket.

"Let's lock them up in the garage—the rats will have a feast," suggested another farmer, short and wearing glasses and a heavy, leather cap, domed on top and with a visor; it made him look like a sunflower.

"What about just burying them out in the cornfields," a third farmer, wearing a leather jacket and some crappy jeans, chimed in.

"All right, all right," said Vlad, who was evidently the voice of reason around here. "Is Kotovsky in?"

"Yep," went the lanky guy.

"How's he been doing?" Vlad asked warily.

"Fuckin' shitty," the sunflower guy answered.

"He's been hurting," the crappy jeans guy confirmed.

"Well, we're gonna go see him anyway," Vlad said, shoving them aside and opening up the doors to let us in.

This was clearly their headquarters. The wallpaper was nailed on, but it was drooping down or peeling off in many places, like flags lowered to half-mast to mark some tragedy. Up against the walls were long benches covered in old rugs and goatskins, and there were more farmers sitting or lying on them, as though they were anticipating something, hoping to hear some good news. Winter clothes such as pea coats and furs were heaped in a corner. A small window let in too little light, and the room was full of the harsh yellow hum of electricity. By the far wall, across from the door we'd come in, there was a desk cluttered with papers and disposable dishware. A guy with sharp, unshaven features and a strange, contorted smile was sitting behind it. He had a leather jacket wrapped around his shoulders and a knockoff Armani sweater underneath. Other farmers, one of them wearing an artificial leather jacket and the other a heavy leather police officer's hat, hovered over him. There was no way he could be a cop, though, because his fists were colored with blue prison tattoos. When he saw us, the guy's face contorted even more. Vlad ordered us to stand by the door and headed over to the desk. The farmers were watching us from every direction, just in case we tried to pull anything.

"Kotovsky," Vlad said, fiddling with the rod as he spoke. "We caught them down by the garages. They say they were on their way home from church. They're Shtundists. They were coming from over by the border."

Kotovsky looked at us apathetically.

"Grisha," he said, "you see what these Shtundists are up to? We gotta take 'em out."

"No fuckin' way, Grisha," the man in the artificial leather jacket disagreed. "We'll get busted. Let's take them over to the garage and keep them there for a bit. Maybe then they'll start talking."

"Start talking about what?" the tattooed guy asked. "What do you want them to tell you? We gotta take them out and torch their car."

"Grisha," the man in the jacket continued stubbornly, "why the fuck should we go around torching cars? You guys are a bunch of fuckin' clowns. Let's keep them in the garage until tomorrow, and see if they start talking then."

"No fuckin' way," the tattooed man insisted.

"I'm telling you," the man in the artificial leather jacket insisted just as strongly.

"Listen," the presbyter tried interjecting, taking a step forward before a farmer grabbed him by the collar, as if to say, "Don't interrupt when farmers are talking business."

"Kotovsky," the rod man volunteered, "We gotta do something. Soon enough their friends are gonna go looking for them, and they'll definitely be coming by our place."

"All we gotta do is take them out," the tattooed guy said, clenching his fists, making the ink on his fingers stand out even more.

Kotovsky sighed heavily. The guy in the artificial leather jacket, knowing what was going on, opened up one of the desk drawers and took out a bottle. The edge of Kotovsky's mouth grazed the bottle, and he attempted to pour some vodka down his gullet through a funnel. The alcohol started trickling down his face, however, and none of it seemed to go down his throat. After another sigh, Kotovsky kicked back in his swivel chair, giving the bottle back to the man in the jacket.

"What's wrong with him?" the presbyter asked Vlad.

"He's hurting," he answered coldly. "Can't you see that?"

"Paralysis?"

"You're paralysis!" Vlad said, in a schoolyard-comeback tone. "They busted up his jaw. Can't you see that? We had a run-in with your Shtundist clan over by the border. Someone thumped him real good with the butt of a sawed-off."

"I even know who it was," I thought.

"Give me a sec," the presbyter said, and took off for the desk once again. The farmers tried holding him back, but the presbyter fended them off: "Hold your horses!" he barked. He out-maneuvered Vlad, who looked dumbfounded, easily pushed past the tattooed guy, and leaned over Kotovsky, who stared up at the presbyter with a doomed expression on his face but maintained his tough façade.

Seeing this, the farmers on the benches all stood up, gravitated toward the desk, and readied themselves to rip the presbyter to shreds if he dared harm a hair on their dear Kotovsky's head. Vlad wanted to pull the presbyter back, but Kotovsky raised his hand and Vlad stopped, keeping his rod at the ready.

The presbyter put one hand on Kotovsky's head, leaned in, and touched his busted jaw delicately with the other. Kotovsky trembled slightly. Vlad seemed to be trembling along with him.

"Does this hurt?" the presbyter asked Kotovsky. The latter moaned faintly. "The thing is," the presbyter continued, "people don't even know what their bodies are capable of. We consider the body a fixed entity—something given to us at birth that we can't change. Consequently, we view any ailment as some sort of irreversible disaster that takes away the most important thing in our lives—harmony with oneself. However, the body is an instrument in the Lord's hands. The Lord calls forth magnificent sounds by pressing invisible keys. Like this." The presbyter pushed hard on Kotovsky's jaw, which clicked and fell into place. Kotovsky didn't know what hit him.

The presbyter stepped aside and took a self-satisfied look at his handiwork. Kotovsky touched his jaw sheepishly, opened his mouth, and started inhaling greedily. Absolutely mesmerized, the farmers' glances shifted back and forth between the presbyter and Kotovsky.

"Listen," the presbyter said, giving them no time to come to their senses, "I wanted to say something to you." He turned toward us. "You go on ahead, I'll catch up."

"Father," Seva replied, dumbfounded. "What about you?"

"I'll catch up, don't you worry," the presbyter repeated, more assertively. "Go back to the car."

I made for the door. The punk, standing behind me, peered at

Kotovsky inquisitively, but the latter nodded apathetically, as if to say, "Whatever. Let them go. Quit it with all the tough-guy shit." Leading Tamara out with me, I went back into the open air. Seva followed us. As we were leaving I noticed the farmers forming a tight circle around the presbyter. I would have darted back inside, but the presbyter was watching us leave, calmly and graciously, encouraging us to keep going. The punk squeezed through the doorway with us. Flustered and irritated, he didn't bother answering the other farmers' questions as he led us back to the Volga.

The sun had set on the other side of the garages, its harsh, farewell glare reflected in the moat of black fuel oil around us. We walked over to the car. Seva popped open the hood and started taking stock of the damage as Tamara took a seat in the back. I flopped onto my seat too. The punk was standing next to Seva, evidently not knowing what to do with himself anymore.

"Are you sure they aren't going to do anything bad to him in there?" Tamara asked quietly.

"Don't you worry," I said. "Everything's going to be all right."

"Thanks for sticking up for me," she continued. "I was so scared."

"Don't mention it."

The punk came over to Seva and started poking around under the hood as well. I took out Tamara's phone while he was otherwise occupied. I flipped it open and found the last number dialed. I hit the green button, and it began to ring.

"Hello."

"Injured, it's me. Can you hear me?" I was trying to keep quiet so the punk wouldn't catch on.

"Herman," Injured said. "Speak up."

"I can't talk any louder. What's going on back at the station?"

"Herman," Injured shouted, "they came around looking for you this morning."

"Who?"

"I don't know. They weren't the police, I can tell you that. They were in civilian clothes. They came by in the morning and were asking tons of questions."

"What'd you say?"

"I said that you'd gone to see your brother, and I didn't know when you'd be getting back."

"What'd they say?"

"They said they'd come by again, and that they really needed to talk to you. Then they drove down into town, Herman."

"So what should I do now?"

"Stay away from the station. I think they'll be coming back soon. It'd be better for you to go someplace a few more days. Lay low until it all blows over."

"Where am I supposed to go?"

"Dammit Herman, you can go anywhere you damn well please!" Injured snapped. And then, "Okay, okay. Sorry. When are you supposed to be getting back?"

"Don't know. Late tonight sometime."

"Give me a call when you're getting close," Injured said. "Get them to drop you off by the tracks and walk over to the train station. I'll be there waiting for you. I'll bring you your dough and your passport."

"Thanks, Injured."

"Don't mention it." And his voice clicked off.

"What was that all about?" Tamara asked.

"Just some problems at work," I said.

Time seemed to be dragging on, as though catching on all the garage roofs and agricultural machinery on its way past. It was already dark, and the air was brisk. I was almost nodding off when I saw the dog, wagging his loyal tail, run out from behind one of the nearby structures. Behind him came the presbyter, taking powerful strides behind the animal, and after him a pack of farmers followed. The presbyter reached the car and waved to everyone. "Let's go!" Seva said cheerfully. One of the farmers came over and gave him back the car keys. The farmers all looked a bit confused, actually—shifting from foot to foot, coughing awkwardly, not saying anything.

Seva slammed the hood shut and walked up to the punk.

"My cell," he said decisively.

The punk was getting a bit flustered.

"Gimme my cell," Seva repeated.

The punk cast a sweeping glance at his friends. Failing to rally any kind of support, he took Seva's cell phone out of his pocket sheepishly. Seva took back his property, got behind the wheel, started the car up, and put the pedal to the metal, taking a victory lap around the farmers before rolling out of their greasy settlement.

★

Once we were in the clear and the cornstalks were rattling against the sides of the car again, I leaned in toward the presbyter.

"You doing all right?" I asked.

"Yep, everything's just fine," he answered cheerfully.

"What were you guys talking about for so long?"

"Ah, nothing really," he said lightly. "About the roads we must walk. About the divine providence that guides us along our journey. But mostly we talked about the latest agricultural reforms."

"Nah, for real—what were you actually talking about?"

"Herman, your time will come—you will find the answers you seek," the presbyter told me, taking a Zippo lighter out of one pocket and a clean handkerchief out of the other. He wrapped the lighter carefully and tucked it away into his pocket.

Then he dozed off as if he didn't have a care in the world.

★

The air was as black and stony as anthracite coal. Our headlights flushed the road with thick, golden rays; foxes were running out of the fields, their eyes giving out a brief, frightened twinkle before fading dejectedly away. As for Seva's eyes, he kept them fixed on the crumbling road, and the presbyter was still snoozing peacefully in the front seat next to him. Gradually, I felt Tamara's hand slide up my leg. I looked at it—Tamara's hand, I mean—but she turned away and started staring intently out the window. It was as if she wasn't even in the car, as if she wasn't the one riding along with us, as if it wasn't her hand moving resolutely to undo my belt and buttons, to slip underneath my T-shirt, as if those weren't her rings burning my stomach with cold and danger, and as if those weren't her long, sharp nails touching my skin, scaring and exciting me. I tensed up, though the men in front seemed entirely oblivious. The infamous Tamara, on the other hand, hadn't forgotten a thing—she remembered all her old tricks, clutching me and inching up my leg, slow and steady. Her hand held me firmly, not letting me exhale or relax at all. It was as though she was afraid I was on the verge of breaking loose and escaping from her. I heard her breathing and felt her hand shaking, either due to fatigue or to the mounting tension. But it kept moving, continuing to perform its mechanical work and pouring all of its energy and tenderness into its task. She still wasn't looking at me—she was searching for something in the darkness; she saw something out there. She was with me, yet she also somewhere far away; I couldn't reach her, couldn't tell her to keep going, to maintain her rhythm no matter what. I wanted to tell her to push on for just a little longer— then she'd be able to rest. But every time I wanted to tell her to keep it up, she'd seem to freeze, as though on purpose, to catch her breath and then let some hot air out of her lungs. Those few seconds were just enough for me to cool off. Then it'd start back up again; she'd have to start all over again, continuing her exhausting act of love. Her rings had warmed up. Now she was moaning almost inaudibly; she turned to me at last, staring at me for what seemed like ages. This was it—this time there was no stopping her, because we had to put an end to all of this. How much longer could we hold out? We had to put an end to this, otherwise we would die from exhaustion and desire. A moment before putting an end to it, after she felt that she'd reached her goal, she laid her hand gently over my mouth, so that nobody would hear me. After that she ran her damp hand along my stomach in a sweet caress, breathing softly. Then she turned back to the window to observe the falling stars that lit up the dry corn.

3

To my left I could see the dark wombs of the railroad sheds, pumped with blackness pure as oil. Lampposts sliced through the gloom, filling the air with sparks that flew in every direction, lighting up the windows and the metal components of the trains. Railroad sidings stretched out to my right, leading to dead ends in grass that was yellow from the diesel and tracks that were black from the smoke. Apartment complexes started a bit farther down—a kingdom of alcoholics and petty crime. I could hear some loud music mixed with dogs barking and locomotives roaring. A train loaded with Donbas coal rolled on by, heading north. The air smelled of rain and wet stones. I put the collar of my jacket up and headed down the tracks, escaping the industrial zone and moving toward where the station's lights burned in the darkness.

Injured was sitting in his car parked by the station sleeping soundly, his head cocked back. I hid behind some trees, scampered by, and then hopped in the car. Injured woke up and looked at me with obvious interest.

"What's with the getup?" he asked.

"This suit? It's Kocha's."

"Get changed," Injured advised me. "I brought you your stuff," he said, pointing at the back seat. "Here's your passport and dough. The Donetsk train will be leaving in an hour. Take the economy-class car—there'll be more people there."

"And where am I going?"

"Get off at the last stop, I guess. My brother will meet you in Donetsk. Tell him you've come to pick up the car. Just lay low this weekend."

"Injured, what do I have to hide out for, anyway?"

"Do you know what they want?"

"No."

"Me neither. So it's time for a little weekend getaway. And hey, I'll get a little break from you, too."

"Where's Olga?" I asked, ignoring his jab. "Maybe she knows something we don't."

"She doesn't," Injured said. "I asked her."

"Maybe we should tell Kocha's relatives?"

"What could they do? Herman, this is some real serious shit. At least I think it is. People don't just go around torching gas tankers for kicks, and with one of us in it, no less."

"All right then," I agreed. "I'll ride in the economy-class car. I'm gonna get changed, okay?"

"Go for it," Injured replied, looking away.

★

The chilly October air became denser; voices seemed to bounce right off it, as off an invisible surface and ricochet back into the darkness, echoing until they disintegrated. The train station attendant made announcement after announcement over the PA system, reading off messages, telling passengers to be careful while boarding, informing them about delays, and repeating route numbers, but all her efforts were in vain, everything she said was incomprehensible, just syllables spilling out of the speaker like bird poop, frightening the passengers more than enlightening them. I stood on the platform in the shadow cast by the main building, wary of staying inside yet unwilling to risk venturing out into the open, where someone might see me. I looked at the floodlights burning through the black fabric of this October night, observed the silhouettes of the railroad employees from afar, watching them disappear behind the crossing on the other side of the tracks, overhearing their jargon. Meanwhile, I kept asking myself, "Who came looking for me? Who suddenly needed to have a talk with me? Maybe it was one of my brother's guys? But why didn't they say so? And if it was the corn guys, then what are they up to now?" And so I felt the calm, peaceful pattern of the last few months being wrenched apart, and everything was suddenly back to normal, or what passes for normal these days. I guess life didn't want anyone taking it by the horns, after all. "This is some tangled business," I thought, as my train finally rolled into the station. Tangled like the grass between the railroad ties.

★

The car was half-empty. My fellow riders were mostly shady salesman types who had thrown canvas bags stuffed with priceless Chinese-made goods right on the floor, then sprawled out on top of them. The train's wheels were squeaking like park swings: it rolled on for a time, then stopped and reversed, as though it had forgotten something. After a bit of this, though, it started pushing forward again.

As for me, I'd curled up in a quiet corner between the sales-men's bags and various boxes of cold meat that stank of death. I settled in, peering out a window at the black swaying of the tree branches and the heavy mass of the moon tumbling across the Donetsk railroad. The autumn air, permeated by the smell of vegetables, was kind enough to allow freight and passenger trains alike to pass through it, gracing them with a ripe scent, the ripe scent of decay, and driving a dry, eastern wind through them. The train was at last gaining momentum after a stop and retreat at yet another crossing, where lights nearly unable to bear the weight of the darkness above them shone in on us through the windows. We were rushing now into the inexpressible blackness, before the train decided to stop dead again, rattling its metal body and awak-ening the already restless dealers in dead animals.

I was just on the verge of falling asleep when we braked at a small, two-platform station. There was the usual pre-departure hustle and bustle under the lampposts. I crawled out from among the boxes of death and stepped into the vestibule. I stuck my head through the broken window. Some men in uniform were walk-ing along the platform, coming from the front of the train. There were three of them. The man out front was holding an AK, the other two were tucked in behind him. Their stride was purposeful and swift, yet unhurried, as though they knew where they were going and what for. When a loud alarm sliced through the silence, though, announcing our imminent departure, the cops got nervous all at once, running up to the nearest train car and banging on its locked doors, which were opened almost immediately. Something told me that they had been waiting for me on this God-forsaken platform—somebody might have tipped them off, or maybe it was just dumb luck. Three train cars separated us, three whole minutes for them to cross. The train was about to head out. Once it left the station, I'd have no way out. I tried opening the exterior door. It wouldn't budge. I found the lock in the darkness, slid it aside, and tried the door again. Success—I hopped down onto the asphalt, and just in time: the train set off almost immediately afterward, crawling away and leaving me to fend for myself. After the last car passed by, I noticed that there was another train, consisting of just three dark and mysterious cars, parked by the second platform. There wasn't a single sound coming from over there, not a single ray of light emerging from its silent innards. "That's odd," I thought to myself. "Who travels on a train like that?"

The train I had just hopped out of stopped a bit farther down the tracks. Once again, screeching metal disrupted the nighttime silence. I saw the cars freeze for a second and then begin rolling back, slowly, toward the station and me. I panicked: I had to make myself scarce. I turned toward the station building and suddenly saw a stream of light flooding the darkness, headlights coming out of the night and approaching the platform. The train cars were already parked by the first platform. Now there were voices and footsteps everywhere—three train station employees rounded the corner of the station building, running toward the train carrying heavy-looking cardboard boxes. One of the men was visibly struggling with his load, his three boxes cutting into his hands. Seeing the dark train parked at the platform, they picked up the pace. The first two men hopped down onto the tracks, scurrying over to the second platform and scampering along beside the unmoving ghost cars. The third man, still holding his three boxes, couldn't muster up the courage to dip under the train, so he stopped for a second. At which point he caught sight of me.

"Hey, give me a hand here, buddy," he said.

I ran over and took one of the boxes out of his arms. I heard a clink inside. "Ah, he's got some booze in there. Champagne or dry wine," I thought.

Meanwhile, the guy hopped down onto the railroad ties and was trying to duck under the train like his friends. I hopped down after him. The green, dusty hunk of metal had already been set in motion, but right then we popped out onto the other side and were now running alongside its black windows, dodging all of the dangerous traps set for us by the ministry of railways.

The doors of the last ghost car were open. The guys with the boxes tossed them on board and hopped in. I gave the last guy a boost, then grabbed my box and followed him onto the train. I found all three of them standing there in a dark corridor with doors on both sides, leading to the train's compartments. The car attendant's compartment was open, but no one was inside; on the other hand, a tough-looking guy with a scowling, bashed-up face and a handgun in a shoulder holster, most likely a security guard, emerged from the void. He nodded at one of the guys as if to say "Come with me." The first sleeper compartment in the car was open too. The tough guy with the gun stepped inside, and we started squeezing our way in behind him. We placed the boxes on the top bunks. I was the last one to slip in—there wasn't much room in there. I tossed my load on top, not knowing what to do next. I stepped back and wound up in the dark corridor.

"Close the door," the security guard said.

And one of the men did so, softly, right in front of my face, leaving me out in the corridor all by myself. I could hear their voices nonetheless. They had evidently forgotten about me. We were passing another train; I saw some shadows whip by the nearest window, some lights burning through the darkness, some footsteps resonating in the vestibule between the cars. I headed down the corridor, away from the closed door. It was an odd car, with no sign of life. The sleeping compartments were open and packed with stuff. There was a Xerox machine in one, on the table, and some binding machines, as well as heaps of heavy paper, were resting on the bottom bunks. The next compartment was stuffed with bunches of newspapers and magazines, all covered with a camo net. The rest of them were closed. I walked down to the last one and slid the door to the side as softly as I could manage. I stepped inside and locked myself in—the voices from the other end of the car were getting closer, most notably the guard's. He was asking the guys who'd been carrying the boxes about something. "Maybe he's asking about me," I thought. I could hear the guard moving down the corridor and checking the sleeper compartments as he went. He would get to me in just a moment or two. "Why now?" I asked myself. He tried yanking open the door to the compartment next to mine, but it turned out to be locked, as it was apparently supposed to be. He came up to my compartment and tried the door, but it wouldn't budge. He made one more attempt at opening it. The compartment was securely locked.

"Good to go," the security guard said to himself. The sound of his heavy, resolute footsteps started fading down the corridor.

The voices disappeared and complete silence descended. I lay down on the bottom bunk, closing my eyes and plummeting into green pits of sleep.

★

It seemed like dark beasts covered in prickly fur with flashlights in their skulls and hot nighttime breath steaming from their mouths were peering through the curtained windows of my compartment as they passed, blinding and intimidating me.

The light that would occasionally flood in, like plaster filling up a mold, submerging my eyes in its abrasive liquid before disappearing almost immediately, leaving the surrounding blackness looking as thick as pond water. The ghost train on which I'd so improbably wound up had been rolling down the tracks for the past few hours, slowly but surely, in who knew what direction, taking me farther and farther from the events of the last two days. What would I remember from this trip? The mixture of glare and darkness, the aftertaste of autumn air, and the sensation of my skin being touched. It felt as though I had been riding along that well-traveled route for a hundred years, taking refuge in deep, secret chambers to keep hidden from predators' hungry eyes. It was like I was holding my breath in someone else's closet, my head resting on my knees, with fancy suits and fur coats, untouched since last winter, hovering over me in the dark like cow carcasses in a meat locker. I felt protected by the clothes hanging above me, permeated with other people's smells, luring me closer and scaring me away at the same time. Voices and songs echoed in my head, looping and returning . . . all the hymns they sang, all their toasts, their goodwill, their secrets and revelations: all those miraculous people, all their peculiar circumstances—why should I have cared about their struggles, about their attempts to stand their ground? And why should they have cared about my problems, helping me to escape, to hide? Whoever we are, we're always moving along our own routes, finding ourselves in foreign lands, reaching beyond the curtains of our own experience; everyone we meet along the way remains in our memory, their every word and every touch. Even if I never get out of this train compartment, even if I have to spend the rest of my days on this bunk, caught in this trap of walls and rails, nobody will ever be able to take away my memories of what I had seen—not such a bad deal, all things considered.

★

Closets looked like aquariums and they had a musty smell. Oddly enough, the smell of ironed dress shirts was somehow overwhelmed by the smell of store shelves, just like the smell of life is overwhelmed by the smell of death. My best childhood memories are the ones where death gives way to life. Then those thoughts vanished, along with the old, worn clothing in the closet. "Why was I thinking about a closet during this particular trip, still feeling a sense of alarm and excitement?" The past was blinding me like lampposts casting their light into the dark corners of train cars.

Back in the day, during what felt like another life, I experienced many different things—and they may have always been there in the back of my mind as I tried to understand how danger and satisfaction could come together in one lump at the back of my throat. The woman I was thinking about was older than me—though, actually, maybe it'd be better to say I was much younger than her. How old was I then? Fourteen or so. Pretty much just a kid. But someone had planned our itinerary; somebody made sure I was in the right place at the right time—I don't even remember how I got there, anymore. It was just one of those insignificant instances; life is full of them. I had to give someone something, or tell someone something, or bring someone some books, or something like that. It went something like this; she was sorting through some old clothes in a closet, spreading her parents' things across the floor and stepping over her mom's fancy dresses like the banners of a defeated adversary. When I came by she asked me to wait for a bit. I took a seat on the couch, carefully observing her as she bent over her parents' coats and dresses, taking out their suits and hats, stepping over them with her bare feet, a whole haze of unfamiliar smells and images flashing by. We barely even talked, but as she was seeing me out, she touched my shoulder in a particular way—as though she was pushing me away from herself and all of that clutter spread out on the floor, but drawing me in at the same time. But that isn't the real story; the story came some time later. Ever since our first meeting, I had been absolutely convinced that something was going to happen. She wouldn't have been stepping over her parents' yellow and red dress shirts so carefully, her hands wouldn't have been so hot when she was touching my shoulder if something wasn't going to happen. Her hands were hot again when we wound up sitting next to each other on a nighttime Ikarus bus heading from who knows where to who knows where. The boisterous kids riding along with us couldn't seem to settle down—they were passing spirits and apples down the aisle, yelling over each other, shouting curses and confessions into the summer night. Our merry bunch, all the neighborhood kids, was coming back from some celebration: there was the gold of the evening suburbs, the pine trees, the night wrapped up in black, the cool air pushing through the open hatches, and somewhere in the middle of this darkness she put her head on my shoulder, pretending to be asleep, the oldest trick in the book. As was usual for me, it didn't look like it was going anywhere, but suddenly her hand slid underneath my shirt, and all of this without her so much as opening her eyes. I tried sliding my hand under her sweater, but she removed it with a tired yet definitive movement, letting me know who was going to pleasure whom; I, naturally, had no objections. She was a grown woman with soft skin and green, sensible eyes. She was wearing a sweater and jeans, and she'd had her experiences and would have her own future— it just so happened that I was lucky enough to fall in between the two, however accidentally. Later on I would think about how life is made up of such things, of older women's adept and passionate movements that turn luckless kids from the outskirts of town into men; they taught us how to love, so we wouldn't think that life consists of nothing but struggle and vengeance. Over the years, there were moments when we had to stand up for them, our older women, protect them from the passage of time. We couldn't retreat or desert them when they were really down in the dumps. I don't know whether the majority of us actually realized what we were doing when we enjoyed their devotion; most of the time we didn't feel as though we were doing anything special, and we'd quickly forget about it. Nobody paid particular attention to their relationships with women; they were consumed with the task of understanding their relationships with life and death. Nobody knew that women *are* life and death. Neither did I, not yet, —but I realized that important and serious things were happening, and that neither the lethargic animals peering into our windows with flashlights in their heads, nor my friends who would occasionally call out my name during my dream, nor my complete immobility and utter helplessness could negate the importance of those things. Because nobody could deny the importance of becoming a man. We had to make sure we stayed still, we had to make sure we didn't wake anyone up, and most importantly we had to make sure we didn't wake her up.

I wonder what Tamara was up to back then.

★

I forced myself to get up and step out of my compartment. A thick blanket of fog had settled outside, the morning sunlight barely poking through it. I walked down the corridor, stepped into the vestibule, opened up the door, walked through, and found myself in the next car. The light was harsh. I shielded my eyes with my hand.

I was now in a dining car that had a bar off to the side with a few stools, and some tables, most of which were bare as fields in wintertime. The exception was the single occupied table, at which I saw two sluggish and sleepy men. One of them, who had a beard, was wearing a black suit, while the other man was wearing a black army sweater; both had crew cuts. They had a couple of cups of coffee on their table, as well as a Kalashnikov with its stock sawed short. Another man, wearing a long, black jacket was sitting on one of the bar stools, drinking his own coffee and skimming through some newspapers. Seeing me, all three tensed up. The two men closest to me both stood up, reaching for the Kalashnikov simultaneously and keeping their eyes fixed on me. I groped for the door handle behind me.

"Freeze," the bearded man said, getting to the Kalashnikov first. "Who are you?"

I had no clue what to say.

"How'd you get in here?" the bearded man demanded.

"I was over in the next car. I guess I got on the wrong train."

"What the fuck are you trying to pull? What do you mean you got on the wrong train?" the bearded man asked, justifiably skeptical. "This is a special train, buddy boy. What are you doing here?"

"Well, what can I say . . . we were carrying some boxes in, and then I fell asleep."

"Are you drunk or something?"

"Who me? Nah, I'm not drunk."

They exchanged glances, clearly not knowing what to do.

"Nick!" the man sitting at the bar called out.

The bearded man looked over at him.

"Check him," the third man said, though it was more a request than an order.

"Hands up," Nick said, giving his partner the gun, coming up to me, and searching me thoroughly.

"This feels awfully familiar," I thought. "It's a good thing I decided to change . . . it sure would have been hard to explain what I was planning on doing with a pair of Bosch electric scissors."

"He's clean," Nick yelled and stepped aside.

"Okay then," said the dude at the bar. "Go out to the vestibule—man, security on this train fuckin' blows. And you"—he meant me—"come over here."

I walked over to the bar, feeling more self-assured. The dude nodded at the empty stool next to him. I sat down.

He was roughly the same age as me. He was giving me an angry, prickly look, but it was somehow detached from his personality, as though he was wearing anger-tinted contact lenses. He was clean-shaven, actually so clean-shaven that he had a few red cuts on his neck. He didn't have too much hair, but he had slicked back what he did have fastidiously; everything about this guy was slick, combed, and washed. I noticed his jacket immediately, a long Milan jacket—the same one One-Eyed Tolik had been wearing, the only difference being that I could instantly tell that the one he had was authentic. One of his sleeves had been stained by blood . . . or, maybe, red paint. Under his jacket was a dark, expensive suit, a mellow-colored tie, and a snow-white dress shirt. The best of the Russian financial press was laid out on the table in front of him. Eventually he finished whatever he was reading, abruptly folded it in half, tossed it onto the bar, next to all the other printed matter there, and clamped down on it with his small hand. As he did so, I saw that his nails were finely trimmed like those of a surgeon. I also noticed how clean his dress shirt was.

"What's your name?" he asked, looking me straight in the eye.

"Herman."

"Herman? You got your passport with you?"

I reached into my pockets, silently thanking Injured once again.

"Korolyov," he said after examining my papers. "Sounds familiar. How'd you get in here? How'd you get past the security guard?"

"Dunno," I answered. "I missed my train, so I hopped on this
one. It was dark."

"Sure, sure," he said without believing a word I was saying.
"And you came here on business?"

"What do you mean?"

"Well, maybe you want something from me?"

"Nope, not a thing."

"Yeah? Everybody always wants something from me."

"Nah," I tried my best to sound reassuring, "I don't need anything from you, not one thing."

"You sure?" he asked.

"You bet."

"It's a good thing I wasn't asleep," he said after a thoughtful
pause. "If I had been, they would have thrown you right off the
train without waiting for a stop. You know, I just can't seem to fall
asleep while I'm out here," he complained. "I don't like this place.
Where do you live, Herman?"

"Not too far from here."

"You're a local?"

"Yep, you could say that."

"Why haven't you gotten the hell out of here yet?"

"Why should I?"

"So you could get a good night's sleep," he said.

"I sleep just fine. Slept the whole night through in the next car. And I own my own business out here now. Kinda stuck here."

"You own your own business?" he asked, suspicious. "That's good. It's nice to have something that belongs to you. But . . . are you positive you don't need anything from me?"

"I'm positive."

"Wanna have a drink?" he suggested out of the blue.

"Yeah, sure."

He slid off his stool and went behind the bar. The selection was a bit weak—the bar evidently wasn't used all that often. The bottles stood in sparse ranks, some vodka, wine, and one bottle of cognac, which was what he grabbed. He took out two glasses originally meant for serving tea on passenger trains, tossed their spoons off to the side, and poured us a round.

"Haven't had time to restock the bar," he said, handing me a glass. "Every time I come back, I promise myself I'll get a good bartender and buy some decent booze, just so I have it. But I forget every time. Too busy," he said, downing his drink.

I followed suit, not knowing how to answer. There he was, pouring me drinks like a bartender, but that didn't make the slightest difference—it was still his cognac, and he wasn't being hospitable for its own sake. The scornful way he was looking at me kept me uneasy.

"Do a lot of folks take this train?" I asked.

"Why do you ask?"

"Just wondering."

"Just wondering? I'm the only one who takes this train. Well, me and the security guards. I don't even have a bartender, see?"

"And you don't have any car attendants either?"

"Nope, no car attendants either."

"Who checks the tickets then?"

"Herman, this is my train, so *I* check all of the tickets."

"It's your train," I said, a bit surprised. "So, you're like Trotsky—you've got your own train and all."

"Yeah, I guess so."

"Where are you going?"

"Where am I going?" he parroted, thinking for a bit. Maybe he was deciding whether or not he should tell me. "Nowhere really. I'm just checking my sites."

"But how do they let your train through? I mean, how do they announce you at all the stations? Do you have a train number?"

"Do you even know where we are right now?" he asked.

I looked out the window. A strand of pink light was warming the fog; it was impossible to make anything out.

"Nah," I said, "I haven't been here before."

"You sure haven't. These tracks lead to a dead-end. They were built in case a war broke out, to move the factories east. Down there," he said, pointing somewhere into the fog, "the tracks just stop. So, I'm the only one who takes this route."

"Oh, wow."

"Uh-huh. This is a strange area. I really don't like coming down here. It's just kinda empty. You're going, going, going, and there's nobody in sight. Just cornfields. You don't actually like it around here, do you?"

"What do you mean by 'around here'?"

"In your hometown."

"Yeah, I like my hometown."

"You guys are an odd bunch," he said, pouring another round. "You're happy to keep jerking me around forever, but you never really want to find common ground. You can't even imagine how many problems I've had. Somebody always wants to screw me over, or stiff me. This one guy, a local, was so damn stubborn—he just wouldn't fuckin' budge."

"Maybe you were part of the problem?"

"Maybe, maybe. Let me tell you, Herman. I think the whole reason you guys have to deal with so much shit is because you're too attached to this place. You've got this crazy idea in your heads that the most important thing is to stay here, not give an inch—you're clinging to your emptiness. There's not a fuckin' thing here! Not a single fuckin' thing. There's nothing to cling on to—how come you can't see that? You'd be better off looking for a better place to live. You'd save me a lot of hassle. But no. You're hunkered down in your foxholes and there's no getting rid of you. And you're always causing trouble!"

"I don't see what the problem is."

"The problem is that you underestimate the power of big capital. You all think that just because you were born here you automatically have the right to stay living here."

"Don't we?"

"Nope, you fuckin' don't, Herman," he said, pouring us another round. "If you wanna get by, learn how to do business the right way. It's really not that hard. Just try to understand that you're not the only ones who have the right to be here, got that?"

"Got it."

"You have to be able to compromise and give something up to get something back in return."

"Obviously."

"And you shouldn't be so damn stubborn. Especially when someone makes you a really good offer, you got that?"

"Yeah."

"All right then," he said, downing his cognac and calming down. "*You* get that, but they don't," he motioned out toward the fog. "They don't fuckin' get anything. They're always causing me trouble!"

"Well, I don't know," I said. "Maybe part of the problem is that you don't give them much of a choice?"

He looked even more scornful.

"Herman, I do give them a choice," he said. "I give them tons of choices. You think I like putting people in body bags? You're all just fuckin' crazy—it seems like time has stopped for you guys. You're stuck in the past, hanging on for dear life, and there's no dragging you back to reality. Ah, what's the point in lecturing you, anyway?"

The door to the sleeper car opened and the bearded man stepped in and stood silently by the door.

"What's up Nick?" the boss asked him, already sounding a bit tipsy.

"You asked me to remind you about breakfast."

"Oh," Mr. Slick said, "you see, we don't have any bartenders, cooks, or car attendants. Okay, let's go."

He headed down the corridor, swaggering like a sailor. Nick let him by, then let me by, and closed the door behind us.

★

Something had changed since the start of our conversation; the air had become hot and turned the color of death—an intense, hopeless color. We were walking along the aisle when I heard some strange sounds coming from some of the locked compartments. I heard some chirping and some animals breathing apprehensively, sensing that there were monsters out in the corridor. Mr. Slick was banging his fist on the doors as he passed, and I could sense the bodies behind the walls, quivering and sighing in reply. The security guard was waiting for us at the end of the car. He was surprised to see me, but didn't say anything, making it seem as though everything was just fine.

"Well?" Mr. Slick said.

The security guard opened the door hastily and stepped back, letting Mr. Slick slip by. Mr. Slick stood in the doorway for a moment, peering in.

"Just like you asked for," the security guard said.

"Well, what do you want me to do with it?" Mr. Slick asked, irritated.

Flustered, the security guard shrugged his shoulders. I looked into the next compartment. There was a table there, to which an unhappy black sheep had been tied with a long rope that looped all around its body.

"Fuckin' cunt," Mr. Slick said. "Nick, couldn't you buy some regular meat?"

"We really couldn't, boss," Nick answered. "There aren't any markets or anything around here."

"Well, you better get a move on," Mr. Slick said. "You brought it, so you do the cooking."

"Me?" Nick asked, terrified.

"Well I'm not gonna do it, obviously," Mr. Slick answered coldly, stepping aside, taking out a toothpick, and starting to dig around between his straight, tiny teeth.

Nick was at a loss. He was clearly afraid of his boss, so he nodded at his bearded partner, who had just come in. The latter got him a big bread knife, and they approached the animal together.

The sheep was oddly submissive. They both grabbed it; Nick was holding the knife, but he was so anxious that all he could manage to do was stab ineffectually the poor animal, not kill it. The animal wasn't happy about this, and it finally tried to break free. Eventually Nick stabbed like he meant it and the sheep began shuddering. Nick sank onto the floor, so his partner took over. He grabbed the still-struggling animal by the neck, like an American paratrooper capturing a Taliban fighter. He pressed the blade up against its throat and jerked the knife toward him. The sheep's head lolled, but it was still kicking, and the security guard also fell to the floor. The knife skidded off to the side, landing at Mr. Slick's feet.

"You morons," Mr. Slick said. "You can't do anything right. Give me that," he told Nick, gesturing at his holster.

Nick gave him his Makarov pistol and stepped out of the compartment, humiliated. Mr. Slick zipped up his jacket, flipped off the safety, and fired wildly. Blood sprayed all over, dousing Mr. Slick's jacket, but he was unfazed, continuing to fire bullet after bullet into the animal. Ringing, morning silence set in. I peered into the compartment. Mr. Slick, covered in sheep's blood from head to toe, was standing there and examining his victim. Oddly enough, it was still alive. The compartment had acquired a strong smell of gunpowder and intestines.

"Herman," Mr. Slick said, without turning around. "Finish it off. Or are you too much of a pussy? I don't want it to suffer anymore." He handed me the pistol.

"I guess I'm too much of a pussy."

"Yeah? How come?" he asked. "Are you afraid of a little blood?" He turned to face me. "What are you going to have for breakfast?"

"Dude," I said, "there's no way I'm having breakfast with you."

"Is that right?"

"Yep, that's right."

"You're all a bunch of pussies," said Mr. Slick. "Every single one of you. If you're afraid of blood, you're never gonna get anything fuckin' done in life. That goes for you, too, Herman. You're never gonna get anything fuckin' done."

"Whatever," I answered.

"Whatever?" the drunken Mr. Slick asked. "Okay, whatever. So, you're not going to have breakfast with us?"

"Nope."

"Fine," Mr. Slick said. "Nick, call up the engineer and tell him to stop the train. One of the passengers will be getting off." He looked back at me: "You aren't gonna get anything done, ever," he repeated.

"You've got some blood on your chin. You might want to wipe it off. It doesn't look too nice."

★

At first I thought they were going to open fire on me, but no, the ghost train rolled away down the tracks without a shot. Shortly afterward, the train disappeared, leaving only the smell of hot metal to remind me that it had ever existed.

4

At the beginning of October, the days are as short as a soccer player's career; the oily sun flows past overhead, weighing down the shadows on the ground, bringing the grass to life, and warming the asphalt's broken heart.

I veered away from the tracks, heading down an old highway almost completely overgrown with cattails. Some bewildered wasps were buzzing along the road and sun-warmed spiderwebs grabbed at my face and clothing, sticking to my skin and getting caught in my hair. The highway stretched through boundless cornfields, and the landscape was featureless—no trees, no towns, no signs of life or death.

Farther along, I found a fork in the road. To the right, the highway pushed on into a valley, looking just as endless, sun-drenched, and webbed-over as the portion I'd already crossed; I decided to bear left instead, following the sun and walking between bare fields where the harvest had already been gathered. The road here was well-worn, so it was easy going, though the sun, moving along the sky's smooth surface, began to blind me. I stopped a few times to rest on the dry grass and look up at the sky, feeling the juice in the grass cooling and going still. "I have no idea where I am anyway," I told myself, so it makes no difference where I pop out. Just keep heading west, away from the border."

The fog started rising again at dusk. At first it cropped up in the distance, out in the yellow fields, hanging there as thick as smoke, gradually expanding; soon enough I couldn't make out a thing except the sun's crooked rays cutting through this white film, filling it with light from the inside. My long shadow stretched out behind me like a crashed kite that didn't want to fly anymore. The fog crawled out from the lowlands, and the sun was glimmering, chopping through it like an underwater flashlight. In time the sunlight faded and the fog went dark; I found myself in the middle of a great milky film.

I stuck to the main road as long as I could, trying not to lose my way, but soon enough the fog became all-encompassing and impenetrable. All I could do was continue to move forward, slowly, pushing the heavy evening air aside with my hands. I couldn't help but feel as though I was always about to collide with something or someone in that milk, at any moment I would run into some barrier, touch someone's face or calf or pull some object out of the fog. When this feeling became too much to ignore, I stopped dead in my tracks in all that silence and dampness swimming around me, sent swirling by the west wind. But, after all that, I didn't hit anything—something reached out for *me*. Someone's hand, in fact. I leapt back, but quickly regained my composure. I touched the extended hand, and as I did so, three children emerged from the sheets of fog. The kids were wearing filthy tracksuits—the first in red, the second in white, and the third one in both red and white, though he was so filthy I could hardly tell. Two of the kids were obviously younger than the third; they were barefoot, while the older boy had wooden sandals. Judging by their Asian features, they were Mongols or Buryats, and they had coarse, black hair and dark skin—though, again, this might only have been because they were so filthy. There was a degree of apprehension in their intrigued eyes—they looked at me like I was a moose that had roamed into their backyard. At last the oldest boy grabbed my hand firmly and led me into the fog. I allowed myself to be pulled along, peering into the milky film, trying to make something out, but I couldn't even see my own shoes.

★

Some soft lights were glimmering up ahead; they grew more and more intense as we approached, singeing the nighttime air. We ascended a hill, leaving most of the fog behind in the valley, and then found ourselves in the middle of a wheat field filled with faint noises. The lights were revealed as campfires drying out the damp gloom; this was some kind of camp, and a rather large one at that—there were dozens of military tents there with household appliances, dishes, old travel bags, and other miscellaneous bundles heaped around them. Sparks were rising into the black and white sky where the thick, dark void was mingling with the few patches of fog that had drifted this high; the men and children of the camp were mainly huddled around their fires, arguing and trying to keep warm, while the women were bustling out of their tents and disappearing into the disquieting twilight. The men were small in stature, and most, like their children, were dressed in tracksuits, though some also sported hats, and one or two were wearing camouflage. They sat around their fires, apparently arguing, while the women were calling back and forth. The children would run out into the darkness, come back with clumps of dry grass, toss them into the bonfires and dive back into the inky hole.

It was hard to say just how many people were in this camp; the fires seemed to reach all the way out to the horizon, and all the voices were blending into a tense hum, as at a railway station. Nobody paid any attention to me: apparently, they didn't find outsiders suspicious. The three kids who had led me there took me to one of the larger fires and ran off. The men sitting there were speaking some Asian language, no doubt discussing the pressing Mongolian issues of the day, and giving no outward sign of either hostility or welcome. I stepped away from this group and headed farther into the camp. It was obvious that they intended to leave at any moment—their things were packed: pots and pans, wooden furniture, toys, and drums all tucked away under the tents. I saw bicycles parked on the outskirts of the camp. The flags of some unknown republics were flying over the camp, blending in with the dark landscape. And yet the ground by the tents was well-trodden—however temporary this stopover, they had been hanging out here for quite a while, though the real mystery was how they'd gotten here and how they intended to continue their journey, since there weren't any cars, buses, or trucks in sight. Maybe they were traveling by bike? Who knows?

The women cast cheerful glances at me as they rushed by, though immediately dropped their heads again and continued on their way as soon as I took notice. Now and then I also began seeing what looked like servicemen, enlisted in some inexplicable army, wearing gray uniforms with uncanny insignia that meant nothing to me, ducking into and out of the tents. They too paid me no mind. Unsettled by something, they only ever looked up at the sky or at their watches. The tension was palpable in the camp; and I knew why this place had reminded me of a railway station: it was as if everyone was all ready to go, all packed up, hanging anxiously around the platform, but the train was running late, and no one knew why.

One of the tents had a particularly large band of these nomads hanging around it: men, women, and children alike. The men were talking, the women yelling, the children bobbing around between them. Some dark-skinned teenagers stood off to the side, not daring to come any closer, while dogs sniffed at the men's sneakers apprehensively. Even farther off I saw a couple of the men in military uniforms, a few bald-headed guys in long robes, and some old women holding bundled herbs and decked out in funky dresses. Everyone in this crowd was peering at the curtain covering the entrance to this particular tent. A light was glimmering in the window and aromatic smoke was coming out of an opening in the middle of its canvas roof. Something important was going on in there; perhaps the fate of this whole tribe hung in the balance? I was trying to squeeze my way closer to the entrance when somebody called out to me.

"Hey, I know you."

I turned around and saw Karolina, wearing a gray camouflage top and high army boots. She had a black beret on her head, and dyed red dreads, robust and durable like nautical rope, poked out from its sides. She was holding a heavy flashlight and shining it straight in my eyes.

"What are you doing here?" she asked.

"I could ask you the same question."

"I work here," she said.

"I'm going home."

"Have you been on the road for a while?"

"Yep, sure have. My train took off without me. I've been walking all day."

"What train?" Karolina scoffed. "There aren't any railroad tracks around here."

"Are you for real?"

"Uh-huh. Why'd you come here?"

"I didn't mean to, it was an accident."

She stood there for a bit and then turned off her flashlight.

"All right, come with me."

She headed back into the center of the dark camp. She skirted around the fires and waved in greeting to her friends. She stopped by another big tent that had crosses and letters stenciled on its walls.

"Cross the threshold," she said, before disappearing inside.

She hung her flashlight in the middle of the tent, where it sent heavy, sweet shadows creeping along the walls. It was spacious and warm inside. The tent itself had been divided in two—off to the left were a few sleeping bags with sweaters, dress shirts, and thick army socks heaped on top of them, while the right half of the space was crowded with seemingly random things—athletic bags with hand planes poking out of the top, as well as tennis rackets, sickles, and neatly organized books. The multilingual remnants of someone's library had been stowed away in the corner: American and French classics accounted for the bulk of the collection, but there were many well-worn occult, theological, and liturgical texts scattered among the cookbooks and tourist guides.

On both sides, I could see electronics, appliances, and the local equivalent of everyday household junk: irons, transistors, table lamps with their cords hopelessly tangled, a few saddles and bridles, razors, combs, and a chandelier. A large map, poorly sewn onto the canvas wall, hung over everything: "Eurasia," I read to myself. Routes outlined with a red ballpoint pen stretched from the east, from Tibet and the regions bordering China, from the Great Wall and Mesopotamia, all the way to Rostov, in Russia, and continued on through our area. "The great migration," I thought, and turned toward Karolina. She was watching me, standing in the middle of the tent, next to a big, ancient black and white television. The fascinating thing was that it worked, though it was only displaying static, filling the room with a domestic, shiny gray light.

"How does that thing work?" I asked.

"It runs on gasoline," Karolina said. "There's a small generator over there, on the other side of the wall. The only thing is that our antenna is so weak that we can't get any picture."

She slipped out of her army jacket, tossed it on the floor, picked up a heavy, knitted sweater, put it on, and sat down on the jumbled sleeping bags.

"Well," she said, settling in. "Let's hear it."

"First off, who are these people?" I asked.

"Refugees. Mongols, Tibetans, even some Afghans."

"Where are they heading?" I asked.

"West," Karolina answered.

"Isn't that against the law?"

"Of course it is," she said, packing a pipe with tobacco. After taking a few solid puffs, she sprawled out on her makeshift bed. "If it weren't for us they would have been sent back a while ago."

"What do you mean by *us*?" I asked.

"We're a special EU delegation," Karolina said, exhaling acerbic smoke. "We oversee human rights cases. Actually, we're convoying these people: they'd never make it, otherwise. They don't have any documents or normal names. Those Mongols really are strange, but they're kind."

"How come the Mongols are heading back to Europe again?"

"What's your name again? Herman, right?"

"Yeah, Herman."

"Herman, they're nomads. They gotta keep moving, never stopping—it's in their blood. They're stuck here, though, for the time being. We've been loafing around here for the last week or so."

"What happened?"

"Sivila's expecting. She should be going into labor any day now," Karolina said, now drowning in a thick cloud of tobacco smoke. I walked over and took a seat next to her. She offered me a hit. Remembering her beverage in the thermos, I declined.

"Who's Sivila?"

"She's their representative."

"What do you mean?"

"Well, like their member of parliament," Karolina explained.

"Technically, they have a representative government. Everyone here respects her, and they're all very concerned about her well-being. They don't want to leave before she gives birth. They're afraid the Hungarians won't let them in if she's pregnant. So, they're all sitting around and waiting. And we're stuck here with them until they're willing to get back on the road."

"Who's the father?"

"There is no father. I mean, nobody knows who the father is, but that doesn't matter—they have different customs. The whole tribe cares about every child. That's matriarchy for you, Herman," Karolina said, her laughter filling the tent. "So, you need to get to the city?"

"Yeah, probably."

"Spend the night with us," she said. "We'll head out as soon as Sivila's baby comes. They need to cross the Carpathian Mountains before winter sets in."

"Okay, sounds good."

She took a black, winter sleeping bag and tossed it to me. "Here. You'll sleep in this one. Let's go brush our teeth."

After grabbing her toothpaste and sticking her toothbrush in her mouth, she sprang to her feet and headed out of the tent, sticking her still warm pipe in her pants pocket. I didn't have a toothbrush with me, so I followed her, empty-handed.

★

Karolina passed the big fire, which was now petering out, and headed down along the dark, prickly stubble fields. She skirted past the last tent, outside of which were sitting a few women wearing orange overalls and puffy shawls, thumbing rosary beads and smoking filtered cigarettes. Then she dropped down into the valley. Her gray sweater, made of thick wool, shone warmly up ahead; she glided down the nighttime dirt path, crushing the occasional fallen kernel with her hard heels. As I followed behind her it seemed as though everyone's eyes were drawn to her dreads, as though their glances were themselves television signals being yanked out of the air by antennae tinting her hair silver and illuminating the lines of her body. A few black metal barrels filled with water had been placed down below the camp next to two portable toilets—the nomads must have been hauling them along their entire Trans-Siberian voyage. Karolina approached a barrel and scooped up some water. It was slow and obedient in her hands, dripping between her long, dark fingers, moving in slow pulses along her thin, delicate wrists, flowing down the sleeves of her heavy, furry sweater, and running down her body, appearing again at her waist, emerging into the night like fragile electric light. Karolina uncupped her hands and water crashed down into the metal pit of the barrel, the droplets shattering the reflected night inside.

"Hold this for a sec," she said around her toothbrush, taking off her sweater and shirt and tossing them to me.

She leaned over the nighttime water, bathing like a soldier in the field, legs spread wide, breathing heavily with pleasure. Her skin was glowing, the water lit by the brittle, white flame that illuminated her, grazing across her flat, tense stomach and her heavy breasts marked with tiny droplets, touching the veins on her arms, and glistening on her hands, white as chalk.

"They never bathe in the river," Karolina said, drying herself off with her own shirt, still not taking her toothbrush out of her mouth. "All this, bathing with water out of barrels, is incredibly unhygienic. Don't you think?"

"Yeah. Do their women bathe like that, too?"

"What's that supposed to mean?" Karolina said, apparently offended. She pulled her sweater back over her naked torso and continued brushing her teeth.

Up on the high ground, the air quivered and suddenly broke as the camp roared in jubilation.

"It's a girl!" somebody yelled, and dozens of other voices passed along the news. "It's a girl!"

Flames rocketed into the sky. Quick, ghostlike silhouettes scurried around the camp, livestock started bellowing, and happy pop music came blasting out of various speakers.

"Let's go," Karolina said. "We really ought to be there for this."

★

The children were carrying snacks and bottles over to the main tent, the women were heating up some kind of stew in huge cauldrons, and the men were embracing and telling each other the news. People were crowding excitedly around Sivila's tent, everyone buzzing and trying to squeeze ahead, everyone concerned and wanting to get a closer look—and if a few of them got trampled along the way, well, nobody really seemed to care.

Some of the men were holding torches, others were holding up their cell phones; everyone's anxious eyes were fixed on the tent curtain—knowing that the long-awaited child was on the other side. Karolina strode between the men, pushing them aside gently, yet with authority. I hurried along behind her, and the nomads parted without objection, clearing the way for the servicemen and us. Karolina stopped at the entrance.

"It was forbidden to go into her tent while she was in labor—even for EU liaisons. Got it?"

"For sure."

"Cross the threshold," she said once more, disappearing behind the curtain.

★

Inside the tent were more people whispering. Karolina told me that these were the ones closest to Sivila—her girlfriends, sisters, female lovers, as well as her bodyguard and accountant. They were beaming; a common feeling of joy united them at this late hour.

A potbelly stove stood in the middle of the room, its metal chimney disappearing somewhere at the top of the tent. A young woman wearing an Adidas jacket was sitting on top of the stove and tossing dry grass into the fire, which filled the air with a marvelous scent. As for Sivila, she was lying on the synthetic carpets, sheepskins, and Chinese-made blankets that had been heaped on the left half of her abode. She was an older woman with a swarthy, Mongolian face and deep, black eyes. She was wearing a Dolce & Gabbana T-shirt. The birth had clearly been difficult, but her tender feelings, which were only accentuated by the thick layer of makeup caked on her face, prevailed over her exhaustion. Her daughter was lying next to her, swaddled in a German down blanket with her tiny face poking out, snoring through her miniature nose. The first gifts brought by her many visitors were in a pile next to Sivila's daughter on the blanket—there were silver Chinese coins, a silver (though not new) Parker pen, a silver glove with an embroidered FC Shakhtar Donetsk emblem on it, and a little silver spoon with some meticulously engraved runes on both sides. Karolina slipped by the crowd of well-wishers, leaned over Sivila, touched the new mother's cheek lightly, and took a silver army token (which could supposedly ward off snipers' bullets) out of her pocket, adding it to the other gifts. Sivila nodded appreciatively, and Karolina returned to her spot. Then the woman who was sitting on top of the stove, tossing grass into the flames, hopped down, bent over the fire, and inhaled deeply, filling her lungs with smoke. She headed over to the newborn and exhaled white, smoky air over the girl's head, so that she even smiled in her sleep. The rest of the nomads smiled with her, and so did I. Karolina, touching my elbow, couldn't help but laugh. Meanwhile, the woman who'd breathed the smoke over the baby's head sat down and began speaking to her.

★

"You, who arose from nothing," she began, "and who came from nowhere, sweet like light and invisible like the night . . . Everything that has transpired around you—all the air you breathed through your mother's pores, all the clouds that coasted by above you, and all the rocks resting beneath the ground—it all fits inside your dreamland. Everything that you're now seeing in your sleep, everything you will engender when you wake, will serve you on this night; everything is circling overhead like stars spinning in emptiness. Incredible warmth rose off the rivers so that you wouldn't freeze during your voyage. Grass sprouted out of the earth so you could tread across it, heading west. Animals followed your breath, warming the black womb of the night with the heat of their flanks, and spirits flew up above like swallows, seeking out a place of respite.

Your head was created from the starry sky. Your right eye was created from rays of moonlight and your left eye was created from the yellow sun. Your teeth were created from comets and fallen stars. Your skin was molded from the October fog. Rain formed your lungs and your joyful heart beats on through the drought. Your arms grow out of the stems of bitter plants and juicy cornstalks shape your calves. When you open your eyes the moon waxes, when you close them fishermen's boats sink. When you sigh, women touch the hair of solemnity and regret, and when you see the skies in your sleep, cows' udders fill up with milk.

Everyone who came to welcome you into this world, everyone who will follow you up and down mountain trails, now sings for you alone. They all have swallows hibernating below the roofs of their mouths, for we all have to persevere together, forging through the snow together, leading our animals across frozen rivers, shepherding endless throngs of animals, guiding them through the mountains, through deep winter nights, through cities buried under feet of snow, and across railroad tracks. Keep sleeping until the birds resting on weary men's shoulders wake you. Keep sleeping until the hearts of those who love you stop beating. When you awake, the morning air will quicken and flow westward, taking with it all our desires and all the secret words we have spoken to you. When you awake, you'll show us the way out of this barren land, you'll draw us a long, narrow line that will lead us to all those from whom we once were parted."

★

When she finished, everyone got the message and started leaving the tent. Their excited friends and families awaited them outside. The woman who had spoken over the newborn was the last one out, and the group made room for her; she stood before all the other nomads, her attentive gaze enveloping each of them in turn. They were all anxious for her to say something.

"She has golden eyes and swarthy skin," the woman pronounced. "Since we've already reached this distant land, since we've already stopped over in this field, let her name be Moka."

A gust of hot wind rushed by after her announcement, rustling the women's hair and knocking the men's hats off. Then the women lifted their hands to the heavens and started shouting ecstatically, and the men threw their clenched fists into the black, October air, thanking the local spirits for their benevolence and forbearance and praising their newborn princess, Moka, their guardian, their ticket to Europe, the queen of the Mongols, the bearer of the FC Shakhtar Donetsk silver rings, the gold-eyed sleeping beauty who gave them all hope and faith.

And amid all of these joyful cries, all this commotion, Karolina took my hand and tied a thin, red band around it.

"Here's a little something for you to remember this night by," she said.

Then she shoved me forward, right into the happy, bustling crowd, which immediately spun me around and carried me along, out into the night, past the glimmering firelight. They were all celebrating, embracing each other, hopping on each other's backs, and running into the thick, low-hanging blanket of smoke that was settling around them. I looked back, but Karolina had vanished. In her place there was only the wind, fluttering the EU flags, kicking up dust, and clearing the way for happy men with copper voices who circled around me and sang incomprehensible songs with incredible energy. Children raced by us, slipping through the men's legs and dodging the women's embraces, screeching and laughing. They plunged down into the dark void, churning the fog, knocking stars out of the sky with their long, bony fingers, and the stars, spilled down, thudding onto the tents' canvas roofs, falling into the fires like chestnuts, where they produced spark after spark, gliding into pockets and falling on men's hats, where each one burst with a splash of cold, bright juice. The herd, distracted by the racket, moved lazily through the camp and down into the valley, with its serenity and water barrels. Lethargic cows ducked away from the women trying to tie ribbons and shawls around their horns and lowed as they descended those insane hills. Sheep and goats trotted along after them, and the children, true nomads that they were, rode on their backs, barely visible, like ghosts, a unit of devilish cavalry that would forge on through the rainy season and the long drought alike, into the most fertile valleys and farmlands. The women danced gracefully by the campfires in their robes and raincoats, slipping into a trance drawn together by shared movement that imitated the birds of the air and the beasts of the land.

★

I was already tired out from all the festivities, so I cut through yet another drove of children and headed back to Karolina's tent. I crossed the threshold. The television was still pumping the nighttime air full of its soft, weightless glow. Karolina was lying on a sleeping bag, passionately kissing some muscular blonde woman in orange overalls. She had already taken off Karolina's sweater and was now kissing her dark, heavy breasts, while Karolina was ruffling her short hair and unbuttoning her overalls. I pretended I was watching the TV, but Karolina noticed me at once and became even more passionate. I tried slipping out of the tent as unobtrusively as possible.

"Herman," Karolina called, sounding amused. "Where are you going?"

"Don't mind me," I answered. "Keep doing your thing."

"Don't be scared," Karolina said. "Come over here."

"I don't want to disturb you."

The blonde swiveled her head and started looking at me too. "You're not disturbing us."

"You're really getting us going," Karolina added and started laughing again. "All right, just go to bed."

They just lay there entwined, waiting for my next move,

intrigued. I figured it wouldn't be right to just get up and leave. "Everyone celebrates in their own way," I thought. I found my sleeping bag, slid inside it, and closed my eyes, turning indignantly to face the wall. I could still hear them kissing when I fell asleep.

5

". . . she said you decided to stay."

"Decided to stay?"

"Yeah."

"Why didn't she wake me up?"

"She said she couldn't bring herself to do it, you were sleeping like a baby."

"Like a baby? What is that supposed to mean?"

"Well, that you were sound asleep."

"At least she didn't take my passport."

". . ."

"That EU commission . . . they're just a bunch of frauds."

". . ."

"Why did they leave me here?"

"Herman," Tamara said wearily, "what do you want me to do about it?"

"Nothing," I answered, dissatisfied with the whole situation.

★

Recalling the past and piecing it all together isn't a pleasant task. Up above, the sun's bronze torso coasted by like an airship, drifting through warm currents of air. I'd woken up around noon and now I thought back to yesterday and last night, the night that lasted for an eternity. I thought back to the songs, names, and faces, imbibing all the while the scents of the dwelling in which I found myself, taking in a silence so profound as to be incredible. The silence scared me. "Are they all still sleeping?" I asked myself. "Maybe they celebrated all night and now they're resting up for the long, arduous trek to come." I slipped out of my sleeping bag and saw that neither Karolina nor her blonde girlfriend were in the tent. In fact, there was nothing there, no sleeping bags, no clothes, no ancient black and white TVs, no books, bags, maps, or socks. It had all just disappeared. Expecting the worst, I went outside.

There was nothing left of the camp except ruins and piles of ashes. Black, skinny strands of smoke stretched toward the sky like hungry cobras. The well-worn paths the nomads had tramped into the ground during their stay formed an odd, incomprehensible pattern now that pilots and birds could use to reconstruct the route taken by wild eastern tribes heading who knows where and who knows why. I couldn't tell when they'd managed to pack up and move out, how they could possibly have gotten away without my noticing. The only things left were two big tents, inflated by the afternoon air, and those poles with the EU flags flapping on them in the middle of the field—while off in the distance, down in the valley, I could see a few soldiers circling around the blue portable toilets, about to load them onto an army flatbed truck. Next to the truck, where the barrels of water had been, I saw the shimmering, white, church-issued Volga. I went on over.

★

Tamara looked despondent. She wasn't in the mood to talk, but I had to get her to explain the whole situation to me. She said that Karolina called her that morning, asked her to drive over and pick me up, explaining where we were, saying she was sorry for being such an inconvenience, and assuring Tamara that taking me along with the tribe was out of the question, since the Mongols believe it would bring them bad luck, and were basically threatening to sever all ties with the EU Commission if I were to continue on the trip with them.

"All right, fine," I said, already sitting in the back seat and counting the October poplars as we drove by. "But how did she know to call you?"

"It's a long story," Tamara answered reluctantly. "She and her team did some work with us back in the day. Some charity work for the church. They had a good relationship with our presbyter; he was always helping them out with paperwork or just saying a kind word. Who else could she have called, anyway? Just think about it, they can't have people poking around their camp."

"That's for sure. I guess dumping me on the church looked pretty appealing."

"Right."

"But they could just have taken me along, too."

"No, they really couldn't have," Tamara said. "The Mongols were worried you'd latch onto them. They don't need outsiders—they've got a code. You should be counting your blessings. It's a good thing they didn't turn you in, or just get rid of you. Where do you get off wandering around like that?"

"Take it easy," I said. "What's going on back home? Are they still looking for me?"

"Yep," Tamara answered. "They even stopped by the church and talked to the presbyter."

"What'd he tell them?"

"Nothing," Tamara assured me. "He said he didn't know anything."

"So what am I supposed to do now?"

"Nothing," Tamara said. "Now you just gotta wait it out. What are you getting so worked up over?"

"What am I getting so worked up over? Let me tell you what I'm getting so worked up over! Have you ever slept in a tent with two lesbians?"

"Yeah, I have. And I didn't like it one bit."

"Can we make a pit stop here?" I asked. "I'm thirsty."

★

A little green food truck was set up on a brick foundation. Long benches stained with ketchup and butter stood off to the side under some trees. It was a kind of rest stop, a safe haven with amiable female dancers, children's songs, and soft-spoken birds, where travelers could share the latest news, warning their fellow sojourners about upcoming traps and danger.

We were the only customers right now, though. A heavyset woman with pink hair and red nails came out of the food truck, gave us a deeply skeptical look, took our order, and disappeared back inside. Tamara and I were sitting on the bench in tense silence; Seva had decided to stay back in the car, but he asked us to bring him back a hot meal. The sun was warming up the autumn fields the best it could and the warm eastern wind brought us the smells of smoke and dry grass. Barren black soil spread out around us, and out on the horizon red-tinted pine trees soared upward.

The air seemed to be woven out of varying smells and shades of color, like the fabric of burning flags still flapping in the October wind. The emblems on those flags were long, sticky vessels made from spiderwebs and thin bundles of fatigued plants cut and assembled by women's hands. There were birds too, flying over vast expanses, heading south, deserting the thick, stagnant air that drifted along over our hair. Lethargic autumn insects crawled over the cloth flags, blending in with the earth and sky. The ragged banners smelled of silt and wet sand—there was a river flowing nearby carrying leaves and severed plant stems downstream.

Tamara was wearing her usual cherry-colored sweater and long dress, hiding her eyes behind big sunglasses, which made her look like some mobster's widow; her heart still belonged to him, how could she ever move on? She sat there, smoking a lot, drinking tea out of a plastic cup, refusing to eat, and watching the butterflies gravitating toward the sugar cubes on our table.

The sun and the autumn air made the rest stop feel ghostly and unwieldy, as though the whole place was liable to collapse and fall to pieces any second now. The last few days were like a sugar cube that had been left outside, and now that sugar cube was flashing in the sun, blinding us, agitating our imaginations, reminding us that any moment might hold unexpected and unforeseen events.

"You'll stay at my place for now," Tamara said. "They probably won't look for you there."

"It'd be better for me to just go home. What could they really do to me? At least that way I'll figure out what the problem is."

"Don't be ridiculous. Why stick your neck out? Wait it out for a few days at my place and then you can go back home. I told Injured about my plan—he's fine with it."

"Well, as long as Injured's fine with it."

"You'll go back in a few days. All right?"

"Okay," I said. And then I asked, "Tamara, why haven't you gotten out of here yet?"

"Where would I go?"

"Anywhere. I don't know . . . you could have gone abroad. Why did you stay?"

She took off her glasses. It struck me again that she was already well over the hill—she wasn't as young and carefree as she had seemed in the Volga at twilight after two days of celebrating. Her face was pale, and she had a troubled and uncertain look about her. Her cigarette was quivering ever so slightly, right between her two big black and silver rings.

"You must have wanted to leave at some point. What could be keeping you here?"

"What do you mean?" she answered after a second's thought. "There always are things that keep us in a particular place."

"Listen, isn't it the future that keeps you somewhere? I mean, the idea that you'll have a future there? Do you really think there's a future for you here?"

"No," she admitted, "but there's a past. The past can also make you stick around."

"What do you mean by that?"

"It's hard for me to explain," Tamara said. "Let's just go home."

★

I hadn't been to Tamara's place since her mom's funeral. Remembering how everything played out that night, I crossed the threshold of her apartment feeling rather uneasy, would everything that went down that night make being here together uncomfortable? But Tamara was walking from room to room, too preoccupied to pay any attention to me, so that uneasy feeling soon passed. It was replaced by a newborn sense of confidence and an odd touch of melancholy, clearly caused by sweet memories and aching anticipation.

I chided myself for thinking of those memories as sweet. It was a funeral, after all—we'd buried Masha, who was a stranger to me at the time, but who was someone's mother nonetheless. I continued chiding myself, thinking, "Go thank her for picking you up and taking you away from that Tatar-Mongol haven of debauchery, for taking care of you and not turning you over to the cops or the local gangsters. Lay low for the next few days until everything blows over, and then go back to your gas pumps with a clear conscience. Make sure not to traumatize her by bringing up her mom, and—above all—don't promise to marry her."

"Hey Herman," she said, bringing me out of my reverie. "I'm gonna head out. You'll be in charge for the day. Don't open the door for anyone, don't answer the phone, and don't walk past the windows."

"Wait—where are you going?"

"I've got stuff to do, Herman. Were you thinking I'd just sit around here all day with you?"

"Well no, not really," I answered, my feelings a bit hurt. "All right, I don't wanna keep you . . . but when should I expect you back?"

"Why should you be expecting me?"

"Well, I'll have to open the door for you."

"I've got a key," Tamara said, matter-of-factly. "So, don't wait up. I'll be back late."

"Well, what should I do all day?" I asked.

"Do some reading," Tamara said. "There are a bunch of children's books over there."

★

I found a packed bookcase in the living room; there were indeed a lot of children's books there, bearing stamps from the factory library, as well as musty collections of fairy tales and science fiction stories, books about heroic Soviet pioneers, and historical novels. I started flipping through the books, coming across the occasional dried flower or old birthday card serving as a bookmark. Pages had been ripped out in places, and sometimes I'd find odd doodles or grim pentagrams drawn in the margins. None of the books really interested me, though. I fumbled around the shelves for a while until I found some magazines, LPs, and a hefty photo album all stacked in a bottom corner.

The majority of the photographs in the album had been glued meticulously onto its pages, but a whole pile hadn't made the cut, apparently, and had just been left stuffed between the front cover and the first page. I went into the bedroom, taking the album with me.

A large sofa bed with a dozen or so soft pillows and cushions on it was sitting by the wall, which, in true Soviet fashion, had a rug hanging on it. It was synthetic and looked to be Chinese, judging by the stylized figures—it was a picture of some sort of tea ceremony, and there was something familiar about the profiles of the figures sitting in the foreground. I had seen these faces before and they had said something to me. Two men were passing each other saucers, thick currents of steam coming off them, and a pregnant woman was sprawled out in the center of the image, between the men, her eyes fastened intently on their nimble hands. In the background, I could see yurts and campfires, smoke drifting up and connecting the earth and sky, as well as herds of cows walking between the columns of smoke, bearing milk inside them like bitter truth.

I flopped down on the bed and opened up the album.

★

Caught, like birds in a net, their eagle eyes stared up at me—both still and attentive, not knowing what to expect from me. Grown men and women, children and old people, students, soldiers, blue-collar workers, high school seniors wearing white graduation aprons, the deceased in coffins with silver coins placed over their eyes, and infants with their favorite toys—they were all waiting for someone to meet their eyes, some color, some black and white, to ascertain what it was that kept them together, what they were living for and why they'd passed on.

The loose snapshots clearly hadn't been organized according

to any principle. The faces there looked unfamiliar and somehow alien. I know that kind of picture, the ones that are always kept; nobody wants to include them in their family photo albums, but that they don't dare throw out, perhaps because throwing away pictures of the living is frowned upon . . . so they begin to collect, these old photographs—given as gifts, sent by mail, or just taken for no particular reason by camera enthusiasts—and wind up in a pile surrounded by other nearly forgotten relatives and family friends. I glanced through them briefly, then set them aside.

The rest of the prints, however, had been treated with love, and sorted fastidiously; they told the story of Tamara's family and even projected its future to a certain degree. The first pictures, mostly black and white, a little bent, scratched, and ink-stained, featured some insane southern landscapes, as well as the white caps of mountain ranges, roof tiles, high windows, stone walls, beat-up roads, and other exotic things interspersed with self-assured men and young, prideful girls with tar-black hair and white teeth. Some of them looked at me gloomily, some were laughing and care-free, while others were clearly worried or upset about something. I tried finding Tamara's features in her relatives' faces, but she was completely different—something separated her from her fellow mountain dwellers; it may have been her weary eyes or her sun-glasses. Nevertheless, these people were undoubtedly close to her; they were related somehow, something kept them together, and I tried capturing some seemingly inconsequential details that might help me solve the riddle of this family, studying their clothing and combing through whatever notes or dates had been written in; scrutinizing young women with puffy hair as they strolled down wide boulevards, men wearing old-fashioned swim trunks standing still on a seacoast, old Soviet cars, silly children's toys, factory entrances, university lecture halls, school hallways, and train compartments filled with happy faces looking straight at the camera, peering into the other side of time and space.

The prints dating back to the mid-'60s were dominated by two girls, faintly similar, yet completely different. The older girl had black eyes with a serious and focused expression and wore a peculiar medallion around her neck, while the younger one was always looking off to the side, wearing goofy ribbons in her hair—they made her look funny, yet somehow more feminine—paying no attention whatsoever to the photographer. I immediately recognized Tamara and Tamila. Various adults—men and women and the close family in which they were lucky enough to grow up—were always bunched around the sisters, clustered behind them, off to the side, or up above. Someone seemed to have chronicled every step of the young girls' lives—preschool (the hideous furniture of Soviet educational institutions, the teacher spilling out of her sun dress, New Year's decorations, dances, games, and the painful hopelessness of singing in a choir), picnics outside the city (animals and sunflowers, the sun on the lake, and children's shrieks that had developed along with the pictures themselves), vacationing at the beach with their parents (sun-battered landscapes and color photographs faded like flags left out in the summer heat), school (uniforms fit for prisoners, state holidays, poetry readings, their first big exams, friends suddenly sprouting up inside the frames); and the girls changed gradually from picture to picture, coming to resemble their current selves more and more, becoming who they were now, today, in this life, this time: fully mature and thoroughly embittered.

During their school days, Tamara was always surrounded by girlfriends: she would be standing there in the center of the shot, arm in arm with one of them. If she was alone, she would have a self-assured expression on her face or be holding a bouquet of flowers, her book bag, or something more substantial. She was mature and looked older than she really was; by the time she was in high school, she had the fully formed body of a young woman and wore jewelry that the administration clearly frowned upon, without ever managing to ban it outright.

Tamila was just the opposite—a timid little girl, a late bloomer of sorts, even in the pictures taken during her last few years of high school. She never took the ribbons out of her hair and she wore oversized sweaters, and worn-out shoes—she always stood off to the side, in the corner, trying to slip out of the frame unnoticed.

Judging by the murky faces, blurry hair, and rushed movements, the pictures that followed clearly hadn't been developed professionally. Tamara wore her white lab coat; occasionally, I'd recognize familiar buildings and scenery, and if I wanted to I could even recall where I was when it was taken and what I was up to. Over time, the number of male faces increased. At first there were some community college guys who barely looked old enough to shave, wearing short, black jackets and holding tape players, then came male classmates in the same white uniform that Tamara wore. Eventually there were more and more men, mature and established ones. They stood by their Volgas, wearing light dress shirts and heavy black suit jackets; they ate in restaurants, drank cognac, wore digital watches and brightly colored ties, and displayed gray, stone-cold expressions and battle-worn fists. All the men flocked around Tamara, standing still just long enough to project themselves into these pictures and become part of her past. Tamara always looked light and stunning, despite the hideous haircuts that were fashionable back in the '80s, and wore long coats and short, nearly nonexistent skirts, or else tight dresses and light-colored sandals that she took off and held in her hands as she stood on the hot, summer asphalt. She had deep and brash eyes, a tender yet dismissive smile, and a body that drove all the men wild—all the professors and truck drivers, thieves and Communist Youth League leaders, budding capitalists and alcoholics who hung around her, trying to make it into one of her pictures at any price.

Tamila, who by this point was starting to look more like a woman, would occasionally make an appearance, but she was still overshadowed by Tamara. There were hardly any pictures of them together. That was probably how Tamila wanted it, but who knows. Generally, Tamila had her picture taken with adults—her parents, teachers, and other men and women, God knows who they were to her. In one print, she was standing in a park that resonated with the abundant sun and greenery of summer, between two rotund women who were squashing her between them, so Tamila simply evaporated among their flashy dresses. I took a closer look and, to my surprise, recognized Angela Petrovna (her thick, ash hair spiked up, her piercing gaze, and heavy, autumnal breasts) and Brunhilda Petrovna (her hot, copper-colored curls glistening in the sun and her hips protruding out of the disappearing fabric). Then I came across Kocha and Injured (the hardened gait of a young thug and the supple torso of a star forward, respectively), Sasha Python, Andryukha Michael Jackson, and a multitude of other friends, acquaintances, classmates, neighbors, relatives—an endless throng of faces, portrait and profile, shadows from the past, from every moment of my life, every moment of my memory. And a surprised Tamara, squinting with pleasure, her hair black like tea, wearing no clothes at all, half-submerged in the nighttime waves; or else wearing a formal suit at various award ceremonies, wearing sweaters and jackets at work, holding umbrellas, sunglasses, and bags during trips, celebrations, weddings, and funerals—she was always standing right in the middle of the action.

By the time *he* made an appearance, I'd reached one of the last few prints; Tamara was already a mature divorcee, much more attractive and intelligent than she'd been before her wedding, as is often the case. Her eyes were a bit weary, her face a bit puffy from chronic insomnia, her movements had slowed down a little and she seemed to have acquired a mild sort of melancholy, as though anticipating that, though he'd left her life, he would eventually come back. And then, there he was again, a constant presence, overwhelming her. He went everywhere with her, upstaging her in the photographs, trying to squeeze her out of the frame, which was a first. And yet she seemed perfectly fine with this new arrangement—judging by her face, at any rate. Maybe she needed his protection, or just his presence, as though she was willing to yield space in her own life to him, viewing it as a given, a necessity. They were always together, sharing each place, moment, shot. Sometimes Tamila's despondent face would crop up, over to the side, as though caught in the same photo with them against her will; and every time she appeared, she looked somber, and slightly pained, as though blinded by the sun.

And then something must have happened, since the man vanished as mysteriously as he'd appeared, and without any images suggesting why he might be absent. Then everything ran together in the last pages, there were some old girlfriends, other familiar faces, some houses, someone's funeral, various cities, winter landscapes, but Tamara herself was gone, save for the occasional rare appearance. It was as if she'd decided to avoid having her picture taken, as though she didn't want anyone seeing her during those years. Only at the very end of the album were there a few relatively recent pictures of Tamara and Tamila. They looked much the same as ever—worn out yet sultry, incredibly similar yet totally different—but now they were sticking together, literally: their arms entwined, always leaning on each other, their hair and clothing pressed together, looking into the lens attentively, intelligently; keeping their eyes fixed on you. They were odd women, I thought, with a past as black as their eyes; when they looked at you, you felt they were looking at you alone, and you in turn saw them and nobody else.

★

When she came home in the middle of the night, when I heard her from inside my dreams, jingling her keys like Saint Peter searching for righteous people up and down the city streets, stepping into the room where I was sleeping, still dressed and still clutching her photo album, I could see her, could see how she moved, how she looked in her skin-tight outfit, her hair blowing in the wind like a flag, even in my sleep ... So when she stole timidly across the dark room and stopped by the bed, hovering over me, watching me a while in the dark before eventually deciding to pry the album out of my grip, I was able to intercept her hand and pull her toward me without opening my eyes, and she submitted to the darkness I was pulling her into. Once her lips found mine she started kissing me greedily, holding nothing back. She had been waiting so long for this moment, dwelling on it, so it was bound to happen. She didn't even bother getting undressed, she just pounced on me still wearing the long jacket that covered up her heavy sweater and long dress. Her hair was falling in my face, blacking out the dim light setting the night into motion. Running my hands up her legs, I felt thick socks going almost all the way up to her knees, and then there was nothing else—no stockings or anything, which rattled me for some reason. I felt all of her at once, all of her weight and weightlessness, felt the warmth of her skin and the slightly damp panties that she slipped out of gracefully, continuing to kiss me, stepping out of them in just a few efficient motions, leaving them to dangle on her left calf, then she slid her hand down toward my jeans and quickly took care of them too. She started riding me, her hips clenching me powerfully. Occasionally she'd lean in, kissing me with abandon, gasping for air, and then drawing back again, caus-ing her hair to spill down onto her shoulders. Her face and neck glimmered in the dark, while her hands pressed firmly down on my chest, as though she was pushing me away or rejecting me, but, lacking the willpower to hop off of me, she could only bounce up and down, her gray jacket swaying like a sail in the wind and her rings catching on my shirt buttons. Her kisses smelled of strong tea and booze, and her clothes felt rough against me, contrasting with the softness of her skin; her teeth were sharp and her nails were bloody and predatory. Her hands slid underneath my shirt, leaving long, painful streaks on my back that glowed in the dark like electric wires. She screamed as she was about to finish, looking at me as though surprised. Her movements became jerky and painful; I got the sense that she was looking past me, moving automatically now, like a sleepwalker. I kept moving with her, keeping pace, staying with her, following a new rhythm with her, and we reached its finale together.

★

She lay down next to me, exhausted, and I ran my fingers through her hair for a while, not knowing what to say. More precisely, not knowing what she wanted to hear. She fell asleep after a bit, breathing warm air onto my shoulders, but when I let my fingers graze her cheeks, she quivered and sat up in the bed, looking fearfully at my face, as though trying to figure out who I was. She sprang out of her bed, dashed toward the door. Her panties were still dangling on her leg, but she didn't seem to notice.

"Tamara." I got up and followed her.

She ran through the living room and disappeared into the bathroom. I tried going in after her, but the door was locked from the inside. I leaned against it to listen and heard her turn on the water, sit down on the floor—her back against the door—and start crying.

"Tamara," I called, "open the door."

She didn't reply. The running water made her crying sound far away, made it almost inaudible.

"Hey," I said, leaning in toward the gap between the door and its frame. "What's going on? Just tell me. Did I hurt your feelings somehow?"

But she flatly refused to answer my question, so I started banging on the door, because I didn't want to leave her all alone in there. Leaving a woman in that kind of state all alone in a room by herself would have been an irrational and short-sighted decision; she was probably pretty lonely in there, so I was convinced I was doing the right thing by continuing to bang on the door. Suddenly, she turned off the faucet.

"Herman, everything's fine," she said firmly. She wasn't opening up the door, though. "Go to bed. I'll be out soon."

"Okay," I answered, taking a seat on the floor to wait.

She turned the faucet on again, rearranged some things, rattling around for a while, muttering to herself, then turned off the faucet a second time, opened the door quietly, saw me sitting there, and took a seat next to me without saying another word.

"I hope your feelings aren't hurt," she said, touching my knee. "I just get emotional sometimes."

"You all right now?" I asked.

"Yep. I'm all right. You okay?"

"Let's go to bed," I said.

"Give me a sec." She took a pack of cigarettes out of her coat pocket, lit one of them, and started kissing me, and her kisses tasted like tobacco and toothpaste; her skin was salty from her tears and her hair was as wet as a fisherman's net.

"I didn't want to tell you," she said. "You'll probably leave if I tell you."

"What happened?"

"Are you going to leave?" she asked.

"I won't, don't worry," I assured her.

"I just know you'll leave," she said. "Well, I'll tell you anyway."

"Could ya just tell me already?"

"Your accountant . . . something happened to her."

"You mean Olga?"

"Yeah. Injured called me and told me to tell you. Now you're going to leave. I just know it."

"What happened to her?"

"I don't know. She's in the hospital."

"Is it serious?"

"I don't know," Tamara said quietly. "I don't think so."

"Could you be a bit more specific?" I asked anxiously.

"What are you yelling at me for? All I know is that she's in the hospital. Injured told me to tell you. He said he's gonna pick you up in the morning."

"Let me have your phone. I'm gonna give him a call."

"Don't call him at this hour," Tamara protested wearily. "Wait until morning. He'll come by and give you all the details."

"Well, what if it was something really serious?"

"Wait till morning," Tamara repeated.

"That's easy for you to say."

"Why do you say that?" Tamara asked.

"Well, your accountant isn't in the hospital."

"I just knew you'd ditch me for her. She's young and you like her."

"What makes you think that?"

"Well, I can tell," Tamara said. "I really thought you'd stick around, you know? Since you're already here and all. But now I can see that's just not going to happen. I'm too old for you, isn't that right?"

"What are you talking about? You're crazy."

"Yep, I'm way over the hill," Tamara said. "No need to make any excuses. I'm doing just fine. I wasn't really counting on anything. Do what you want to do, okay?"

"Okay."

Still distraught, though calmer, Tamara finished her cigarette and put it out right on the floor.

★

"I wanted to ask you. That tall, dark-skinned guy in the photographs. Who is he?"

"The tall guy?"

"Yeah, the tall one."

"Arthur," Tamara answered. "Tamila's husband."

"Tamila's?" I asked, surprised. "I thought he was your husband."

"Well, then he was my husband. At first he lived with Tamila, and then with me. He loved me a lot."

"Where's he now?"

"He was murdered," Tamara explained. "About ten years ago. They wanted to take his business away from him, but he wouldn't give it up. So, they blew up his car with him in it."

"Oh, man."

"But that was so long ago," Tamara said.

"What about your cousin?" I inquired. "Are you on speaking terms?"

"Yeah, she forgave me. She loved him a lot too. We only truly bonded after he died. It's funny how things work out. So," she asked after a long pause. "Are you going to see her?"

"I don't know."

I didn't want to lie, but telling the truth would have been even worse.

6

The sun blinded us awake and Injured was charging through the apartment like a guy who knew exactly what his time was worth and exactly what he could accomplish with it. There was fresh air nestled into his leather jacket as though he had come carrying scraps of an October morning in his pockets. He gave me a hearty good morning, as if to say, "I'm glad to see you still in one piece," then went over to the kitchen, filling the tiny space with his body, moving between the table and dishwasher, so tight a squeeze that his jacket squeaked, and peered out the window.

He had called Tamara a little past midnight, asking if I was at her place, if everything was all right, and said he would be stopping by in the morning. Now he was sitting down at the kitchen table with me, letting the wide, crooked rays of sunlight tint his skin gold and copper. He looked us over, first taking in Tamara, who was still half asleep, standing in the corner, before getting down to business with me:

"You know," he said, "it's a good thing you didn't wind up going all the way to Donetsk. They picked my brother up a few days ago. I had no fucking idea what was going on. I kept calling him, see? And some cop kept picking up. At first I thought maybe my brother had dumped his phone on someone again, or that he'd lost it somewhere, or something like that. But actually, they've been keeping him at the station for three days now. His wife called me yesterday and said everything was fine, that I had nothing to worry about, that he's doing all right . . . he's still got a healthy appetite, his own lawyer, and they'll be letting him out soon."

"What'd they get him on?" I asked.

"I couldn't tell ya," said Injured. "Last year they got him on his annual tax return—he wanted to file it a year early to save time. Before that they got him on bribing a government official. He's in the cell phone business, you know."

"He works for a carrier?"

"No, he sells phones," Injured explained. "Used ones."

"Stolen ones, too?"

"Sure, that comes with the territory."

"Maybe you should pay him a visit?"

"Nah," Injured said. "He'll figure it all out. He's a big boy. I've got enough problems of my own. Isn't that right, Tamara?"

But Tamara too had problems of her own. She'd been up practically the entire night, worrying, wondering whether she had said too much, thinking about how she didn't know what to expect from me now. She stood there, dejected and engrossed in her thoughts, nodding her head and agreeing with everything Injured said. I don't think Injured picked up on the fact that something was up between Tamara and me, but he still looked uneasy, and this quickly rubbed off on me. I immediately started bombarding him with questions about what was going on; it's not like I could ask about Olga directly while Tamara was around . . . Still, it would've been nice for Injured to take the hint and tell me what had happened to her. I guess he didn't consider the matter pressing. He mainly seemed to want to tell old stories.

Soon, Tamara realized that we were just killing time until we could get back on the road; she made us some strong and hopelessly bitter tea, then disappeared into her room, visibly distressed.

"Hey Herman," Injured said, "what kind of job did you have back in Kharkiv, again?"

"Why do you ask?"

"Ah, it's nothing. Just that some folks from up there have been looking for you, asking about you back at the station. And you know what I think?"

"What's that?"

"It'd be best if they found you."

"How come?"

"The way I see it, you weren't actually the one who screwed up. They probably only need you as a witness."

"A witness? What for?"

"I couldn't tell ya. You got anyone back there in your pocket?" he asked hopefully. "I mean, you ever bribe any government officials?"

"Damn it, Injured, I would have, but I didn't have the money."

"All right," Injured said. "Well, it's probably fine either way. It's just that those guys came by again yesterday. There were two of them. They want a word with you. They said you had nothing to be scared of."

"Well, I'm not scared anyway. Did they talk to you?"

"They talked to Olga."

"Did they stop by her office or something?"

"Yeah. At first she wanted to kick them out, but then she wound up listening to what they had to say. *Then* she kicked them out."

"Who are they?"

"Well, all they said was that they wanted to talk to you. Some loose ends they want to tie up, or something. They didn't give any specifics, but they said it'd be better for you if you met up with them, and Olga more or less told me she agreed."

"You really don't have any idea what it's all about?"

"If you meet with them, you can find out. It's not like they came out here to strangle you, right?"

"That's the question. But where do I find them?"

"It's pretty damn simple. They're staying at the hotel. You'll find them there."

"At the hotel? Maybe it'd be easier just to call them?"

"They didn't leave their number," Injured said, after a moment's thought. "These are some shady dudes. They stopped by and sniffed around like they were trying to find something."

"Like what?"

"I really don't know. Like I keep saying, it'd be best for you to talk to them yourself."

"Okay, I'll stop by the hotel today."

"Go for it," Injured said encouragingly. "Don't be scared."

"I'm still not scared."

"You've got nothing to lose."

"You've got that right." Taking a quick look around to be sure Tamara hadn't snuck back into the kitchen, I asked, "How's Olga doing?"

"Bad," Injured replied, without even a moment's thought, as though he'd been ready with the answer all along, and had just been waiting for me to ask. "She's in the hospital."

"And how the hell did she manage that?"

"It happened yesterday, when she was trying to kick those two guys out."

"*Trying* to kick them out?"

"Well, yeah. She didn't even listen to their whole spiel, you know? She showed them the door, and when she was slamming it after them, she got her foot caught, somehow, and broke her toe."

"She broke her *toe*?"

"Yeah, her toe. Now she's in a cast. I mean, you have to think about what you're doing when you do it!" he added, nonsensically.

"Maybe they said something that pissed her off?"

"Herman," Injured said, now sounding a bit anxious, "I don't know what they said to her, okay? All I know is that Olga told me to tell you to meet up with them. She seemed concerned, was asking all sorts of questions about you."

"She's worried about me?"

"Maybe."

"I guess I'd better stop by and visit her."

"Yeah, pay her a visit," Injured said. He struggled to his feet, casting a suspicious glance at the dishes on the shelves before heading for the front door.

"Hold up," I said, getting up too. "I'm gonna go with you."

"You know what? Why don't you sort out your own stuff first, all right?"

"Injured," I said, "you're acting pretty cagey, even for you . . . what's on your mind, anyway? Is there something else going on?"

Injured hesitated for a second and then sat back down at the table with me. It turned out that there was more to the story—some serious things had happened while I was hiding out. The corn guys had started really playing rough. They hadn't touched our gas station, though Injured had reason to believe that they would any day now. Instead, they'd cracked down on Ernst, the friend to all aviators—they tracked him down at the airport and proceeded to inform him, without providing any supporting paperwork, that the airport did indeed belong to the state. So, despite the fact that it had obviously gone to shit, and despite the absence of even a single passenger flight in or out of the city, the runway itself was still on the state's balance sheet . . . meaning that, one way or another, Ernst would have to hand it over to the official representatives of the people. And all of Ernst's attempts at getting the corn guys to fuck off had come to nothing. Moreover, he'd been issued a tough ultimatum: Ernst was told that if he even contemplated putting up any further verbal or physical resistance, this matter would be turned over to the authorities, and, naturally, there was no need to explain who the authorities worked for around here. Ernst was given three days to gather up his stuff and vacate the airport he had unlawfully occupied.

"How's he holding up?" I asked.

"He's hanging in there," Injured said. "He's set up some

barricades outside the entrance and he's gotten out his prized grenades. Now he's holed up in there, waiting. We're trying to do something for him. We went to the courthouse and did what we could to push back on the corn guys, but they just froze us out. We've got nothing we could use in court, because the airport really is a state asset."

"Injured, I just don't get it. What do they need the airport for?" I asked. "What do they need our gas station for, come to think of it? They just wanna take over everything in sight, is that it?"

"They've got their own vision for the development of the region," Injured said, a little vaguely. "They're going to build an asphalt plant where the airport is, I hear."

"They couldn't build their asphalt plant someplace else? Is the airport built on holy ground or something?"

"Herman," Injured said, like an older brother. "They could build their factory wherever they wanted. Seems like they want to build it at the airport and nowhere else, got that?"

"Got it. So what now?"

"You know what. You don't have to get involved. You've got your own problems. What do you need the airport for?"

"What do you mean? What do *you* need it for?"

"Well, I live here, man," Injured replied.

"I live here too," I said. "What the fuck, Injured? Do you still not trust me? I'm staying."

"I trust you. It's just that I've got a bad feeling about this one."

"A bad feeling about what one?"

"I feel like we're not gonna get anywhere on this."

"So what if we don't? We should at least try, right?"

"Right."

"We can't just roll over, right?" I asked.

"Well, yeah, you're right," he said. "Just chill out, okay? I've been thinking it all through . . . about why they backed down this summer."

"So, why'd they back down?"

"I don't know," Injured replied. "I just can't figure it out."

"Well, they backed down," I said, "and that's all there is to it."

"Yeah, sure. But there's no guarantee they'll back down this time."

"Look, Injured, if they don't back down then we'll cross that bridge together, all right?"

"Sure," Injured said hesitantly. He got up again, and this time he made it all the way out the front door. I made to follow him, but Tamara appeared and stopped me as I was crossing the threshold.

"Wait up," she said. Injured saw what was going on, so he bounced down the stairs and left the two of us alone. "Sorry if I said more than I should have yesterday."

"Everything's fine, Tamara. I'll give you a call later on, okay?"

"You do that. Try not to forget."

"I won't forget," I told her.

"Okay," she said. "Well, it won't be a big deal if you do. And, look, I almost forgot, but the presbyter brought you a book. He said he wants you to read it closely."

"Some church book?"

"Dunno," Tamara answered wearily, handing me the book and pushing me out the door at last.

★

The metal gate with the black stars on top looked orphaned. A feeling of emptiness and neglect permeated the place, despite the fresh tire marks leading straight up to the entrance. A spiderweb hung in the air, as if anchoring the metal to the ground. It was quiet, and seemed devoid of life, at first glance; the air was heating up slowly, like in a room where nobody lives. Autumn was setting in, I guess. And despite the apparent desolation, I could sense life behind the gate, as though a besieged army were hiding there and observing us nervously through gun slits. Injured beeped his horn, but to no avail—there wasn't a single movement behind the black gate, and no one called out to us from beyond the moat. Injured took out his cell.

"Hello?" said a flat and mistrustful voice on the other end of the line.

"Come on, open the gate already," Injured said by way of greeting.

It occurred to me that Injured hadn't been acting right, lately; for the past few weeks, really; he'd been quieter than usual, though you'd have had to know him well to notice. Where had his rough exterior gone? "Maybe our star striker is showing his age," I thought to myself. Like this back and forth with Ernst—instead of hassling the guy, who must've already been scared out of his wits, Injured was sitting and waiting patiently for him to let us in.

Ernst too wasn't at his best. He was masked and already dressed for winter. He was wearing a cut-off overcoat that covered a red, stretched-out T-shirt. I could see high army boots on his feet.

He was holding a pioneer spade and his pockets were drooping, weighed down by what I hoped weren't really live grenades. He was happy to see me. He said it was a good thing I had showed up, that he had a lot to tell me, that he had just gotten back from a terribly interesting expedition, which I, as a historian, would find particularly fascinating. He was planning, in other words, on talking my ear off, but at that point Injured interrupted him, declaring that he didn't want to hear anything about any fascist tanks or about fascism at all, for that matter, that he'd prefer it if we could just shut our traps. Once Ernst opened the gate, Injured pulled in and stopped his car on the cracked asphalt inside—all summer the grass had been pushing its way up, waging a furious struggle with the hard road, only to freeze as soon as it reached the surface, with winter on the way.

Injured got out and sat on the hood of his car; we took up positions around him. We looked like a few old friends who'd just happened to meet up on the way here or there, and so decided to stage an impromptu reunion. The gas guys were on their way, however, they were supposed to show up any minute now. Injured was listening intently for the sound of any traffic on the highway. He told Ernst to keep his spade ready and try not to make a fool of himself. He told me to keep my mouth shut and not get in the way.

"I'll do the talking," he said. "All you guys need to do is chuck some grenades at them when I give you the signal." It took me a second to realize he was joking.

They showed up half an hour later. Ernst tensed up, and Injured went quiet, keeping a cautious eye on our guests; nobody knew what to expect from them, and nobody was entirely sure why they'd bothered making the long trip out here. The same old Jeep pulled up first; I took a closer look, hoping to see Nick at the wheel, but it was some other guy; he looked about fifty, with short hair, a heavy leather jacket, and an equally heavy look in his eyes.

The back door of the Jeep opened, and Nikolaich fell out. He too was wearing a leather jacket, and also sported a black cap that neatly covered his pale, autumnal baldness. Seeing me, he froze for a second, as though verifying some information stored away in his mind. Then he hurried over to the Beamer pulling through the gate. Nikolaich opened one of the back doors, and a tall, gray-haired man, wearing a long, dark jacket and holding a briefcase, stepped out of the car. This fellow buttoned up his jacket while Nikolaich held his briefcase for him, hugging it against his stomach, looking like a trained German shepherd holding something in his teeth, after which the gray-haired man took his case back and moved decisively toward us with Nikolaich in tow. He didn't have any bodyguards with him.

They greeted us reservedly—no handshakes or anything. Nikolaich, who kept looking at me but avoiding eye contact, was bustling around the gray-haired man, making various short comments, addressing only Ernst and Injured. He looked flustered and not at all sure of himself, which must have been because I was there. A few months back he'd been offering a fair down payment on my soul, throwing his weight around, making a show of being tough and decisive to puff himself up in my eyes—but now the shit had hit the fan, so he had to do some serious ass-kissing to avoid taking the blame. The gray-haired man, unlike Nikolaich, actually looked self-assured and prudent, like he didn't have anything to prove to anyone. He was there to get something that already belonged to him—no need for displays of strength. He approached us, treading firmly across the beat-up asphalt, and put his briefcase nonchalantly on the hood of Injured's car, but the owner gave him such a withering glare that he removed it again without comment, handing it back to Nikolaich, who stood planted behind his superior, occasionally peering out from behind and trying to keep up with the negotiation process. He was scared.

The gray-haired man started the conversation. Quickly determining that Injured was going to be acting as our esteemed yet glum representative, not the joker in the cut-off overcoat, he brushed Ernst and me aside and got down to business, still radiating an absolute confidence that everything had already been settled, and that this little show was only being put on out of respect for us. In fact, he didn't much want to be talking to any of us—but he apparently thought that we deserved to know why.

"Well, what have we got here?" he asked, as though resuming a previous conversation. "This is the government decree, and these are the resolutions from the public prosecutor's office. And here's a statement from the utilities department." Injured accepted all the documents without so much as glancing at them; he already knew what they said. "We'll have a car come by tomorrow and, our guys will help you pack up your stuff. What time would be good for you?"

"There won't be a good time," Injured replied. "And there won't be any cars coming by, either."

"How's that?" the gray-haired man asked, a bit put out, but clearly taking great satisfaction in our misfortune just the same. "Of course there will. I've already arranged for it."

"Who'd you arrange it with?" Injured asked coldly.

"I arranged it with the driver," the gray-haired man answered just as coldly.

"And what about us?"

"What about you?" He was acting like he didn't even understand Injured's question.

"Did you arrange it with us?" Injured asked.

"I'm pretty sure we did," the gray-haired man replied.

"No, in fact, you didn't," Injured assured him. "Nobody cleared anything with us. So keep your car back in the city."

"What about the statement from the utilities department?"

"We don't give a rat's ass about the utilities department," Injured said, "or their statement."

"Is that a fact?" the gray-haired man asked.

"Sure is."

"Sasha," Nikolaich said, stepping out from behind his shadow with the briefcase clenched loyally in his teeth, "what the fuck are you listening to all this cheap fuckin' rhetoric for?"

"Shut your trap," the gray-haired man snapped. "You're a reasonable man," he told Injured, "you must realize that if you don't let our car onto the premises tomorrow, we'll just bring in the bulldozers. And you'll have to pack up by yourselves and leave anyway. You realize that, right? We've got all the paperwork right here."

"You're also a reasonable man," Injured said, doing his best to ape his opponent's calm, credible tone of voice. "You know perfectly well how you got those documents. There's nothing legal about any of this. It's a goddamn land grab, and you know it."

"A land grab, you hear that Sasha?" Nikolaich cried out from behind the gray-haired man's back, nearly dropping the briefcase in his mouth. "This isn't a fuckin' land grab."

The gray-haired man paused for an instant, ignoring Nikolaich's cries, then asked, his voice metallic:

"So, you're trying to say that you're refusing to vacate the premises?"

"We're not messing around," Injured said, making a show of getting even more comfortable on the hood of his car.

"Okay, then," the gray-haired man said, almost kindly. "Nikolaich," he ordered, "give Mr. Pastushok a ring. We need to settle this."

Nikolaich seemed to shrivel up. He put the briefcase on the ground and lowered his eyes.

"Hey," the gray-haired man addressed him again. "Are you listening?"

"Yeah." Nikolaich was scared to death, but he forced out a reply, terrified of breaking the Young Pioneer code.

"Well, what are you waiting for? Call him already," the gray-haired man ordered.

"No," Nikolaich answered quietly, sweating profusely. "I'm not going to call him."

"What'd you say?" The gray-haired man became rigid where he stood.

"I can't," Nikolaich whispered. "I can't call him. He calls me."
"What?"

"I said he's the one who calls me," Nikolaich replied, gradually starting to regain his usual demeanor. He knew that as long as he followed Mr. Pastushok's instructions he'd be in the clear.

"I can't just call him up." The subtext was plain: "You're the one screwing this up, so you fix it yourself—there's no fuckin' way you're going to put me in the line of fire again, which is exactly what would happen if I were to have another conversation with our dear Mr. Pastushok."

"All right," said the gray-haired man. "So now what?" He wasn't used to backing down. "He's going to call," Nikolaich replied after gathering his thoughts. "Soon. At twelve."

The gray-haired man jerked his arm abruptly, taking a look at his watch.

"Forty-five minutes," he said, a bit flustered. "So we'll just hang around till then, okay?" he asked, addressing Injured, who apparently held enough cards now that his approval was necessary.

"All right," Injured said. "That's fine. Let's go," he said, turning to me. "Let's have a smoke."

Hopping down onto the asphalt, he passed the gray-haired man quite lackadaisically and headed behind the building, toward the runway. I followed him. Ernst, who was just standing there nervously between the gray-haired man and Nikolaich, eventually ran after us, flagrantly neglecting his duties as host.

★

The grass by the runway had been mowed recently and everything smelled strongly of still plant juice. The buildings, dark and empty as unused pots and pans, stood spectrally amid the autumn vegetation, amid the cornfields that circled the airport, threatening to invade all the cracks in the asphalt with their dry stems and hot roots, to grow through all the windows and manholes, stretch out onto the walls and tin roofs, and erase any sign that a few generations of pilots had been here. The smell of the grass on the wind was mixed with the scent of sun-kissed fuel oil that had burrowed into the ground and made it insensate.

"Who was that guy?" I asked Injured, looking back to where the gray-haired man would have been visible had the main building not been in the way.

"Their lawyer," he said.

"What about what's-his-name—Vladlen Marlen or Marlen Vladlen—who's that?"

"Their boss. Mr. Marlen Pastushok."

"You know him?"

"Nope. He hardly ever shows his face. But everyone's afraid of him."

"How old is he?"

"Couldn't tell ya," Injured said. "I've heard he's a really young guy."

"Well, that lawyer of theirs is a real shady dude," I said, trying and failing to catch sight of him around the corner of the building.

"Their lawyer's fine. It's that bald fag I don't like. You can tell he's just waiting for a chance to screw us."

He stuck his hands in his jacket pockets and set off, kicking some empty beer cans down the runway with his heavy shoes.

"Hey," I said to Ernst, who was still all bundled up in his old overcoat. "Did you know Arthur, Tamara's husband?"

"Arthur?" he asked, his mind on other things. "I knew Arthur, sure. We even had a business together. It went under, though."

"How did he and Tamara get along?"

"They had a good marriage," Ernst said. "It didn't last long, though. He left her for Tamila, her cousin."

"Seriously?"

"Yeah. That sure was something else. *Sturm und Drang*! They nearly killed each other. Tamara even started cutting herself. You ever notice how she's got all those things on her arms? That's so you can't see the scars. They didn't talk for about two years or so, but then they eventually made up."

"Did he die?"

"Arthur? Nah, he moved to the Netherlands. He sold cars for a bit and then opened up his own restaurant. Sometimes he writes them letters. He always writes both of them at once."

"How do you know?"

"Know what?" Ernst asked.

"Well, about the scars and the letters."

"Well, Tamila and I lived together for six months or so. Then she told me she wanted kids, but I wasn't ready for that—well I've got my aviation stuff to worry about, you know what I mean."

"Who would have thought," I said, surprised by his story. "They didn't seem like the type to freak out over anything."

"Yeah," Ernst mused. "Life doesn't make a whole lot of sense sometimes. You never know what's down there below the surface. You think you know all there is to know, that you see what's really going on, but no, usually we're all completely in the dark about what's right in front of us . . ."

I looked around. So what was actually going on right in front of me?

★

The wheat, tough and thick, which had been growing here for years, slowed them down, blocking their path, so they had to tear through the dry, intertwining stalks. The boisterous, happy group walked along under the sunbeams, tripping over their shadows, which were getting underfoot like hunting dogs. Young, smiling pilots wearing leather caps and jackets, with heavy watches on their arms and brown clipboards in their hands, emerged out of the golden waves of sun, out of the bitter October air. They passed by, yelling back and forth, joking about something that had happened here at this particular airport some twenty odd years ago— they couldn't really remember it in detail anymore, so they'd come back here to jog their memory.

The wheat stalks were finding their way into their boots and pockets; spiderwebs wrapped around their fingers and rested on their hair. They lifted the webs gracefully toward the heavens, doggedly attempting to extricate themselves from the clutches of these endless fields. Mechanics wearing black overalls were bringing up the rear, carrying canvas bags filled with letters and parcels that they had preserved all these years. The bags caught the sunlight, igniting a green flame in their wake. The mechanics were laughing, squinting ever so slightly behind their sunglasses, eyes on the sky that rang like porcelain in the crisp, autumn air.

But they weren't the only ones out in the field; an odd-looking aviation team, who had fallen even farther behind the mechanics, was rolling the swaying carcass of an Antonov An-2 airplane out of the sunny haze, its bodywork and paint glimmering despite its orange coating of dust. They pushed the plane along, dripping with sweat, coughing in its cloud of dust, but they wouldn't give up, couldn't stand to abandon their machine in the middle of the field, no matter how difficult their task.

The pilots continued striding down the runway, heading for the empty, resonating hangars, full of dark air like sluices clogged with river water. After their voices had disappeared behind the buildings, the mechanics arrived and tossed their mailbags onto the asphalt before wandering off to their respective garages, filling them with laughter and happy shouting. Then the ones bringing up the rear finally reached the runway, leaving their low-flying aircraft right in front of the airport's administrative buildings.

The machine, dried out by the drought and scorched by the sun and cocooned in spiderwebs and tufts of grass, sat there in the middle of the runway as though it was trying to figure out where it should go next and how it should get there. Soon an insistent rustling sound came from the airplane's innards—it was as if somebody was clawing at the upholstery, groping for a way out. The airplane's doors burst open, allowing a bright beam of sunlight into the black, stuffy pit of its interior. Red foxes and black cats started hopping out, doves and swallows flew into the sky, toads leapt onto the runway and bats spilled out like pears falling from a tree. All the beasts of the sky and earth who had been hiding on board and, who had suffered due to the extreme heat, the stuffiness, scattered now, trying to get as far away as possible from that infernal machine, and all the sky along the border with its patches of turbulence like traps set for their souls.

★

"Herman," Injured said, tapping me on the shoulder. "Well, are you coming?"

The gray-haired man and Nikolaich were still just standing there opposite each other like two dancers on a parquet floor, waiting for the music to start. The gray-haired man was glowering at Nikolaich, practically hissing through his gritted teeth. Nikolaich was squirming and nodding his head dejectedly. If they were talking, they both went quiet when we came up to them.

"Well?" Injured asked.

"Let's wait for another five minutes," the gray-haired man said.

"Sure." Not that we had much of a choice, after all.

We stood there, counting off the seconds, trying not to look each other in the eye, examining the cracks on the asphalt that were deep like wrinkles on a clown's weary face.

Nikolaich's cell rang. He reached into his pocket and held the phone up to his ear, looking as though he was having a panic attack, sweating profusely.

"Hello," Nikolaich said, and much too loudly considering how quiet it was at the empty airport. "Yes! Yes, Mr. Pastushok, he's here. He's standing right next to me. Yes! I'm handing him the phone now!" he said frantically, doing precisely that, with evident relief.

The gray-haired man's movements were no less hasty, now. His neat, lawyer's fingers grabbed for Nikolaich's cell phone awkwardly.

"Yes, Mr. Pastushok," he said, trying to sound firm and unconcerned; this quickly became something like a hysterical whine, however. "We're here. Everything is fine, Mr. Pastushok. They don't want to, Mr. Pastushok. They're waving their dicks around, Mr. Pastushok." Injured took umbrage at this last comment. "I said that they're refusing to cooperate, Mr. Pastushok. What? They said it's some sort of protest. They're saying it's the local community. They're saying we have no right to . . . What? I already told them that we do! I showed them the papers! Mr. Pastushok, I'll definitely sort this all out. I'll figure it out, don't worry. Definitely. I don't know yet. Maybe we can make a deal, Mr. Pastushok. Tell them to what? Tell them to fuck off? That's clear, Mr. Pastushok. Yes, everything is clear, don't you worry one bit! Sorry for all the hassle. I'll figure it all out! Yes! You too, Mr. Pastushok, you too!"

The gray-haired man turned off the phone and handed it back to Nikolaich, his hands pale and bloodless. He took a snow-white handkerchief out of his jacket pocket, and his trembling hand wiped a copious layer of sweat off his face. He struggled to fit his handkerchief back in his pocket, but he eventually managed to stuff it in more or less as neatly as before. He took his briefcase back from Nikolaich, who, expecting the worst, curled up behind him like a dog encountering a group of strangers. Injured was smiling in a rather peculiar manner.

"Well, this is how it's gonna go down," the gray-haired man declared, addressing Injured. The fingers that clutched the handle of his briefcase had turned blue. "I warned you. Don't say I didn't warn you. You have exactly twenty-four hours. We are going to bulldoze everything tomorrow. And you'll be held liable for failing to cooperate with the lawful representatives of the utilities department."

Once again he reached for his handkerchief and started wiping the sweat off his neck, his hands shaking all the while. He headed for his car without saying another word. Nikolaich, trotting along at his heels, gave us a strange, threatening look before hopping in the Jeep. It was as though he wanted to say something but lacked the courage to do so. Instead, he decided to bide his time.

"Well," Injured said, "now we've got some real problems."

7

He knew what to do. He had calculated everything precisely and knew that his friends would have his back if things got rough. Because business is just business, but the blood they shed together during fights on the soccer field and around the neighborhood bound and united them. This had nothing whatsoever to do with business. The cry of bloodlust far outweighs the voice of reason—that's what Injured thought, anyway, and he was proved correct. It was confirmed the very next day when the entire gang, all the guys I'd known since I was a kid, crawled out of their dens, offices, stores, and markets to come back us up, like it always was in the good old days. Except, of course, that this wasn't the good old days. It was now.

As soon as Nikolaich and the gray-haired man left the airport, Injured and I also headed back to the city. He let me out by the community college dorms; I dove into the echoing October air and came out from behind the college buildings into a quiet, empty street. I pushed on until I reached the stone wall around the hospital. "There are times when someone's expecting you," I thought to myself, "and you just have to come back whether you want to or not." The buildings were quiet and spiderwebs were coasting by. The patients peering out the windows looked like fish in an aquarium.

★

The nurses couldn't wait to tell me about Olga. They griped about her bad manners, lack of discipline, and generally grating personality. They couldn't be sure what my relationship to her was, so they didn't go into too much detail. Mainly they did a lot of sighing, not really expecting any sympathy from me.

★

Olga was alone in her ward—perhaps the kind-hearted nurses couldn't bear the thought of inflicting her on a roommate. She was sleeping in her bed, a carefree smile on her face. She was wearing worn Levi's jeans and a heavy baseball jacket. Her right pant leg had been torn all the way up to her knee and her cast looked like a new sneaker. Her hair flamed in the afternoon sun, and her skin faded into the snow-white sheets like milk on rice paper. Vases filled with flowers rested on the chairs and floor. The wasps and butterflies that wavered around the flowers were torpid and inattentive—like they usually get as winter comes on. I cautiously took a seat on the edge of the bed. There were oranges by the bed, open books resting on the floor, and Olga was still clutching her cell phone, even in her sleep. There were apple trees outside the hospital windows, their branches, quivering dryly in the light breeze, been picked nearly bare by the nurses and patients. Nearly bare, as just then a tiny apple fell off one of them and plunked down onto the windowsill. Olga opened her eyes.

"Herman? What are you doing here?"

"I decided to pay you a visit. Who brought all the flowers?"

"Nobody," she said, after a second's delay, as though she'd opted against fabricating any stories. "I asked the nurses to bring them. I wanted you to think that somebody had been worrying about me."

"That's more or less what I thought."

"Great. That's just great."

"How's your foot?"

"It's fine." She checked her phone for new messages and then set it off to the side. "I asked them to let me out yesterday, actually. I said I was absolutely fine, but they wouldn't hear of it. They just went berserk."

"They said you were the one who went berserk."

"Yeah, sure," Olga said, a bit offended. "Like I don't have anything better to do. Well, whatever—one more day in here and I'll be going back home no matter what. I've got a ton of work to do, you know? It's not getting done while I'm stuck in this goddamn place."

"How'd you break it, anyway?"

"I wanted to close the door, that's all. Those bastards got me so worked up."

"What'd they even want?"

"Who knows." She fiddled with her phone again aimlessly before putting it back down. "They were real nosy, sniffing around, asking tons of questions. They were some real nasty guys. Also, one of them had a bald spot on the side of his head. Ever see anything like that?"

"What do you mean *on the side?*"

"Well, not up top, in the middle, like normal people have—off to the side, right above his ear. And he kept on asking me to repeat myself like he was a little deaf or something. He and his bald spot—they really pissed me off. Finally, I couldn't stand it anymore, so I kicked them out."

"Sorry for causing you so many problems," I said.

"It's no big deal. It's my own fault, really. At first I was just so mad at you . . . It's a good thing you decided to come by. Are you going to stick around for a while?"

"If you let me, yeah."

"Sure, stick around for a while. My relatives loaded me up with oranges. I feel like it's New Year's."

"Why New Year's?"

"I would always eat oranges on New Year's when I was a kid. Or when I was sick and had to stay home from school. It makes me feel like a schoolgirl again. Help me eat some of these, okay?"

"Sure," I said and started peeling.

The oranges were warm like fluorescent lamps. Juice squirted out of them and the wasps immediately started swarming over our heads. Juice dribbled down Olga's fingers as she ate; her fingers were so long I watched the drops trickle down for what felt like an eternity. Finally, she swept the drops away.

"Hey," she said, "I know that Injured's got some scheme going on out there . . . at the airport."

"Yeah. So what?"

"Are you going to be there with him?"

"Well, yeah."

"Keep an eye on him, all right?"

"What do you mean by that?"

"He's been acting strange lately. Maybe he's getting old."

"Maybe," I said.

"Stick with him, okay?"

"Sure."

"And watch your own back too."

"Whatever. What could happen to me?"

"I hope nothing," she said. Then, "Read to me a bit?"

I picked a book up at random. It was something to do with accounting. Countless passages were marked both by coffee stains and underlining in pencil; it was as though somebody had wanted to rewrite practically every sentence.

"Got anything interesting?" I asked Olga.

"I grabbed whatever I had in the office."

"Oh, hey," I said, "I just remembered. The presbyter gave me some kind of book. Want me to read it to you?"

"The presbyter?" Olga asked, looking upset for a moment. She quickly collected herself, however, or at least pretended she had. "All right, go for it. What's it about?"

I took out the book Tamara had given me. The pages were well-thumbed and yellowish; a few of them had even come loose from the binding and would fall right out if I wasn't careful. It was pretty obvious that the book's owner had used it heavily, marking certain passages and maybe even rereading it, but hadn't taken very good care of it. It was probably even taken along on trips, but it had never been left behind or forgotten. It had a rather peculiar title, too—*The Development and Decline of Jazz in the Donetsk Region*. I flipped through its yellow pages.

"I don't know whether or not you'll find it interesting," I said. "It might be better just to read about accounting."

"I'm so damn sick of accounting. What's your book about?"

"About the development and decline of jazz. In the Donetsk region."

"People played jazz down there?" she asked.

"I guess so."

"Well, c'mon," Olga said. "Just start reading from the middle, though. It's more interesting that way."

It seemed as though the October sun had gotten irrevocably tangled in the tree branches, its rays moving along the floor like seaweed in transparent water. I remembered that Olga and I had been in a hospital together once before, and that things had ended rather strangely that time; or, rather, everything had taken a strange turn around then and had continued being strange to this day and would probably go on being strange for some time to come. Olga made herself comfortable on the hospital pillows, looking somewhere past me, somewhere toward where the slow shadows of apple leaves were moving along the white wall.

So, I opened the book to a random page and started reading:

The development of the jazz scene in the Donetsk Region has traditionally been accompanied by climactic events and scandalous details. It is doubtless this scandalous quality that accounts for the almost complete lack of substantive research on the rise of jazz in the industrial south of what was then the Russian Empire.

The story to be told in this book is particularly odd and has yet to be exhausted.

Our primary concern here will be the nearly forgotten 1914 spring-summer tour of the region by the Abrams sisters. However, one could not start this account without providing the reader with a little context by describing the events leading up to the tour. The Chicago Methodist Church found itself the focal point of these events, as one of its smaller congregations was at this time running a soup kitchen that had formed a close partnership with a local branch of the Anarchist Black Cross (ABC), a charitable organization created to provide support for imprisoned anarchists, primarily those incarcerated in Tsarist Russia. The ABC was tasked with raising funds, hiring defense attorneys, and spreading anarchist literature across Europe. During the winter of 1913, one Mr. Shapiro, as well as his son—both active members of the ABC—met Sarah and Gloria Abrams, who were both singing in the Chicago Methodist Church's choir. The meeting took place in the aforementioned soup kitchen.

Gloria and Sarah Abrams had gained recognition on the North American musical scene as two of the most famous and original singers of spirituals—it was they who were largely responsible for the genre becoming a mainstream, rather than strictly religious, musical phenomenon. The Shapiro family immediately took an interest in the sisters' musical talents, seeing in these African-American sisters' popularity an opportunity to further their own political agenda. After much persuasion and numerous threats and bribes, the oldest member of the Shapiro family, Lev, managed to strike a deal with the sisters. The plan was simple—recruit the sisters and arrange a tour of the Donbas Region, a predominately industrial part of the Russian Empire, in order to spread anarchist literature among the working class, and in the process transfer a large amount of money to local anarchist organizations to finance revolutionary activities. Initially, the sisters categorically ruled out the idea of collaborating with émigré anarchist organizations. However, Lev Shapiro managed to woo Sarah, the younger sister, who was facing the possibility of being expelled from the Church at the time. Gloria and Sarah agreed to take part in this dubious operation and reach an accommodation with the church leadership on all the finer denominational points.

The head of the Chicago Methodists greatly appreciated the sisters' willingness to spread the teachings of their church among members of the Donbas proletariat and the German colonists of northern Russia. So, upon receiving the assistance promised to them, the sisters began preparing for their tour.

Olga, who had seemed to be listening attentively, chose this moment to break in: "There's something I forgot to say. Don't you find it a bit strange how closely their little gang has stuck together, through the years? I remember back in the '80s, when we were still young, their whole crew—Injured, Ernst, all those guys— didn't want anything to do with me and my friends. They didn't want any more problems. For instance, I remember how Ernst got caught for selling contraband jeans once . . ."

"Contraband jeans?"

"Uh-huh. He would buy designer jeans, rip them in half, pack

them up, and sell each leg separately. Actually," Olga added, "busi-
ness-wise, it was a pretty good idea."

"So what happened?"

"Well, they paid off the cops. They didn't leave Ernst hanging. They stuck by him. And I think that's why they've always had
so many problems . . . because they always stick by each other, no
matter what. They stick together and dig in. Think how many of
them are gone already—most of them didn't even make it to forty.
I think that they'd be better off if each of them would just look
out for themselves, you know?"

"Yeah, maybe we'd all be better off."

"All right," she said. "Sorry. Keep going."

In March of 1914, the sisters set off on the *Mesopotamia*,
a vessel owned by the Russian-Malaysian Steamship
Company. Barbara Carroll, an Irish-American and one
of their oldest friends, as well as Maria de las Mercedes, a
fellow singer and church member of Mexican descent—
and who had good reason to leave the country after the
church administration accused her of embezzling dona-
tion money—joined the Abrams sisters on their religious
mission.

The steamship that took the quartet across the Atlantic
Ocean was primarily used by Russian émigrés, living near
the ports of Crimea and Pryazovia in the hope of securing
passage to somewhere, anywhere, else. On the return trip
from America to Eurasia the vessel would be half-empty,
which naturally led to a spike in the number of contraband

goods on board, and facilitated a close bond between the majority of the crew and various smugglers. Back in New York, the *Mesopotamia*, primarily operated by Greeks and Gypsies, would be partially loaded with canned meat, manufactured goods, and mail sacks. Phonographs, which were highly sought after in Europe at the time, would also be shipped across the Atlantic.

The *Mesopotamia* happened to be one of the company's oldest vessels and was long overdue for repairs. It was designed to accommodate one hundred first-class passengers and roughly five hundred émigrés. The Abrams sisters were allotted a room in one of the empty holds; they rarely came out and had almost no contact with the crew. One should note that the sailors, who received a rather hefty sum for agreeing to transport the women, were quite apprehensive about this particular venture, and even rather belligerent toward them at times.

According to the younger of the Abrams sisters, Sarah, the voyage was arduous and interminable. The steamship sailed sluggishly through the green March Atlantic, its half-empty metal womb jangling. Scavenging seagulls had been trailing the ship all the way from New York. The Greek sailors would shoot them down with their revolvers, and they'd drop into the cold water like white roses. Terrified, the Abrams sisters locked themselves in their hold, which was as big as a gymnasium, listening to the shots and quietly singing their spirituals.

The steamship made its first stop off the coast of

Newfoundland. The island was covered by its usual blanket of fog, and as soon as the crew found themselves surrounded by this fresh, thick, milky substance, they stopped, not daring to venture any further into that wet, churning haze, populated by whales and icy mountains. The next morning, the Abrams sisters stepped out onto the deck, and on seeing the glaciers all around them, they started singing hymns. The sailors, who were bewildered at first, eventually joined in. Shortly afterward, the fog rolled out to the west, and the *Mesopotamia* reached the coast safely.

The ship set off again after a few days. The women divided their time between singing and chatting. They hardly had anything with them except for a change of clothes, some psalm books, their anarchist pamphlets, and two canvas bags stuffed with American dollars. The younger two, Barbara and Maria, asked Gloria endless questions about what awaited them. Gloria said that she didn't know a whole lot about Russia, but she had heard that life in the cities they were going to tour differed significantly from life in the United States. According to her, the local women were all fantastic singers and had perfect pitch, while the men usually accompanied them on their instruments. Unfortunately, sharp class disparities and cruel exploitation of the masses by their capitalist rulers had kept these men and women from being able to perfect their musical talents by singing the Lord's praises. Barbara and Maria were excited, greatly anticipating their arrival and performances in faraway lands, but the younger Abrams sister,

Sarah, was struggling with life at sea, crippled by seasickness and exhausting bouts of insomnia.

She would roam the lower reaches of the ship at night, stepping into spaces forgotten even by the crew, stealthily edging down dark, metal hallways, opening secret doors, behind which she found chambers of stagnant gloom. When she discovered the cache of phonographs, she took those odd, elaborate apparatuses, placed them on the floor in a ring all around her, wound them up, and turned them all on simultaneously, catching a rhythm, as imperceptible as a draft, in the resulting cluster of sounds and songs, and slipped into a deep sleep at the very bottom of the ship's floating metal heart. She would take out new needles for the phonographs, sharp and shiny, and pierce her palms. Her raspberry-colored blood would glimmer dimly in the dark glow of the lamp, dripping down onto the floor and attracting vulnerable ship rats.

One night, as she was walking down the hallways in an insomniac haze, Sarah came across yet another hold, one that she hadn't seen before. She could hear some whispering and moaning behind the door. Frightened as she was, she mustered up all of her courage and opened it. The black metal room beyond was filled with terrified and exhausted sheep. They were all bunched together, standing completely still and murmuring relentlessly into the void. Turning on the light, Sarah saw sparks ignite in their eyes, and only then did the blood become visible—they were up to their knees in it. The room was awash in a sea of blood, which rolled back and forth with the boat's motion, and the sheep, convinced that they were doomed, just stared at Sarah, not even bothering to rush for the now open door. The girl dropped to her knees, hugged the nearest animals, and started singing them spirituals. Gloria only found her the next day, in among the herd. Her sister was whispering to herself, tears trickling down her face. Gloria tossed a heavy Scottish blanket over her shoulders and led her back to her bed. Sarah fell asleep immediately, and slumbered until their arrival in Liverpool, as if she didn't have a care in the world

The ship was halted in Liverpool and deemed a health hazard by the authorities. The captain, an old Bessarabian Gypsy, instructed his crew to raise the yellow and black quarantine flag. Port doctors who came aboard diagnosed many of the crewmembers with syphilis, so the sailors were strongly encouraged to remain on the *Mesopotamia*. The crew was trapped. In the evenings, the whole choir would get together on the deck and sing quiet, despondent spirituals for them, making their hearts burn passionately and drop into their stomachs like golden stars falling into the emerald Atlantic. The sailors organized feasts and treated the women to contraband rum and pungent Turkish tobacco, telling them about their escapades in the brothels of Odessa and the yellow Bessarabian sun that sears the apple orchards white like a child's hair. After a week in the harbor, the *Mesopotamia's* crew mustered up enough courage to make their escape. The sailors raised anchor at night, and left the unwelcoming city of Liverpool behind, continuing along their planned route.

The ship made its next stop in Marseille, where the crew got themselves into a rather unfortunate jam when they went to the local markets to refill their provisions and tried selling some canned buffalo meat that they had been hauling for a good month or so. Some customs officers happened to get their hands on the sailors' contraband and detained the men as smugglers. The crewmembers were quick on their feet, however, and so started a massive fight, which allowed them to make good their escape, carrying their injured friends back with them. The *Mesopotamia* was forced to vacate the port of Marseilles immediately. The voyage was quickly wrapping up; the Americans took to gazing into the distance apprehensively, catching wind of the disquieting African heat.

Shortly thereafter, the steamship reached the Black Sea, passing the golden Crimean coasts and winding up in the bitter, frothy waters of the Sea of Azov. At the beginning of April, the *Mesopotamia* arrived in Mariupol.

"My mom used to go to Mariupol all the time," Olga said. "For work, mostly."

"What'd she do for a living?"

"Something to do with the railroad. She was hardly ever home. I don't really remember her all that well. She died when I was real young. She was always running off somewhere, and I would get this feeling when she was just about to leave, knowing I'd have to wait and wait for her to come back again . . . I remember that real well. I'd always be running to the train station and looking at the trains, hoping I'd see her there. I was pretty young, obviously. From then on they've been these terrible things you can just find yourself in, but you can't ever seem to get out again. What were you most afraid of as a kid?"

"Americans," I answered after thinking for a bit.

"What's wrong with Americans?" Olga asked. "Americans are fine. They invented jazz."

"Dunno. I didn't know anything about jazz as a kid."

"I was scared of train attendants," Olga said. "I still can't stand them. And conductors. And accountants too." And then, after a bit: "Hey—can you take me home tomorrow?"

"Yeah."

"Just make sure you don't forget."

"I won't."

"Okay," she said. "Okay."

The port of Mariupol, which was always packed with Turkish and Moroccan vessels at the time, truly impressed the Abrams sisters with its celebratory hum. The outdoor bazaars and cramped shops were filled with high-quality, affordable goods from Asia Minor and Western Europe; the dock buildings concealed treasures that had been shipped there from all over the world. Right there, in a port restaurant, the Abrams sisters signed a contract to sing their spirituals at concerts for the workers of the Novorossiya metal works and the French-Russian Association's mines. The missionaries settled in at the Tsar David, an inexpensive yet cozy hotel in town. According to Sarah Abrams's personal account of the trip, the local promoters, who were most likely coming into contact with African-Americans for the very first time, did their utmost to ensure that the women's stay was as pleasant as possible. The sisters immediately got to work, truly embracing their new audience. Their first performances at the metal workers' clubs were wildly successful and allowed the sisters to win them over at once. They flocked to the sisters' concerts, terribly enthusiastic about the North American spirituals, while the Americans in turn began to pick up various local customs and church practices, though they found them rather strange, as they combined aspects of more orthodox Christian teachings with paganism. The peculiar fusion of religions and literary traditions that had arisen as a result of a most fortunate confluence of circumstances and conveniently placed seaports provided the Abrams sisters with an abundant source of new inspiration. Within weeks, Gloria Abrams had written a few new songs that eventually became classics.

At the end of May, the sisters moved from Mariupol to Yuzivka, which Sarah Abrams described as "mostly a city of one- or two-story buildings, most notable for its fabulous stores, offices, banks, and constant improvements. The first-class hotels, the Great Britain and the Grand Hotel, attracted a multitude of businessmen from Belgium and Britain seeking to get rich quick. Yuzivka was a real goldmine for Western businessmen who were lacking opportunities in their

native countries. We were housed in one of the Novorossiya Company's cottages, along with skilled workers, engineers, and the company's British specialists. The Coliseum
and Saturn movie theaters were packed every evening with
dynamic, boisterous crowds, happily showing off their new
outfits from the ports of America and Japan. The workers,
on the other hand, preferred teahouses, public libraries,
and bathhouses, while on the weekends they frequented
churches and numerous gospel halls. Our music was well
received and the locals expressed their solidarity with the
working class of the United States of America."

One can only guess why those unfamiliar African-
American rhythms appealed to the Eastern European workers. Possibly it was that the Abrams sisters sang about life
in America's proletarian neighborhoods, about the working man and his daily struggles and concerns. The senti-
ments expressed by these North American vocalists were
easily understood and shared by a large cross-section of the
local working class. The sisters' popularity rose; they could
always be found at union clubs and Sunday services. The
Methodist Church had discovered an incredible tool for
propagating their religion—the girls spread the word, and
jazz would ultimately secure yet another convincing victory, winning over a completely new audience who had
never encountered anything like it before.

But when summer came, the situation became more
precarious. First of all, the Russian anarchists, tired of waiting, tracked the girls down and expressed their eagerness

to receive the funds intended for them. Surprisingly, the choir refused to transfer the money to the revolutionaries. Maria de las Mercedes was particularly adamant about this. She was the one who convinced Gloria to hide the bags stuffed with American dollars at their friend's apartment. She happened to be a member of the local Lutheran church's choir, and the insulted anarchists decided to take Maria out to intimidate the girls. Her body was found in one of the Novorossiya Company's warehouses. Gloria realized that the revolutionaries weren't going to stop there. Moreover, Sarah, who had developed a close relationship with the manager of a local bathhouse, announced that she was pregnant. Going against her sisters and the church, she opted to keep the child and return to America (in fact, she made the passage on the *Mesopotamia* again). Barbara Carroll, the fourth member of the choir, wound up accompanying Sarah home.

All by herself in a foreign land, Gloria Abrams decided to hold auditions for new choir members at the local churches. Meanwhile, she agreed to transfer the hefty sum she had received in America to the appropriate anarchist organizations. As planned, Gloria bought a ticket to Rostov, where she was supposed to pass the money along. Accompanied by local smugglers, she got on the train and headed east. She didn't make it, however. By the time the train arrived in Rostov, she'd vanished. Neither the train attendant nor her fellow passengers could provide any useful tips. All subsequent efforts made by the anarchist groups to track down Gloria Abrams or find out what had happened to the money she'd been carrying came to nothing—she had disappeared into the black hole of the Donetsk railroad along with those bags stuffed with dollars, not to mention her handwritten sheet music. Nevertheless, some of her work has survived, primarily thanks to Sarah, who preserved her sister's legacy as a relic of early jazz music.

The following spiritual (translated here from the original English) is one of the last extant pieces written by Gloria Abrams. Composed just before her sister departed back to the United States, it is rightly considered one of the most lyrical and socially charged masterpieces of choral jazz, and the underlying melody has become something of a standard, seeing use by such world-famous musicians such as Chet Baker and Charlie "Bird" Parker.

> Who stands on the piers by the anchorage as the sun bows out?
>
> It's us, Lord, the fishermen and workers after an exhausting day,
> returning from the wharfs,
> stepping on the banks and singing to
> the river water that has deserted us forever.
>
> What can men sing about on these quiet evenings?
>
> Lord, we remember our cities and we long for them.

We hang our horns and guitars upon the trees and
step into the river.
Standing in the warm waves, we sing to the fleeting
green water that flows past us.
Standing in the warm waves, we sing to the life that
slips between our fingers.

And when the passersby ask you to sing for them,
what will you say?

We'll say that our voices are bitter like prison tea.
Music squeezes our hearts like Moroccan oranges.
All of our songs serve merely as a reminder of those
hot city blocks
we left behind, merely as a mourning song for the disappearing water.
And if we forget our homes, then what are we supposed to sing about?
We ask our memory to stay with us and not leave us
alone.
All of our hymns about banks and shops eroded by time,
about markets and warehouses filled with goods.
About our women whom we are willing to die for,
and our children who will take our places at the factory one day.

We are all linked together by the rivers that flow
through our past.

And our women stand alongside us on their banks.
The prophet Zechariah leaves the factory for his lunch
break,
wipes away a manual laborer's sweat,
and washes oil and coal dust from his black hands
and nails,
scissors jingling in the pockets of his overalls.
For now, while he's not on the clock, he can look up
at the sky.
For now, he can take a break from the heavy work
that people count on.

Let the city remain etched in our memory.
Old train cars took us away from you,
and whoever forgets you will never be at peace.
Every one of them vanishes, their hearts torn to shreds.

It's so easy for us to share the past.
Life is a machine made for us,
and we know that there's no need to fear this machine.

Golden factories open up their gates to us,
the sky flies high, above our schools and stores.
The only things awaiting us are emptiness and
oblivion,
the only things awaiting us are love and salvation.

8

They had dark jackets, white dress shirts, and worn yet durable shoes. Their cars were the same—worn yet durable. Mercedes and Volkswagens. They were like a funeral procession. I walked around the hangar, stepped out onto the runway, and immediately locked eyes with them. They were standing by their cars like taxi drivers waiting for fares outside a train station. They were smoking and shooting the shit.

"Hey, Gadjo!" Pasha, Kocha's relative, yelled to me. Everyone came over. "Gadjo, a little bit late, aren't ya?"

I greeted them all one by one, starting with Pasha, who was holding a phone in each hand, then Borman, a fat guy whose red hair had grown out over the summer; he kept touching it as if he didn't believe it was there or that he couldn't quite believe it had actually grown out. After that I said hello to Arkady, Prokhor, and our other guys from the church, all those committed, well-intentioned members of the congregation, gathered in the middle of the runway; their black jackets made them look like guests at a wedding who had stepped outside for a smoke break between dances. I greeted Ernst, too, who looked like the groom—he looked very uncomfortable with this whole operation, even though he was the one who got us into it. I greeted Injured last and then stuck by him. Injured wasn't saying anything; it was obvious he felt self-assured with his whole gang there. He was wearing a light, comfortable black windbreaker, perfect for a rumble. He touched my hand.

"A letter came for you," he said, taking an envelope out of his pocket and unfolding it. "I forgot to give it to you yesterday."

The letter was from Katya. Her handwriting was round and childish. I put the envelope in my jeans pocket.

"I'll read it later," I told Injured, and he nodded.

The sun burned evenly above us, and the wind whipped across the men's tanned, nearly black faces. Everyone was focused and calm. Pasha was telling some story about how he bought a used Fiat for his daughter as a wedding present. He said the guy who sold it to him was from Moldova, from somewhere around Bessarabia, and he drove the car all the way up here, but he had forgotten all the documents for it at home, but he only told Pasha that after the money had changed hands, and now they didn't know what to do—the guy had to get home to pick up the documents but he didn't have his car anymore. Well, the wedding was set for a few days from now, and the Fiat was almost brand-new and the color of blood. They all tried consoling Pasha, telling him not to worry, saying forget the documents; they'd buy him all the documents he needed just as long as he didn't get all worked up. They said the Fiat was a good gift, a modest and necessary thing—they completely supported his decision to buy his daughter a car and promised to give the newlyweds a present of their own, something useful and almost brand-new. To the casual observer, the guys might have looked as though they were just about to go celebrate the marriage—as if they were going to finish their cigarettes and then they'd head back inside where their wives, sisters, and lovers were waiting for them. Pasha, however, still holding two cell phones, reminded us all that we had to live long enough to make it to the wedding first.

The corn guys were running late, and deep down I was already starting to hope that they just wouldn't show up—that everything would resolve itself without any hunting knives or bike chains, that we would all smoke one last cigarette and then shove off toward the old airport cafeteria, where Ernst would roll out his strategic alcohol reserves to celebrate the successful completion of our region's latest reprivatization case—not to mention the end of this hot summer, and the beginning of a warm autumn. We'd express our solidarity and deep, abiding friendship. The wine would linger on our lips like dried blood, and we would reminisce about all our women, ask each other about our families, and tell stories about mutual friends. The short, autumn day would flow into the thick early evening, a cold twilight would stretch out across the runway, and everyone would be tipsy, alive and kicking.

★

They pulled around the corner and advanced slowly. Ernst had left the gate open; we were all gathered on the runway now, behind the fence where nobody could see us. Maybe the corn guys took that as a good sign, as though the enemy had opened the gates of their city and given the marauders three days to pillage the hangars and garages, secure the runway, and establish their own little authoritarian regime. They only saw us after they pulled behind the hangars.

Their column was headed by a yellowish MTZ tractor equipped with two buckets—one lunging forward like a set of tusks and the other lagging behind like a tail. Two guys, one wearing a sailor's shirt and the other a robe, were sitting in the cab.

Nikolaich came next in his Jeep, and a truck brought up the rear with what appeared to be soldiers riding in the back—each of them equipped with a shovel. They were a ragtag bunch who clearly didn't want to be there; they looked like an old Soviet penal battalion, or maybe more like high school girls wearing their mother's dresses to prom, given how badly their uniforms fit. Perched on their raised flatbed, they gazed warily at the Gypsy crew waiting for them by their Mercedes and Volkswagens.

The tractor pulled up right in front of us, its buckets agitating the calm air. The engine kept running, though. The man wearing the sailor's shirt and the other guy in the robe were in no rush to step out of their vehicle—they sat there, like starlings, waiting for instructions from their superiors, who stood off to the side. Nikolaich, their little runt, was the first to hop down onto the runway. He was dressed for battle—decked out in a camouflage jacket with a heavy collar and matching pants with blue sneakers peeking out at the bottom. Borman started cracking up at the sight of him, and the rest of us joined in with his contagious laughter. Nikolaich, realizing that it was him everyone was laughing at, scampered anxiously around the Jeep, opening up the other door and letting their head honcho out. The gray-haired man sprang onto the asphalt, holding his briefcase in one hand and buttoning up his jacket with the other. He looked ready to get down to business, but then his manner also struck me as a bit affected—he didn't even close the car door behind him after getting out, as though he wanted to make sure he had an escape route open. The muscle he had brought along didn't look too intimidating either. They hopped down onto the asphalt and slinked along after the gray-haired man, who kept glancing back at them, unsure why they were taking the rear, as though hiding behind him.

"Injured," I asked, "what now?"

"Dunno. We'll see."

"They've got all their government decrees and orders after all."

"You know," Injured said, "they may not have any of that crap."

"What do you mean?"

"I mean they might not have jack shit. They might be bluffing."

The gray-haired man stopped short. Nikolaich ran up from behind. The penal battalion continued cowering behind their commanders, feet shifting uncomfortably in their mud-caked boots. The gray-haired man turned, struck a dramatic and overly theatrical pose, and began shouting at Nikolaich without even looking at him. Nikolaich barked back in reply. They continued shouting at each other for some time, glaring at us all the while, until one of them finally realized that we couldn't hear their performance because the tractor engine was still running. The gray-haired man went red in the face, while Nikolaich flapped his arms like a caged bird. Finally, the tractor drivers realized that they were getting the signal to turn off the engine, which they did. It got quiet.

"Nikolaich," the gray-haired man said after clearing his throat, now really hamming it up for the crowd, "what are they doing trespassing on these premises?" He waved his briefcase at us.

"It's unheard of!" Nikolaich snapped, soldier-like, and stomped his feet.

"Present these gentlemen with the order issued by the council and begin the demolition," the gray-haired man hissed.

"Yes, sir," Nikolaich answered, sweat dripping off his skin, breaking out into red blotches.

The gray-haired man popped his briefcase open, took out a piece of paper, and handed it to Nikolaich. Nikolaich struggled to swallow, as if the dry autumn air was clogging up his windpipe, and headed toward us. He was at a total loss by the time we finally came face-to-face. He didn't know who to show the order to— Ernst, who was considered an official airport employee; Injured, who had no official ties to the airport itself, but might slug him in the nose at any moment; or the Gypsies, whom Nikolaich didn't know personally and who terrified him anyway. Our crew stared him down, laughing right in his face. Nikolaich started sweating even more profusely. After a lengthy pause, Pasha finally pocketed one of his cell phones and extended his hand. Relieved, Nikolaich gave him the piece of paper. Pasha perused the decree and then handed it to Borman, who also scanned the page. The document was passed farther down the line.

The decree looked pretty unconvincing. Firstly, it was a Xerox copy; secondly, the seals on the signatures had been smeared like sauce across a tablecloth; and thirdly, the signatures were very dubious. The wording of the decree was rather hazy: it primarily focused on Ukraine's gross domestic product and improving the country's investment climate, on democratic reforms and the government's approval rating, but there was absolutely no mention of transferring the deed to the airport to another party or the need to drive tractors down its runway. The page made the rounds and wound up back in Pasha's hands. Pasha then went back to staring at Nikolaich intently, refusing to lower his eyes, black as death in that light. Nikolaich stood his ground, also refusing to lower his eyes—a generous dose of hatred, overwhelming his tired and uncertain gaze, spread slowly and thickly across his pupils. Then Pasha lifted the decree up to his mouth, stuffed it between his teeth, and started chewing it, watching for Nikolaich's reaction. When it came, it wasn't quite what I expected—his face lost what was left of its color, yes, and he seemed to sink back into his camouflage outfit, his eyes losing their malice and looking only weary and timid now; but the overall effect was one of petulance—as though the whole world were ganging up on him. Meticulously chewing the last bit of top-quality copy paper, Pasha swallowed the decree and grinned. Nikolaich threw his arms up in desperation, looking back at the gray-haired man.

"They . . ." he said. "Did you see that? They ate it. They ate it!"

The gray-haired man seemed lost in his thoughts. Evidently, Injured had been right—they were bluffing. They couldn't even rally the cops; all they had were some small fry with shovels. They thought they'd just waltz in here and we'd go along quietly. They hadn't gotten off to a great start—and, based on the gray-haired man's reaction, there was no turning back for them. His eyes started wandering; he got all squirmy, making an immense effort not to lose face. The soldiers looked deflated—they had come out here expecting that their day's work would just entail some manual labor for the benefit of the local oligarchs, but now that they realized that some punches were going to be thrown, and most likely they'd be the ones to take them, every one of them started hopping from one heavy, muddy boot to the other. When Pasha finally swallowed the decree the last flicker of hope whizzed past their crew cuts.

"Begin clearing the site," the gray-haired man said, after he'd had a moment to collect himself.

Nikolaich waved to the tractor drivers, as if to say, "Come on, start the engine. Now we're gonna mow every fuckin' thing down!" But, oddly enough, the drivers just waved back, as if to say, "Fuck that shit, you mow it all down yourself."

"Nicky boy," Nikolaich shouted at one of them. "Rev it up, c'mon Nicky boy!"

But both drivers shook their heads desperately, as if to say, "Boss, we're on break for the rest of the day."

"Hey!" Injured called out at Nikolaich. And then, to the rest of us, "Chill, guys." He was speaking calmly, as though trying to get us all to be friends. "They've got nothing."

"What do you mean 'they've got nothing'?" Nikolaich asked, offended.

"You know exactly what I mean," Injured said. "So beat it already. We'll sort everything out ourselves—we don't need any lawyers."

"We got nothing, huh?" Nikolaich asked, not hearing a word Injured said. He ran up to the tractor, which was yellow as the sun, and started jumping up and down, waving at the drivers to come down. "We got nothing, eh?"

"C'mon, you fuckin' bitch," the gray-haired man sputtered at Nikolaich, "do something. C'mon, you son of a bitch!"

Nikolaich stopped his hopping and considered the members of the penal battalion: his last line of defense. They did their best to disappear, lining up behind the gray-haired man, but the latter took a step off to the side, propelling them into Nikolaich's field of vision.

"You hear that?" Nikolaich asked his troops. "What are you standing around for? Forward!"

The penal battalion swayed and headed straight at us, but stopped after just a few steps, holding their shovels indecisively. Pasha exchanged scornful glances with Borman. And at that point, Arkady, pushing himself off his Volkswagen, moved forward. Prokhor followed suit. Unhurried, Arkady took out a pack of Camels, taking one for himself and then extending the pack to Prokhor, who took one too.

"In all honesty," Arkady said, "the seal was just fine. But that signature—man, that was something."

"Not at all," Prokhor said, gesturing for a light.

Arkady took out his lighter, lifted it up to Prokhor's cigarette, and then lit his own cigarette from the tip of Prokhor's. I could already tell where this was going.

"The signature was just fine," Prokhor continued, taking a luxuriant drag. "The seals, though—the seals were fuckin' shit."

"The seals were fuckin' shit?" Arkady repeated, adding a hint of poorly concealed sarcasm.

"That's what I said."

"The seals were absolutely fine," Arkady said heatedly. "Come on, dumbass, did you even look at them?"

"You're the dumbass," Prokhor replied—likewise heatedly, it must be noted.

Arkady neatly put out his cigarette and nailed Prokhor with a right hook from nowhere. Prokhor spun down the asphalt toward the penal battalion, his Camel flying out of his mouth in a wide arc—but he recovered almost instantly and pounced on his assailant. Arkady sidestepped Prokhor, who flew past him, charging like a bull. He pivoted and darted back toward Arkady, essentially hopping into his arms. Both of them wound up rolling down the warm asphalt like kids on the beach, Arkady trying to choke Prokhor, Prokhor repeatedly boxing Arkady's ears, maybe trying to make him go deaf . . .

The soldiers just stood there and watched, shocked, trying not to breathe, because they naturally didn't want to disturb those two ferocious lions of organized crime. Nikolaich, the old prick, knew all about our local gang's antics, and shouldn't have been unnerved; he stood there dead still, all pale and green, as though he had broken out in camouflage. The tractor drivers were peering intently out of their windshield, already quite invested in the struggle playing out in front of him. At last realizing how much these Gypsies were making a fool out of him, the gray-haired man spat onto the asphalt and tossed his briefcase from one hand to another.

"That's enough," he said, just loud enough for everyone to hear. "You're fuckin' dead meat. I wanted to settle this peacefully, but now you're fuckin' dead meat. You don't even know how fuckin' dead you are, you can't even imagine. And you, you fuckin' bitch," he hissed at Nikolaich. "Go hang yourself. You got that straight, you fuckin' bitch? Go and hang yourself right this minute."

He turned around and climbed into the Jeep. It peeled out, and disappeared behind the hangar. The troops scurried somewhat timidly off to their truck, hanging their heads. They tossed their shovels up first, then hopped inside and disappeared around the corner.

It got incredibly quiet. All we could hear were Arkady and Prokhor trying to catch their breath down on the asphalt.

Nikolaich looked us over, taking in each face in turn, stopping at Ernst. He zeroed in on Ernst, even though he hadn't actually done anything to Nikolaich—Ernst was only standing there alongside his friends, just killing time. But Nikolaich was staring directly at Ernst, who intercepted his scornful look and answered in kind. So there they stood, nobody paying much attention to them—Pasha had gone over to help Arkady and Prokhor up. Borman was surveying our guys, talking over the fight in detail, and Injured was talking with someone too, but something struck me as wrong about the way Ernst and Nikolaich were still standing there, glaring at each other like dogs before a fight, as though time had stopped and this whole situation pertained only to them, as though it were up to the two of them alone to decide how we were going to finish this.

It was obvious what Ernst was thinking. Ernst was thinking, "Something bad is going to happen, something real bad is definitely going to happen. For now, nobody can really tell—they all think that the worst is behind us and that the storm has passed. But that's not true at all." Ernst was very familiar with this feeling, with the sense of impending danger. It was coming, all right, and there was no way to avoid it. They'd have to run this gauntlet one way or another. There would be no way to speed the process up or avoid it altogether. All you could do was look the ominous beast in the eye and wait. Its terrible snout would sniff you for a while, then it'd just walk away, leaving fear and stench behind. Ernst almost immediately had a flashback to when he once felt the rotten breath of brewing trouble. He recalled that trapped feeling that clogged his lungs, he recalled that deep-seated fear that encroaches upon new territory like swollen rivers in March. Also, he remembered that the most important thing is to keep fighting and maintain eye contact. Then everything would be fine, and then everything would pan out—the most important thing is to be ready for the worst.

It was just as obvious what Nikolaich was thinking: "I still have time to fix everything. I'll get the job done, everything is going to be all right." Even while everyone was jeering at him, while everyone was humiliating him in front of his superior, in front of the army guys he'd arranged to have sent over, he kept thinking the same thing: "I'll get the job done. I'll fix everything." What was he planning on fixing? Nikolaich had no clue. Over the past two days, he'd made his life so complicated that he no longer knew how to make things right again. Those cunt Gypsies had made him look like a fool in front of the gray-haired man. Nikolaich could picture it now—the gray-haired man regaling everyone at the office with the story, giving Mr. Pastushok a report on how Nikolaich had handled himself, making him look like a total asshole in the eyes of all those bastards at work. If people didn't laugh at him so much, if they didn't humiliate him so often, he'd persevere somehow, he'd get through it. Now they were just ripping his heart out, though, right through his throat, and stomping on it. And this was a never-ending, vicious cycle. He stood there with tears of desperation in his eyes, remembering the throbbing pain of endless humiliation—he could barely admit that to himself that he had always lived with it.

Ernst thought back to the old German military positions: trenches covered in springy pine needles that crunched under one's feet, poorly preserved fortifications, completely forgotten. He'd hunted for them for a while because he knew that there had to be some trenches still around, at least according to the military maps. However, none of his friends who were digging around in the woods and marshes here from dawn till dusk—unearthing weapons, medals, and most importantly, unaccounted-for Wehrmacht soldiers who were worth big bucks—knew anything about those positions. Moreover, they would all laugh at him, saying, "Dude, this is just like you and your tanks. Quit dreaming—there aren't any trenches still out there." But Ernst took it upon himself to talk with the locals, and one of them eventually admitted that there *actually* were some trenches, deep in the woods, but now they'd be nearly impossible to find. After the war, they purposely planted a ton of pine trees out there, because they didn't feel like extracting all of those shells and bombs that had fallen into the sand dunes near their posts back in '43. The trees were just there to keep people from wandering around. Ernst combed all of the nearby forests and windbreaks, on all fours no less, and finally came across a few heaped trenches that were almost completely concealed by the pine roots. He set up camp for two days, meticulously digging through hot sand infused with bullets, shell casings, and army uniform buttons. In the evening of day two one of the locals called the cops, who sped on over and nabbed Ernst Thälmann, the renegade archaeologist. Maybe that was when Ernst had felt a similar terror, and when he'd learned how to master it: when they were taking him back to the station. He knew that the next few months would be rough and that he'd have to prepare himself for the worst. He'd have to live through that nagging sense of impending doom, knowing that it would recede, eventually. Just wait it out. Persevere.

After wrapping up his stint at sea, back when he was a promising young specialist with dreams of becoming the captain of a commercial ship, Nikolaich had gotten to know it very well. No matter how much he tried to be one of the guys, no matter how accommodating he tried to be, he was always rejected outright, accused of pursuing his own greedy interests and lacking a sense of camaraderie. And he couldn't say anything in his defense, because it was true, on some level—he really didn't have any sense of camaraderie; he didn't have any, and that was that. His whole family was the same—his whole greedy family. His mom didn't have any sense of camaraderie, and neither did his dad. Nothing—not even active involvement in the Communist Youth League and the management position he finally achieved—could make him feel like less of an outsider. In any new group of people, under any imaginable circumstances, he felt rejected; people refused to accept him, no matter what he did. And all of his unsuccessful attempts to be part of the gang only made things worse—he'd quickly become the butt of all their jokes. His superiors didn't care for him, his underlings didn't respect him, and women wouldn't put out for him, although, truth be told, he didn't really want anything to do with them anyway. He didn't have any friends, any kids, any pets. He was afraid of the people he worked for. Moreover, he was afraid of revealing his fear of them. And now here he was, standing there in front of us, all of these panicky thoughts racing through his mind. His eyes were red with hatred and helplessness.

He recalled his run-in on the Hungarian border in '90. He was coming back from Munich via Vienna without any money, food, or smokes. He had been visiting an old girlfriend, Rae Stern; he'd been in the same class as her, and she'd changed her last name and left for Germany after graduating from college. Now she was a singer who did regular shows at the Samovar restaurant. After spending a few reckless days and sleepless nights fueled by gin and whiskey, Ernst was finally starting to make his way back home, where Tamila was waiting for him. Things were just getting started between the two of them back then. Some Croatian nationalist picked Ernst up at night, took him down to Vienna, and dumped him out at the train station. That's where he decided to risk it, taking a seat in the Belgrade-bound train, figuring he could ride for three hours or so, get off in Budapest, and avoid any document checks. Miraculously enough, he managed to cross the Hungarian border—the stars aligned for him. It was as if he had vanished into thin air amid the drafts billowing down the train corridors. He put one over on the border guards, and they wound up stamping his passport and even forgetting to check his tickets. The ticket collectors couldn't track him down in the vestibule or any of the bathrooms, so he stepped off the train victoriously at the Keleti railway station, celebrating his incredible luck and ultimately relaxing his vigilance, which proved fatal. He even managed to strike a deal with the train attendants on the Moscow-bound train, and they agreed to take him to the border and drop him off there. He didn't have the money or audacity to get any farther. So, Ernst solemnly promised them

9

he'd get off at the border. "It'll be all right," he thought. "It's not like they'll chuck me out of the train in the middle of a field. Just make sure to cross the border, and then it'll be smooth sailing." That's where he went wrong. He was sitting in an empty train car, bound for Moscow, looking out the window where the warm, March afternoon was giving way to a brisk evening. The red sun was sprawling out on the horizon, its bloody hue reflected in the windows. The closer he got to the border, the more a disquieting feeling started overwhelming him, because he knew that he wouldn't be able to pull the wool over everyone's eyes indefinitely; he'd have to take responsibility for his behavior.

They didn't actually wind up dropping him off at the border. Instead, the train attendant's heavy glare bore down on him and he knew what was in store. At night, the train was rolling along a railway bridge and the heavy lampposts were piercing the black, stuffy compartments, like unidentifiable animals trying to peer through the cars' window shades. He was sitting in the dark, tuning in to the churning of the wheels and the churning of his own heart and already knowing that he couldn't escape what was coming, and that he always had to be prepared for the worst.

The worst part was that the feeling of helplessness was surfacing and growing. He saw then a well-defined image of what he had been trying to forget forever, what he had to avoid every time he started rummaging around in his memory—what he was afraid of even thinking about. Singapore, 1993.

Their rusty, Greek-made vessel, which they had bought for

pennies off the Germans, had been in the port for a whole week, its cheerful Liberian flags flying. They were a motley crew—a Greek captain and some sailors from the Philippines, with the balance of the crew made up of his countrymen. Nikolaich, the second officer, ridiculed by the sailors and hated by the captain himself, was an odd bird with multiple bald spots who didn't seem to have a friend in the world; even the ship's rats avoided him. How he tried to be one of the guys! How he bent over backward so the crew would just accept him! And that's the thing about bending over backward—it makes you look rather foolish. In his compatriots' eyes he was still a cheapskate and a lousy motherfucker. In the narrow, slanted eyes of the Filipino crewmembers, he only was a dick and cheapskate. What made them experts on lousy motherfuckers all of a sudden? Nikolaich heard them all snickering behind his back, he saw their mocking and scornful eyes, he imagined what they were saying about him, and his eyes filled up with tears and hatred. But the worst thing happened in Singapore. And he remembered every detail.

Three guys beat him up; Ernst remembered that quite clearly. It didn't last long, and they weren't particularly adept fighters, so he only came away with a fat, slightly bloody lip. Then he picked up his empty backpack and set off for the train station, to keep pushing east, where they were still anticipating his arrival.

After a week of waiting, watching the sun scorching the waves they still weren't ready to leave port, the crew finally convinced Nikolaich to go ashore with them. "C'mon, boss," they said, "come along with us. We'll have some fun. We'll find you the best girl in town. An officer on the best ship should have the best girl." And he, piece of shit that he was, fell for it.

There was that one time back in the '80s when he was doing some fieldwork in Crimea. It came rushing back to him all at once, as if he had returned there: the nighttime air, the Crimean vegetation suffering through its long summer, and the incredible, bitter water in the bay knocked the wind right out of him. The wind was herding low-hanging columns of cloud along the sky, making them sail past the fishermen's boats, the empty, nighttime beaches, above the scorched steppes and black, scarred roads. It all started the way these things typically do—bravery, joy; Soviet Crimea, before the tourist industry and displaced Tatars: bad wine, collective farms, ceramics, and bones in the dry ground.

The archaeological expedition was a big group, and most of them had never met before. Ernst was the youngest one in the party, and everyone treated him accordingly. Being pushed around didn't even bother him much anymore—after all, there was no hope of changing anything, really, so why bother complaining? And there was one really young teacher's assistant in the group. Her name was Asya, yeah, Asya, that was it, and she was responsible for their team. They were constantly ripping trail markers off the trees and systemically violating all of Christ's commandments. And Asya was always taking abuse from everyone—her superiors, her colleagues, and the locals too, which is worth noting, though that isn't what this story is about.

It all got off to a rather inauspicious start. Ernst was always helping Asya out at camp, trying to be around her as much as possible. He'd walk her out to the bus stop when she went into town and meet her there when she came back. He'd sit next to her by the campfire in the evenings, be ready with a towel whenever she was swimming in the ocean, do all kinds of stuff for her, like a brother would—without a hint of unprofessional behavior, without counting on any reciprocation, and all the while being bullied by his older colleagues. He was pretty much doing what any sexually frustrated seventeen-year-old boy would have done. And Asya was always apprehensive in his presence. Sometimes it'd seem as though something was just about to happen between the two of them, like she was dropping hints, but it came to nothing, she'd change the subject every time, steering the conversation back to work, dashing all of Ernst's hopes. It was hard on him, but he bounced back pretty quickly—he had to, since the local guys were already moving in on her, and they, unlike Ernst, were adept and energetic, giving her rides to the city in their Kopeika and walking her back to the camp at night . . . The older guys in the expedition were quite amused by the whole situation and would mock Ernst mercilessly. The worst part was that it was *love* she was rejecting. She wouldn't have anything to do with him, romantically speaking, but she would let him do odd jobs for her, and would encourage him to wait for her at the bus stop. And that's just where a bunch of local guys trapped him one day as he waited.

They made it quite clear that they didn't want Ernst hitting on their woman anymore (yeah, they called Asya *their* woman). They told him to stop causing trouble, that he should just head back to camp and jerk off like usual. That got Ernst all riled up. First he just yelled at them, and when that didn't do any good, he started waving his fists around. The locals were surprised at this show of force, but that didn't stop them from knocking Ernst down and giving him a good beating. He went back to the camp, picked up his spade and without saying a word, despite the jeering of his colleagues, he headed back to the bus stop. The crew, now realizing that the locals might wind up doing something permanent to the youngster, followed him, genuinely concerned. Ernst already knew that he had to fight until the end, that he couldn't back down now, otherwise he'd go on being the camp pushover who always got sent to the store for wine, and who never got anywhere with the ladies. He figured the worst would be over fairly quickly—after which things would finally go his way.

He marched straight at the little circle of his tormentors, who were still congregated around the bus stop, by their car, celebrating their easy victory. Obviously, they weren't expecting a return visit from Ernst, let alone the whole expedition. Ernst bolted toward them and smashed the fuck out of their windshield. The locals panicked and hit the road, deciding it wasn't advisable to mess with those lunatic archaeologists.

The air was equatorial, warm and thick, and the sun's yellow reflection was swimming in the water like oil in a frying pan. Suffering from a lack of stimulation, they asked the old Greek captain for permission to disembark. The port's thousands of bars, coffee shops, and pubs greeted them. They walked down Clarke Quay, but not for long. They stopped at the first pub, where three Chinese whores fell right into their laps: two regular ones, and a really young one—a girl, not a woman. It was the girl who set off Nikolaich's eternal anxiety; he knew that in Singapore you could get away with doing just about anything to anyone, but not with minors. His stinginess was acting up too, despite his best intentions, and was just about to get the best of him when his crewmates managed to calm him down. Nikolaich wanted so badly for them to accept him, he wanted so badly for them to like him, it was bound to happen, and happen it did.

Nikolaich was already loaded on rum. After the pub, they all—sailors and prostitutes both—got in a taxi and headed to Chinatown, passing through numerous teeming city blocks before winding up, somehow, in a shady apartment. Someone produced some awful Chinese vodka, and that's where Nikolaich's recollections of the evening got fuzzy; they kept pouring him more and more, laughing and patting him on the back, so he eventually just let himself go. One of the prostitutes was fat and had a booming voice. She sat on the floor yelling something incomprehensible and kept hiking up her short, red dress. The next woman was skinny, with big breasts that sagged piteously, distracting and intimidating everyone. And the third, the youngest of them, was quiet and sad; she stood by the window where the hot glare of the streetlights tinted her skin gold. She wore her hair short, which made her look even younger, like a girl just going into high school. She had too much makeup on her face, but Nikolaich liked that about her, since it gave her a childish, endearing, and approachable look. She was wearing a short, red shirt with shoulder straps, a tiny emerald-colored skirt, and bright pink stockings. She had on a pair of light sandals that flapped whenever she took a step. Her shoulders were covered with a thin, soft down, and there was a tattoo portrait of Jesus on her right shoulder blade, although Nikolaich assumed she was a Buddhist. She had pouty lips and a long, thin neck encircled by a leather collar with metal studs. That collar just drove Nikolaich wild; he kept bobbing around her, desperately trying to strike up a conversation, racking his brain for the few nautical terms he knew in English, and all the while his shipmates were egging him on, saying, "C'mon boss, be a man. You're one of us!"

Finally, he went in for a kiss. Her breath had a bitter and acerbic scent to it and a lingering taste of fire and ash. She was a good and eager kisser. So they made out for a while, there by the window—nobody had ever kissed Nikolaich like that before. And after a few minutes of this, the sailors went wild, hooting and hollering and pointing at Nikolaich, who was quite excited as well as flustered. He didn't pay attention to what they were shouting, at first, but gradually it dawned on him that it sounded as though they were saying "C'mon boss, fuck that boy's brains out! You're already sucking face with him, now take him by the balls and give it to him!"

The other prostitutes were cracking up; the fat one was rolling around, her head banging on the floor hysterically. Even Nikolaich's schoolboy with the Jesus tattoo enjoyed a light and scornful laugh; however, he wasn't about to let Nikolaich go, not for anything, and the sight of him clinging to the mortified second officer sent everyone into fresh hysterics. Nikolaich, who'd sobered up instantly, felt absolutely drained, unable to move an inch—he wanted to sink deep down into a pool of murky, warm water where nobody would ever be able to find him.

And it has to be said that it really worked. The older guys quit sending him to the store for booze. They even developed a kind of restrained but sincere liking for him. He had gained their respect. Everyone now realized that he wasn't on the bottom of the social food chain anymore, that he wasn't totally hopeless when it came to getting along with people, since he'd had the guts to stand up to the locals all by himself. Most importantly for Ernst, Asya realized it too, although she was the last person anyone expected to notice.

Ernst remembered their last night there, at camp, when her skin was already as cool as an autumn night, absorbing the sand like bread soaking up milk. They made love for the first time, trying to make up for all the missed days, high tides and low tides, cyclones and anticyclones, sunny afternoons and foggy evenings. They didn't even take off their clothes—she just unzipped the fly of her jeans and let him in, and he felt, much to his surprise, how easily and deeply you can enter a woman. He could see her bra through her shirt, glimmering in the moonlight like a seagull, while the wet Crimean sand clumped in her hair and shamelessly infiltrated her clothes.

It wasn't just what happened. Just about anything *could* have happened, especially after so much drinking. What mattered most was that he had genuinely liked it. He couldn't get that damn Chinese boy's soft skin and long legs out of his head. Sometimes Nikolaich would dream about him and sometimes it'd keep him up at night. That's what he couldn't forgive his shipmates for. And even after so many years, after he'd long ago quit and started a new life, after he found himself working for Mr. Pastushok—fearing him and not daring to show his fear—he couldn't forgive his crew for the shame and, worse, the nightmarish excitement they had made him feel that night.

And that's when Ernst really put it together, that the most important thing is to not back down, and to view everyday problems as givens that will inevitably appear and then just as inevitably disappear again. The most important thing is to not be afraid. Well, and preferably have a spade ready.

And now, standing there in front of them, he was going through it all once more—the port, the pubs, and the underage transvestite. He felt the humiliation of it again—he couldn't seem to rid himself of that feeling. That's how it had always been, hadn't it? All of his attempts to do things the right way had ended poorly. Just like now. Everyone had ditched him: the gray-haired man took off into town to complain, and the penal battalion was gone too. Just the Gypsies were left, but they were laughing at him too, at his petrified expression, his stupid-looking camouflage outfit, all of his attempts to look competent and decisive. They were humiliating him like everyone always had, backing him into a corner, beating him with sticks, refusing to give him a chance to fix things.

Not that it was all about the spade, mind you. What matters is that the guys had seen all of this as they were growing up and observing their parents' and older friends' behavior. It's pretty simple—stick together, keep outsiders out, and protect your land, women, and homes—then everything will be all right. If it's not all right, it'll at least be fair.

Nikolaich, like a rat stuck between metal fuel tanks, was giving them a look filled with fear and hatred, thinking that they had gone too far this time and that they simply hadn't given him any other choice.

Because nobody has the right to come onto your turf and take your women and homes away.

Because, really, he'd done everything right. It wasn't his fault it never panned out. It wasn't because of the camouflage outfit, he could've worn anything else, after all. And it wasn't about the Makarov pistol that he had borrowed from the security guard especially for the occasion, and was now keeping in his pants pocket, feeling its heavy, cumbersome metal against his hip.

It's just that when you grow up with all of that, when it starts molding your consciousness at an early age, certain things are easier for you to take—you don't let them get to you. There's the life you lead, which you can't compromise, and there's your death, which you'll always have time for, so there's no sense in rushing it.

They reject you, not even trying to find common ground, because you're an outsider, and there's nothing that can ever bring you together.

Those things are right, understandable—they're constants. People have always lived like that and so they'll try to teach their kids the same things.

Because only sharing life and sharing death can bring us together.

★

"What's the deal, ya little wimps, cat got your tongue?"

The tractor drivers hopped down on the ground, landing stiffly, and started shouting happily, greeting Injured, Pasha, Borman, and even me, like we were long-lost relatives, although I'd never seen them before. Arkady and Prokhor greeted the drivers back, laughing and treating them to a free smoke. Nobody was paying any attention to Nikolaich, who was standing off to the side with a stupid grin on his face. Even Ernst had forgotten about him by now, and the drivers then went over and greeted Ernst as though he too was a long-lost relative, because he essentially was. I'll never forget the look Nikolaich was giving Ernst; there was something heavy in his eyes, something that gave me the chills.

"Well, how are you guys doing?" the drivers asked Injured with an affected tone of exuberance. "Sasha, my fuckin' God, how the hell are you?"

It seemed as though they wanted to hug everyone there, pull them up close to their sailor's shirt and robe, respectively. Our guys appeared to be happy to see the drivers, but they didn't look as jubilant about it.

"Nicky, is that you?" Pasha was talking to the guy in the sailor's shirt, "fuck man, who the hell are you working for?"

"Come on, Pasha—you know I'm a decent guy," said the one in the sailor's shirt. "That motherfucker over there," he said, pointing at Nikolaich, who continued smiling awkwardly, "put us up to it. How could I have known this was your turf?"

"You knew perfectly well," Injured replied severely.

"Injured, c'mon," whined the guy in the sailor's shirt. "Honestly, we didn't know. We wouldn't do a thing like that to you guys . . ."

"All right, all right," Pasha conceded reluctantly, "just pick your friends a bit more wisely next time."

"Yeah Pasha, like I'm friends with those guys?" Nicky said, nodding at Nikolaich.

"You never know," Pasha answered.

"Guys, don't be like that," the driver said anxiously.

"Everything's fine, just quit your bitching," Injured told him.

"Thanks fellas, thanks a lot," Nicky said.

Then they told us how they got here. They said this was the first time they'd met Nikolaich and would certainly be the last. They thought they were just going to do a routine job, and it was only once they'd gotten to the airport that they realized just how deceitful and dishonest those two fags, Nikolaich and the gray-haired man, really were—saying that it was a good thing the gray-haired man had booked it on out of here, because otherwise they would have turned their buckets on him. Because they're decent guys and wouldn't sell out for the money Nikolaich and the gray-haired man were offering them. Well, and they wouldn't have sold out for more, either.

Injured didn't bother listening to their story. He stepped back and took a seat on the hood of the black Mercedes. He looked satisfied and lethargic, and seemed to be basking in the sunlight, as though he was trying to savor these last few hours of day, store them up in his memory. I sat down next to him.

"What now?" I asked.

"Nothing," Injured replied.

"What if they wind up coming back?"

"I don't give a fuck," Injured answered calmly. "Let 'em come back. You know, your brother was never afraid of them. What can they actually do to us, anyway? They can try to buy you out. But nobody can buy you out unless you want them to. Right?"

"Right."

"That's what I thought. But that's not what they think. Ah well, who cares," he said, changing the subject. "What'd little Katya have to say?"

"Dunno. Haven't read her letter yet," I said, surprised by his question. "I'll tell ya once I get around to reading it."

"Okay, sounds good."

★

Nikolaich finally came to his senses around then, deciding it was time to hightail it out of there.

"Hey!" he yelled at the drivers.

They looked over at him simultaneously, but immediately lost interest, pointedly turning back toward our crew and continuing to tell them their tall tales.

"Nicky!" Nikolaich yelled again, his voice trembling.

"Yeah?" the guy in the sailor's shirt answered, peering over his shoulder.

"Let's go," Nikolaich barked succinctly.

"Go fuck yourself," Nicky answered just as succinctly.

Pasha and Borman exchanged a glance and continued talking with the drivers, pretending everything was just fine.

"Nicky!" Nikolaich exploded. "I'm fuckin' talking to you. I said, 'let's go'!"

There was a new note in his voice that forced the drivers to wrap up their pleasant conversation, say good-bye to all of us, and shove off toward the tractor. Nikolaich waited as they waltzed on over to their steel friend, kicked its heavy tires, and climbed into the cab. He was observing the rest of us out of the corner of his eye, tracking our movements. The veins on his skinny neck were bulging. There he stood in his camouflage outfit—ready to take his resentment out on the first person to cross him.

Nicky tried starting up the tractor. It sneezed and spat up some fluid, shuddering and stalling, utterly exhausted. Nicky ducked out of the cab.

"It won't start!" he yelled at Nikolaich.

"Don't tell me about—just do something about it already!" Nikolaich said, feeling mocking glances pelting his back.

"What am I supposed to do?" Nicky asked indignantly.

"Do *something*!" Nikolaich yelled at him. "Fix it!"

"With what? My fuckin' dick?"

Our guys started laughing. Pasha practically fell over, right on top of Borman, and Ernst folded in two, like he had just taken a punch in the stomach. Arkady and Prokhor started cracking up too, as the spectacle continued.

Not even Injured could contain himself, letting out a string of chuckles from his position on the hood. "Alrighty then," he called to the drivers. "Let me see what's up."

"Don't!" Nikolaich said, putting his hand out, seemingly as a warning. "Don't come any closer!"

Injured stopped, then called out, "Are you out of your fuckin' mind?" And then he kept on walking.

"I told you not to come any closer!" Nikolaich repeated hoarsely. It was like his vocal cords had all dried up.

"I'm just going to take a look," Injured said dismissively, still approaching the tractor.

"I told you not to come any closer!" Nikolaich cried out hysterically. Then his sweaty hands pulled a Makarov with some strange markings on the grip out of his pocket.

Everyone shut up and stood still, even though, in Nikolaich's hands, the pistol somehow looked like a toy. I think nobody believed it was a real Makarov. Borman even gave a scornful snort, but after exchanging a glance with Pasha, he realized what was going on. The wind picked up from time to time, carrying some bitter, autumn smells along with it.

"Hey, what the hell are you doing?" Injured asked, quiet but stern. "Put the piece away, okay? I just wanted to help."

"Don't come any closer," Nikolaich repeated, pointing his pistol awkwardly at Injured.

"What the hell are you doing?" Injured asked again.

"Hey, you prick!" Pasha shouted. "He said put the piece away!"

I think the word "prick" set him off. Everyone had been pressing down on the coiled metal spring deep inside him too hard, he had been containing himself for too long, and finally the spring snapped, destroying every failsafe and kicking an internal mechanism into motion. As soon as Injured moved again, taking a microscopic step forward—a shot ripped through the air. Injured grabbed his side. One of our guys immediately dashed toward Nikolaich, hitting the Makarov out of his hands onto the warm asphalt and knocking him right on his balding head. The other guys dashed to help Injured up. He drooped in their arms. They set him down on the asphalt alongside Nikolaich. Pasha unbuttoned his windbreaker, exposing the bullet wound; someone ran for the first aid kit while someone else frantically called an ambulance, the tractor drivers hopped back down onto the ground and hovered around, trying to help somehow, and Ernst was yelling anxiously at me, explaining something and pointing somewhere in town, and I was answering automatically and agreeing with him, although all I could really do was stand there and look at the dark blood seeping out from underneath Injured. I kept repeating to myself the same two questions: "Did he really die? Is he really gone?"

★

What was it that happened, all those years ago? It was in August, late August, with its hot evenings that cool down slowly like trucks parked at a rest stop. It was one of our last years of high school. We'd already developed more than a few bad habits, and were running with the wrong crowd, and though we were all grown up we still spent our long evenings down at the river like a bunch of kids. There wasn't a whole lot to do in town at the time— not that there is now, either. I don't remember anymore why we decided to hoof it all the way out to the bridge. Generally, we'd hang out on the beaches where the water was shallow and the current wasn't strong. But everything was particularly charged that August night—the water was particularly dark and deep, we were particularly carefree, and the sun seemed to swing by particularly fast. We were rushing toward the bridge to get there before night-fall. It was a rickety wooden bridge. We climbed up the railings and dove unhesitatingly into the water, over and over, the water that was dark yellow from the sand. And when the darkness under the bridge thickened and turned to lilac ink, we started getting dressed, pulling our clothes onto our wet bodies. After every-one had gotten dressed, putting on our shoes as we were walking away, Gea, who was only in our class for a year, told us, "Wait up. I'm gonna take one last jump." Nobody objected, so he slid out of his T-shirt, which he had just now tugged over his wet shoul-ders, hopped up onto the railing, and dove off into the yellow and lilac-colored void.

At first we just called his name, figuring he had hidden some-where. Then we got scared and jumped in after him, plunging into the darkness. But it was impossible to make anything out down there, so we retreated to the riverbank, waving flashlights that cast their beams across the river's surface, while somebody ran into town for help. The river was flowing past us, its ripples disap-pearing into the darkness. Gea was hanging there under the water, his body bobbing with current like seaweed. Not wanting to believe that the worst had happened, stubbornly refusing to believe it, we all repeated quietly to ourselves as we gazed into the glimmering water, "Did he really die? Is he really gone?"

10

"Herman, did you know him long?"

The thick grass spread out across the hospital courtyard, concealing apples, cigarette butts, and used syringes. Sometimes cautious and suspicious cats would freeze in the grass, their green eyes pointing up into the sun. Sometimes a window would open up, and some poor decrepit patient could be seen sneaking a quick smoke, waiting for the doctor to come by. Once it was his turn, he'd flick the cigarette out, sending it flying into the yellow grass like a falling satellite. The courtyard was dotted with some old, wind-battered trees. A bench, which had been brought in off the street, sat by the brick hospital wall. In the evenings, patients would sit there, smoking, drinking fortified wine, and telling interesting stories from their lives. Now the presbyter and I were sitting on the bench. He had just gone into the hospital to check up on Injured, although there was nothing to check up on anymore. Now he was giving me the full rundown and waiting for me to say something, but I didn't have anything to say. Injured had died so suddenly that I couldn't keep myself from talking about him in the present tense. The presbyter decided not to correct me. Then he asked me:

"Herman, did you know him long?"

"I guess you could say that," I said. "I've known him since I was a kid. He's older than me, obviously—he was really friends with my brother. They played soccer together. And then I joined the team later on."

"Was he a good player?"

"Yeah, the best, man. You know, Petya," I told the presbyter, "I'm not just saying that because he's dead. He was actually a really good player."

"What about yourself?"

"I wasn't great. I was lacking something. Maybe I just wasn't quick enough. Maybe I wasn't hungry enough. But we won the championship anyway."

"When was that?"

"In '92. They'd already won it a few times, actually, before I joined the team. It was no big deal for them, but me, I was stoked. Can you imagine winning the championship?"

"In '92," the presbyter replied, "I was in the loony bin."

"What do you mean, the loony bin?"

"Well, the loony bin. I had some drug problems. My sister had me committed. She thought they could help me kick it."

"Did they?"

"Nah, they didn't. I helped myself. But I had to work my tail off. I even got recruited by some cult, can you imagine that?"

"Well, how'd you get better? By praying?"

"Praying? You're kidding, right?" the presbyter said, chuckling. "It was all drugs, Herman, it was all drugs. That's how it works— certain drugs always outweigh others. All in all, I have no idea how I got clean. But I did."

"Where does religion come in?"

"It didn't. Religion had nothing to do with it. It wasn't about the church."

"Then what was it about?"

"It was about the fact that I had them and they had me. We're all in this together, you know what I mean? Let me tell ya a story." He took Injured's phone out of his jacket pocket, turned it off, and set it aside, as though he was gearing up to tell me something truly important. "You know why the majority of drug addicts crack? Because they're all by themselves. Well, you probably knew that. That's why there are so many group therapy methods, and some-times they even get results. As for me, I've always been skeptical of group therapy. You know why? Because I'm an adult, and I'm used to taking responsibility for my words and actions. When I decided to get clean, I thought to myself, 'Alrighty then, no group therapy and none of that twelve-step crap.' All of these toxins are flowing through my veins, pumped by my heart, and nobody can loan me their heart, now can they? So, I immediately decided against all of that handholding and sharing. I convinced myself that I was capa-ble of regaining control over my own life and that it was unfair to blame anyone else for my mistakes. That kind of romantic drivel just complicates things. But, Herman, now I'm absolutely sure that I had to withstand that unbearable torture to see what I was made of and what I was capable of, for real. Herman, we sure aren't capable of much. And, even so, we rarely live up to our fullest potential—but that's a whole other issue. Nevertheless, at some point I did get clean after all. And then I realized that noth-ing had really changed—Herman, life is an exhausting everyday struggle against one's addictions. It's only a matter of time before

I fell off the wagon, you know what I mean? Obviously, it's not about getting clean, it's about staying clean. And that's when you need group therapy in the service of God—there's no way around it. You know, I got real lucky finding the church here. Real lucky, you know what I mean? They take those kind of things in stride, and I know I wouldn't have made it without them."

"Ah-ha, so it was the healing power of scripture after all?"

"Nah, you're not getting it. What I'm trying to say is that certain things are more important than faith. Things like gratitude and responsibility. Actually, it was an accident that I joined the church. I just didn't have any other place to go. I couldn't turn to my sister any longer, because she'd just send me right back to the loony bin. I had no real other choice. But the church and I didn't really get off on the right foot. I mean, the church can do wonders, sure, but nobody besides you can fix your problems. Basically, I didn't think I was in it for the long haul. I thought that the holy brothers would give me the boot sooner or later, as soon as they caught on to my act. They knew my history, but they never made a big deal about it. And then they sent me up here. The local priest had just moved to Canada, and the church needed someone who was willing to stick around for a while. I was willing. And I'm sure when they sent me here they were absolutely convinced I'd be heading for the hills in no time. I guess they thought, 'If he disappears, then he's not our problem anymore.' You know, when I first got here we all met up at Tamara's place."

"Who met up at Tamara's place?" I asked.

"Well, the congregation and me. There weren't many of them back then. And you know what . . . They just sat there staring at me, and I couldn't say a thing—I couldn't even force out a single word because I was feeling that fuckin' shitty. And they got that, they understood it. And they weren't even expecting me to say anything. They just got it, Herman. They felt everything, and understood, but didn't expect anything from me. Group therapy is a bunch of horseshit—everyone's just trying to get clean, save their own skin, and nobody gives two shits about the others, about who'll make it to the last session and who'll bite the dust. Because when you're saving your own ass you don't have time to care about anyone else. There's no therapy that can help you. It's all so unfair, you even wind up suffering because you see yourself revealed as a real bastard trying to survive at any cost. But me, my situation was completely different—I understood that they didn't really need me, that they'd get by just fine without me. Well, plus I had been officially assigned to head up their church, so they weren't about to send me packing—back to the loony bin—I could rest assured. Even though I could've been anyone, I was almost a complete stranger. Just some motherfucker from across the border. I immediately realized that if I couldn't stay clean here then I was pretty much a goner. And no prayers would help me."

"Did they know about your history?"

"Pasha knew. I told him myself. On the very first night. I took one look at them and realized that there was no need to hide anything—it'd bite me in the ass later if I tried. Pasha was their leader, like he is now. So, I told him everything. I said that I wanted to be completely honest with them, and that if a dope-fiend priest didn't suit them, then I, naturally, would step down. You know what Pasha said? He said that if all the local dope fiends started quitting their jobs, there would be a spike in the city's unemployment rate. He essentially told me to chill out and do my job—sing hymns with them and baptize their children. So, I stayed."

"I see."

"But that's not the whole story," the presbyter continued. "Herman, that's not the whole story. I still couldn't stay clean, you see? I worked for about six months, and then I fell off the wagon. I even pocketed some of the church's money—not much, but still. Pasha pulled me out of it. He saw what was going on right away and he kept me from going on a bender. He locked me in his house and kept me there until I was clean again. He treated me with his own herbs and stuff. He told everyone I had the flu. And it was around then that I said to myself, 'Look, you don't give two shits about your health, obviously. You don't really care about your career, that's obvious too. And you couldn't care less about God's commandments, despite your professional commitment. But dude, if you don't want to burn in hell, simmer over a slow flame, cook like a TV dinner in the microwave, then stick with these odd, slightly off, yet incredibly genuine and compassionate people. Don't run out on them. Stick with them. Read them psalms or baptize their children, whatever you want. After all, it doesn't really matter what you'll be doing. Just stick with them. They won't send you packing—that's not how they do things around here.' And that's how it all played out," the presbyter finished, and turned the phone back on. "I barely knew Injured, myself. Actually, we hardly ever talked. And I hardly ever talked to your brother, either. But that doesn't matter—they were all here together. Herman, we're all in this together, you know what I mean? I know what I'm talking about.

This isn't about the church or drugs. It's about responsibility. And gratitude. If you've got those two things, then there's a chance you won't be remembered as a total asshole."

"Everything you're saying makes perfect sense," I said. "But, see—Injured got shot and my brother hightailed it out of here a while ago now. They were doing all the right things, like you said, but it didn't help. Look, I agree with you. But the funny thing is that they're down in the trenches thinking they can wipe everyone else out . . . but, it turns out that they're the ones getting knocked down, one by one—they're being squeezed out of this town and soon enough they'll all get squeezed out."

"You think so?"

"Yep."

"Okay, they might get squeezed out," the presbyter said. "Maybe. But still—they'll stick together until the very end, you know what I mean? Herman, I've met a lot of different people in my life. All kinds of people. The majority of them were weak and vulnerable. The majority of them have betrayed their friends and family. I think it was because they were so vulnerable. No matter how you slice it, life makes people wimps and traitors. I'm telling you that as a priest. If they all get squeezed out, like you said, then I'm going out with them, because I'm down in the trenches too, Herman. We have the same sense of responsibility. And the same sense of gratitude."

He took out the phone again and turned it off, listening to the rustling of the grass. The late afternoon sun had rolled out behind the hospital wall, its red edges touching the windows of the intensive care unit.

"Sometimes I'll show them tricks, too," the presbyter said out of the blue.

"Huh?"

"Tricks," the presbyter repeated, "circus tricks. When I was getting treatment they taught us some tricks. That was part of our therapy. They said it was supposed to bring us back to our childhood days. One of the addicts was in the circus. He worked as a juggler. He was even wearing a clown outfit when they brought him in. He taught us how to do it. Look here," the presbyter said, magically producing a bottle of pure alcohol out of his jacket pocket and bending over to fix his shoelace. He took a quick pull from the bottle and hid it. Then he produced a Zippo lighter out of thin air, put it up to his face, and exhaled a heavy jet of blue flame.

Frightened, I leapt back. But a moment later he was his old self, just sitting there, watching me with his calm and pensive eyes.

"Now *that's* group therapy."

I didn't know how to respond.

"Where are you headin'?" he asked.

"I gotta take care of some business. Some very important business."

"All right then," he said, dismissing me. "Call if you need me. You've got my number."

"So, you're saying it's all about gratitude and responsibility?" I asked.

"Yep," he said, nodding. "Gratitude and responsibility."

★

There were slot machines on the first floor of the hotel. A few guys that looked like Communist Youth League members with glassy eyes were sitting on high chairs in front of them, and a girl, who had red-dyed hair and red Keds, was sleeping in an upright position leaning on the windowsill. Some Chechens were scurrying down the hallway, carrying boxes with grapefruits thumping around in them. I went over to the front desk, told the girl there my name, and asked whether anyone had been looking for me. She gave me the room number immediately. "It's nice when people are looking forward to seeing you," I thought as I went upstairs.

The hotel was like a partially sunken ship—not everyone had escaped, but mostly because there really wasn't anywhere to escape to. I walked down a long, dark hallway. It smelled of paint and hotel furniture.

The door was half-open. I could hear a shower running. I knocked, but nobody answered. I pushed it open and stepped inside. There were two beds separated by a desk. It was messy— pairs of jeans, baseball caps, rumpled sheets, and mustard-stained women's magazines were scattered all over the place. One bed was empty, while a guy, younger than me, no more than twenty-five-years old, was sitting on the other one. Sitting there and holding a cup of fruit yogurt, the itchy hotel blanket pulled up to his chin. A laptop was resting on the chair in front of him, playing hardcore porn. The sound was off. It was as though the actors didn't want to disturb anyone. The guy didn't notice me coming in until something—my reflection in the monitor, probably—tipped him off. He dropped his yogurt, which splatted into a sweet half-moon on the floor, and hurriedly adjusted something down there before tossing the shaggy blanket to the side rather abruptly—possibly too abruptly—and hopped onto the floor. He was wearing tracksuit pants, brand-name ones, and a white T-shirt. He looked like a train passenger in first class who had just slid out of his fancy suit and made himself comfortable for the journey. Much as Olga had reported, he really did have a bald spot on the side of his head, but it didn't make him look any older. He had something fitted in his left ear that resembled a heavy hearing aid. Slamming some keys on the laptop in an attempt to shut off the porn, he then deigned to look at me, brashly if not quite confidently. The image on the screen had frozen, a women's golden head interrupted in the middle of desperately sucking on something or other, bobbing in perfect clarity in the dimness behind my host, but he didn't notice.

"Herman?" he asked a bit too nonchalantly, extending his hand. "I'm Dima. Take a seat," he said, pointing to a chair by the door.

I tossed an issue of *Cosmo*, smeared with something sticky, onto the floor. Dima looked as though he was dying to lunge over and to pick up the magazine, but he restrained himself. He just stood there, examining me from head to toe and gradually collecting himself and trying to decide how he should behave around me. The blonde behind him was still sucking on some otherworldly object, her radiant hair clashing with Dima's track pants.

I didn't have a chance to speak before the shower fell silent and Dima's partner, a chubby, long-haired guy wearing blue pajamas and fluffy, girly slippers, barged into the room. At first he just paced around, drying his hair with a striped towel. He didn't notice me at first; it was only after picking up on the tension in his buddy's face that he sent a sideways glance my way and did up all three buttons on his top.

"This is Herman," Dima informed him, doing his best to sound chipper.

"Vladik," the long-haired guy introduced himself coldly.

Then he swayed in my direction without actually taking a step toward me, possibly trying to figure out whether or not it was appropriate to shake my hand. He decided against it. And, really, I wasn't in any hurry to shake hands either.

Dima went right on scrutinizing me. "Well," he said, "we've been looking for you. It's a good thing you decided to come by. Isn't that right, Vladik?"

"Yeah," Vladik agreed glumly.

I understood what they were getting at. Vladik looked plainer. Dima had assigned him the role of bad cop. He was supposed to be breathing down my neck, I figured, intimidating me. And, literalist that he was, Vladik tried to do exactly that, positioning himself by the door so as to actually breathe down my neck, so close I could smell his aftershave. By this logic, Dima must have been the good cop, thinking of himself as a real sly motherfucker—he was supposed to come off as just a regular guy, I guessed, someone I could trust. Dima was the one I was supposed to spill my guts to, while Vladik was just there for show.

"We even stopped by the gas station," Dima said. "And called your brother. Isn't that right, Vladik?"

"We've been dicking around here for five days already," Vladik said resentfully.

I looked back at the laptop, for lack of anything better to do.

The blonde was still shining on the dark screen, refusing to let her prey out of her mouth. Vladik couldn't help but glance over at whatever I was staring at, so he noticed the blonde then too. Dima, seeing that we were both intently examining something behind his back, looked over his shoulder. Before he could react, Vladik burst past him and slammed the laptop shut. Now they were both standing in front of me like a couple of schoolboys being chewed out by their headmaster. They felt that immediately, and they didn't much like the feeling, so they sat down on Dima's bed simultaneously, carefully maneuvering around the spilled yogurt. The problem was that they didn't feel any less like schoolboys in this position, sitting there and not knowing what to do with their hands. I mean, when it came down to it, we were all feeling more than a little uncomfortable. But we had to move the conversation along.

"Yeah," Dima said, "you should at least get a phone."

"What for?" I asked.

"Well, so people could get hold of you," Dima said. Vladik was, in the meantime, trying to stare me down.

"What do you two want, anyway?"

"We'd like to ask you about a few things," Vladik said. "Do you know Borys Kolisnychenko?"

"Bolik?"

"Borys," Vladik corrected me coldly, "Kolisnychenko."

"Yeah, I know him," I answered, trying to sound just as steely.

"Were you having some money problems?" Dima asked, going back to trying to sound cheerful and unconcerned.

"What makes you think that?"

"They came right out and told us," Dima said, chuckling.

"Yeah?" I asked. "What'd they tell ya?"

Dima said, "They said they cleaned you out."

"They said you were a real sucker," Vladik added.

"They actually said that, 'a real sucker'?" I asked.

"Well, they didn't exactly say that word for word," Dima conceded. "But they said something along those lines."

"But they didn't call me 'a real sucker,' did they?"

"No, they didn't," Dima admitted grudgingly.

"Well, there you have it," I said.

"What's the difference?" Vladik asked. "They cleaned our clients out too. They screw everyone over."

"Yeah," Dima seconded him, "they're in line for a long overdue beating. We just can't seem to catch them in the act—they're sly bastards."

"What does this have to do with me?" I asked.

"Herman, here's the deal," said Dima. "It looks like we'll be able to slam them if you help us out."

"Listen up," Vladik added threateningly.

"It looks like if you testify against them, they're fucked. And they really screwed you, didn't they?"

"They sure did," Vladik answered for me.

"And they screwed our clients too!" Dima said, enjoying himself now. "Basically, we gotta take them down together, okay Herman?"

"You got that?" Vladik asked sternly.

"He's got it," Dima said. "Don't you worry. We'll take care of everything. All you gotta do is testify in court and you'll get your money back. Then we'll handle it from there, all right?"

I kept quiet for a bit, examining the little doggies on Vladik's slippers. Then I said, just for clarity's sake, "So, you're asking me to testify against Bolik? That's what this is about?"

"Yep," Vladik confirmed, "against Boris."

"Now what the fuck would make me do a thing like that?"

This really surprised Dima, for some reason. "They screwed you!" he said. "And took your money!" he added, redundantly.

"And you think that's reason enough to sell out my friends?"

"Some friends you got there, Herman," Dima said. "They took you for a ride."

"Made a real sucker out of you," Vladik interjected yet again.

"Shut your mouth," I told Vladik. "You hear that? Shut your mouth."

Vladik withered.

"Hey, hey," Dima said, trying to back his partner up. "Easy now. Let's all calm down."

"Nah, I'm not gonna calm down," I continued, addressing Vladik. "Shut your mouth. You understand?"

Vladik tucked his head into his shoulders, causing his wet hair to flow out over his shirt. He finally did, in fact, shut his mouth. But I decided I couldn't leave it there. I wanted to put an end to all this nonsense once and for all.

"Nah man, do you understand, for real?" I asked Vladik. "You really understand me?"

"He understood you," Dima said warily. "Herman, he understood."

"Well, that's good," I said. "Because this is how it's gonna go— you can spend the night here, but you better catch the first bus out of here tomorrow morning. If I ever see you guys in this town again, you are going to be royally fucked."

"Herman," Dima objected rather limply, "what's your deal? We've got your back. We want to punish *them*. Herman, they took you for a ride."

"How old are you?" I asked him.

"Twenty-four," Dima answered.

"And I'm twenty-three," Vladik volunteered for some reason.

"You shut your mouth," I snapped. "Dude, you're only twenty-four and you're already a complete piece of shit. You realize that? You think I'm gonna start ratting on my friends for some dough? You think I'll turn them in over some money? Where do they even find guys like you? What'd you major in at college?"

"Pre-law," Dima muttered. He was getting flustered. He had pictured our conversation playing out rather differently.

"Motherfucker! Where do all these lawyers come from?" I wondered incredulously. "Well, you heard me—I want you to get the hell out of here. By tomorrow morning. My friends and I will take care of ourselves, without any lawyers."

I stood up and headed for the door. Dima sprang from the bed as I went.

"Herman," he called desperately, "we have all the documents right here! We filed for all of them! You should help us out. We have your best interests at heart! Why don't you get that? Look here!"

He grabbed the laptop, opened it up, and handed it to me, trying to show me something. The computer woke up, rumbled a bit, and the familiar blonde popped up on the screen, sucking even more vigorously at whatever fluids remained unsucked.

"Why don't you finish up, jerkoff," I suggested, and closed the door behind me.

★

I also told him: "You're absolutely right. I agree with almost everything you're saying. But you said they're all vulnerable. I'm thinking, What the fuck makes you think they're wimps like that, anyway? And why the fuck is that the case, Father? Why do you say they're vulnerable? They were all born and raised here. They're all scurrying around like their train is about to leave, you know what I mean? But it's like the train is parked at the station and they're saying all of their good-byes. Now they don't owe anyone anything, and they can start fuckin' bashing things up and burning things down because the train's already there, waiting for its passengers. That's how they behave. I have no idea why. Those bastards live here. In these towns. They grew up here. They went to school here, skipped classes here, and played soccer here. They lived their whole lives here. So why, why would they burn the land they've lived on for so long? All those fuckin' cocksuckers have started walking around like they own the place. All of those finance pricks, pig cops, corporate shits, young lawyers, up-and-coming politicians, analysts, business owners, fuck all those capitalists—why are they acting like they've on vacation and are just about to hop on the train and go home? It's not as though they're really leaving. They're not going anywhere anytime soon. They're staying put—we even frequent the same stores. And you think they're weak and vulnerable, Father? My ass they're weak. They've got steel jaws and they'll rip you to shreds, if need be. How are they vulnerable?"

"I absolutely agree with you," he replied, "but you're forgetting about one thing—vulnerability fuels aggression, and so does weakness."

"So, you're saying they've gone fuckin' bonkers because they're actually weak?"

"Yes. And because they're vulnerable."

"What can we do about that?"

"Herman, keep doing what you've been doing," the presbyter answered. "Keep doing what you've been doing. Don't slight the living, and don't forget the dead."

★

In the evening, Seva and I went back to the hospital to pick up Olga. She'd already heard about Injured; she was quiet and had obviously been crying. She let us carry her out to the car and put her in the back seat. She lived only a few blocks from the hospital. Seva drove cautiously, trying not to hit any of the numerous potholes along the way. Seva and I carried her over her spacious yard, all covered in grapevines, stepped onto and passed through her veranda, brought her into the living room, and carefully placed her on her couch. Two women were waiting for Olga in her little house, and they whizzed around us, bringing Olga a pot of freshly brewed tea and some small, puffy pillows, disappearing and returning with water, or producing a frail black cat and handing him to Olga. Finally, Olga could take no more and asked everyone to leave—except for me, that is.

"When's the funeral?" she asked quietly.

"The day after tomorrow. On Saturday."

"Pick me up, all right?"

"All right."

"Why don't you get going?" she said. "Come by later."

"I'll wait until you fall asleep, and then I'll get going."

"Sounds good."

Olga lay there, wrapped up in a warm, wool blanket, peering out the window at the thick, lilac-colored darkness sprawling out around us. I could hear the women waiting outside, talking.

"You remember how you told me about those postcards?" Olga asked suddenly.

"What postcards?"

"The ones for tourists. Those sets of all different cities. You said how you would talk about them in German class."

"Oh," I said, "sure, the Voroshilovgrad postcards."

"Yeah," Olga confirmed, "the Voroshilovgrad ones."

"What made you think of them?"

"I found a whole stack of them."

"For real?"

"Uh-huh. I couldn't remember for the life of me where they came from. But then I remembered. My friends and I had some German pen pals. One boy from Dresden would write me. He kept inviting me to come visit and he sent me some postcards. I sent him some too. I'd buy whole sets of them. I'd pick out the ones with tons of flowers because I wanted him to think that Voroshilovgrad was a fun city. I would just keep all the other ones, with all the monuments and stuff. And I just found them. A whole stack of them. It's funny," she said, "there's no such city as Voroshilovgrad anymore, and the boy from Dresden doesn't write me anymore, and it's like none of that even happened, or it wasn't even part of my life. It's like it happened in another life, or someone else's life. Someone else's city, someone else's country, and someone else's friends. Maybe these pictures *are* my past. Something they took away from me and forced me to forget. But I haven't forgotten, because those really are a part of me. They may even be the best part of me," she added, after a second's thought.

She touched my hand and stayed quiet for a while, looking out the window.

"I knew that something was going to happen," she said suddenly. "I could just feel it. But there was nothing I could do."

"What could you have done?"

"I don't know," Olga said. "I don't know. And I don't know what to do now, either. Don't forget to pick me up, okay?"

"I won't forget," I reassured her. "Don't worry."

She took her cell out of her pocket and handed it to me.

"Put it somewhere."

I looked it over, then asked "May I?" I quickly found Injured's number in her contact list and called. It rang once, twice, three times. I was about to hang up when I heard an odd sound, like an answering machine clicking on, and then a nearly imperceptible rustling, like a draft, a hum that began almost imperceptibly and gradually mounting until it felt like a cold ocean breeze was blowing all of the sounds and voices out of the air, clogging everything up with its icy breath. The wind was picking up, howling out of the void. It was as though I'd tuned in to some secret radio channel that pilots used to navigate over this deserted land. Incomprehensible voices could be heard inside the noise. They were shouting to be heard over one other, lost in the faraway ether, desperate to get some important message across. But I couldn't pick out any individual words or phrases, no matter how I tried. Gradually the voices disappeared and a heavy, inexpressible silence settled in. I turned off Olga's cell and placed it on the windowsill.

"What's up?" Olga asked.

"Nothing. Nothing at all."

She was lying there in the darkness, her eyes wide open, for some time, touching my hand, sighing softly, and faintly humming something. She fell asleep shortly thereafter, her breathing smooth and estranged.

★

Seva didn't wait up for me. By the time I stepped outside he was already gone. I walked down the street, ducked under the dark apple branches, took the shortcut, and emerged from the wood out by the hospital wall, for the third time today.

The night had cooled down; clouds blanketed the sky. It was quiet and empty in town; moonlight touched the heavy branches of the fruit trees and the cold, dew-covered road signs. I kept going, trying to remember what was behind the buildings along the way. I passed the other hospital where my brother went when he got appendicitis. I remembered how we'd all run over to visit him, scaling the brick wall. I passed the white block, where the prison was—my brother and I would go there to talk with this one guard. My brother had some business to settle, and I would just tag along. I passed the monastery, which used to function as a barracks and where our dad did his military service. My school was right behind the monastery—the playground, the lines painted on the asphalt, all the places we used to stash cigarettes, the holes in the fence that we used to crawl through. The hotel was barely visible off to the side. I remembered how we'd bring our girls there, once we were fully mature and had some pocket money, street cred, and our own notions about love. The faded phone company building, where they'd opened up a movie theater back in the day, was across from the hotel. We hardly ever went there because they mostly showed movies about karate, which didn't interest us adults. The health clinic, where we used to buy pure alcohol, was farther down the street. Next came the 24-hour convenience store on the corner where they'd serve anyone who was thirsty, regardless of their physical state, their age, or their religious beliefs. Off to the right, the fire tower popped into my field of view for a second; we once had an epic brawl right over there. Then came the neighborhood police station where we were all taken afterward. Quiet neighborhoods followed, taken over by grass and spiderwebs, and dark alleys with exhaustively cracked asphalt. Then came the highway, heading out of the city; I stepped onto it—how many times had I left all these streets and houses behind? I felt as though I was abandoning the city, deserting my friends, relatives, and lovers. An uncanny sensation, a mixture of alarm and loss, overcame me for a moment, but quickly receded, and I could feel some sweet rhythm in everything, hinting that the highway was just getting started, and I could take it for hours in any direction. Empty fields emerged behind the city's last houses; the dam crossed through the darkness farther down. The surface of the river glistened brightly in the moonlight, beyond the dam. The hills rolled out past the river; the night had settled over them like furniture covers. Nothing had changed while I was gone. The highway had the same glass, metal, and scorched grass on the shoulder. The same streams of light coming from the houses over the dam. The same persistent silence. The same voices and whispers evaporating in the silence. The same wary animals. The same sleeping fishermen. The same high sky. The same black earth.

P.S.

Hi, Herman,

Sorry I haven't written for so long. First, I don't have a whole lot of news. Secondly, I wasn't too sure you'd actually find my news interesting. But I decided to write you to tell you a story that happened a long time ago. I don't remember why, but I haven't told you it before. The story is about Pakhmutova, and since you knew the deceased, I hope you'll think it's interesting and illustrative. My dad brought Pakhmutova over to the TV tower when I was three years old, so we grew up together. I quickly got used to her. Life up at the tower is rather mundane, and there isn't much to do for fun, so I would spend all of my free time with Pakhmutova. We slept together, ate together, and went for walks together. In the summertime we'd always stop by the river and swim forever on our way back to the city. We'd swim over to the bridge, listening to the trucks rattling by up above.

That day was particularly quiet, and the sun seemed particularly bright. The summer was coming up on its halfway point. The days were warm and seemed endless. We went to the river sometime in the afternoon. Pakhmutova had been running up and down the hills all morning, so she was exhausted. She reluctantly followed me into the city, lagging behind and breathing heavily. I went into the water first. I stayed by the bank because I didn't really feel like fighting against the current. Pakhmutova, on the other hand, drove forward, paddling down the river and enjoying the refreshing cold. The current carried her downstream, but I wasn't too worried—our dogs can swim a whole lot better than us. But this time was different—the water carried Pakhmutova farther and farther, all the way down to the bridge, spinning her around like a twig. The river is usually pretty calm, but down below the bridge, where they made the bottom a little deeper, sometimes there are underwater currents. Pakhmutova was sucked into one of them. I got really scared and swam toward her as fast as I could. The closer I got, the more I came to realize that I probably wouldn't have enough energy to pull her out of the water. The current caught me too and sent me down to the deep end where Pakhmutova's head was still barely bobbing above water. I drew even with her and grabbed her around the neck. I was really scared. She must have thought we were playing, so she hopped on top of me, her front legs wrapping around me. I started choking on the water and going under. I tried shouting, pushing her away, and hitting the water with my hands, but this was all useless. I was really tuckered out, and started losing consciousness because I was so scared and frustrated. I was thinking, are you kidding me? All I wanted to do was rescue my poor German shepherd, but not only can't I do that, now I'm gonna drown too.

When I actually started going down, and a ring of blue-green light shut around me, Pakhmutova realized I wasn't horsing around and she dove in after me. It's a good thing I was smart enough to grab onto her and not let go. The current carried us really far down the river. Once we got back to a shallow bend, we collapsed onto the bank, gasping. We were shivering, but Pakhmutova calmed down pretty quickly and ran over to sniff something along the riverbank. I just sat there on the wet sand thinking how funny it is how things turn out sometimes. At first I was trying to rescue her, and then she wound up rescuing me. Now we're bound together by something important and serious, something we'll never tell anyone else, because I'll be too afraid to and because Pakhmutova's a German shepherd, after all, Herman.

I think that's roughly how it tends to play out, right? We're forced to rescue the ones we love, and then we don't even realize when the circumstances have changed and they need to rescue us . . . but maybe that's how it's supposed to be? We form the closest bonds by experiencing life together and facing death together. That's when you know you love someone. Not all of us experience that, but that's a whole other issue.

Meanwhile, it's starting to feel more like fall, the sun can't heat up the trees and rivers as quickly, and it's actually getting cold in the evenings. I practically don't leave the house. I just sit in the kitchen watching nightfall sneak up on us. All we can do is wait for things to go back to normal—wait for the air to warm up and the water in the river to light up. The hills on the bank will catch the morning rays and blind us.

Well, that's what I wanted to tell you.

XOXO

P.P.S.

"Let me tell you a story," the presbyter said, carefully studying their faces. "Well, you're farmers. I just remembered a story about the prophet Daniel that has to do with that. Were you baptized?"

"Well, yeah," their timid voices answered.

"That's good," the presbyter said cheerfully. "Then you'll understand what I mean. The thing is that we often underestimate what we're capable of and we're afraid to cross the line we've already drawn for ourselves. The Lord alone determines the measure of our possibilities, so by underutilizing our knowledge and skills we're actually underutilizing the gifts given to us by the Lord. Am I expressing myself clearly?"

"Yes, yes," they assured him.

"Good," the presbyter said again, and just as cheerfully.

"So what about Daniel? Well, in the course of events, due to, say, local social conditions, he wound up, as one does, from time to time, in a pit with lions. Real, live lions. His death, at the paws of the lions, was only a matter of time. He had no chance. So, Daniel kneeled and prayed to God: 'Lord,' Daniel said, 'these angry and godless lions growling at me—was it their will to be bestowed with such a thirst for blood and hatred? Were you, Lord, the one to fill their hearts with such yearning and rage? Isn't it your voice that wakes them every morning and lulls them to sleep every night? Who else, then, could rescue me? Who else besides you should I ask? Who else should I appeal to, to whom should I address my words of gratitude and before whom will I be held responsible for my actions?' And while he was praying, the animals leaned against him, warming their bodies, and their hearts beat softly as they harkened to his gentle words. And he caressed their golden manes, picking dry leaves and blades of grass out of them. When at last he was drifting off, the lions stood by, guarding his deep and tranquil sleep. I wanted to say that," the presbyter went on, "because it just so happens that you all live together here—baptized and unbaptized people, Shtundists and barefoot, semiliterate villagers . . . I've seen lots of different people. You were born and raised here. Your families and businesses are here, and that's the way it's supposed to be. But you're fighting amongst yourselves, without realizing the most important thing—that you have no enemies here. You've been pitted against each other and made weak and vulnerable—but when you're together as a team, you've got nothing to fear. There's no need to be afraid, none whatsoever. Even when you're thrown into a pit teeming with lions and there's no one to lend a helping hand. Just believe in yourself and persevere. Well, and don't forget to pray when it's time to pray. Like Daniel did. You see what I mean?"

"Yes," the farmers chorused obediently.

"One more thing," the presbyter said, "the real reason the lions left Daniel alone was because he could breathe fire. The lions took that as a sign from God, so they didn't want to disturb him."

"Huh?" The farmers were dumbfounded.

"Like this," the presbyter answered, bending over to retie his shoelace, straightening back up, lifting his hands to pray, and exhaling a blue-pink tongue of flame, the fire of bittersweet joy.

SERHIY ZHADAN is one of the most popular and influential voices in contemporary Ukrainian literature: his poetry and novels are renowned and widely read both at home and abroad. He has twice won BBC Ukraine's Book of the Year (2006 and 2010) and has twice been nominated as Russian GQ's "Man of the Year" in the category of Writers. Writing is just one of his many interests, which also include singing in a popular rock band, translating poetry, and organizing literary festivals. Zhadan was born in Starobilsk, Luhansk Oblast in 1974, graduated from Kharkiv University in 1996, then spent three years as a graduate student of philology. He taught Ukrainian and world literature from 2000 to 2004, before retiring from teaching and dedicating himself to writing. Zhadan has translated poetry from German, English, Belarusian, and Russian, from such poets as Paul Celan and Charles Bukowski. His own works have been translated into German, English, Polish, Serbian, Croatian, Lithuanian, Belarusian, Russian, Hungarian, Armenian, Swedish and Czech. In 2013, he participated in and led Euromaidan demonstrations in Kharkiv, Ukraine's second-largest city, during the country's Revolution of Dignity. He continues to live and work in Kharkiv.

REILLY COSTIGAN-HUMES is a graduate of Haverford College, where he studied Russian literature and culture. He lives and works in Moscow, and translates literature from the Ukrainian and Russian.

ISAAC WHEELER received an MA in Russian Translation from Columbia University, and is also a graduate of Haverford College, where he studied Russian Language and English Literature. Wheeler lives in Brooklyn, NY, where he is a professional business and literary translator.

DONORS, SUPPORTERS, & PARTNERS

SUBSCRIBERS

Adrian Mitchell

Aimee Kramer

Alan Shockley

Albert Alexander

Aldo Sanchez

Amber Appel

Amrit Dhir

Andrea Passwater

Anonymous

Antonia Lloyd-Jones

Ashley Coursey Bull

Barbara Graettinger

Ben Fountain

Ben Nichols

Bill Fisher

Bob Appel

Bradford Pearson

Carol Cheshire

Caroline West

Charles Dee Mitchell

Cheryl Thompson

Chris Fischbach

Chris Sweet

Clair Tzeng

Cody Ross

Colin Winnette

Colleen Dunkel

Cory Howard

Courtney Marie

Courtney Sheedy

David Christensen

David Griffin

David Weinberger

Ed Tallent

Elizabeth Caplice

Erin Kubatzky

Frank Merlino

Greg McConeghy

Horatiu Matei

Ines ter Horst

James Tierney

Jay Geller

Jeanie Mortensen

Jeanne Milazzo

Jennifer Marquart

Jeremy Hughes

Jill Kelly

Joe Milazzo

Joel Garza

John Schmerein

John Winkelman

Jonathan Hope

Joshua Edwin

Julia Rigsby

Julie Janicke Muhsmann

Justin Childress

Kaleigh Emerson

Ken Bruce

Kenneth McClain

Kimberly Alexander

Lea Courington

Lara Smith

Lissa Dunlay

Lori Feathers

Lucy Moffatt

Lytton Smith

Marcia Lynx Qualey

Margaret Terwey

Mies de Vries

Mark Shockley

Martha Gifford

Mary Costello

Matt Bull

Maynard Thomson

Meaghan Corwin

Michael Elliott

Michael Holtmann

Mike Kaminsky

Naomi Firestone-Teeter

Neal Chuang

Nhan Ho

Nick Oxford

Nikki Gibson

Owen Rowe

Patrick Brown

Peter McCambridge

Rainer Schulte

Rebecca Ramos

Richard Thurston

Scot Roberts

Shelby Vincent

Steven Kornajcik

Steven Norton

Susan Ernst

Tara Cheesman-Olmsted

Theater Jones

Tim Kindseth

Todd Jailer

Todd Mostrog

Tom Bowden

Walter Paulson

Will Pepple

FORTHCOMING FROM DEEP VELLUM

MARIO BELLATIN · *Mrs. Murakami's Garden*
translated by Heather Cleary · MEXICO

MAGDA CARNECI · *FEM*
translated by Sean Cotter · ROMANIA

MIRCEA CĂRTĂRESCU · *Solenoid*
translated by Sean Cotter · ROMANIA

MATHILDE CLARK · *Lone Star*
translated by Martin Aitken · DENMARK

LEYLÂ ERBIL · *A Strange Woman*
translated by Nermin Menemencioğlu · TURKEY

ANNE GARRÉTA · *In Concrete*
translated by Emma Ramadan · FRANCE

GOETHE · *Faust*
translated by Zsuzsanna Ozsváth and Frederick Turner · GERMANY

PERGENTINO JOSÉ · *Red Ants: Stories*
translated by Tom Bunstead and the author · MEXICO

FOWZIA KARIMI · *Above Us the Milky Way: An Illuminated Alphabet* · USA

TAISIA KITAISKAIA · *The Nightgown & Other Poems* · USA

DMITRY LIPSKEROV · *The Tool and the Butterflies*
translated by Reilly Costigan-Humes & Isaac Stackhouse Wheeler · RUSSIA

GORAN PETROVIĆ · *At the Lucky Hand, aka The Sixty-Nine Drawers*
translated by Peter Agnone · SERBIA

C.F. RAMUZ · *Jean-Luc Persecuted*
translated by Olivia Baes · SWITZERLAND

TATIANA RYCKMAN · *The Ancestry of Objects* · USA

JESSICA SCHIEFAUER · *Girls Lost*
translated by Saskia Vogel · SWEDEN

MIKE SOTO · *A Grave Is Given Supper: Poems* · USA

MÄRTA TIKKANEN · *The Love Story of the Century*
translated by Stina Katchadourian · FINLAND